The Mad Baron's Bride

MISTY URBAN

All rights reserved.

No part of this publication may be sold, copied, distributed, reproduced or transmitted in any form or by any means, mechanical or digital, including photocopying and recording or by any information storage and retrieval system without the prior written permission of both the publisher, Oliver Heber Books and the author, Misty Urban, except in the case of brief quotations embodied in critical articles and reviews.

PUBLISHER'S NOTE: This is a work of fiction. Names, characters, places, and incidents either are the product of the author's imagination or are used fictitiously. Any resemblance to actual persons, living or dead, business establishments, events, or locales is entirely coincidental.

COPYRIGHT 2024 © Misty Urban

Cover art by Dar Albert at Wicked Smart Designs

Published by Oliver-Heber Books

0 9 8 7 6 5 4 3 2 1

CHAPTER ONE

BATH, ENGLAND, 1800

Customarily, there is little to remark about a lady's companion.

Leda Wroth proved an exception.

The first rebellion lay in her appearance. Lady's companions ought to fade gently into the background. They are to broadcast nothing of their own personality and impose no demands on attention, their role mere support and decorative shadow.

Mrs. Wroth, quite in defiance of this custom, was beautiful, though hers was not a loud beauty that obtruded upon the viewer. A new acquaintance might first concede her handsome, a pleasing aspect to her regular features and clear skin. A second meeting, one found oneself caught by the quirk of a smile that hovered around her expressive mouth, the quicksilver currents of intelligence and, oft, quickly subdued humor in her eyes.

Upon a third meeting, anyone who fell under that steady violet gaze—man, woman, child, indeed any sentient creature—readily surrendered his will to her superior knowledge and obvious mastery of the world. She conveyed the assurance of being steadfast, informed, equipped for any occasion. *Capable.*

And that calm confidence in how the world ticked over, along with her mastery of its intricate ways, accounted for her success in her line of work.

Leda Wroth did not merely companion ladies. She removed thorns from sides. She cleaved through Gordian knots of the most vexing personal or family situations and set one free on the path to their greatest desires.

She *saved lives*.

The life she was currently saving belonged to Miss Charlotte Astley of Little Bolton, Lancashire. And the setting was not a cruise charting the Antipodes, nor a marsh about the British outpost in Calcutta, but the Upper Assembly Rooms of Bath during Monday's dress ball.

Miss Charlotte Astley had descended from the north with the grace of an angel, an angel whose family land sat directly atop a productive seam of coal. A nymph of no more than seventeen summers, Miss Astley possessed the further advantage of showing well in the latest styles, in which young ladies went about in public in a garment that once would have served as a chemise. The soft muslin of her gown clung to her rounded shoulders and breasts, evidence of her well-nourished childhood, and a Kashmir shawl dangled from plump arms. A dainty ribbon bandeau pushed a cluster of curls onto her forehead like the topknot of a little brown quail.

She would have been ravened like an early Christian in the Roman Colosseum in the marriage mart in London, had her mother not possessed the foresight to sample the waters of Bath first, so to speak. Mrs. Astley, furthermore, possessed the acuity to comprehend that her tender maid required a wise champion to navigate the labyrinthine maze of the Bath Upper Rooms, where a gentleman paid for the privilege, either through subscription or per visit, to look over the available young ladies.

It did not take long for inquiries of an appropriate discreetness in the correct channels to manifest a short list of names for said champion, and topping them was Leda Wroth, long-time lady's companion to the estimable Lady Plume. Thus it was that Mrs. Wroth and Miss Astley mingled near one end of the vast ballroom within view of the entrance to the Octagon Room as well as the dancers, the brilliant glare of one of three Whitefriars crystal chandeliers ensuring that the subject of their discussion could not venture by without Mrs. Wroth's notice.

"An earl's son, I grant you, but manifestly unsuitable," Mrs. Wroth was saying in a tone that brooked no dispute.

Miss Astley's face fell into an attractive pout. "Not in the least?"

Mrs. Wroth shook her head decisively.

Leda, in contrast to the prevailing paleness of the room, was sporting the fashionable *habit d'escalier*. Over the requisite round gown of white muslin—hers gorgeously embroidered along the hem with its small train—she wore a half-robe of crimson velvet, with slits in the thigh-length hem and half-sleeves tied with ladders of delicate crimson ribbon. A matching turban bound up her dark tresses.

The effect was to indicate that Leda Wroth, in contrast to the virginal sylphs drifting around her, was a woman of dash and depth who knew her own mind. A confirmed, on-the-shelf spinster who wore her eccentricities with pride, and who regularly engaged in dancing, cards, and strolls with the sort of gentlemen who liked poking things on shelves to see if they could make them tumble off.

Miss Astley stroked her closed fan in speculation. "But he is the Viscount Corry," she said softly. "I should be a viscountess."

"And in time a countess, mistress of Castle Coole, which I hear the current Earl of Belmore has spent vast sums refurbishing," Mrs. Wroth said with meaningful emphasis.

"An envied hostess, then."

"Or an impoverished one."

Miss Astley raised her eyebrows.

"His lordship had visions of leading Irish Parliament," Mrs. Wroth said. "His hopes for that are now dashed, of course."

Miss Astley blinked and waited for illumination.

"Because of the Act of Union. It has forced your viscount to recalibrate his ambitions as well, I imagine."

This too failed to illuminate for Miss Astley. Leda sighed. It was too much to hope that young people followed the political news in addition to the latest gossip.

"The Irish Parliament voted itself out of existence in agreeing to the Act of Union with Great Britain. The British Parliament will now govern the United Kingdom. I'm told that your viscount managed to get himself elected to the British House of Commons for County Tyrone, so he will no doubt be headed to London in January when the new Parliament opens."

"Shouldn't he be in the House of Lords, if he's a viscount?"

"An honorary title, dear. His father holds the peerage."

Charlotte brightened. "Mama wishes to go to London."

Leda delivered her *coup de grâce*. "And so I imagine does Lady Julianna Butler, daughter of the Earl of Carrick. She is first cousin to your Viscount Corry and the most likely candidate for his wife."

Charlotte widened her eyes. "You *are* terribly well-informed, Miss Wroth." She sounded admiring rather than vexed.

Leda touched the ruby pendant filling in the low neckline of her half robe. It was not hers, for Leda Wroth had precious few possessions of her own, but she would upon grounds of their long friendship consent to let Lady Plume decorate her now and again in jewels.

"Thank you, dear. I hope you are not too much disappointed."

Charlotte considered the room before her. Couples swirled in the cotillion while music spilled from the gallery. Conversations borne on breathless laughter floated toward the lofted ceiling, and genial smiles descended from those strolling and looking down from the balconies above.

"I gather Mama wants to air me here and there in London, mostly so we can visit the shops." Charlotte's mouth turned up at one corner. "But if I return unengaged, perhaps she might let Toby pay his addresses. He is apprenticed to a solicitor in Shrewsbury, and no more than the younger son of a Shropshire squire, but..." She flicked her fan before her face.

"He is very dashing," Leda guessed.

Charlotte giggled. "A bit dashing. *Very* would be overstating the matter. But he is kind, and he makes me laugh, and he has the truest and most generous heart, and—" She sighed, wafting her fan beneath her chin as her eyes grew dreamy. "I think he would like me just as much even without Papa's pig iron."

"A veritable paragon," Leda said, wisely keeping her own opinions on romantic love, youthful or otherwise, out of Charlotte's dreams for her future.

"Oh, not by far," Charlotte said. "But of all the blokes who have cast out their lures, I think I like him the best. Do you not think that the most important consideration?"

Leda debated sharing with the younger woman what she, in fact, held to be of paramount consideration: a woman's freedom to direct her own life, to dispose of her own property and person as she wished, without being compelled by law and custom to submit her goods, or her body, to an at best indifferent and at worst hostile spouse. Leda herself had been seventeen when the world, or rather her parents, disabused her of romantical notions that she might marry a man she *liked*.

And now, after the tempest of blood and horror following

that ill-advised venture, she was very much committed to never marrying again.

"At any rate, you are here tonight in Bath, with no Toby in sight," Leda said. "Off with you to dance the minuet, and if the Viscount Corry should partner you, you shall be very firmly and distantly polite. Perhaps a touch distracted, for men detest when they should have less than a woman's full attention."

Charlotte closed her fan with a fond look. "You have been exceedingly kind, Mrs. Wroth. I wonder that you are not married yourself, and raising daughters equally wise."

Mrs. Wroth, though Charlotte could not have known this, did an excellent job of hiding the quandary of feelings these words provoked. Miss Astley could not possibly know that educating the youth was the one calling Leda Wroth felt firmly lodged in her breast, and the one future which she was utterly denied.

"Shoo." She made accompanying motions with her hands, as if Miss Astley were a chick. Charlotte chuckled and obliged.

Leda threw a glance about to locate her ladyship, it being incumbent on her post to have a bead on the woman who paid her a generous salary, though Lady Plume was the easiest of companions. She would call upon Leda if she required a fourth hand at cards, a partner for tea, or someone to gossip with during a dance. At the moment, Lady Plume's distinct headdress was not in evidence.

But the strangest man leaned against one of the marble pillars behind her, staring at Leda.

She did not recognize him, and they had not been introduced. She would not have forgotten this man. He was not terribly tall, yet he occupied his space entirely, solid and rooted, as if the pillar drew strength from him. A dark cutaway tailcoat buttoned over a chest that, while not excessively broad, still seemed substantial, in that way some men had. Dark grey satin breeches and white stockings hugged legs powerful in their shape. His physical presence was enhanced by the air of quiet, steady authority he projected as he watched her with a gaze both thoughtful and speculating.

And disapproving. Stern disapproval rippled from him in waves.

How rude. Leda lifted her chin and moved her gaze along as if it had never landed on him. No acknowledgement, no expression; the cut direct. She had mastered several varieties of the cut, but had small opportunity to use them, as lady's companions are meant to be obliging.

"Mrs. Wroth." A damsel appeared before her, drooping in her demeanor. "Mr. Sedley did *not* make me an offer. He was seen walking in Sydney Gardens with Miss Summers while I, like a perfect wigeon, waited for him to call."

The damsel's mouth trembled. "You advised me that he was inconstant. And worse? Mama made me come tonight, where I am in danger of seeing him, *and* she insisted I wear fruit in my cap, when everyone else has feathers."

The girl bent her head to display a silk cap bound with elaborate rosettes and sporting an unwieldly cluster of perishable items above the brim.

"My dear Miss Edham. Mr. Sedley is notoriously inconstant. Last season he wooed Lady Macbeth, and next season it will no doubt be Cordelia. I expect your parents wish you to look beyond a theatre actor for your future happiness at any rate. In the meantime." Leda deftly removed the plums and cherries from the girl's headdress, leaving only the apricots, which blended better with the peach silk.

"I do believe that is an improvement. Now go smile at every young man you find seemly, dance the minuet, and if Mr. Sedley should approach you, pretend for the first instant that you have forgotten his name."

Miss Edham's face brightened. "I shall do so. Mrs. Wroth, you are splendid. How is it you have not been wooed and won by someone perfectly lovely? I cannot account for how you are overlooked."

"Neither can I," said Leda. "Run along now. You can still make up the next set."

"Mrs. Wroth." An elegant older couple filled the space before Leda as Miss Edham departed. The woman wore powdered gray curls in defiance of fashion, and red rosettes fell in plaits down her muslin gown, with long sleeves peeking beneath a velvet half robe that fell into a train behind her. Three small feathers waved gently atop her head.

"Sir Peregrine and I cannot thank you enough. You were entirely correct in the matter of Lizzie's jewels. Her maid was being blackmailed by the butler—blackmailed! Can you imagine? The insolent ape replaced her pearls with paste in order to pawn them."

The lady waved a delicately painted fan. "Gladly, we have recovered the necklace, the maid has been scolded, and the butler has been turned off, without a character, I must add. And quite a lecture you read him, did you not, my love?" She looked adoringly at her husband, who nodded emphatically, giving Leda a grateful grin.

The woman reached out a gloved hand to clasp Leda's, her voice dropping further. "And we are in your debt for the word you put in our Lizzie's ear. She turned down the baronet's son, who was every bit the rogue you said, and is in transports of happiness with her captain. I do wish you could have accepted our invitation to the wedding."

"I am sorry that Lady Plume did not wish to leave Bath that week, but indeed happy I was able to be of some small service to your family, Lady Partridge. Sir Peregrine." Leda dropped a small curtsey. "Please give Lizzie my fondest regards."

After more thanks were exchanged, with exhortations to visit them in Cheltenham, which Leda was too wise to tell them she would never accept, the Partridges moved on.

"We shall tell anyone who shows interest of the great kindness you have done us, of course," Lady Partridge promised with one final squeeze. "With such absolute discretion."

"You are worth your weight in those rubies, Mrs. Wroth," Sir Peregrine confirmed.

Leda stroked her pendant, considering whether, at some point, it would be prudent to begin hinting that her invaluable, very discreet services might be worth a token of gratitude, money or jewels. Perhaps a small annuity. Lady's companions who do not have property of their own need to think about ways to secure their future, if they hope to have one.

"I cannot detect your employment, madame, but it is manifestly *not* matchmaker."

The rumbling male voice behind her shoulder sent the strangest shiver down Leda's spine. Not foreboding, but something else she couldn't identify.

"In fact, as far as I can ascertain, you are engaged in unmatching. Keeping couples apart, or so it would seem."

She turned to face the man in the dark cutaway coat. The pillar-leaner. Up close, too close, he had caramel-colored hair and eyes of an unsettling pale shade. Eyes that stared directly into her own.

"An unmatchmaker," he said.

Her gaze skipped over his countenance. Strong face, straight nose. A jutting brow. Lips precisely shaped and a deep coral, lips a woman would envy, yet which balanced his rugged features.

The shiver was not foreboding. Not quite.

"We have not been introduced," Leda said archly.

He nodded. "Does that then forbid us to have intercourse?"

He meant, of course, mere interaction, but something about that word—*intercourse*—suggested twining things. Closeness. For a moment her vision blanked of anything except him, as if the rest of the room had disappeared. Leda blinked, disconcerted.

"In a ballroom, yes. Were we in a position of peril, I imagine the niceties could be dispensed with. If I stood in the path of a runaway cart, suppose, or a burning—"

Proving he had no regard for the social niceties in the least, he *took her hand*. Another shiver skittered up her glove, past her elbow, skimming her shoulders. How very drafty this room had become.

"We are in peril. If I am not mistaken, that is the Master of Ceremonies approaching, and that is a young woman he intends to introduce to me."

"Well, yes, that is Mr. Tyson's duty, and that is Miss Hotham with him. She has only just arrived today—I met her in the Pump Room this morning—and you are being incredibly rude—good evening, Mr. Tyson, Miss Hotham. Please excuse us."

She smiled at the miss and a surprised-looking Mr. Tyson as her partner whisked her toward the couples daintily arranging themselves in lines on the dance floor.

"Rude? Hardly. You invited me to dance the minuet with you. I accepted."

He led them toward the top of the room, keeping a firm grip on her hand. His fingers were warm and strong. Leda offered a smile to everyone she knew, which included quite a few people, and struggled to catch up the loop on her train before she trod on the embroidered muslin and took them both down.

"I asked you? Bold of me. Quite against custom."

"Ah, but you heard I also am newly arrived in town, and know no one."

With a flick of the wrist he raised his forearm, turning toward her, and automatically Leda placed her palm against his. Her gaze collided with his as their limbs connected, hand to elbow. They fell into step as if they were performers who had rehearsed for hours.

The breath deserted her body. The sensation that slammed her was, she imagined, much like being hit by a runaway cart.

"You know the figure," he murmured as he stepped forward, gently pressing her hand. She circled him, taking mincing steps.

"But you did not know that. It would serve you right if you dragged me into the set only to discover I cannot manage the minuet."

"You," he murmured, his lips twitching at one edge, "have never in your life encountered a situation you cannot manage."

His eyes were gray, the color of spring clouds fat with rain, but his lashes and brows were dark brown, a startling contrast. He was clean-shaven but for clipped sideburns that descended to his jaw, giving his beauty a decidedly masculine cast.

Leda's stomach turned in time with the music. Indeed, she was the managing sort, yet she had the distinct sense there wasn't the least thing manageable about this man.

"Explain yourself, sir," Leda murmured. Her voice sounded oddly faint, as if she could not catch her breath.

Absurd. She was the mistress of every circumstance. She had built her reputation as being such.

"You kidnapped me," she began.

"Kidnapped! We are dancing. I have hardly carried you off to my lair." He dropped his arm and took the requisite step back.

She disengaged as well. His warmth lingered against her palm, and the notion of being alone with him, anywhere, sent a thrill after the shiver. This man, with a mere flick of his hand, threatened her hard-won aplomb, her careful defenses.

"Abducted me, in plain sight," she emphasized, gathering her skirts, "and I wonder if you even know who I am."

He bowed, one fist behind his back, leg straightened just so. He was an elegant dancer, a man aware of his body. He had a care where he stepped.

Like a predator.

"I know who you are." His voice held a velvety edge, quite disarming. The men she knew made a point of being boisterous, unable to miss. This one had a watchful air about him.

"I asked. You are Miss Wroth."

"Mrs. Wroth." She curtseyed, dipping her face to hide the stab of pain those words brought her. "I am a widow."

"Recently?" His brows rose.

"No. I have been widowed these many years, Mr.—"

He failed to take the hint to supply his name. Instead, one arm still clasped behind his back, he circled her stealthily, gaze trained on her face.

"I pity Mr. Wroth. To possess such a gem, then lose it so early."

Unaccountably, she flushed. This dratted enormous ballroom, first full of odd chills, and now too warm for comfort. He held out his hand, and she took it.

"For all you know, Mr. Wroth ascended to heaven singing praises to be released from his earthly chains."

His gaze moved over her brow, the proud slant of her cheekbones, the decided jut of her chin. There was nothing soft about her features, Leda knew. Much like her heart.

"Oh, Mr. Wroth did not go willingly," the stranger murmured.

What followed was a downright shudder, apprehension shaking her entire body.

He couldn't know. No one knew what her husband had

thought in those frantic, final moments. Not even Leda, and she'd been there.

"I still await your explanation, sir."

He weaved behind her while the other men circled their chosen lady, and the back of Leda's neck prickled, sensing his gaze upon her. She'd never been so aware of a man.

"Of why I accepted your invitation to dance?"

She tamped down the curl that teased her lip. He was either a bit whimsical or a bit mad. The touch of ridiculousness, in a man who otherwise appeared so proper—and possessing more beauty and address than any one man should be allotted—was enormously appealing. She was not immune to a man's charm after all, it would seem.

"Exactly."

The men resumed their line and began a sequence of moves which Leda took note of, knowing the women were expected to follow. It was difficult not to fall into pure reverie simply watching him, his elegant grace, his self-possession. He was a man measured in every movement, thoughtful, deliberate. Much like her.

Say something ridiculous. An impetuous inner voice Leda had not heard in a very long time sprouted suddenly in her mind. It spoke to her distantly, as if shocked at having a window of air and light after so many years of being buried.

He held his out arm toward her in the prompt, and Leda executed the flowing set of movements he'd demonstrated. She let the music ripple through her body, along with a sudden, wild sense of release, and concluded with her own arm stretched toward his, palm up.

Say you were struck by my beauty. She'd forgive the plumper, for she was sure she was not beautiful, only handsome to the generous, a touch prepossessing at best. *Say you saw me and felt a strange and inexorable pull.*

Let him not have a problem he needed her to solve.

Let this man, if only once, and only *this* man, approach her for any of the other reasons a man might whisk a woman onto a dance floor and into his arms.

He stepped toward her. She stepped toward him. Their gazes held, melded.

"I have a matter on which I require advice," he said. His voice was deep and warm, and his eyes glowed as if the sun sat behind clouds. "Actually, two."

She tore her gaze from his and trained her eyes straight ahead as she moved into the promenade. Pointed her toes, telling herself to lift her heels and not let any part of her slump toward the floor.

"Of course you do," she said.

CHAPTER TWO

He'd lost her.
　　She'd been *there*, so present, so in tune with him. She moved with him in the dance as if they were mirrored halves that together made a whole, a perfect complement.

And then he'd said something to make her face shutter. What had he said?

Jack searched his mind, which was usually a very disciplined place, but something about this woman made his senses unable to assemble the proper information. His gaze snagged on the arresting shape of her face, particularly those full lips with the ever-present pucker, as if she were amused by everything she saw. The scent of almonds, rising from her neck, made his mind blank and his mouth water. The husky sound of her voice feathered his ears and riled his brain to all sorts of fevered imaginings.

And the feel of her, so much sweetness. Warm, pliant skin. Supple muscles in her arms, a delicate strength in her fingers as she clasped his. Every sensation cloaked in a veil of silk, from her gloves, his. It was a sweet provocation, tender and thrilling at the same time. Like walking through a field with tall grasses brushing lightly against his body. Like floating beneath the water of the estuary, warm and still, his entire being weightless and alive.

It had been too long since he'd touched a woman. And longer still since a woman had looked deeply into his eyes, held his gaze as if she meant to search his being. As if she wanted to know his secrets, and would keep them close once she knew.

Since a woman had looked at him with interest, real interest, as if she took delight in him? That had not happened since his mother set aside his baby gowns for short pants.

And as for sharing his secrets—he never would.

Perhaps she sensed that, and so the iron wall crashed down in her eyes, like a gate locking in a prisoner, or a door locking out a supplicant.

He wanted a way back in.

She was speaking. "Do go on."

She stared straight ahead, eyes fixed on the far wall, where guests lined in chairs along the wall watched the dancers with languid attention.

Jack swallowed hard. His damnable mind would not function. It circled one thought: how soft and delectable her skin appeared on the slope of her elegant neck and that soft hollow beneath her ear, where a crimson eardrop dangled. The luscious sweep of warm beige skin across her decolletage, the delicate divot between her collarbones, the way the setting of the ruby pendant drew his eyes to the faint shadow of cleavage. Most women pushed their breasts up and out for a man to admire, but Mrs. Wroth kept her bosom tucked away as if it were her own business, and only a favored man would be allowed to view.

Or touch. His mouth went dry.

"Go on about what?" What would bring that curious sparkle back to her eye?

"The problem you need solved, of course." They reached

the end of the promenade and she turned from him to walk behind the line of other women.

By the time they reached their place at the top, he had it. "Where did you and Mr. Wroth live?"

She met his gaze, startled, and reason fell out of his head for a moment. He'd thought her eyes were brown. Now they appeared a deep-blue gray, the color piercing.

"Northeast of here," she said tersely, holding her palm a fraction from his.

He curved his fingers against hers. He wanted to touch so much more of her.

"What brought you to Bath?"

"Employment." Her lips pursed, flattening that pucker he'd noticed. Full, delicately drawn lips, the color of a primrose in spring. His head went hazy.

"You must have married young."

She faltered in a step as they circled one another. "Too young." Her brows drew together. Fine, feathery brows, black like her lashes.

"That was my error as well. Were you happy?"

She froze, then stepped back. The pattern required him to step back also, but he wanted to hear her answer.

She refused him. "You are married?"

"Widower."

She withdrew to the ladies' line, and he wished the musicians would play faster, so he might draw near her the sooner.

"I am seeking a governess for my—daughter," he said as soon as he could take her hand for another promenade. He liked her firm grip, the strength of mind it suggested.

"How old is the child?"

"Almost ten."

"Have you considered a girl's school?"

"That is not for us. She is—shy."

He glanced to the side as they passed smiling couples, wondering how much of their exchange was being overheard. With the music, the click of heels on the floor, the chatter of conversations flowing through the large room, he doubted anyone paid any attention to them.

Anyone not paying close attention to Mrs. Wroth was a fool. She carried herself with a steady grace, as if she held a weight on her shoulders, but bore it gently. A widow—did that account for the faint shadow of sadness in her eyes? A woman who had knowledge of the ways of men with women.

Of the ways a woman could pleasure a man, and he her.

His gut tightened at the thought, heavy with heat. This would *not* do.

"She is an intelligent child, but rather solitary. I believe she would prefer to remain at home."

"And home is—?"

"Norfolk." He pictured it in his mind's eye, the pebbled front of Holme Hall, battered by the salty winds of the North Sea. He wondered what she would think of the red hulking block of it, that haunted shell.

His companion blinked. Her eyes were a deep blue after all. "Norfolk is the other side of the country."

He nodded, keeping his expression carefully neutral. She narrowed her eyes and peered into his face as she stepped close. The scent of almonds and honey assailed him.

She swayed back. He clasped his fingers around her hand without thinking.

"Why come to Bath for a governess? Surely there are clever and capable women in your area." She appeared to search her mind, her brows drawing back over her startling eyes. Their wide setting gave her a look of deceptive innocence. "Norwich. King's Lynn. Even London would be closer."

"I have family here. And—" He paused. "I've had difficulty engaging a local woman. Or rather, not engaging, but keeping."

She tugged her hand free and moved in her figure, dipping her torso with a bend of one knee. The fabric of her gown rustled with invitation.

"Tell me about this child," she said.

His aunt had been exactly right to recommend Mrs. Wroth to him. She appeared every inch the intelligent, capable woman he needed. Difficult to intimidate.

Impossible to scare away.

"My daughter is not to blame. There are—legends that circulate about the house. Wild stories, no basis of truth."

Lies.

He had her full attention now, her eyes locked on his. He wondered how much more time he had. He'd been warned that the last dance was called the long minuet for good reason. Long enough to persuade this woman to be his?

Governess. His governess. Muriel's governess.

"We've gone through a dozen women," he admitted. That was counting the vicar's daughter from Swaffham, who changed her mind before arriving, and the gentleman's daughter from Greater Yarmouth, who turned around and climbed right back in the cart after she saw Holme House.

"That would make the next thirteen," she murmured.

"Only a concern for the superstitious." His chest grew heavy. If she were the superstitious sort, there was no hope here.

"Then you must find someone not easily frightened."

Not her, he was certain. Mrs. Wroth seemed as steady as the sea. Moving forward, always, her rhythm unchanged, assured.

Now that was a foolish image. The sea changed all the time, from calm to roaring, from glassy pools to waves that pulled a man under. The ruins of the shipwrecks off the beach below his house gave proof of the tide's implacable power.

If ever a woman could soothe a savage beast, Jack fancied, it was Mrs. Wroth.

"My aunt recommends I find a wife," he blurted.

That proved precisely the wrong thing to say. She wheeled from him early and went back to her place in line, her face sharp and gleaming as diamond in the light from the chandeliers. Confused, the other women scurried to follow.

He noted this. Other women followed where Mrs. Wroth led.

He danced her way, curling his fingers into a fist behind his back. The minuet was a tortuous dance, much like wooing. The man pursued, circling, pleading, while the woman stepped forward, then back, never quite coming into his arms.

Not that Jack had much skill with wooing. Maybe his wife would have been happier with him if he had.

"It has been six years," he said, surprised at the touch of desperation in his voice. Six years since one nightmare ended and another began. One burdened half-life giving way to another.

It had been many years, far longer than six, since Jack had harbored dreams for the future. What was it about Bath, about this ballroom—about this woman—that suddenly planted notions in his head? He hadn't given a thought to a *wife*.

"Oh, high time you remarried, then."

Her voice cracked, and her lovely jaw drew tight, as if she clenched her teeth. She stared over his shoulder as they wove the figure, a step together, a step apart. How maddening she was.

"And do think," she said, when she'd finished a turn with the ladies and come back to him, "a wife would resolve the governess problem nicely. You should have someone to teach and guide your daughter. As well as a housekeeper, a chatelaine, and a hostess. A cook, in a pinch, and possibly a secretary. Not to mention a body to warm your bed."

Ah, God's teeth. She was talking of beds. Jack's mind fogged with the heat rolling through his body.

Devil take it, he hadn't been interested in a woman for years, but with her floating about him, just beyond reach, he could barely keep himself under control. He wanted to yank her to him and mold every inch of her body to his.

In a crowded ballroom, sultry with the heat of many bodies and the smolder of wax candles.

Maybe he was what everyone said.

"That is what a wife does," he said, trying to bring his mind back to the conversation. "All those things you say."

It would do no good to yank this one about, he could see that. She had too strong a mind. If he wanted this woman he would have to woo her with words, lure her toward him with curiosity and interest and the offer of his own self.

Tempt her with promises, then keep those promises.

She turned away, arms lifted precisely before her, self-contained, wanting nothing. Certainly not him.

"All those things and more." The words floated back to him. "An onerous list of tasks, wife."

Onerous? "The most exalted status a woman can have," he replied. Every woman sought to be a wife, did she not? He'd been taught since birth that the greatest gift a man possessed was the offer of his hand.

Of course, Jack's hand held a paltry offering. A crumbling manor set on crumbling cliffs, howling with wind and clouds. A tiny title and properties whittled down almost to nothing by the previous owner of the estate. A motherless child who feared the world, and—ghosts.

So many ghosts.

"I can think of loftier titles," she said when the pattern

brought her back under his nose. So many colors shimmered from her hair, highlights of gold and undertones of red among the tresses of dark brown. They gleamed like silk.

"Queen," she said. "Empress. Ruler of realms."

He was ready to kneel before her, like a knight of old seeking favor from his lady. He was ready to stretch out his neck for the sword.

He was clearly addled. He hadn't been in company like this for too long, genteel, elegant, witty. He was acting an uncouth buffoon.

"I could make you a baroness," he said, because it was the only real item of value he had. But what would that mean to a woman with ambitions of rule?

"That is, my wife. Would be a baron's wife. Not a baroness proper, with a title of her own, but a lady nonetheless. Mine."

"How lovely for her," Mrs. Wroth said.

They froze, gazes locked, her nose at the level of his neck. Then she swept into a careful curtsy, ending the dance.

"Will you help me find someone?" He'd come to Bath with one hope and been given one name: hers. He had nothing else.

"No." She turned away.

He did it then, lost himself—again—and caught her hand. That warm, firm hand in its elegant glove. He could not let her walk away.

Desire punched him in the gut, hard. "Please."

She threw a look over her shoulder, eyes narrowed. Her eyes were violet. *Violet*. Jack reeled.

"I can think of no acquaintance that would suit your needs, sir," she said. "I wish you luck in your search."

And she stepped away, head high, her red-rimmed gown rustling in her wake.

A gentleman intercepted her on her way, making no

attempt to modulate his voice. "Mrs. Wroth! A vision tonight. Met the mad baron, did you?"

Jack's entire chest clenched. So it had followed him here, the whispers, the mockery. That sobriquet he could travel the country and not escape. His feet rooted to the floor as if trapped in damp clay.

"Mad indeed," Mrs. Wroth murmured.

And that was that.

Mad.

What Anne-Marie had reduced him to, and all he would ever be.

CHAPTER THREE

Lady Plume rustled into the dining room wearing her favorite morning dress, a loose muslin gown draped with lace and pink ribbons, with a lace chemisette swathing her bosom and a delicate lace cap pinned to her silver curls. She draped herself in a chair across the polished wooden table from Leda and gave a small yawn.

"Anything interesting?"

"In the *Chronicle* this morning?" Leda sipped her coffee and flipped a page. "An armistice has been proposed with France. There's a new treaty of alliance with the Emperor of Russia. The royal family is returning to Windsor and Lord Nelson is at his estate near Ipswich. And word has it that the property the new Chinese emperor confiscated from his father's minister, Ho-Ching, is worth 300 million pounds sterling."

"Imagine. Thank you, Gibbs." Lady Plume accepted her hot chocolate from the butler, who tenderly tucked in her chair, then went to the sideboard to assemble his lady's breakfast.

"Such a fortune would not go as far here as it once did, I'm afraid," her ladyship remarked.

"The mayor has been asked to organize a meeting of Bath

citizens to petition the king to convene Parliament and address the high price of provisions." Leda scanned the page. "Mrs. Smith has returned from London with an assortment of new furs and laces."

"She's opposite King's Bath, is she not? We could visit today."

"Reverend Warner is taking subscriptions for his history of Bath. One volume, royal quarto, with engravings. Shall I put us down for one?"

"Put us down for two, and we'll give one away as a gift for Yuletide."

"And there is a brew house for let on the quay."

Her ladyship smiled. "You already have enough to do, darling. You know I depend on you." She raised her cup to her lips. "Anything of interest transpire at the ball?"

"Nothing beyond what I told you already on our long journey home." The Upper Assembly Rooms lay one short street away from the Crescent, where Lady Plume had her house, and in her brief walk alongside her ladyship's chair Leda had communicated the events she felt of interest.

She had not, curiously, said a word about the strange man who danced the minuet with her and set her hackles up in the most unexpected ways. For one thing, against every rule of politeness, she had not learned his name. For another, she did not intend to assist him on his hunt for a wife.

Never mind that she regularly participated in pursuits of wives for friends and strangers alike. She was not going to recommend a wife for *him*.

Rude, offensively handsome, and possibly mad. His wit would no doubt prove aggravating upon prolonged exposure and his beauty and charm would come to constitute an offense. She could not in good conscience subject any woman to that.

"Hmm." Lady Plume smiled as Gibbs set a loaded plate

before her. She tucked in as a knock sounded at the front door. "You do not mind taking callers, my dear?"

Leda tugged the mob cap covering the tresses she'd efficiently brushed and pinned up. "I am half-dressed, at least."

She and her ladyship were accustomed to callers at hours in and outside fashionable times. The needs of supplicants did not adhere to the forms of *ton*. Thus Leda had donned a morning walking dress of sprigged muslin and was prepared for exercise either in or out of doors.

"Mrs. Limpet, your ladyship," Gibbs announced, conducting a petite, nervous-looking matron into the room.

"At your breakfast, you are! Indeed, I hate to disturb you. But you suggested, your ladyship, and I confess I hoped—"

"Sit," her ladyship said in welcome. "Gibbs will fix you a plate. I know you are eager to hear what Mrs. Wroth has discovered."

Leda rolled her paper to the side. "I wish I had better news."

Mrs. Limpet's expression fell into lines of dismay. "I knew it."

Very often they did, Leda thought. A woman knew when a man was false, when a man was lying, when she was being bamboozled with fanciful words or gifts while a man she relied on, a husband or brother or guardian or son, took from her with the other hand what should have been hers.

Leda did not hate men as a class, nor did she detest the sex. Women were just as capable as perfidy. But it was women who sought out Leda, again and again, wanting confirmation of something they suspected but hoped was not true. Needing another set of eyes to peer around a corner or see into the dark.

Leda was never surprised by what she found there. After all, she herself had escaped the worst demons. It was her privilege and her duty to keep other women from falling into the same maw that had once swallowed her and which she had eluded by no others means than the grace of God and her own determination.

Gibbs placed a plate of buttered toast near her elbow with a sympathetic gaze, and Leda recalled herself. Gibbs tended to her ladyship with complete devotion, but he never made kind gestures toward Leda. He still, after six years of her employment, had never given Leda one sign of approval.

"Thank you, Gibbs. I regret to say, Mrs. Limpet, that his friends confirm that Mr. Crutch regularly lives beyond the means of his quarterly allowance. A great many of his acquaintances hold his vowels, and he has not paid his tailor in two years."

Mrs. Limpet clenched her jaw. "Doubtless he sees my chemist shop as a way to line his pockets."

"Your cordial Balm of Gilead is selling very well, is it not?"

Their guest nodded. "That and the True Scots' pills. I've found a formula that reduces the griping other Scots' pills can cause." She added a large lump of sugar to her tea and stirred, frowning.

"Of course, many women might be glad to share their worldly goods with a husband." Lady Plume regarded Leda over her chocolate. "In return for the protection and—other advantages a man may provide."

Gibbs, at the sideboard loading a plate with sausage links and coddled eggs, raised his eyebrows.

Leda crunched her toast, relishing the sweet, creamy butter. All these years later, she had not learned to take for granted the luxury of good food and regular mealtimes. The price of provisions might be dreadfully high, but Lady Plume's kitchens had so far not suffered. Sir Dunlap Plume, though departing the world perhaps too soon for his own liking, had, through the many wise and well-managed investments he left behind, ensured a long and comfortable widowhood for his lady.

One argument for marriage. Perhaps the only one Leda could think of.

The most exalted status a woman could have, her partner with the gray eyes had said. So confident that his attentions would send a woman into transports.

With that very symmetrically pleasing face of his, that solid physique, that strange effect of his regard, as if one had imbibed a liquor that sent warm, languid effects to every part of one's body—perhaps a woman subject to his attentions *would* enjoy transports.

Leda had never been transported. She tamped down the oddly weakening memory of his hands holding hers.

"What would the advantages be, in Mrs. Limpet's case?" Leda asked.

"I fail to see any." Mrs. Limpet's eyes widened as Gibbs set a loaded plate before her. "Smoked salmon? Lady Plume, you do set a fine table."

"Leda and I enjoy feeding people," her ladyship said serenely. "And providing assistance wherever we might to our friends."

There was a broad hint there, but Leda could not follow. She would be the first to admit what she owed Lady Plume. Her employer did not know Leda's full history in Bath, how she'd arrived in a stained gown with her borrowed slippers worn through and nothing but a ragged shawl holding all her worldly goods. How she'd fallen by luck and grace into the hands of a schoolteacher who asked few questions but guessed much.

Leda had come quite by chance to the attention of Lady Plume, who was searching for a young and amusing companion, and in her ladyship's employ Leda had come into the full extent of her powers to manage other peoples' affairs. She had through many quiet but steady successes built her reputation as a sensible, well-mannered woman who knew everything, heard everything, and could be trusted with a secret.

A formidable, enviable status, to be sure.

An unmatchmaker. Just what her beguiling and quite exasperating dance partner had called her.

That way lay reflections in which Leda did not wish to indulge, and from which she was fortuitously saved by another knock at the door. Lady Plume cocked her head and smiled into her chocolate.

Mrs. Limpet attacked her eggs, as if determined to polish off her plate before she must concede the table to another guest. "I daresay I look a fine catch to a man with pockets to let. I own my shop and the rooms above. I have a respectable trade." She sniffed. "I'm not hideous to look upon, nor so long in the tooth I might not catch a man's eye yet. Were I willing to trade the advantages of widowhood for a yoke."

"The freedom to set your own schedule, go where you wish, and keep what company you please," Leda offered.

"To wear what I like." Mrs. Limpet patted her black lace cap, trimmed with beads.

"Take your meals when you feel disposed, and enjoy a menu designed to your tastes."

Mrs. Limpet's eyes glowed with a fierce light. "Attend the theatre whenever the fancy takes me."

"But to have no companion at bed and board," Lady Plume said. "No children to brighten one's days and years."

This seemed an unnecessary intrusion of sentiment, since Lady Plume did not, to Leda's knowledge, have children.

"No fears for a child's health or future," Leda said. "No worries they will not take a trade, or will make a poor marriage, or will shame their parents."

"No man to warm your bed on a cold eve," said Lady Plume.

"Or pushing you out of bed on a cold morn to fix his breakfast."

"No bedsport," Lady Plume pointed out.

Mrs. Limpet sighed. "I do miss the bedsport."

Both women looked at Leda. She scowled.

"No man importuning you with his needs and reading you sermons on the marital debt."

Lady Plume shook her head. "You had the most abominable husband, my dear. That is not the general condition."

Mrs. Limpet regarded her plate. "I am too old to catch a babe did I marry again," she said. "But you, Mrs. Wroth—if you will forgive me? Did you never wish for children?"

Toast choked Leda's throat, as if she had swallowed glass. Lady Plume watched her curiously.

Did she lie now, or later? To reveal the truth would invite questions she was not prepared to answer. "Do I appear the type to have a secret child tucked away?" Leda finally managed.

"But you could marry again," Lady Plume said.

Leda pulled her mouth into some semblance of a smile. "But then I should be obliged to leave your ladyship, and you are a far more genial companion than a husband."

Gibbs coughed from the door. "Your ladyship. John Burnham, Baron Brancaster of Holme Hall."

Leda looked up. It was *him*.

The strangest sensation overtook her body. As if she were a flint that had been struck, and sparks flew from her.

Lady Plume smiled widely. "Brancaster."

He made a small, correct bow. "Your ladyship. Jack, please."

"And you must call me Aunt Plume. Do join us."

Leda's thoughts piled atop one another like squealing piglets. His name was Jack. He was a *baron*. Lady Plume was his *aunt*?

"Brancaster," Leda repeated. "*Lord* Brancaster."

His gaze met hers. "Of Holme Hall, Norfolk."

"Gracious me, I've a shop to open." Mrs. Limpet half-rose and, when no one stopped her, reluctantly completed the motion. "*Lord* Brancaster." She fluttered her eyelashes. "A chemist shop on Paternoster Row. I've a botanical syrup you must try for bathing, and a nervous cordial should you have need."

"Would it aid one contemplating matrimony?" Leda asked, prodded by a contrary impulse. She was all afire now.

Mrs. Limpet nodded with a touch of surprise. "It does, though I recommend the botanical syrup for those approaching the altar of Hymen. My syrup lays to rest the slightest apprehension and leaves the system entirely sound."

"Then I daresay Mrs. Wroth would appreciate a dose," Brancaster said.

She glared at him and thus could not miss the shape of his thighs outlined in cashmere breeches, his calves in leather top boots and small spurs. His riding coat of dark green everlasting sported a tall collar, his one concession to fashion, for otherwise his waistcoat was a muted velveret and his cravat simply knotted beneath his chin. Neither a dandy nor a peacock, and he seemed a man who would pay his tailor in full.

"I marvel that I somehow missed your telling me you have a nephew in town, mum," Leda said to her ladyship, watching Brancaster as he dropped easily into one of the painted Maltese chairs. He seemed bigger in the dainty dining room than he had in the ballroom last evening, his chest broader. Perhaps the coat was padded.

"I told him to find you last night and make you dance, for I was engaged at cards with Lady Oxmantown," her ladyship said. "Did he not locate you? It was rather a crush."

"He found me," Leda said.

"Coffee, tea, or chocolate?" Lady Plume inquired. "If there

is anything you might want, Gibbs can produce it. Leda, do hand over the paper. Are your rooms in order, Jack? I wish you would put up here while you are in town. It seems so poor to let family take lodgings."

"Coffee, please." He met Leda's gaze as she pushed the *Chronicle* toward him. "I did not want to intrude on any arrangement you have here, aunt."

Leda raised her brows. "You refer to me? I am the arrangement?" The thought of him staying in the house, looming in their quiet and orderly space, made her wish a dose of Mrs. Limpet's nervous cordial was at hand.

His hair was combed back in the latest style, slightly wavy. She wondered if he used curling papers. A woman of lesser fortitude might be taken in by that sensual charm and easy grace, the impression that he walked calm and confident in his own skin.

"I suppose lodging with an unmarried woman might handicap your search for a bride," Leda said.

He scowled. "I am in search of a governess. I was told you could help me locate suitable prospects."

She scowled back. "You told me you wanted a wife."

"*I* told him he wants a wife," Lady Plume said serenely. "I thought you might help with that, Leda."

"I am not in the business of making matches."

"No, rather unmaking them, from what I detect."

"Choosing the wrong partner can be ruinous to a woman's entire future," Leda snapped.

He tasted the coffee Lady Plume passed his way. "The same might be said for a man."

"At least here you can escape the silly rumors that follow you all about Norfolk," Lady Plume said.

His lordship stared at his plate, his brows pulling together. "If only that were true."

The brooding aspect suited him exceedingly well. Leda groped for her wits. "The Mad Baron? The Earl of Howth called you that at the ball last night."

"So my fame has spread all the way to Ireland," Brancaster growled.

"His eldest daughter, Lady Sydney, is widowed," Leda said. Lady Sydney was also older than his lordship by at least a score of years. "And his youngest daughter, Lady Frances, is I hear in search of a husband. She is likely past child-bearing age, if that is a concern, but unlikely to listen to gossip."

"Leda," Lady Plume said reproachfully.

"I am endeavoring to be helpful," Leda said. "To that end, perhaps I ought to know why they call you the Mad Baron, milord."

"It is not Jack," Lady Plume said softly. "He had a mad wife."

"Independence in women is often mistaken for madness," Leda said, speaking from her own experience.

"Leda!"

"That is your name?" Brancaster forked up a slice of smoked salmon. "The queen seduced by a swan."

"My given name is Caledonia," she said, throwing him an arch look. "No reference to despoiled women."

"It gives me a fanciful impression of Mr. Wroth." Brancaster chewed. "The much lamented, dearly departed Mr. Wroth, buried in—"

Leda set her jaw at a mulish angle.

"Cheltenham," Lady Plume supplied, repeating Leda's lie.

"The seat of your marital bliss as well?"

"I have never detected," Lady Plume said, "that Leda was acquainted with marital bliss."

"That would make a pair of us." Brancaster regarded Leda. That level gaze of his was so very unnerving, and the gray bars in his iris seemed to shift, light to dark, depending on his mood. "You have no wish to repeat the experiment?"

"None."

"I feel the same." He looked to his aunt. "If my reputation has tagged me here like a hound at my heels, Aunt Plume, I hardly think it will speed my suit among the Bath beauties. Better to confine myself to seeking a governess."

"So long as you do not drive her mad also," Leda said.

That was a blow below the belt, as it were, and she knew it before the words left her mouth. Yet her jaw locked on the thought of apology. He'd dismissed his wife as mad. She knew how that felt.

She knew what that meant, to a woman.

But Lady Plume's astonished stare shamed her into a retraction. "That is unfair of me to presume," Leda admitted, "since I am unaware of what caused Lady Brancaster's demise." She waited.

Brancaster scooped into his dish of coddled egg. "A topic I've no wish to discuss, as it would turn me off my breakfast. Aunt Plume, you have a splendid chef."

"Only a plain cook from Dorset," his aunt returned, "but I am very happy with her. Gibbs, please tell Mrs. Skim that Brancaster enjoyed her cookery."

Gibbs gave his assent, and Leda refrained from shouting and hurling her china cup across the table. The unfeeling cad. The *brute*. He showed no more concern for his wife's troubled state than Leda's flint-hearted nephew had shown when damning her to the asylum.

Men drove women to madness, then punished them for it.

Best to remember that, and steel herself to the strange melting feeling that contemplating Lord Brancaster was wont to induce.

"To the question of a governess." Lady Plume offered her

cup to Gibbs, who hastened to add more chocolate. "I intended for you to ask Leda."

"To recommend candidates, you mean? He may as well inquire directly at Miss Gregoire's, though I could introduce him, I suppose."

"My dear." Her ladyship's lips curled into a delighted smile. "I meant he should ask *you*."

The sensations inside would suggest Leda's heart was clambering into her throat, a place it had no business being. "I am already employed."

"I would be willing to loan you to family, for a time. I have the highest faith in your intelligence as well as discretion. And we all know there isn't the least touch of madness about you."

Her ladyship *didn't* know. Leda intended for it to say that way.

"I'm afraid my skills aren't the least suited to governessing. I am incompatible with small children, as my time teaching at Miss Gregoire's Academy for Girls will attest. If you will excuse me. I have letters to write."

"You'll join us at the Pump Room, I hope? Brancaster has to take the waters and write his name in the book."

Good sense pressed her to say no. To avoid this man who unsettled her, though he sat doing nothing but methodically scooping eggs. He'd known madness in a woman; he might sense something in her. She already felt a bit daft, the way her thoughts cleared as she watched his jaw flexing as he chewed. Noting his hands, solid, strong, and as well-shaped as the rest of him.

"I have errands to attend." Like hiding from Lord Brancaster until he went away.

He met her gaze, and a strange thickness clung in her throat. It felt like despair.

Not *his,* certainly. What did a comely, well-heeled lord of the realm have to despair of?

Yet she could read his expression, the slight flattening of the lip, the twitch of one dark brow. He expected her to run from him. He was resigned to it. His reputation had taught him to expect nothing more.

He came to her for help, or at least came to his aunt, and Leda went skittering off like a bedbug seeking cover.

"You might at least give him some introductions. Your acquaintance is broader than mine," Lady Plume said.

That was true, for while Lady Plume had lived in Bath far longer, she tended to swim in the shallow pool of the upper class, while Leda, like a chameleon, had forged friendships across many ranks. And was that reproach in her employer's voice? Her ladyship had scooped Leda from the doorway in which she found her barely holding body and soul together and had set her upon the plump cushion of No. 14 Crescent Place like a favored house cat, where she was petted and well-fed and allowed to preen at her own cleverness. And she could not now turn around and help another in need?

Yet drawing near this man would be dangerous to her hard-won peace. Leda knew it by instinct. She would approach, thinking herself on solid ground, and fall through into a pit of— she knew not what. Something overwhelming, she was certain.

She reached for her remaining piece of toast, meaning to take it to her room while she wrote. Gibbs, his nose in the air, removed the plate and carried it to the sideboard.

Whatever small gain she had made in Gibbs' estimation, Leda had promptly lost by denying Lady Plume this simple request.

"Ring for me when you wish to leave. Of course I shall accompany you." Leda ignored the strange kick in her errant heart as it made its way back to the proper locale in her chest. She would spend more time with him. Long stretches.

For the purpose of turning his attention from herself and sending another woman home with him to Norfolk.

As it should be. She had known near a decade ago, when she stood in a stone church saying vows that banged as heavy as a bell clapper in her mouth, that a future of love and happiness was not for her. Yet, as Leda refilled her cup and removed herself to the library to complete her correspondence, she found the dregs of her coffee very bitter.

CHAPTER FOUR

It was generally Leda's ambition to be no more than sufficiently smart in her attire, as she wished to be found unobjectionable and in no way setting herself up as an example to be emulated. Yet she felt overly self-conscious of her fashion choices that morning as she walked down Milsom Street beside Lord Brancaster, with Lady Plume, who found the prospect of a walk over half a mile fatiguing, carried alongside in a sedan chair.

Leda had grown accustomed, in the years of her employment, to the different ways that tradesmen, peers, and passersby regarded a lady as compared to a common miss or mistress. Lady Plume's way was smoothed considerably by the aura of wealth and consequence she imparted. But that was nothing to the eminence by which a lord swept all before him.

Gentlemen who would have merely tipped their hats in a perfunctory greeting met Brancaster's eye and smiled with the shared, secret knowledge of men. Ladies bobbed their heads, dispensing smiles coy or serene. Misses colored and whispered behind their bonnets. Merchants came to their door to hover with inviting smiles. Boys tagged behind in the street, remarking on his riding whip, his spurs, the precise roll to the brim of his top hat.

And this was Bath, where, during the season, it was not uncommon to come across a duke, an earl or two, and any host of officers in uniform. In Norfolk, in what she supposed must be quite remote country, he would be worshipped as a lesser god.

He bore it well, nodding in return, touching the brim of his hat, answering the occasional "good day" and "how do." Leda was glad she had worn her spencer of buttercup cloth and, for her head, the capote with the wild poppies along the small brim, though she worried how much dust kicked up from the road would coat her muslin frock by the time they returned home.

She was glad also that Brancaster was courteous. It would go far in procuring him a wife.

"Bath is rather new," he remarked as they passed the Palladian edifices of Queen Square.

"Wood rebuilt Bath the way Augustus turned Rome from mud into marble," Lady Plume replied.

"In Bath stone, which is easier to cut than marble, and has that distinctive honey color," Brancaster said. "Found only in Somerset. Our carrstone is red, though it's also a limestone. There's a great chalk shelf running under Britain from here to Norfolk, some believe."

"Indeed," said Lady Plume, who was more interested in waving to her acquaintance and studying their dress.

"Why would you think so?" Leda asked, curious.

"Have you seen the hillside carvings in Wiltshire? That's chalk giving the horses their white coat. Same with the White Horse of Uffington and the Cerne Abbas giant. And we've chalk pits near my estate, very good for brick making, so very likely the ridge is contiguous."

Leda wondered how a lord knew anything about stone. How easily, too, he remarked these mythical sights. As a gentleman, he had the leisure and the means to travel wherever he wished. So he assumed the same privilege available to everyone, never mind that some people had salaries to earn and depended on the protection of others for their every last need, which left no room for whims and very little leisure.

For a moment—a moment only—Leda contemplated what advantages might be offered the wife of a lord. Travel in her own carriage. Pin money. The title of her ladyship, and the accompanying respect.

But she knew well what was demanded of a wife—at least, a gentleman's wife. The duties demanded of a lady would be compounded. Only the rare and fortunate woman achieved Lady Plume's combination of wealth and liberty as a widow. Leda lacked the fortune as well as the liberty, and one gambled on being a lord's wife, for the fate of the lord's widow rested all too often on the sufferance of the heir.

No, she was better off where she was: quiet as a mouse in her bolt hole in Bath, outside the notice of any feral cats that might be hunting her. She was safe here.

And she would keep Brancaster—Jack—safe from her as well.

"I've a package to send," Leda said as they turned into Westgate and neared the White Hart Inn. "Shall I meet up with you at the Pump Room?"

"We can wait." Brancaster watched her produce the packet she'd been carrying in her cloth bag, wrapped tightly in oiled brown paper.

"One of the orphans you're supporting, I suppose? Come along to the Pump Room when you're finished," Lady Plume said. "Brancaster must have his name in the book, so everyone will know he's arrived."

"My packet is worth more than five pounds, so I must register it, but I oughtn't be long."

"You do not fear being left on your own, Mrs. Wroth? Here's a busy place."

The White Hart was the oldest coaching inn in Bath, at the heart of the medieval borough, and the coach to Gloucestershire departed in half an hour, with all the attendant bustle as ostlers readied horses and passengers readied themselves. Leda blinked at him.

"I am quite accustomed to being on my own, Lord Brancaster."

"I wish you would call me Jack."

"On no account will I assume such familiarity, sir. It would hardly be proper."

He drew nearer, his gray eyes lightening as his gaze touched each feature of her face. His look was as warm as a candle.

"I confess," he murmured, "the word I associate with you is not *proper*."

Her breath caught in her throat. "What vocabulary would you employ?"

He sketched a brief bow. "I will divulge that at another time. I await your company, madame. Something tells me I shall need you to navigate this place."

"I expect you will do sufficiently well on your own."

"But my own company cannot possibly yield the same pleasure. Adieu for now."

Lady Plume emerged from her chair, deciding she could brave the short distance to the Abbey Churchyard, particularly since many of her acquaintance were converging on the same point. Her ladyship took little interest in Leda's errands, so long as her companion was available to her when she wished, but Leda feared Brancaster had seen the address written in her bold hand on the front: Tytherton Kellaways.

But that could mean nothing to him, as it would mean

nothing to Lady Plume should he remark on it. Only Leda knew what the place meant.

Her nerves were stretched thin as thread on a spindle, so perhaps that accounted for the trick her imagination played. Emerging from the coffee room of the inn was a man she hadn't seen in eight years. A man she had hoped never to see again.

A man she'd been certain she'd never see again, because she'd killed him.

Leda nearly dropped her package in the yard, where the dirt had been churned to mud with the passage of hooves, feet, and roaming dogs. A hen in a cage, waiting to be loaded atop the next coach, screeched and fluttered its wings. Leda's insides did the same.

That hair, slick as oil. That dark brow and long nose, the small eyes with their heavy lids, the pink lips puckered in perpetual distaste. That visage was burned into her memories, into her deepest fears. Her skin went cold with apprehension.

He turned toward Union Street, away from the Roman Baths, and Leda rushed to the counter inside to lose herself in what small crowd she could find.

He could not be here. He could *not*. For if he were alive and recognized her, her freedom was at an end.

In a shaking voice, Leda required pen and ink of the agent coordinating the mail, and for an excessive sum, he rendered them. Her hands shaking just as badly, Leda opened her package and scrawled a quick note inside, a desperate question, a plea. The two people who could help her were in as much danger as Leda if their secret were discovered.

Her ears rang with the buzz of wasps as she stepped into the Pump Room. Light falling through the far windows blinded her momentarily. The high ceilings dwarfed the occupants of the room, the noise of conversation a gentle susurration no stronger, or more important, than the lapping of the baths next door in their concrete basin.

Gentlemen clustered around papers, discussing news of riots and sailing ships and war, while ladies promenaded, striving to engage the attention of the gentlemen. Someone's dog rushed past, yipping, while a small tiger in livery and a riding whip tried to clear a path for a servant pushing a Bath chair containing a master whose affliction, one would guess at the sight of him, was gout. From his alcove high in the wall the statue of Beau Nash smiled down upon what he had wrought, and his marble smile said he found it good.

The man, the black shadow, could step inside any moment. Everyone came here, the newly arrived to make themselves known, those settled for the season to survey the new arrivals. He would come and he would see Leda and he would—what?

What power could a dead man have over her?

He would know that Caledonia Toplady had not died as they'd been told.

He would ask what else she had lied about.

He would ask where the child was.

"Mrs. Wroth. Are you quite well?"

The words filtered through her fog but didn't register as belonging to her. A form loomed in the corner of her eye, and out of instinct she shrank away.

"Leda," a voice said quietly, and she turned toward it.

Brancaster, so splendidly solid, like a wall that could keep back the dark. She blinked and focused on his steady eyes, his concerned frown.

"Forgive me. You seemed very far away."

He held out an arm to her, and she took it.

That was a mistake, for once she had him, a steady support, she did not want to let him go.

"What has upset you?"

She forced her lips to move. "Did you write your name in the book?"

"Yes, I—"

"I want to see." Leda fairly dragged him toward the register on its small table. The newest signers moved away, slow as treacle, and she peered at the list of names. Ink danced before her eyes.

"The Duchess of Gordon is in town." Lady Plume gave Leda a start, showing up at her shoulder. "It's been an age since I saw Jane. I do hope she's not ill—that would be such a shame. She was looking forward to leisure once she had all her daughters married."

"Be advised that is your one duty as a parent, milord," Leda said, her voice hollow in her ears. "Raise the girl to be married."

He raised his brows. There was something wicked in the gesture, and her stomach curled in on itself. Perhaps she ought to have eaten that second slice of toast.

"The philosophy of your parents, I take it?"

"And your wife's parents also, I am sure."

"So it was." His jaw set, and he looked out over the small crowd assembled in the Pump Room, but his gaze was distant. "Yet I suspect that was not her goal for herself."

It was not here, the name she dreaded to see. But that did not mean he was not in town. It could mean he had only just arrived and had not yet signed the register.

It could mean he might enter the room at any moment. Would he recognize her, after all this time?

What man would not recognize the woman convicted of his murder?

She pulled Brancaster away from the ledger, her fingers digging into his arm with unnecessary tension. "Tell me more about the qualities you desire in a wife. The next to hold that privilege may well be in this room."

"The qualities I wish in a governess, you mean."

"I thought I persuaded you a wife was the better bargain. All that labor, and for free."

"Rather your comments persuaded me that wifehood must be the most dreaded and overworked status in the kingdom, and no sane woman would willingly lash herself to that mast without the greatest inducement."

"You forget what an inducement bed and board can be, all on its own," Leda answered. "And a companion who cannot be objectionable—or so I assume," she added hastily, realizing she had said too much.

He didn't miss a thing, drat the man. His brows lifted. "You find me unobjectionable?"

"I am assuming the perspective of the dainty young maiden who will become your wife, and presuming she would not find you so." She turned to survey the crowd about them.

"Who said I would wish for a maiden?" he murmured.

"Every man does. Come, here are Sir Charles and Miss Hotham, whom you slighted last night, and may now repair the breach."

Leda stepped forward, and he stepped with her, as if they were a matched pair and had been in harness together for years. He wore Eau de Cologne, and on him the notes that emerged were grapefruit and bergamot, with a hint of tobacco.

A wall of longing hit Leda in the face. The faint scent of tobacco took her back to her father's study, one of her favorite places in the world, once her shelter and escape.

She had no refuge now. Only this tiny space in Bath where she crouched like a child closing her eyes in a game of hide and seek, praying she wouldn't be found.

"Sir Charles, good morn. How are you finding the waters today?" A sulfurous odor drifted from his cup, dispensed to him by the matron behind the wooden bar at one side of the room.

"Miss Hotham, I hope you enjoyed the assembly last night. Lord Brancaster had already engaged my hand for the minuet or I would not have bustled away from you so hastily."

Leda made quick introductions. Sir Charles's brow worked while Miss Hotham regarded Brancaster, a blush rising on her cheeks. She could not seem to decide how deeply to curtsey.

"Miss Hotham, I detect that your days in the schoolroom passed under the tutelage of a wise governess. Would you be willing to share the name of your friend? His lordship is in search of a proper person to instruct his charge." She pulled her lips into a smile. "Though I have counseled him that he might instead seek a wife."

Miss Hotham turned scarlet.

"Brancaster!" Sir Charles's brow cleared. "The Mad Baron, eh? 'Swhat Howth called you. Rowdy good story there, I'd imagine?"

"Not at all." Brancaster's voice was as smooth as melted butter, but his arm beneath Leda's hand felt like a catapult primed to spring. "Too much time walking the cliffside with one's thoughts will lead a man's friends to call him mad, and style themselves wits for it."

Sir Charles looked disappointed that a salacious tale was not in the offing. Meanwhile, Brancaster regarded Miss Hotham with no more interest than he had regarded his cutlery at breakfast; there was need to interact in socially acceptable manner, and that was all. He seemed unmoved by the delicate slope of her nose or the susceptible fairness of her skin.

Leda wondered why she felt faintly smug about his lack of interest in the girl.

Miss Hotham appeared desperate to remedy this. Her fan fluttered. "I find madness very poetic. Like in Mr. Wordsworth's *Lyrical Ballads*."

"Your governess had a romantical interest, then?" Leda asked, determined to set the conversation on its proper course.

More blushes painted Miss Hotham's sweetly curved cheek. "Oh, no, my mother oversaw my education, mum."

"Ah, a pity, as I imagine she is not eligible for either of your open positions, your lordship," Leda teased Brancaster. "Would you care to walk with Miss Hotham about the room and hear more about her education? Sir Charles might take me to get my daily dose of the waters."

"Now see here, Mrs. Wroth, I won't have you pitching my daughter at the Mad Baron," Sir Charles chortled. "I know your reputation as a matchmaker."

"I had thought her a match unmaker, rather," Jack murmured.

"A red coat's good enough for my gel, should there be a government pension behind it," Sir Charles said. "Look you, there's Captain Handfield below the statue. Come and I'll introduce you, El." He nodded to Jack, then Leda, and towed his daughter away.

"Are you going to encounter that reception often?" Leda considered the knight's departing form and Miss Hotham's wistful glance in Jack's direction.

"I fear so," Brancaster answered, his jaw etched in hard lines.

"Perhaps you'd best tell me why people call you mad."

"I'm sure I cannot say."

She tugged him into a promenade with her so he did not stand there like one of the Corinthian pillars of the colonnade, sturdy, strong, imposing. She brushed aside the observation that he was the ideal height for her to twine her arm in his and walk comfortably.

She could make no sense of him. The men used his sobriquet to poke fun. They didn't fear Brancaster's madness, whatever strain it was presumed to be.

But they wouldn't marry their daughters to him, either.

"Will you make me resort to consulting Lady Plume? I have yet to sort out that line of relationship. Never say you inherited a family strain of madness from her, for I have seen no sign of disordered wits. She never even has the vapors."

"She is a great-aunt, and my grandfather was her youngest brother. I do not think they were close, but Lady Plume has kindly taken an interest in my branch of the family, which none of my other relations, aside from Aunt Dinah, have proven eager to do."

"Because of your reputation, or because of something else?"

He looked at her bleakly. "Can a man ever be separated from his reputation?"

"Yes, if the grounds of accusation are false."

She waited for explanation, which was not forthcoming. There was some basis to the claims of madness, then. But what?

False shadows and old scores, as had been the case with her?

Not that she was about to tell him they shared that taint.

She turned to survey the room of its female population, identifiable by the many varied ornaments in their hair. A young maid would not do for Brancaster, so it would appear. He required a woman of experience, of developed character and steady mind, one inured to gossip and bandied words. A comely widow, or a maid of advancing years, someone who would not be shocked by a man's occasional eccentricities. A sensible sort who would provide a gentle guiding hand for his daughter, a thrifty eye on the running of his house, and companionship for himself on gloomy afternoons when the cliffsides were no good for walking.

Such women existed all over, in droves. She could present a handful of them to Brancaster before the morning was out. She tugged his arm to draw his attention to the first one, and when he turned to her a sudden vision soared into her mind, driving out thought and sense.

Brancaster, across the breakfast table, sliding her the morning paper with that look of warm attention, that small smile upon his well-defined lips as she handed him his toast, buttered just as she knew he liked it.

She felt off balance, like she'd stepped into a punt on the river. She'd never known domestic tranquility for herself, not until she found Miss Gregoire's here in Bath, and she'd certainly never imagined male companionship for her future. Not of the sort that shared breakfast after sharing a bed.

The mineral scents of the waters must be addling her brain. Sharing beds, indeed. She received her fair share of subtle hints and invitations, as a widow still in possession of her looks, but nothing yet to tempt her.

Not until Brancaster, with that look in his fog-gray eyes, that lock of caramel hair curling over a jutting brow, that precise slope to his jaw and his scent of citrus and the way his gloved hand left a brand on her back as he steered her in a circle in the minuet, causing all her breath to fight its way up her chest.

Good heavens, it was time to bring her thoughts in order. She'd been off her stride since the White Hart, and no surprise. "I believe it is time to introduce—"

"Mrs. Wroth. Infernal gossip and peddler of lies."

A man bore down on her, a tower of indignation. Every part of him trembled, from the tight curls sprouting about his red face to the ribbons dangling from the knees of his breeches. A double row of buttons studded a tight coat with a high stand-fall collar and tails cutaway over a crimson waistcoat lined with smaller buttons, all of them quivering with the force of his indignation. He loomed before Leda, looking down at her beneath the brim of a tall, conical black hat.

"You—you *harpy*."

"Here now," Brancaster said sharply. "I'm sure that's uncalled for."

"You turned her off me. Told I was insolvent. Told her *lies*."

"I never lie," Leda lied. "Brancaster, this is Mr. Crutch, lately of Warminster. Mr. Crutch, Baron Brancaster of Holme Hall."

"She was sweet on me." Crutch ignored his lordship to glare at Leda. Beneath her fingers, Brancaster's arm tensed, drawing her closer to him. The action seemed instinctive. "Sweet, and you turned her sour."

"Mr. Crutch, I am sure any suit you press will rise or fall on the merits of your own self," Leda replied. "If Mrs. Limpet has changed in her preferences or inclinations, that is within a woman's prerogative to do."

"You're a wrecker." Crutch gripped his walking stick and continued glaring. "You find perfectly happy people, with happy hopes and prospects, and you—you *destroy* them."

"I do no such thing," Leda snapped. She had made her mission in life—her new, reclaimed life, at least—to help women find freedom and purpose, relief from persecution, encouragement to follow the paths that would best funnel them to their dreams.

She did not destroy. And she paid penance every day for the destruction she had done.

"I have not yet had my cup," Brancaster announced, "and neither have you, Mrs. Wroth. Crutch, is it? Good day." He steered around the irate bachelor as if he were a goat in a farm lane.

Leda made the mistake of glancing behind. Crutch had, predictably, turned to deliver a fulminating glare.

He could seriously damage her reputation with his accusations that she had meddled and manipulated. Her name came to lips as the soul of absolute discretion. Those who sought her advice or fixes did so with the promise that their difficulty without be solved with the utmost quiet and lack of fuss.

If Leda lost the trust of the people who came to her, she would not lose income, true. But as a conventional lady's companion, overlooked and unremarked, she would be a deal less interesting to Lady Plume, and *there* lay all her security.

"Do all your unmatched take it so poorly?" Brancaster asked, holding her arm close to his body. A distracting heat arose from him, hotter than the waters of the spring pouring beneath their feet.

Leda couldn't respond. Her lungs seized when she saw a shadow slip through the tall doors, pass through the morning light slanting on the floor. Greasy black hair. Small, close-set eyes. The black stock at his throat, as if he were a military man or religious. As if he had the authority and discipline of either.

A cold, quivering sensation wound up her body from her feet, as if she'd stepped into an enormous chilled pudding, and she was drowning.

He was here.

"Do you know, I believe I might dispense with my daily dose today." Leda was astonished that her throat worked to form words, which moreover sounded perfectly sensible, when her senses had taken flight like a screaming hen. "There is so much more to see in town, Brancaster. Let us find your new lady somewhere else."

She had to get him out of here. She had to find him a governess and send him off packing before the ghosts grew any closer, before there were any chance he might learn who Leda was, before Lady Plume learned.

Bath had been her refuge for six years, where she clung like a red squirrel in its tree. Now the kite was on the loose, hunting with his keen eyes, and that refuge would disappear. Where could she go next? Where would she be safe?

Nowhere will be safe for you, if you leave me.

He'd sworn that, hadn't he? Made her a promise. And now he meant to keep it, even from beyond the grave.

CHAPTER FIVE

Leda laid her selection of evening gowns on the bed and studied them. Her cache of possessions was small, but each was dear. If he made her run, she would lose all this: the beautiful things, the small trinkets that held meaning, this pretty room with its walls of robin's-egg blue. A life she had built for herself—on Lady Plume's generosity, that was true, but *hers*, the way nothing had been hers in her early life, nor her married life, either.

She didn't want to run. She wanted to stay.

It had been grueling, keeping her mask on today. Lady Plume wanted Brancaster with them as they paid calls on Lady Plume's extensive acquaintance and new arrivals. Very often a host or another guest, or sometimes a servant, pulled Leda aside for a small conference. Lady Plume smiled beneficently upon these exchanges; it pleased her to see her companion in demand, to know her resources were of benefit to her friends. Lady Plume was born to be chatelaine of a medieval keep or some rich Dark Age abbey, save that she never could have borne the absence of basic hygiene.

Brancaster observed these conferrals with a blend of

curiosity and suspicion. Were he at all possible to ignore, Leda would have done so. But there was little choice to pretend he did not exist when her ladyship paraded her nephew as if he were a prime stud she had won at auction, determined to display his fine form and bloodlines to full advantage. Her ladyship regaled her friends at length with the prosperous and colorful history of the Burnham family, which Leda had never before heard her praise; she itemized the honors her ancestors had achieved at court; and she spoke of Holme Hall, perched upon its carrstone cliffs far away, as a veritable Hampton Court of Norfolk.

Brancaster listened to these recitations with his features bland of expression but a curious muscle ticking below his jaw. This only drew attention to the truly splendid lines of his face and neck, representative of his well-knit form altogether, and since not one female missed an opportunity to commend him or attempt to draw his approval toward herself, Leda soon grew irritated by the unfailing praise.

She chided herself now for her jealousy. Had she set herself to the effort, Leda could have had a governess for him lined up in the first hour of their day, and at least three eager candidates for his wife by the time their calls were concluded. Two further candidates appeared as they strolled around the Bath Vauxhall Gardens, Lady Plume in her chair, Leda on Jack's arm as if she were any friend of the family and not a paid employee. Regrettably, Leda could not in good conscience recommend any of these eager young girls pursue Brancaster, despite their charms of person and manner, for who knew but that she would be sending some unsuspecting maid like a lamb to slaughter.

Brancaster was not in the least unpleasant to be around, and his daughter did not seem to be difficult. From the few words he had spoken of Muriel, Leda gathered she was an imaginative but deeply sensitive child at a point in her life where she crucially needed the guidance of a sensible female.

Still, Leda thought as she made her selection for the evening, she would not send any female into the clutches of a man who was dangerous, no matter how poetically his castle on the cliffside was described.

A woman would require a staunch set of morals to be cast daily in the company of such a well-proportioned, appealing man and not begin to harbor untoward fantasies. She must be too wise to fall under the spell of gray eyes and a beautiful mouth that twitched in the most beguiling way when he was amused. She must not be too entertained by the sly, wicked sense of humor in his comments after they departed a particularly silly company. And she must not, on any account, be the melting sort who would be unduly conscious of the many small, kind attentions a gentleman might pay a lady, especially when one had gone without such attentions before.

The way he might, for instance, steer her around a soft spot in the path, warning her not to soil her shoe. The way he might lean too close to comment that a friend's feathered hat, fluttering in the breeze, appeared about to take flight. The way he might buy treats for all of them, but give the first to the companion, rather than his aunt, the knight's lady.

And she must not mark, and thereafter recall at inopportune moments, the way his eyes widened and his face brightened with luxurious appreciation as he experienced for the first time the divine revelation of sugary dough that was the famous and unrivaled Sally Lunn bun.

No, Leda could *not* in good conscience put any woman in his company who might lose her admirable self-control at that look of sensual joy. The man was a pit of crumbling rock, and a woman could fall in, unsuspecting.

In the event this was her last night with him and she might

indeed be on the run tomorrow, Leda wore her newest evening gown to dinner, a delicate red silk gauze draped over a silk chemise. Jet beads decorated the bodice, which was modest by most standards, and the small puff sleeves left her arms bare. Beaded embroidery around the hem made the skirt flare about her as she walked, and she chose her black silk fan for a dramatic accent.

"Good heavens, are we at a Venetian masque?" Lady Plume remarked when Leda came down to join them in the parlor. "I expect any moment a harlequin will cartwheel into the room and breathe fire."

"Are you telling me I look ridiculous?"

Her ladyship had sent her own lady's maid to curl and dress Leda's hair, a boon which was not uncommon, and another mark of how Lady Plume confused the issue of Leda's status, far too often treating her as a friend or relative in the Crescent for an extended stay instead of an employee who earned a generous quarterly wage.

"I say you look delectable," Lady Plume announced, loudly enough that all her guests could hear the proclamation. There were ten of them in all: Mr. and Mrs. Warren, newly arrived in town with their two unmarried daughters; Lord and Lady Oxmantown, Lady Plume's cronies and a fixture at her table; and Mr. Ravelli, who was attempting to set up a small conservatory where he taught art, music, and the Italian language to any who would pay tuition.

It was soon clear from the vein of conversation that the Misses Warren were there to tempt Brancaster, and Mr. Ravelli there to flatter Leda. He eagerly took a seat beside her at table and monopolized her through both courses, leaving Leda very little time to grill the Misses Warren on their accomplishments and determine whether either was suitable to be sent off to the wild fringes of Norfolk as a bride.

"Norfolk!" Lord Oxmantown boomed when Brancaster was introduced. "Must admit I've never been. What's the business, then? Fishing? Can't imagine you raise cattle there."

"We can and do," Brancaster replied. "And there's a deal of effort to try to fence and drain parts of the coastline to turn the salt marshes into cropland. I believe there's better luck with the fisheries on the eastern seaboard, Yarmouth side."

"Farming," Mr. Warren scoffed. "No man's going to advance himself by farming these days, no matter how many acres he can enclose. It's industry will run this country in the next century, mark my words."

"And that we have in Norfolk as well," Brancaster said. "There's a cordwainer in Norwich, I heard, who has set up a factory for making shoes. Can you fancy? Machines punching and sewing your leather, just like the wool industry, which your Midlands have learned from Norfolk. Miss Warren," he turned to the eldest, "have you an item of clothing of worsted wool?"

Miss Warren blushed from her neckline to the knot of beads and flowers holding her curls. "I am sure I cannot say."

"I have a shawl and a nice thick pair of worsted stockings for muddy days." Leda spooned up her white soup.

Brancaster smiled at her, gratified that Leda, at least, was not too bashful to speak of lady's attire. "First made in Worstead, Norfolk."

"How marvelous."

"But you're not into wool-making, man."

Lord Oxmantown had only been made baron a few years ago due to his service in the Irish Parliament, but he had been created Viscount Oxmantown shortly thereafter, which elevated him above Brancaster's mere barony. He made no secret that he had his eye on reviving the title of Earl of Rosse, which had died with a male relative of his earlier in the century. "Parliament's the place for a man to advance," Oxmantown announced. "All the more opportunity now with Union upon us. Plenty of matters to be settled and doled out yet." He smacked his lips as a footman placed a dish of larded rabbit before him.

"I confess I've been kept by business and other family matters from taking my seat." Brancaster selected a roasted partridge for his plate. "Been voting by proxy."

"Eh? What business is that, then?"

"Our area is good for flint mining and, in the past, brickworks. Brick making's a touchy trade, however, and I've found it difficult to achieve the correct formula for a brick that is durable and will keep its shape. I've spent several years performing various experiments on my lands, which no doubt have led some of my neighbors to believe I'm a mad chemist of some sort."

"Oh, that would explain the rumors, then," the younger Warren girl was surprised into saying, upon which she immediately blushed a hue rivaling that sported by her elder sister.

"Speaking of rumors." Lady Oxmantown laid down her spoon. "I heard the most dreadful news of Mr. Crutch. A dear, charming man, acquaintance of mine, can always be counted upon to make up a table or cut a fine leg." She addressed this to Mrs. Warren, who nodded as if to agree that these were fine qualities in a man. "He has been disappointed in love, I hear. Had his heart and fortunes set on a young widow, and she spurned him on the poor advice of a friend." She glared at Leda.

"That his fortunes are disappointed I do not doubt." Leda watched Mr. Ravelli place a slender veal cutlet on her plate, along with three dainty olives. He must assume she was delicate, and could not know she adored olives. "I imagine a man may hold ambitions to be elevated in marriage every bit as much as a woman might."

"Oh, I don't think—?" Miss Warren faltered.

"That women endeavor to advance themselves through

marriage?" Leda raised a brow. "If not they, then I assure you their friends and family have that aim."

Brancaster regarded her from his place as Lady Plume's guest of honor. "You do not believe in marrying for love, Mrs. Wroth?"

"I believe it is a fine aim for a heroine in a romantic story," Leda replied. "But I suspect that most of us are swayed by practical considerations, from the Earl of Howth's daughters down to Sally in the scullery, who is counting coins until she can marry her Tom."

Gibbs, standing behind Brancaster, reared and blinked at Leda as if surprised she knew this.

"I assure you I am only thinking of my daughters' happiness," Mrs. Warren said freezingly.

"My Dunlap cut a fine leg," Lady Plume said thoughtfully. "Awfully smart in his uniform. But in the end I chose him because I thought I could help him to a knighthood, and so I did."

"Let us consider Brancaster as an example," Leda said.

"Must we?" Brancaster murmured, carving a leg of lamb for his aunt.

"He is on the hunt for a wife, and no doubt he will narrow his choices to maids of pleasing demeanor and aspect," Leda barreled on. "But in the end, he must have a governess for his daughter and a chatelaine for his castle, and can he depend that his affections alone will land on a suitable woman for this task? Or ought he be guided by practical considerations?"

"You must have been terribly disappointed in your marriage. I do pity you, Mrs. Wroth," Miss Warren ventured.

"Well you might. In my example, my parents married me to the highest man they could find to offer, and we were completely unsuited in temperament or our hopes."

"I imagine you made his life a living torment as a result." Lady Oxmantown sniffed.

Leda decided not to tell her the entire truth. Lady Oxmantown had never much liked her, but the matter of Mr. Crutch had sealed Leda's villainy in her eyes.

"Agnes, I do find myself surprised at the liberties you afford your servants," Lady Oxmantown went on. "Why, here is milord with his glass nearly empty, and your butler has not yet stirred himself to pour more wine."

Gibbs, following Lady Plume's nod, hastened to his lordship's elbow with the bottle of Madeira. Her ladyship abhorred drunkenness at her table and had given Gibbs very specific instructions about fortifying Oxmantown, who would not on his own exhibit the least restraint.

Brancaster, Leda noted, enjoyed small sips from his cup, but at the same slow pace demonstrated by Mr. Warren, whom Leda suspected had not strayed far from his former merchant's shop and more temperate bourgeois values.

"As for your companion, as you call her." Lady Oxmantown was not finished with her diatribe. "Why, here she is in a splendid gown, sitting at your table enjoying your largesse, and telling your friends how they ought to go on. Do you suppose any other lady in town would afford her the same license?"

"No, which is how I have allowed no one else in town to lure her away from me," Lady Plume answered. "Including yourself when you asked, Jane. Leda keeps me very comfortable, and I like to reward her for it."

"And yet you proposed, just this morning, loaning me to Brancaster to set his affairs in order and find him a wife," Leda could not help remarking.

"But who says an excursion to Norfolk would not be a reward," Lady Plume replied, cutting a French bean. "It's lovely this time of year, and Holme Hall is quite charming."

Brancaster took a bracing draught of wine.

Leda could not go to Norfolk, because she had to figure out how to keep her character but leave her very comfortable position with Lady Plume if the ghost she had seen this morning were indeed real, not the dead man but the dead man's heir, here in town, meaning to stay long enough that his path might cross with Leda's. She had changed a great deal in ten years, at least on the inside; she was wiser, calmer, and would not be commanded. She must take a moment to think, not blindly rush into the cold and the darkness when she felt she was under threat.

But if older and grown she still possessed the same dark brown hair and unusual eyes, the same shape to her face and form, the scar her husband had left in the hairline at her left temple. She, too, would look a ghost come alive to the interloper, since for the last six years he had thought her dead.

She had left the express command that he be told this.

And she would die in truth did he make her go back.

The beads decorating Leda's gown grew constricting, though she had worn her most comfortable stays. They lay against her skin like so many small needles, and the swoop on her bodice that had in the shop looked so beguiling now seemed to outline exactly where a man might plunge a knife to best pierce her heart.

Brancaster watched her curiously. Damn the man and his all too perceptive eyes. Why could he not be preoccupied with food, wine, and his own importance, like Oxmantown?

She had been safe in Bath, or if not safe, at least hidden. But Lady Oxmantown reminded her how precarious her position was. Lady Plume had petted Leda because Leda's skills at managing and fixing—oh, all right, some would call it meddling —kept Lady Plume at the center of interesting schemes and the best gossip. Her ladyship could, and would, turn Leda off in a moment if Leda were no longer a credit to her establishment or in any way brought discord into the luxurious comfort that Lady Plume enjoyed.

What poetic justice that it should be Brancaster—the man who drove women mad—who had stirred up this hornet's nest for her. If she had to give up the life she'd built and leave once again with nothing, Leda might go mad in truth.

LADY PLUME DID NOT fancy herself a literary sort, but she housed a few shelves of books in the smaller drawing room on the second floor. It was here Leda repaired after the guests at last departed, Mr. Ravelli far overstaying his welcome to persuade Leda to perform one more duet with him, and then one more. She was only a passable musician at best, no compare to Mr. Ravelli's truly fine tenor, but if he were not attempting to recruit her as a music teacher for his school, then he was doing a creditable job of showing her what life as his wife would be like.

If Leda married again, she could not fall into the clutches of the ghost. By law she was free to marry, she thought. Or at least, she was no longer bound to a husband. She was not entirely apprised of the finer points of law when it came to marrying a woman who had been locked away for being mad.

The library might offer her ideas, so she stole there with her chamber candle after she hung up the delicate red gauze, wondering when she might have occasion to wear such a beautiful gown again. Certainly she couldn't take her fine things on the run, and the goal of her foray into Lady Plume's tiny library was to find a map to tell her where in the world she might go.

Wales? She'd heard it was an uncharted place, filled with trolls and wild men in caves. The farthest reaches of Cornwall, where land dropped into the rocky sea? She might be trapped like a fox at bay there. Perhaps she ought to consider going north, to the untamed Highlands, to hide herself among the craggy mountains and misty moors and vast tracts of unpeopled land. Toplady would never look for her there.

A light shone in the drawing room around the deep upholstered chair. Brancaster sat within it, ankle crossed over one knee. In what was no doubt a nod to Lady Plume's sense of propriety he had worn knee breeches with silk stockings and black pumps to dinner, and the fabric stretched over his muscular legs. She oughtn't look at his thighs.

Leda moved her gaze up and lost track of her breathing for a moment. He'd set aside his coat and cravat and sat in his shirtsleeves, which ended in a small ruffled cuff at his wrist, and a beautifully embroidered brocade waistcoat. She hadn't had an opportunity to appreciate it at dinner, but she took a moment now to admire the delicate swirls of thread, and the masculine strength in his broad shoulders and chest.

He looked up from his book. His hair was slightly mussed, the waves not as smooth as they'd been over dinner, and a small shadow of stubble cloaked his jaw, making him seem a bit rakish. She hadn't seen a man in undress in years, and never a man who appealed so completely to her sense of aesthetics. Sally the kitchen maid would call him a prime article and no mistake, and she would not be wrong.

"I've interrupted you."

He didn't speak, so she did, needing to break the spell his steady gaze cast over her. She was undressed as well, having pulled over her undergown the morning gown she would never actually wear in the morning, because it was likely Lady Plume would receive callers or want to go out. The loose neckline revealed more of her decolletage than she was accustomed to showing in company and, while the voluminous folds concealed the outlines of her body, the sheer fabric showed the form beneath despite herself.

The candlelight shivered and danced, much as Leda's pulse was doing.

"You are welcome to interrupt me."

The low rasp of his voice raised the hair on her arms and shoulders, a thrill of alarm.

She had never encountered this before, an imposing man in her private spaces. She hadn't realized they could take up so much space in a chair, in a room, even when sitting still, emanating a sense of strength leashed and waiting beneath that touchable fabric. She'd forgotten, or pushed aside, the memory of the ways of men, their big hands, their scents of spice and tobacco, their deep voices.

She'd never been around a man who made her so *aware*, as if her nerves had been tapped alive.

A scent of sulfur wafted from her candle, promising her that moving forward was a step toward temptation, one step toward hell.

"Come in," he said, and she did, temptation be damned.

"Your aunt has persuaded you to trade your poky lodgings for one of her soft beds?" She drifted along the bookcases, pretending to look at titles. She already knew what was here.

"I hadn't wished to impose on her, but she offers several amenities that the rooms I found did not." He rested his gaze on Leda as if she figured among these amenities. Heat rippled across her collarbone.

"At the price of your bachelor's independence. She will mark all your comings and goings, you know."

"I have found that the pleasures of the bachelor life, whatever they may be, have lost their appeal."

"Thus the wish to marry again. Did neither of the Misses Warren show promise? It cannot be there is not a single lady you met today who has piqued your interest."

He closed his book but put a finger in it to mark his place. "I've met one."

She studied a row of leather-bound titles, conscious of how she held her candle, how her body moved in this space. She was accustomed to being looked at, but the weight of his regard was different. It lay on her skin like a touch.

"Do you mean to make an offer?"

"I am not certain she would encourage my suit. She has not spoken highly of marriage."

He stood, his body unfolding from the chair, and she was treated to a full view of the powerful swell of his shoulders, the strong square of his chest. The waistcoat hugged a flat stomach, and she suspected he did not rely on stays. The stretch of the fabric suggested that what lay beneath was pure muscle and virile blood.

Now why was she having notions that he was *virile*.

She turned to glance at him over one shoulder, arching a brow. "Is she the type to consider an association outside of marriage?"

That was very daring of her. Leda hadn't once contemplated having an affair, though she knew widows like herself could take such liberties, if they stayed discreet. Leda herself looked the other way, and occupied herself in her room, when Lady Plume now and again entertained a male caller late into the night.

"I do not know if she could encourage those attentions, either. And at any rate, I ought to occupy my time with finding a companion for my daughter. Not for myself."

"Yet the right wife would fulfill both of those functions, and so admirably," Leda murmured.

Heat teased her senses first, sending a tingle down her spine. Then the scent of tobacco and warm male curled beneath her nose as he drew close. A spicy undertone came with it, a scent unfamiliar but which conjured images of the dark undergrowth of forests, wild animals, hunter and prey. She shivered as he spoke, and his breath wafted over the part of her shoulder left open by the loose neckline of her gown.

"What are you searching for?"

Safety. Like all cornered creatures, she wanted safety: a burrow in which to hide. A companion to protect her.

She turned her head away, scanning the titles without reading them. "Something to lull me to sleep. My imagination is overactive tonight."

He held out the volume in his hands, gilt tooled on the green leather. "My aunt had a copy of the *Lyrical Ballads*. I was curious about it."

"Appropriately soporific?"

"Not so. The first poem is about an ancient mariner going barking mad. Lack of water, I gather, and something about having to wear a dead bird about his neck."

Leda scrunched up her face. "Then by comparison, you must feel quite mundane. The utterly normal, average baron. Nothing like what they say."

"The accusation is not that I am mad, so much as I drove my wife to madness."

"I am sure that is not true."

He lifted a brow. The hairs were dark, like his lashes, startling against the pale color of his eyes, which caught the shadows in the room. "No? Yet you said almost as much over breakfast."

"That you drove your wife mad? Did you?"

He turned away. "She died believing I did. Of a certain, I did nothing to help her."

"Surely you tried."

"Perhaps I did. But if a man cannot change his situation, or his nature—what could I have done?"

"If you were not cruel to her, but made attempts to secure her happiness, then you did as much as any could expect. The rest is on her to come to peace with her situation."

He lifted his head. "Did you? Come to peace with your situation?"

Leda refrained from giving an answer. She had murdered her husband and run away. That was how she made her peace.

He moved along the bookshelf with her, casting a penumbra of sensation about her, as when moon swam before the sun.

"Would you come to Norfolk if I asked?"

She breathed in the scent of him and again had a notion of wild creatures on the run, damp forest leaves, spicy pine, an earth rich with dark secrets.

Yes. She wanted nothing more than to burrow against him, wrap herself in his warmth. Let herself be safe in his powerful shadow.

"No."

For how could she trust herself? She had her own strain of madness. She woke one day holding a knife tipped in blood, with the body of a dead man in the parlor. She couldn't trust herself in a house with a man, and certainly not an innocent child.

Women were safe. Lady Plume was safe. And if Bath was no longer her bolt hole, if the nephew of the man she'd slain might recognize or, worse yet, had come to find her, then she would not be going to Norfolk or any known land. She would have to disappear.

"There is nothing that would persuade you?"

He was too close. His nearness disordered her brain, sent her thoughts jumping like wood mice. She wanted to anchor him right here next to her, never let him leave, so she might stand indefinitely in this state of awakening, her entire body coming alive.

"I have no experience as a governess. I have no interest in being a wife. Anything else, as you say, is a distraction."

"Sometimes I think our distractions keep us alive. Keep us from truly going mad at the state of things."

She cast her eyes about anywhere, to keep from closing her eyelids and losing herself to the seductive spell he cast. She didn't know what this was, this glow of heat that moved along her skin, as if she were bread set into an oven. She'd never known this. A hollow ache appeared in her core, the longing for something she'd never possessed.

"Ah—found it."

"An answer?"

"A book of interest." She couldn't tell him she needed maps to find a port where she could sail away to far lands. She set the candle on a small table and reached for the title she'd deciphered in the shifting dark, but it sat on a shelf above her head, just beyond her fingertips.

He stepped toward her and lifted his arm. The action brought her face close to his neck, bare without the cravat, a smooth column of skin. If she leaned forward but half an inch, she could bury her nose in the dip between his collarbones. Press her lips to his skin, breathe deeply.

He froze, arm in the air, as if he sensed her thought. The scent of him was maddening, awaking the sly animal that lived inside her, the little fox that had been sleeping for going on ten years.

He stood there, waiting, a hitch in his breath, the weight of his gaze burning into the side of her face. Leda surrendered to the madness. She darted out her tongue and touched it to that skin waiting just beyond her lips, like a delectable trifle served up only for her. His neck was smooth and warm and salty.

He groaned at the contact, as if some sleeping animal were rousing to life within him as well. She lifted her head and he stared into her eyes, his gaze a swirl of shadows. Then he bent his head and she didn't flinch but met him, took his mouth as it clamped across hers, met his force and heat and instant, hungry need.

She didn't know what possessed her but it roared life in an instant, flames leaping out from banked coals, and this, *this*, his mouth on hers, was the thing she'd been craving since that moment she saw him leaning so carelessly on that pillar, as if he held up the room, and she wanted him to hold her up, too.

His lips were firm and sure of their mission, nothing like other lips she'd known. She grasped the lapels of his waistcoat so she didn't fall over or dissolve at the onslaught of heat. Desire poured through her like mix into a cake mold, thick and sweet and languid, sinking to every corner of her body. The warmth crept to that deep, secret crevice between her legs and she felt a sharp awareness there, like a mouth opening, the way her mouth opened beneath his as he tilted back her head and coaxed apart her lips and plunged his tongue against hers. The room spun and lifted away.

She clung to him, awash in heat, drowning in it, aware of nothing but the press of his mouth, the heat of his body, the delirium of plunder as he sipped from her essence and she felt every part of her body rising to meet him, as if she might crash and melt against him like a wave breaking on a dock.

He broke away first, lifting his head and hauling in air. "Leda."

He sounded dazed, like a man who'd taken a blow. She felt no less shocked.

"Dear heavens," she whispered.

He stared into her eyes, his gaze searching out every line of her face, and she feared what she revealed in the light of the flickering candles. Her need and hunger, immodest, insistent.

The way he'd spun her like a child's top and she could scarcely stand on her feet.

He dropped his forehead to her shoulder and she reveled in the weight of him, in the sign that he too was overset. His hands rested on the backs of her shoulders but he slid them down her back, gathering her close, an embrace and a caress. She molded herself to his body, to his hard chest and powerful thighs, then felt it between them—his *man's* part, thick and hard. She froze.

"Leda." His fingers curled into her soft skin, his voice a ragged gasp. "Will you—"

"*No.*"

She wrenched away. He was attractively built, indeed beautifully sculpted, but she had fallen under his ensorcelling spell and forgotten: he was a man, possessed of the traditional parts of a man, and the ways to inflict pain on a woman.

"Forgive me. I forgot myself," she whispered.

He drew back. He didn't scold, or rage, or beg. How unusual. He merely sucked in air, his nostrils flaring, and squared his shoulders.

"I forgot myself as well. I beg your pardon."

"Don't," she said swiftly, then held her fingers to her lips, abashed.

"Don't what?"

"Don't regret this." This kiss. This magic that had fallen over both of them for a moment. The pleasure that danced in her veins even now, waltzing with her horror and fear.

"My only regret, Mrs. Wroth, is that you are not leading me directly to your bed."

Insolent man, to leave her with the images that conjured. Of him leaning back in her widow's bed, his body gleaming as she peeled off those gorgeous fabrics to inspect the muscle and warm skin beneath. More of those drugging kisses, and what he might taste like if she put her mouth elsewhere upon him.

But she knew what came after, and it wasn't worth the rest.

He held out her candlestick and the book, and she took them. His brow lifted.

"*The Blazing World,* by the Duchess of Newcastle? I am not familiar with that title."

"It is a strange fantasy, written over a hundred years ago, about a woman kidnapped to another world where she is made an empress. Written by a woman, Margaret Cavendish. She called it one part romance, one part philosophy, and one part fantastic." Exactly what Leda wished her life could be, in that same balance.

His other brow rose to meet the first. He was being so blasted calm.

"I am not sure you are in for a quiet sleep," he said.

"I never am." Leda curled the book to her chest, where her heart still raced like a runaway colt, and left the room before she did something utterly mad. Like pull his mouth to hers again and beg him to kiss her senseless, or worse yet, bring him to her room.

CHAPTER SIX

She hadn't had the nightmares in a while.

She was locked in his wine cellar again, too cold for comfort, not cold enough to kill her, knowing that if she raged and smashed the bottles, she would be as mad as he said.

She stepped through his dark house on a dark night, knowing something watched her, something with inimical intentions. White, thin hands that might reach out at any moment and touch where they had no business to be.

She walked through a misty dawn in a frozen garden, knowing she'd left something terrible locked in the house, but not knowing *what*. And when it might rise and follow.

She plunged a knife into his chest and withdrew the triumphant, bloody blade to see that she had stabbed Brancaster, and she watched as the warm flush left his face and the light left his brilliant eyes, leaving him a corpse before her. Terror like she'd never known.

She screamed for help, so many times, and her voice was a whisper, the scratch of one bare branch on another on a winter afternoon.

"You look quite knocked up," Lady Plume said sympathetically when Leda joined her in the breakfast room in her plainest morning dress, a cotton round gown with hand-painted red buds patterning the fabric. Her hand mirror told her the bright gown did not detract from the violet shadows beneath her eyes.

"We did not entertain all that late last evening," Lady Plume added, her gaze wandering to Brancaster, who tapped a rim around a soft-boiled egg.

Leda's stomach turned at the thought of eggs or meat, and she selected a piece of toast from the side rack. Gibbs offered her butter, the merest sliver, and by this Leda knew she was not yet back in his good graces.

"I stayed up too late reading." Leda avoided looking at Brancaster. The memory of that kiss flooded her senses, and she feared the evidence of it would appear on her face.

Evidence of how she had completely, if momentarily, lost her mind. Kissing a man! Her employer's nephew! In her own house!

Brancaster scooped out the soft innards of the egg, and Leda stared at the way his lips closed around the spoon, his cheeks flexing. Good Lord. Nothing about him was out of order, his cravat a tidy fold, a morning coat of dark blue brocade fitted over a waistcoat of dove gray silk, and yet the man could tempt an angel to sin.

And Leda was far less than an angel.

"We have made no headway in finding Brancaster a governess," her ladyship observed.

"I thought he wished a bride."

Her ladyship sniffed. "He need be more selective this time. He chose too quickly before, and mostly for pity, I think."

"My error was letting my parents choose," Leda murmured.

She wondered how her parents fared, for they, too, would have thought Leda dead all these years. Of a certain they believed she, and they, were better off that way.

"This time, he can choose from his heart," her ladyship said.

"Or from a list of requirements, which would be the sensible way to go about it."

Leda sat at the table. With a huff Gibbs moved the kettle of chocolate out of Leda's reach and toward her ladyship. Leda sighed and wondered if she could make a move for the coffee, but the pot sat before Brancaster.

"I do think at the least you could travel to Norfolk with him and help him get his affairs in order. Meet the girl, and determine what sort of governess she needs."

"Travel alone with a man for days? Staying at public inns?"

Brancaster lifted his head. The cravat didn't disguise the bold slope of his jaw, the set of his chin. And the tousle of hair falling over his jutting brow did nothing to detract from the piercing cold in the glare he tacked on her.

"That would be a terrible idea."

The toast scratched all the way down as she swallowed. Last night he'd wanted her. He'd kissed her. She'd felt his hunger in the way his mouth drew on hers, in the press of his big hands across her back, in the press of his—what was the word, *manhood*, between her thighs.

Traitorously, appallingly, a heat flickered there, like a tiny flame rising from coals she thought long turned to ash. She didn't lust as other women lusted, she knew that. Her passions ran bloody.

But if there were a way she could stand in that moment and kiss him infinitely, with the flicker of candlelight sculpting his face and that delicious heat weaving through both of them, with none of the pain and humiliation and wounding that came after —she would still be in the parlor, kissing him.

"See?" Leda said. "Brancaster agrees."

Lady Plume sighed and stared reproachfully at her nephew. "Did you tell her?"

"Tell her what?"

"How the former Lady Brancaster...never mind." Her ladyship rose. "We must check the book. Perhaps there are new arrivals who will suit our needs."

Leda fixed him with a glare as her employer departed. Brancaster studied the bottom of his egg. Gibbs fiddled at the sideboard, ears pricked.

"Tell me what?" she asked.

He pushed away his egg cup. "Why no woman of sense will come with me to Norfolk, as my bride or anything else. Ever."

"OH, it was a terrible tragedy. I don't know the details, only the rumors, of course, but they say there is quite a stretch of cliffs alongside Holme Hall, situated on the seaside as it is. And the poor woman—" Lady Sydney lowered her voice— "*threw herself* from them."

"She fell off the cliff?" Leda raised a hand to her mouth.

Lady Sydney shook her head. "She *jumped.*"

Leda looked about to see who in the Pump Room had heard this awful disclosure. The Earl of Howth, Lady Sydney's father, strolled with Lady Plume, regaling her with some amusing tale. Brancaster had been trapped in conversation with Mrs. Warren, who was certain that last night he had been captured by at least one of her daughters and would, in the light of morning, be able to detect which he preferred.

Leda watched his straight back in his tailed coat, the courteous tilt of his head as Miss Warren trilled up at him. He did not droop as a man bowed by senseless tragedy. Or crushing guilt. He had, to all appearances, held up manfully.

"Then why do they call him the Mad Baron?"

"Because he drove her to it, of course."

"He drove his wife to destroy herself?"

Lady Sydney blinked. "Well, why else would she? If there were any possible recourse, she would have gone to her friends for aid, or found a way to escape. Only complete despair could drive a woman to end herself."

Leda nodded. She had known it herself, even in extremity: that desperate, animal instinct to survive.

"How long ago?" Leda asked.

"Five years, I think, or is it six? I can't say, as he goes about so little in society. Even before it happened he was practically a recluse, which was part of her problem, I don't doubt. Loneliness from living tucked away at the bare fringe of the world."

Lady Plume had not, in the years Leda had known her, mentioned this nephew, or his title, or his bereavement. Almost as if he were a family secret. Why was she set on helping him now?

"And this is why no one of any station will consider his bid for a wife," Leda mused.

Lady Sydney nodded. "Not even Frances, and you know how she is."

Another of the earl's daughters, Frances, made their way toward them across the room, giving Brancaster and his companions a wide berth. Lady Frances was notorious for her want of a husband, a prize which has thus far eluded her despite her family name and her father's elevation. Frances wore a gray silk round gown, Lady Sydney a dark purple, both of them mourning a third sister who had died the previous year, leaving small children.

As Brancaster's wife had left him a daughter. Was the girl thought to tend also toward madness, and that was why no governess would stay at the house? Such things were said to be inherited.

Another reason that Leda's parents and sister had had

nothing to do with her. They wished no questions, no nervous gazes, to fall their way.

Mrs. Warren, who had made the recent and still quite dizzying hop from merchant's wife to gentlewoman, saw little beyond his title and a daughter who might style herself Lady Brancaster. But the higher families had closed ranks, and Howth was the worst of them, joking about the Mad Baron, in search of another wife to drive out of her senses.

What had his first wife suffered?

What had *he* suffered, as a consequence?

Brancaster turned, having been freed from Mrs. Warren. He scanned the room, and his gaze halted on Leda. As if she were the one he sought.

She stared back at him, her insides churning. Terrible images danced in her head. Had he witnessed the leap? Had he known his wife was lost to despair? Had he been the one to find her, or had the report come later, leading him to her broken form at the bottom of the cliffs?

"There is a new gentleman in the book," Lady Frances announced, joining them. "They say he is possessed of a lovely estate in Gloucestershire, near Cirencester. The name stirs recollection, Izzy. A Mr. Toplady. Do we know that family?"

A wave of cold shock doused Leda, as if the waters of the lake near her childhood home had closed about her head. She couldn't breathe.

He was here.

"I do recall a thread of gossip, at that." Lady Sydney had married well, to a rising peer of Ireland awarded two baronies and a diplomatic post, handsome, or at least prepossessing, if the painting by Reynolds were to be believed. He had died a month after their marriage, extinguishing the two peerages, leaving the estate to his cousin the admiral and his wife to enjoy a long widowhood at the sufferance of her father, amusing herself by taking an interest in the lives of those around her.

"He came by his estate when his father—or was it his uncle?—was found murdered by his wife. A horrible spectacle, they said. She was locked up in a madhouse, of course, where she could hurt no one further, and I heard she died there."

"My word," Lady Frances breathed. "What an unnatural creature she must have been."

"We must pity such creatures, Fanny, rather than despise them. Not every woman has the constitution or capability for good sense. If they were, the universal reputation of our fair sex would be much higher, I must believe."

Leda stood immobile, her feet melded to the floor like hot wax, her body engulfed in flames. Madness. Murder. An insensible, unnatural creature. Would they say these things if they knew it was Leda? Would they say these things if they knew the whole truth?

Likely they would. Women were not to fight the yoke that marriage put upon them, however heavy a burden it conferred. They were meant to bear it, because of Eve, cursed for the first disobedience. They were not to turn mad like animals and fight for their freedom with bloody claws.

This was why she could never marry again. One of many reasons. Because of this animal within her.

Brancaster joined them, and Leda's nerves fired at his nearness. He seemed so large, difficult to harm. He could not be overpowered by a mere woman.

But what might he, with his own power, do to a woman? There was strength in his shoulders, in the chest straining the buttons of his morning coat. There was power in his hands.

Hands that had led her so gracefully in their dance. Hands that had raised wildfires of lust across her skin the night before.

"Lord Brancaster." Lady Sydney cooed as if she had not

nearly accused him of murder moments before, when his back was turned. "You are bringing us the fashions of London, I think."

"I wear what my tailor makes me, madame." Brancaster made the ladies a brief bow. His suit lacked much embroidery or ornamentation, the dark blue cloth of his tailcoat cut away to show a gold-striped waistcoat and pantaloons of a muted buff color tucked into tall black boots. Beside the heavy embroidered silks and bright patterns of the other gentleman in the room, he looked severe and commanding, a watchful kestrel among a flock of bright warblers.

Dangerous. A warning rippled across Leda's neck. She could not throw herself on his mercy.

"Which of the Misses Warren is making her bid to be your bride?" Leda asked.

"Fanny, my dear, I believe you might be permitted to make the acquaintance of our interesting new arrival," Lady Sydney said. "If that is the gentleman staring so fixedly in this direction."

Leda looked toward the counter where the cups of mineral water were dispensed and felt she stepped out of her world into a pantomime. The figures around her grew blurred and misshapen, mere blobs of bright color with leering faces, paper-thin mockeries that might be shredded away. From across the room, his dark eyes sank into her like claws.

He was large, a brown suit with a high collar and ruffled cravat cradling his round face with its heavy jowls, the insolent set of his rosebud mouth. He looked a man who demanded to be given his due.

She knew she must be seeing the nephew, and yet he was so much his uncle come to life that she was certain she faced a ghost. Cold trails of fear raked down her spine.

He'd found her, after all this time. He'd come for justice at last. Or revenge.

"Brancaster." Her throat was tight, her voice high with panic. "I would like to leave."

"Where to?" He offered his elbow, and she took it before her knees collapsed. He was firm and solid.

"The—King's Bath. You have not seen it yet. And the Abbey. You must visit the Abbey." She tugged futilely. He was too large to push.

He searched the room for the focus of her stare, and found him. Toplady's beady glare moved briefly to Brancaster.

No. No, no. She must not make Brancaster a target. And she must not allow *him* to come anywhere near her.

"The Baths," she said desperately. If he pursued her, she could push him in. It would make her a murderer twice over, but he must not, *must not* be allowed to speak to her.

"What has upset you?" Finally, to her great relief, Brancaster steered her toward the pillared doorway and the promise of light and air beyond.

"Upset? Not at all. I have made a decision." She hauled him out the door. "We will not find your governess here, or a wife. I am coming with you to Norfolk."

CHAPTER SEVEN

He didn't know what led her to change her mind. He didn't trust she was being honest with him about her motives.

But Leda was with him, and while Jack reminded himself to be on his guard, he couldn't find it in him to regret that he was now forced to spend several days on the road with her.

Alone, he'd taken the stagecoach along the main roads down to London and through to Bath. It was a slow, clumsy way to travel, and it was also the cheapest and least dangerous means available, when a man alone on horseback, traversing the entire width of southern England, was simply asking to be robbed, beaten, and left for dead. But he couldn't ask Leda Wroth, a gently bred woman, to hack alone with him on some shambling hired nag across fields and country lanes, subject to who knew what weather or other threats.

Lady Plume expressed her doubts about the stagecoach option, but she did not address her remarks to Leda's delicacy. It was clear to anyone who knew her that Mrs. Wroth was not in the least delicate, in constitution or sensibility. The woman had steel in her backbone.

"But in a coach, you'll be subject to anyone who can pay the fare inside," Lady Plume said when Jack outlined his plans over breakfast. "Not to mention those who pay the outside fare and overcrowd the roof. Pirates. Ex-prisoners. Someone inside your coach will undoubtedly smell of onions, and someone atop will almost certainly be drunk. Then there will be the cub who imagines himself quite the whip and badgers the coachman to let him take the ribbons, and will no doubt overturn the coach."

"If Mrs. Wroth minds the discomfort, I will accommodate her and hire a post-chaise," Jack said, calculating in his head the cost of hiring horses for the miles from Bath to Hunstanton, the tips for the ostlers, the tips for the postboys, the meals in public inns, and how to find coaching inns that could accommodate a lady. The cost would strain his budget until the next quarter rents came due, that was certain.

A baron, nearly broke. What a laughable situation. It was why he couldn't show his face in London for a regular Season, or take his seat in Lords. It was why he couldn't persuade a governess to put aside her reservations about the remote aspect or condition of Holme Hall, nor the difficulty presented by her charge. Not for the first time, Jack cursed the profligate life the former baron had led without a thought for the unknown nephew who would inherit a ramshackle house and the tumble-down farms that remained of the estate after the previous Brancaster had sold off everything he could to live a life of riotous comfort.

But Jack could not, in good conscience, treat Leda like a servant, even if she had hired herself as his interim governess, with the scope of her salary to be settled once they reached Norfolk and she could properly assess the situation.

He had not yet told her fully what she would find. He dreaded the confession, and what it said about him. The light it cast over them all.

But he had to tell her sometime. She had not answered an advertisement and might turn straight back to her father's vicarage once she saw the lay of the land. Leda was a friend of the family, his great-aunt's favored companion, though his aunt had said not a single word about how greatly she would miss her companion of six years, nor made any insistence that Jack swiftly return Leda to her.

Friend of the family, yes. A spinster friend of his great-aunt. That was how he would consider her. He would be polite, formal, distant. Reserved.

This resolve collapsed the moment Leda entered the dining parlor. She wore a wool gray riding habit with the skirt buttoned along the side to convert it to a walking dress. The smart military cut of the jacket emphasized her bosom, and a rakish ruffle adorned her throat, framing a face pale with weariness, spots of color adorning her high cheekbones. Her hair was dressed severely, her outfit completely lacking in adornment, yet she looked capable, efficient, and delicious.

Family friend, his arse. He wanted to kiss her again. He wanted to whirl her close in a dance and feel her body fit to his, warm and pliant. He wanted her in his bed.

He wanted her in his house, buxom at bed and board, bound there by promises of marriage. Heaven help him, he wanted her for his wife.

Her, and none other.

More fool he.

While Leda nibbled on toast, her ladyship spoke at length of the beautiful prospect of Holme Hall (not mentioning the near perpetual and often chilly wind from the North Sea), the grand building itself on the Jacobean pattern (perhaps she did not know how much it had fallen into disrepair since her childhood), and the pleasant neighborhood about (nothing but farms, wind mills, and marshes, dotted with the occasional chalk pit and lime kiln). Clearly, she wanted Leda to look with favor on the place, but Jack feared she was only setting them both up for disappointment. She saw them off with great cheer, as if they were embarking on their wedding trip.

"Why did you change your mind?"

Jack caught Leda in the small hallway while Gibbs levered her trunk down the stairs, looking aggrieved by the manual labor. Jack took her valise and studied her wan face. Violet smudges darkened her eyes to a dull gray matching her dress, and she pressed her lips into a thin line.

"A woman's prerogative," she said.

She was not being forthright with him. But when was a woman ever honest?

"You will forget all about me," Leda said to Lady Plume, who walked with them out of doors to see who was passing in the Crescent. "I'll return to find you've given Mrs. Hobart or Madame Nouçier my post."

"No one could ever replace you, Leda, dear," Lady Plume said serenely, scanning the figures promenading in the vast green across from the Crescent while Jack and Gibbs loaded luggage on the dogcart. "Though you do know I detest being alone. And it would be a shame to let your room sit empty, when it has such a pleasant prospect."

Leda stewed as they rode to the coaching inn, confirming Jack's suspicions that she was not entirely leaving of her own free will. But what drove her, then?

At the White Hart, as they stood in the dirt-packed inn yard while their things were loaded somewhat haphazardly atop the coach headed to Chippenham, Jack recalled the package she had mailed to Kellaways. He wondered again who it was for, and what they meant to her. Women of his station were almost relentlessly forthcoming about their business, themselves a chief subject of occupation and interest. Leda remained mysterious and tight-lipped.

He was bringing a woman of whom he knew almost nothing, of neither her character nor her past, neither her breeding nor her education, into his home, to look after those dearest to him.

He must be daft.

She stepped close, taking his hand as he helped her into the coach, and the scent of almonds swept through his head, clearing every thought. He followed her inside like a stag in rut, led by sheer instinct. Daft, indeed.

The leather seat creaked as he lowered to the bench seat beside her, trying not to press his length along hers. The interior seated only six adults, and all needed to be small adults if they were to avoid banging knees with the person opposite, and each occupy their allotted amount of space. Jack had enjoyed the breath of his shoulders when Leda curled against him in Lady Plume's parlor, her fingers digging into his muscle as she clung to him for a kiss. Now he crowded her unmercifully.

A woman's strident voice sounded from outside the carriage, well before she poked her head inside. "—don't see why you couldn't hire a carriage and transport your family in some comfort. No, my husband must always be mixing business with pleasure. Bringing samples on a family visit. Showing us off like his wares."

The matron, much against current fashion, wore bulky petticoats that filled out the skirts adorning her more than ample form. A younger woman, nearly the same size, climbed in after her, and the third seat opposite was taken by a slender, meek-looking man in a rateen coat and pantaloons, who clutched a large leather case.

Jack hoped his companion, the male voice currently

responding with equal distemper to the matron's complaints, might match the other in size. No such luck. A very fine and expansive figure of a man clambered inside with a significant squeak of springs as the body of the coach depressed. Along with a truly generous girth dotted with an extravagance of buttons, he hauled in with him an enormous duffle surtout and tall round hat. He made two of Jack, even accounting for the shoulders.

"Fustian, Patricia. This is the fastest way to return us home to Sheldon, and you know my darling creatures cannot be left on their own too long. They might pine for us, and what taste would that give the meat?"

He turned to Jack, who was pressed unbearably between them by the gentleman's presence on one side and Leda's soft heat on the other. Of the two, it was Leda who most addled his brain. He was disabused directly of the hope that he might not have to participate in the further torment of conversation while being pressed like a sausage into his seat.

"Heard of Wiltshire bacon, I suppose? I'm a prime producer. Best to be had in these parts. And *we*—" He nodded importantly at the man with the leather case— "my factor and I, we've just struck a bargain to send all our flitches to the estate at Bathwick. Now what do you say to that! You're riding with a personal supplier to Sir William Pulteney, one of the richest men in all England! Didn't know when you wed me, did you, Patricia, that one day you'd be rubbing shoulders with baronets, did you, love? I fancy one day you'll be proud to claim your shackle is Mr. Horace Clutterbuck, esquire."

Jack now placed the smell emanating from the leather case and the attire of their fellow travelers. The features of his seatmate, rounded and prominent, put him in mind of his porcine charges.

Leda, it seemed, could not let this self-importance swell

without taking out a pin. She leaned forward to address the newcomer.

"You will be pleased to know, sir, that you and your family are in company worthy of your eminence." Jack shook his head, and she ignored him. "For here beside you is the Baron Brancaster of Holme Hall."

"What! A baron!" The gentleman also leaned forward to peer around Jack, which had the effect of compressing him further into his seat. He turned his small, surprised eyes on Jack. "You don't say."

"Oh, your lordship." Patricia drew out an enormous silk fan and waved it, further decreasing the available space to breathe. "An honor, I'm sure."

"A baron," Clutterbuck marveled. "Jenny, sit up straight and make your curtsey. An unmarried baron, did you say? Unless you..." He attempted to survey Leda, crushing Jack further.

"Mrs. Wroth," Jack muttered. "I don't suppose it would be more comfortable if you—" He made a helpless gesture in the small bit of space before him. Her almond scent grew richer in the confined area, beneath it whatever herbs she stored in her wardrobe with her clothing, and under that, some deeper scent of her own, the arousing scent of woman.

"I suppose I might." She squirmed in her seat, trying to free herself. Jack solved the problem by scooping her into his lap. Immediately, the pressure eased, and he could breathe again.

Warmth. Softness. A female in his arms again. He'd forgotten, before he came to Bath, how delightful that could be. Longing stirred, seated deeper than mere physical sensation.

Her cheeks reddened, and she held herself stiffly as she faced their companions.

"Mrs. Wroth, his governess," she said crisply. "This is to say, I am not *his* governess, but hired by him to be governess to his daughter."

"Oh. Married, then." Mrs. Clutterbuck's face fell.

"Widowed," Jack said, his words muffled against Leda's shoulder.

Jenny regarded them both dubiously, clearly uncertain as to whether she should lay out her feminine charms for a baron who would travel in a stagecoach with his governess most improperly perched on his knee.

Jack faced a different problem, perceived in full when the horses moved, jolting the conveyance into motion. Leda shifted, her body jounced backward by the movement, her bottom resting directly atop his groin. The thick wool of her skirts shrouded the shape of her, but the mere contact was sufficient to make him stand to full attention.

It had been far, far too long since he'd taken his ease with a woman. He was woefully alert to every sensation caused by this one.

It was nearly fifteen miles to Chippenham, a journey likely to last up to three hours, and he was going to be in agony the entire time.

Patricia took out her knitting and enjoined her daughter to do the same. Clutterbuck and his factor engaged in a discussion of how they might increase production to furnish Bathwick with its bacon. They all, at different points, engaged Leda in conversation. They tried to engage Jack, but his remarks were barely coherent. Leda sat in his lap, her body slender and strong, her body all warm softness, her scent a cloud that fogged his brain.

He didn't want to speak to the Clutterbucks of Holme Hall and the grand life he did not lead, one lacking social engagements, political clout, rounds of visits with important neighbors. He didn't want to reveal to Leda, not yet, the virtual isolation in which he lived, fields on three sides of him and on the fourth a sharp, sheer cliff to a cold sea. She would learn soon enough that neighbors did not call, and the mad Baron Brancaster was not invited to harvest festivals or Yuletide feasts or planting celebrations.

There was no village for him to be the benevolent lord, only Hunstanton nearby, where shopkeepers did him an honest trade, their eyes wary as they conducted business. Around him lived his handful of tenants paying rents he couldn't in good conscience raise when he'd done nothing to improve the land or its buildings, having no means to do so. And with him lived his quiet daughter, bowed into silence by too many losses of her young life, and ghosts.

The image was not enough to quell his body's response to Leda. The consequence of a man deprived. In one respect, he was gratified at the reminder that his manhood still functioned, despite everything. He'd forgotten the sheer pleasure it could be, his shaft thick and hard, his thighs heavy, the back of his mind light with the loss of blood. Such arousal reordered his priorities, centered everything around the sensations of his body. The sway of Leda's soft bottom against his lap, the way he was certain her bottom, even through the layers of padding, slid back and forth along his thighs. Her soft, fast breaths as he held an arm about her waist to keep her from tumbling to the filthy floor.

If he didn't contain himself, the ride alone would work him to climax. And he must not, under any circumstances, imagine a way he could work her skirts around his waist, move aside the heavy layers of fabric, unbutton his fall and slide himself into the warm crevice of her body, burying himself inside her as the coach rocked them both to bliss. That thought would make him spill in his pantaloons, and the stain would show when they arrived in Chippenham. He gritted his teeth and leashed his body, unable to focus on anything but the exquisite torture of Leda rubbing against him, mile after mile, and being denied the ultimate release.

They rolled at long last into the yard of the Angel, the horn trumpeting their arrival. The Clutterbucks clambered out, the men still debating hocks versus back fat and where to source their salt, the women clearly disappointed that riding with a titled peer of the realm had not enriched their lives in any discernible fashion, not even to leave them juicy gossip to share with their friends, much less an offer of marriage for Jenny.

Leda slid off his lap with a sigh of relief, and Jack clenched his teeth at the final caress, and the cold that rushed in after. He might be blue balled for life, unable to service a woman ever again, broken from being over-sensitized for so long.

Well, it was no more than he deserved, wasn't it?

"I beg your pardon." Her cheeks still bore those flags of color, and her eyes were a brilliant, tormented indigo.

"I beg yours," he said through an iron jaw. "I saw no other way to spare us both suffocation."

They were alone in the coach, which rocked again as the horses were unharnessed, their luggage unloaded from the basket in the back. She looked vaguely tousled, wisps of hair fanning about her face, her cheeks pink as if she'd been pinching them. He could yank her to him, press those sweet lips beneath his own, have her skirts up and his torment over in a moment, a few brief, hard strokes. He shuddered at the exquisite agony the picture produced.

"You might bespeak a private parlor for us to collect ourselves." His voice was a dry rasp. A terrible idea. In a private parlor he might press her against the wall or over a chair, toss all that wool out of his way, and finish what the journey had promised. He imagined Leda's cheeks flushing with arousal, then satisfaction as he brought her to a fast, hard release.

Dolt. He needed to bring himself under control. Fast and hard would not satisfy what had built in him. He needed hours. They needed a room.

"We won't have long at this stop, they said. Barely enough time for tea."

"We are not continuing by coach. I am arranging a post chaise."

He hobbled behind her as she proceeded through the double doors into the sturdy inn, lit by several bays of windows all showing an iron-gray, glowering sky. She paused inside the small wooden hall with the innkeep's counter and the doors opening to the common room beyond. Her brows drew together.

"A chaise is an expense—"

"That is well worth the comfort."

Her cheeks flushed again, and Jack could have kicked himself for his insensitivity. "You'll require a chaperone, of course."

"A chaperone? No. You forget I am a widow."

"Not even widows are approved for traveling the countryside with strange men, I am sure. It will appear..." He let the sentence dangle, silenced by the longing that struck him at the image that followed. Leda as *his* companion, sharing meals and carriages and rooms and beds.

Her brows lifted this time. She had such an expressive face. "A dalliance?"

A mild term for what he imagined, which was colored by the hot blood rushing through his ears and, still, his nether regions. Her lips were carmine red, as if she'd been biting them. Precisely as he wished to do.

"No." There would be no dalliance. He had to tell her, at some point, but he could not bear for her to know what a failure he had been as a husband, a lover. What a failure he was now as a father, as a landlord, as a baron. As a man.

She didn't know yet and, when she regarded him with those enormous eyes, there was still a chance he could be something other than what he was, in her imagination at least. Someone better, stronger, a man in truth, not a broken shell.

A man walking in behind them jostled Jack, and out of instinct he grasped Leda's arm to shield her. A mistake. Heat soared between them, like a fire pumped with a bellows. Her lips parted. She was so close. He could simply take her into his arms, take her upstairs, relieve the pressure about to make him explode—

And show her what a failure he truly was.

"There will be no dalliance," he said roughly, squeezing her arm.

She narrowed her eyes. Was she indignant? Hurt? Did she want him, despite everything? Hope leaped up like a wild hare, bouncing off the inside of his chest. If it could be different with her...

But it wouldn't. And she should know, before she subjected herself to hours and days alone with him in an enclosed carriage, what he had done to Anne-Marie.

"But there will be coffee." She separated her shoulder from his grip. "Which I will be drinking while you arrange for the chaise."

Chippenham being a stop on the busy London-Bristol road, all the post chaises were currently in use, Jack reported a short time later as he found her in the tavern. The innkeeper expected at least one return later that day, but could not give them an exact time of arrival.

The lines around Leda's eyes went white, and she gripped the jasperware cup holding her coffee with both hands, as if to steady herself. "I cannot stay here."

Jack looked around the noisy tavern, thronged with all sorts of people, from nattily dressed tradesmen and aproned women in traveling cloaks to laborers in their fustian jackets. He ought to have hired the private parlor for her to sit her coffee in quiet.

Another man worthy of the title of his lordship—or worthy to be the man providing for Leda Wroth—would do this much for her. But Jack was all too aware of the lightness of his pockets, which he would be obliged to empty to deliver them to Hunstanton and hope for no accidents along the way.

Still, he had not thought Leda the type to be bothered by the common press. She hadn't struck him as the supercilious sort.

Some instinct prompted him to glance toward one corner, shadowed under a first-floor balcony with more tables and chairs that looked out over the rest of the room. A man sat in the gloom, staring intently at Leda. He was dressed like a gentleman in a dark cloth coat and grey pantaloons, but wore a hungry, calculating look. Jack guessed him to be an upper servant, perhaps employed at one of the manors hereabout, waiting for an employer to finish a task. His intense concentration on Leda made the hair on the back of Jack's neck stand on end.

He had been thick-headed, again, to assume her conscious of class. As a woman, she must be conscious always of her well-being. Anne-Marie had taught him this much.

"Of course," Jack said. "What do you wish? We could wander the market and see the Shambles and the Yelde Hall, if you like quaint medieval relics. If you wish newer, we could look at the canal, which I hear was just completed. Or visit the shops?"

He hoped she would not ask him to purchase her anything. As it was he hoped they would find a modest place for dinner, were they forced to wait that long for a vehicle.

As they stood, the man in the corner stood also and hastened over, barring their way. He made no acknowledgement to Jack, his gaze pinned on Leda.

"Mrs. Toplady," he said, his voice low and somehow menacing.

Leda didn't freeze so much as recoil, as if absorbing a blow. She blinked and swallowed. "No. You have mistaken me for someone else."

The man leaned close and peered into her face. "Them eyes. Who's to forget them eyes?"

"I am Mrs. Wroth. Good day." She tried stepping around him, but the man didn't move.

Jack came between them. He was not quite the eye level of the other man—his kind father had bequeathed Jack many gifts, but not height. Still, the breadth of his shoulders counted for much.

"You heard the lady," Jack said. "She is not who you think."

The man straightened and regarded Jack, the look of calculation returning. "Or perhaps she's not who *you* think."

Jack glanced back to find the man watching as he escorted Leda out of the dim tavern to the yard, which was currently quiet, only a boy sweeping away remains from the last visitors and an ostler grooming a horse. Past the arched gate that admitted the horses, on a wooden bench along the street, two gaffers sat smoking their pipes and observing the street.

"You do not wish to be in this inn, or you do not wish to be in this town?" Jack inquired.

She'd been stiff as a scalded cat since the morning, when he announced the first leg of the journey was Chippenham. When the man confronted her, she'd reared like a shrew flushed from its burrow, ready to sink in its venomous teeth.

She braced her shoulders, as if bearing up under a heavy yoke. "I—know people in this area. From my marriage, and—before."

"Was Chippenham where you and Mr. Wroth made your nest of marital bliss?" Why he was so dratted envious of a dead man, Jack could not say. It sat ill with him. "Then surely there is some acquaintance you would wish to look in on. It would fill the time while we wait."

She turned toward the open market square, avoiding a tradeswoman approaching with a young boy in tow. "There are people I would wish to see. And others I would not. My marriage did not...end happily."

Her expression was as stoic as the Sphinx, but tension tightened the corners of her eyes.

"You and Mr. Wroth did not get on?"

Now why should that twist so in his chest? Glee that she had not been happily married, no more than Jack was. She would not still carry a torch for a man she disliked. But alarm, also, for what she might have suffered in her marriage. God alone knew what Anne-Marie had gone through, and Jack had done nothing to offer her ease.

"Let us not speak of him." She drew her shawl closer about her shoulders, though the spring day was turning warm.

"Very well. Where can we find these friends of yours? Avoiding the people you do not wish to see in the process."

She slanted her head. "They live outside town, in Tytherton Kellaways. I suppose I could arrange to meet you back here."

"You'd leave me to wander town all on my own, and deny me the honor of being your escort? There's only so long one can be entertained gazing into a canal." He was desperately eager to spend the day with her. To meet these people who had known Leda Wroth well before he did.

She bit her lip, and Jack heroically conquered the urge to tug the tormented flesh free and soothe it under his thumb. *Get a hold of yourself, man.*

She pressed her hands together, fingers plucking at her beaver gloves, practical for traveling. "I would beg you not to ask questions."

This time his brows climbed. Leda Wroth was a woman of secrets. He was hardly surprised.

"Keeping in mind," she added, twining her fingers together, "that as someone who is hiring me to come into your home and have the keeping of your daughter while I arrange a true governess, you would be right to ask as many questions as you wished. Under normal circumstances I would advise it."

"I will be content with what you tell me, but now I cannot be kept away. The curiosity would consume me."

She smiled, though only one side of her mouth quirked up. She was still tense as a harp string. "That is a woman's weakness."

"Oh, mine as well. Very much."

He offered her his elbow, and she took it. The weight of her small hand sliding over his skin lit a warmth that echoed in his groin, where his arousal lay banked, like hot embers that could flare at any time into life. Jack supposed he would always be in a state of near arousal around Leda Wroth.

But the heat spreading through his chest was of a different quality. A surge of protectiveness, and the same sense of triumph he felt when Muriel consented to share his company. Fierce pride that she chose him. Wanted *him*.

"You will have to consent to walking a few miles."

"I have spent days walking Smithdon Hundred end to end. Your tame Wiltshire countryside does not intimidate me."

She glanced at his feet. "You may get your boots wet."

That gave him pause. "Just where did you say you were taking me?"

"To a cottage of my sister witches, where we mean to cook you and eat you, of course."

"I'd rather an orgy," Jack replied. "Would you consider an orgy instead?"

She laughed, and a ray of spring sunshine burst in his chest.

Bringing Leda Wroth merriment felt like his greatest accomplishment in quite some time.

"No orgy," she said, completely unconcerned that he had made such a wildly inappropriate suggestion. "With any luck, there will be a child present."

His curiosity heightened, but he curbed his tongue. He wanted to know so much about her. What kind of family had raised this canny, capable woman. If her blighter of a husband had hurt her, and that was why she wished not to marry again. What had driven her from Bath with that desperate, hunted look in her eyes.

What she would say if he leaned down and whispered in her ear what she had done to him, riding his knee those three hours to Chippenham. What outrageous fancies still flitted about his brain.

He had no business attempting to seduce her. He could not marry, either. That was a lark his Aunt Plume had taken into her brain, that Jack would be better served with a wife.

A governess only. A companion for Muriel. Jack did not deserve a companion. He'd not taken good enough care of the last one.

"Where do we begin, Mrs. Wroth?"

"Here, in the market. We cannot turn up empty-handed. Then I will introduce you to Maud Heath and her Causeway."

The square held the wooden stalls called the Shambles that would be full of vendors on market days, and the old Yelde Hall, timbered in the medieval style. Leda led him toward the butcher's shop, marked by the carcasses hanging in the window, and without a qualm stepped over the gutter at the lip of the door, currently running pink with effluvia.

Jack soon realized that Mrs. Wroth knew how to do her own marketing. She bargained with the butcher for two brace of larks, a hare, and something she called Bath chaps, a pink mass enclosed in a jar of brine. Jack grew impressed as she sorted over the birds, returning one that she pronounced stale after flexing its tiny feet. When the butcher rendered another, she tipped up its tail for inspection, then professed herself satisfied.

"How do you know if a bird is fresh or stale?" Jack asked.

"The vent," she said matter-of-factly, and turned to the hare, already stripped of its fur and innards. "Now with these, you look for meat that is whitish and stiff. Blackish and flabby means the kill was some time ago. And look at the claws." She held up a long foot. "If the claws are wide and ragged, she is an older hare. If there is a small knob on the bone here," and she felt just above the foot, "it is a leveret, less than a year old. This is a youngish doe, not hung so long she will be gamey."

"Only dead four days, mum," the butcher assured her. "Can I interest you in a cut of mutton or ham? A side of beef?"

"I will look at your jellies, if you have them, and perhaps some salted fish."

"Calves' foot, hartshorn, ribband jelly, and any fish you want. Herring, plaice, whiting, pike—"

Leda sorted through her purse for the proper coin, and Jack took her packages as the butcher finished wrapping. "You would make a formidable housekeeper, Mrs. Wroth. Are you certain my aunt has made full use of your skills?"

Leda bid the butcher a courteous good day. "I am happy with the employment Lady Plume has given me."

"As a non-matchmaker."

"As a person equipped to discreetly resolve difficulties and settle affairs of the heart." She turned, her face hidden beneath the brim of her capote bonnet, and pointed down a broad street. "That is the other Causeway, the one lined with the burgage houses, the homes of the rich wool merchants, if you want to see them."

"I do not wish to spark envy in my breast. Let us go join Maud."

She glanced at him from under her bonnet, her eyes a bright blue. "I have heard only the highest praises of Holme Hall."

"From my great-aunt, who knew it more than five decades ago, when her father and brother had lands, funds, and proper standing in the neighborhood. Her nephew went some way toward diminishing all of those."

There was no keeping the bitterness from his tone. The previous baron, having no direct issue, had demonstrated a corresponding lack of interest in handing the estate over either thriving or intact.

And as it was attached to the title, the estate would go to the next heirs male. Jack didn't know who that might be, the Burnham family having cut his father when he chose to go into trade. Some clerk in some dusty government office would be busy tracing lines of descent once he died, Jack supposed. He only cared that the estate be yielding income he might leave as a bequest to Muriel, so she would be provided for after he was gone. And she could provide for the others.

"I suppose I shall see it for myself soon enough."

"And go running back to your comfortable position with her ladyship as soon as might be arranged, I don't doubt."

She stopped on the old stone bridge crossing the Avon, a fortification that looked as if it had been there since the times of the Saxons, if not the Romans before them.

"Lord Brancaster."

He faced her. "Jack."

Her lips parted slightly, that delectable red. "Milord Brancaster. I hope you know I will stay as long as you have need of me."

Stay to help him? He'd rather thought she was running from something.

Here in the bend of the river the water flowed lazily, though a small breeze blew from the weir, carrying with it the scent of salmon. Fresh water had such a different character than the pounding waves of the sea. And this town had more of a rugged medieval landscape in the points and angles of the buildings, so different from the expansive neoclassical rectangles that had smoothed over Bath. This was more like Norwich, where he was born, and the familiarity loosened a weight that had long sat heavy on Jack's chest.

So did her promise. He had been carrying his burdens alone for years. The very notion of having a helpmeet, an aid—simply someone to *talk* to—the stab in his chest was also an opening, letting in light and air.

"What if I need you never to leave?"

Now that was absurd. Why was he being absurd?

She stepped close to him as a carriage approached the bridge. "You said there will be no dalliance."

Damn it, *damn it*, he had. He should never have made such an outrageous declaration. His wits had been addled.

"And you said you will not be a wife."

A post chaise neared them, and the lead horse leaned down to snuffle Leda's bonnet as they passed. She laughed.

"Aye, he's an eye for a handsome lady!" The postilion, a gent of many decades, lifted his hat. "Good day, mum. Sir."

"That had better not be a vehicle we could have rented," Jack said, watching the chaise roll past, its occupants tucked behind the front glass.

"You asked them to hold a coach for us, did you not?"

"I promised they would have our business," Jack hedged.

Her shoulders slumped, though she held up her chin. "Do you wish to go inquire?"

He studied her face. "No," he said. "I wish to see Maud Heath's Causeway, and your friends, and I'll go a bit mad if I can't have a bite of that pickled herring, which I can smell through the package."

Her brows lifted. "Is that why you are called the Mad Baron? Because you must not be denied your victuals?"

There was something behind the question, belied by her light tone. She had asked him not to inquire into her past. Did she likewise suspect he was keeping something from her?

"If you are to be allowed your secrets, Mrs. Wroth, I may equally claim the right to mine."

They stood eyeing each other, and Jack had the oddest sense of having been in this moment before. Of watching Leda Wroth step into his life, and knowing she belonged there. As if he had been waiting for her all this time.

Now, that was the maddest notion he'd had yet. Jack held out his elbow. He must shake off these notions crowding his brain, or sense would desert him entirely.

He held his breath, wondering. She clearly did not trust him, nor anyone. Why would she promise him her time?

Then she took his arm, and he breathed in relief and wonder at the sense of something firm and important sliding into place, like one brick fitting perfectly against the next.

He wanted her in his life more than he'd wanted anything. And she was the one thing he could not have.

CHAPTER EIGHT

Jack placed his free hand over Leda's, holding her against him as they walked what was called the New Road. Around them the crowded brick and timbered houses, crowned with the church steeple, gave way to scattered wooden buildings, cottages, and barns. Then nothing but a sea of green pasture dotted with browsing sheep, fields of newly sprouted corn, and verges marked with blooms of wildflowers. The sky shone the color of pale love-in-a-mist, with white clouds roaming like sheep that had strayed into the firmament. Jack did not have a poetical soul, but he like most people could be struck by beauty, and by the sense that he had been gifted a treasure of a day, and a treasure in the woman beside him.

Leda paused before a chalky slab of stone, a metal plaque pressed into its surface.

"Maud Heath's gift, given in 1474," Jack read. "What, the marker?"

"The Causeway," Leda answered, amused. She tugged him down the trail, wide enough for two people, with grass pushing up between the cobbles.

"Maud Heath lived in Langley Burrell, which we'll pass,

and made this trek every week, bringing eggs, butter, and cheese to the market in Chippenham, likely to the very square where we alighted. She was left widowed at her husband's death, and since they had no children, she bequeathed the town a trust paying eight pounds a year to build and maintain a path for other travelers. It goes all the way to Wick Hill, where there is another marker in her honor. This is a floodplain, you know, and it can become quite muddy or even impassable at high water. A great nuisance if not a bar to her income."

"An intrepid woman, Maud." Jack could see Leda doing such a thing.

"Had she children, she would have given her goods to them, and her blood would live on if her name was forgotten. But she granted her money to the community, and now generations have benefited from her vision and her name is remembered through the ages."

Her tone left little doubt which future she preferred for herself. Jack smarted at the implication. "So the best possible status for a woman is a childless widow."

"'Tis the only way a woman might be granted complete freedom over her life," she answered. "Though of course, that life is greatly eased by a comfortable income."

"But not a man?"

She glanced his way, as if surprised by his grim tone. He was surprised himself. He had been taught, as a youth, that man was made to rule the world, and woman made to ease the burden of man. He had known Anne-Marie was not happy with her lot, but not before Leda had he wondered why.

"I imagine many a merry widow has been pleased to adorn her life with a man," Leda responded. "As companion and bedfellow, a lover with whom she might amuse herself, and then send him home where others are obliged to clean and cook and do for him, or he must look after himself."

He flushed. She spoke of beds. Of the pleasures he had imagined enjoying with her, giving her, since their hands first met in the minuet.

They walked the path through the growing grasses studded with wildflowers and the scent of rich, watered earth. "So you enjoy managing people, but not in a housewifely capacity."

"Precisely."

"As a sort of manager of relationships."

"Or a disinterested friend. Without my own motives clouding the question."

"We all have motives," Jack said. "Which way?"

"This way. That road leads to Langley Burrell."

"How is it you know the area? Did you live in Chippenham?"

"A...family member moved here. At her marriage. I visited many times." She walked briskly along beside him, but her manner was stiff and disjointed, not at all her usual grace. "When my marriage...dissolved, our servants needed someplace to go. We found a lodging near here, where they could live in peace."

"They did not wish to stay on at the house?"

She hesitated for a long time. There was something afoot here.

"When my husband died, his nephew inherited. My husband was a harsh, self-serving man, and I feared his nephew might be even crueler."

"He, your husband, left you nothing to live on? No jointure?"

"He left me nothing but scars and shame. My marriage was a horror for me and for the people you will meet. That is why I hope you will ask them no questions. I do not wish to stir painful memories." Her jaw set as if she braced herself against memories of her own.

"I see why you have no good opinion of marriage," Jack said quietly.

"From what I have seen, marriage at best is a yoke for a woman, and at its worst can cost her life, or drive her to madness." She marched on.

They passed a small village, farmhouses clustered near the street, women throwing wash over bushes, dogs chasing boys as small girls picked flowers and herbs. They came to a bridge, no more than boards set over a stream.

"The Clapper Bridge," Leda said. "Not far now."

Jack smarted the whole time. Her remark about madness. An accusation? Did she know what had happened to Anne-Marie? Did she blame him?

Of course she did. Everyone had. He *was* to blame.

They crossed a wider bridge over what Jack guessed was the Avon, breaching its banks in a spring rise. Leda looked with dismay at the wooden boards that had once constituted the Causeway, some planks floating off their wooden piles, some underwater.

"I had not considered this. Oh, dear."

"Hold this." Jack thrust the butcher's parcel into her hands and held out his arms. "If I may?"

Her brows knit together, that sign of exasperation he was beginning to adore. "I don't see what—" Her words ended in a gasp as he swept her into his arms.

"You warned me I would wet my boots."

She clutched his arms. "But I did not mean...*this*."

Her in his arms. The instant, powerful flare of lust, and a certain triumphal possession. He'd wanted her back against him the moment she slid off his lap in the coach. She was light yet substantial, her curves fitting against his, and she *belonged* here.

"Are you glad now you did not leave me kicking my heels at the Angel? I am saving your boots."

"You are giving me palpitations. Please do not drop me."

"Wrap your arms around me."

"Then if I fall, you fall, too."

"You trust no one to look after you, do you?"

A silence followed, then she said quietly, "No one ever has."

He curled her closer to him and kept his balance as a board shifted beneath him. Water, speckled with grains of silt and algae, slipped over his boot. He tried not to wonder if it would stain the fine leather. "Parents?"

"Fine, upstanding people, concerned with one thing only: that my sister and I make marriages reflecting well on them. At least with my sister, they succeeded."

"And your husband was cruel."

She did not answer, which said enough.

He cradled her against him. Almonds and forget-me-nots teased his nose. "And with my aunt, you do the looking after."

"It is the purpose for which she hired me," she said drolly. "Nay, don't step there—that pile is rotten. Try that tuft." She pointed.

"And now you are going to direct me in how I carry you." The tuft gave way, a deceptive mound, and his boot squelched into mud. Water leaked through a seam. The leather would definitely be ruined.

"You needn't carry me at all. I can walk."

He hoisted her more firmly against him, bringing her head closer to his face. He wished to hold her till his arms gave way. "Have you considered that a different husband might look after you?"

"Husbands do not acquire wives to pet and coddle them."

Jack pressed his nose to the buckram of her bonnet over her temple. His breath stirred the wisps of hair peeking from beneath the brim.

"I would pet you. Often."

Her eyes feathered shut and a muscle spasmed in her throat, above the high collar of her jacket. A shiver passed through her into him, a ripple of desire.

She desired him, perhaps as much as he desired her, but she was valiantly fighting.

"Put me down here. By the monument."

Drawing out the effort as long as possible, he set her on her feet on the plank pathway, which held firmer now that the ground had risen to river meadow. She smoothed her bodice and skirts while Jack read the inscriptions on the monument, again dedicated to Maud Heath.

Atop the pillar, metal flags marked a sundial on all four sides, with the usual epigram. "Let us do good while there is time," Jack read. "That is your motto, I think."

"You know your Latin."

"Only what was beaten into me at King's Ely."

She joined him to regard the weathered monument. Warm sun glossed her cheek.

"Perhaps beatings would have improved my French. My governess despaired."

So she'd had a governess who taught her French and parents concerned about how high she married. She'd been born to a gentleman's family, which explained why she had sought employment as a lady's companion and not in trade.

He could marry her. Not that there was much family left to bemoan if he married beneath him, but Leda Wroth would not lower the Burnham name or the Brancaster title. If anything, Jack lowered it. As a baron's lesser son, his father had stooped to trade—never mind it was a profession he loved—and Jack had himself been apprenticing to a trade of his own when a distant uncle's sudden death passed the estate and the title to him. Ten years later, he still didn't feel easy in his role of lord of the manor, certain that behind his back, both his neighbors and tenants referred to him as the shoemaker's son.

Better that than the Mad Baron.

"This one is sadder," he said. "I will return to you never."

"Time will not return? But we always have time, until we die."

So she was not a poetical soul either, which would explain why she had been unmoved by his discussion of Coleridge.

"This moment will never return," Jack said. "Once it passes, it is gone."

She met his steady gaze. In the sunlight her eyes had the shade of the violets clustering along Maud's path.

"A mercy when the time is a harsh one," she murmured. "Its passing."

"And a sorrow when the moment is a joy," Jack replied. "Which is why Horace tells us to seize it, I suppose."

Her lips were the color of the frog orchids that would be blooming soon in the quarries around his home. He wanted to show them to her. He wanted to touch her linen cheek, the rose blush appearing there. He wanted to fit her once more against his body and not let go this time.

He wanted to hitch himself inside her, couple them completely, and stay there.

"I don't suppose," he said, his voice sounding strained to his ears, "you would allow me to kiss you."

For a wild heartbeat or two, as the warm sun beat on the back of his neck, he thought she might say yes.

She broke from his gaze. "Not so near a church." She pointed to the mill near the river, and a simple chapel standing alongside, in great disrepair. "St. Giles."

She didn't want him. Jack braced himself to take the rejection manfully.

"A church beside a mill beside a river? I imagine that structure floods quite regularly."

"And is infested with vermin living off the corn, so Mrs. Blake says."

"That is Bath stone," Jack said in surprise, tugging off his gloves as he approached the church. Anything for a distraction. He was accustomed to being alone, but Leda's rejection went deep. He ran his hands over the face of the building, since he was not permitted to touch her.

"Limestone. A fine chalky texture, but weathers well. Do you see the outlines of shells on the surface here? They are small enough to make an excellent freestone. You can cut it in any direction without splitting, and it makes a smooth surface for dressing."

She watched him with her head tilted to one side. "Knows Latin *and* architecture."

"Not architecture." He brushed a hand across the wall, wondering how long it had stood here, resisting all the forces of nature and time. "Stone masonry. I would have been a mason if the title of Brancaster had not come to me."

She raised her eyebrows in polite interest.

"A more difficult trade than you'd think, making bricks." He dusted his hands and refit his gloves. "There need be precision in the recipe and in the firing, and it is difficult to find both the right mixture and the right baking process. Believe me, I've tried."

Another set of failures, the evidence scattered all about his home, which she would see when she arrived. Was there *anything* he could do that might impress her?

He had carried her quite far without dropping her. That must count in his favor.

"Come," she said. "We are close."

He sensed apprehension in her as they moved away from

the willow and alder near the riverbank and toward an English oak that stood at some distance, crowning the stand of lesser trees around it. As they neared Jack saw the top of a brick chimney, then the cottage attached, a simple structure of wattle and daub, no more than one room stacked over the other.

"It's what they call a squatter's cottage," Leda said, sounding apologetic for the humbleness of the place. "There's a common law that says if you can build a home and have a fire in the chimney in the span of a day, the place is yours to call home."

A nightmare for landlords trying to collect rent from tenants, Jack thought. He didn't know what he had expected of Leda's acquaintances: a gentleman's manor, perhaps, or a merchant's home in town. Certainly not a small English cottage, with no other buildings in sight save a small withy shed. The garden was lovely, fruit trees in flower, vegetables peeking from their beds, and a buzz of insects in the air along with song from the birds swooping among the trees. Voices came from inside, and in the yard a boy's quarrelsome shout.

"Now, Nanny! If you don't kick over the bucket, you daft beast, I'll let you have the beet tops from my dinner. And maybe the beets, too."

They were close enough to hear the response from inside, a woman's voice, amused. "You'll eat your dinner, Ives, if you want to grow sprack, else you'll go no higher than Nanny there."

The path turned a corner and Jack saw the boy, white shirt flapping half out of his breeches, trying to milk a nanny goat that did not wish to cooperate. The yard was tidy, with various implements scattered about: a trough for the goat, a butter churn, a washtub turned on its side to dry, a basket sitting beside the front step as if the owner had been interrupted in an errand. A hen scuttled away from Jack's feet as they approached.

Leda clutched the paper packet to her middle as if she

expected the boy to throw stones and she might use it for a shield.

The lad spotted them and straightened, pushing back his cap. "Hi, here's strangers at the gate! Gander-flanking, are ye?"

"No, we are not wandering or lost." Leda swallowed hard. Her smile was forced and bright. "We have come to visit. You must be Ives. I am Mrs. Leda Wroth."

"Mrs. Wroth?" The boy blinked.

Then his face broke into a delighted smile that revealed several missing teeth. "Mum!" he bellowed at the house without turning. "Me other mum is here! The fancy one."

Setting down the milk bucket, he placed his feet and executed a perfectly courtly little bow, his speech turning formal. "I am delighted to finally meet you, Mother."

CHAPTER NINE

From the corner of her eye, Leda saw Brancaster startle at the term *mother*. She hadn't known how to prepare him. She could only pray he would not make a fuss.

If he would accede to her wish that he not ask questions, it would mark the first time in her life a man had done so.

Two women bustled out of the cottage, and Leda felt the strangest sense of stepping back in time, of crossing a border that had once seemed unbreachable. She was exposing, to a stranger she barely knew, the three people in the world she had built her entire new identity around protecting.

She shied a glance at Brancaster as she gathered her skirts to step over a muddy spot that Nanny had left by kicking over her milk. He wore the expression she'd seen him wear in the Pump Room when greeting strangers: cordial, correct, reserved.

She held out her free hand. "Will you shake my hand, Ives? I have been eager to meet you for a long time now."

He glanced at the women behind him, seeking permission. "Very well, if it's the *done* thing." His speech was stilted, and Leda held back a laugh.

His hand was strong, his body well-formed. He looked a boy

fed with all the proper food, air, and exercise a boy his age needed to grow. His dark hair was roughly cut, a thick thatch standing out every which way, and Leda wondered if he would develop his father's hawk-like nose. He certainly had his father's eyes, so dark as to appear black, but on Ives, they twinkled with merriment and life.

Forgoing the etiquette that said she should introduce Brancaster first, Leda extended her hand to the other women. The elder, shorter and plump, shook it in both of hers, but the younger, Leda's age, held her palms to her cheeks, shaking her head as her eyes filled with tears.

"Mum—we didn't think—we never knowed—and you're here now, aren't you?"

"I'm sorry I didn't send word. It was quite by accident that we came to Chippenham at all, but once we were here...I hope it is all right to see you?"

"Of course it is!" The elder wiped her hands on her apron and beamed at both of them. "Come in, you and your sprawny."

"We are not courting." Leda's cheeks grew hot. "Milord Brancaster, may I introduce you to my friends? This is Mrs. Blake," she indicated the elder, "and this is Betsey Cowper—Mrs. Cowper, that is." Betsey, gaping at Brancaster, wobbled her head in assent.

"And this is Ives. Or rather, Master Ives...Toplady. My dears, this is the Baron Brancaster of Holme Hall, Norfolk."

The boy executed another bow, his eyes round as eggs. "Gor! A real British lord? In our yard?"

"Heavens, and us with naught but tatties on the table for nuncheon," Mrs. Blake cried. "Well, it's all a huckmuck, but you'd best come in anyway, aye? There's tea, at least, some of the bohea you last sent us. Quite tasty."

Betsey, awed, made her curtsey, and then, as if fearing it was not deep enough for a lord, made another, deeper obeisance.

Her head was clearly turned by him, and Leda could not blame her. In his striped coat with its broad lapels and cutaway tails, a pair of buff breeches, and his tall traveling boots, Brancaster cut a fine figure.

For the life of her, Leda could not move to answer Mrs. Blake's invitation.

She had felt that figure curved against her body for the hours of the coach ride that morning.

Then again pressed against her when he carried her in his arms through the water seeping over the causeway.

That figure was burned into her arms, into her skin. When she inhaled, he invaded her nose, citrus and cedar and some rich earthy tone that whispered *man*.

She had never had a sweetheart, as Mrs. Blake had jokingly called him, but Brancaster was the one man she'd ever met who could overset her, sending her pulse aflutter and her nerves alight.

And he was the only person she had ever let in on her secret. Blood thrummed in her head at her madness. She had led him here blithely, thinking only it would be lovely to see her friends in person, not thinking ahead to the consequences. Not thinking that he could as easily lead someone else here as well, now that he knew.

She tore herself from her frozen state and turned to him. "Mrs. Blake was our cook-housekeeper, and Betsey our maid during my marriage."

Let that be sufficient for the moment. She had told him too much of the state of her marriage, and he had seemed sensitive to her plight. Disturbed by it, even.

"And Master Toplady is your son, Mrs. Wroth?"

The tight set to his lips and his narrowed eyes spoke of his displeasure. He'd guessed at her lie. Would he make a scene about it? Storm away? Reject her offer of assistance and leave her here?

Or would he pin her down and extract the entire painful, sordid, bloody truth?

Somehow, on the basis of no logical evidence, she was certain he could no more easily walk away from her than she, right now, could walk away from him. Some thin but strong filament bound them together. She couldn't explain what had led to such an act of trust on her part as to bring him here, and she couldn't explain why she felt bound to him. But she did.

"Ives is my adopted son," she said in a low voice. "I will explain everything later."

His mouth relaxed a degree. "Will you."

She held his gaze. "Yes." As much as she dared.

"I want tea," Ives proclaimed, "but I s'pose I've to finish with Nanny first."

Brancaster turned to the boy. "I will help you."

Ives stared. "A fancy lord? You'll muddy your boots."

"Mrs. Wroth has already ensured their ruin by traipsing us along Maud Heath's causeway. What's more mud?"

Ives eyed his lordship's footgear, a thoughtful twist to his mouth. "Them's fine boots. A shame, that is."

Brancaster stepped aside to attend to the goat, and Leda followed the other woman into the cottage, pulled by their whispered questions.

"Lady Plume is well. I mean to return to her when this errand is done. Brancaster is her nephew, or grand-nephew, rather. I am going with him to Norfolk to help him arrange a governess for his daughter." Betsey opened her mouth, and Leda squeezed her hand. "We can trust him. I am sure of it."

Betsey closed her mouth. Leda looked around the cottage, humbly furnished, but snug and clean.

"You are comfortable? I worry about you all, tucked away here. So different from what you knew."

"Aye, but it's safe and out of the way, and that's what we wanted." Mrs. Blake patted Leda's hand as she took the butcher's package. The motherly gesture left her with a surprising ache. Leda had not had someone to mother her since she traded the nursery for a governess.

The single room of the cottage held a kitchen on one end, a door leading to a scullery and larder beyond. A sturdy table stood in the middle of the room, with a sideboard against one wall to hold dishes and a spindle and loom opposite. In the second half of the room reposed a pair of upholstered chairs, a smaller chair with a woven seat for Ives, and a bright rag rug thrown over the flagged stones covering the floor.

It was so different from Lady Plume's home in the Crescent, yet something about the place felt more welcoming. More like a home.

"You have what you need?" Leda asked. There were few luxuries or ornaments. A cross hung on one wall, an embroidered sampler on another. Wooden stairs led to the room above, no doubt a shared sleeping chamber.

"We've that and more," Mrs. Blake exclaimed as she unwrapped the package. "Larks, a rare treat! I'll roast them and they'll make a tasty morsel. And a hare civet for dinner, I'm thinking. Betsey, tell that nineter of yours to pick us gooseberries when he's put Nanny away, and I'll make the young scamp and his strapping lordship a stir-in pudding, too. A feast, to celebrate the missus paying us a visit.

"Now, then." She fixed Leda with a stern gaze. "Sit you down and tell us what is afoot. We received your message yesterday to be on our guard."

"I saw Toplady in Bath." Leda sank into a ladderback chair, plucking her gloves from shaking fingers.

Betsey, on her way to the door to call to the boy, whirled with her eyes wide.

"No, not my husband," Leda promised. She squeezed the words past the tight band of her throat. "I am not yet to the point of seeing ghosts, though at first I thought I might have. They are very like, but there is something more sinister about Eustace. If Bertram had had that quality, or I had seen it, I never would have consented to marry him. I would have run away much earlier."

She stared at her hands, splayed on the nicked oaken surface of the table. "None of it might have happened if I had."

"Aye, but it did, and naught's to be done now." Mrs. Blake shook her head.

"And I have my Ives," Betsey said. "Will you have eggs for your pudding, Patience?"

"I'll make a cake if you find a handful, but you might pull some greens for our dinner. The rhubarb's at its best now, and the strawberries just coming on." She winked at Leda. "Mrs. Wroth always did like her strawberries."

"It feels so strange. Calling you Mrs. Wroth," Betsey remarked, handing Leda a basket from a table near the hearth. "With Ives I call you Mrs. Toplady, as you said to."

"I've been Mrs. Wroth so long that I've forgotten I was ever Mrs. Toplady," Leda said. "When I hear the name now, it gives me shivers."

She paused. "Someone at the Angel knew me, or thought he knew me. And I know him, though for the life of me I can't recall how."

She looked back and forth between the two women. Mrs. Blake deftly placed the cooking frame in the hearth, then pulled her roasting pans from a cupboard. Betsey tied the strings of her cloak at her throat, her mouth turning down. It was hard to believe they were all eight years older, and these women so much the same. Only Leda had changed from the inside out.

"If you forget, maybe that's a mercy," Mrs. Blake remarked, her cheeks pinkening as she poked the fire to life.

"But I might also make a mistake," Leda said. "I don't know if Toplady was looking for me, precisely. People come to Bath for the waters and the society. But if he finds me—how long till he finds you? And then what happens? We chose this place because we thought you would be safe. That Ives would be safe."

"And he will be, until he comes of age and can claim his birthright." Mrs. Blake straightened to stare at Leda. "That was always the plan, aye?"

Leda hesitated. Then she nodded and followed Betsey outside.

From outside, the cottage looked so neat, the wattle and daub freshly whitened, the thatch of the roof secure around a gently smoking chimney. A field of corn on one side, a stand of tall trees on the other, with the river and other houses not far away, this small plot of land seemed a corner of Arcadia. Blooming fruit trees behind the house promised a summer's supply of apples, pears, and damsons. Bushes lining a masonry wall along one edge of the garden blossomed with currants and raspberries. A blackthorn tree dangled clutches of tiny sloes.

A pain pierced Leda's chest, as if a spade dug beneath her ribs and turned. What a pleasant thing this was, to step out one's own door into one's garden and orchard. To choose the food that would appear on the table for a dinner shared with family, or the closest thing to family that she had.

Across the yard, Ives led Brancaster on a tour of the hens, introducing each one and explaining her personality and heritage. Brancaster listened, asking serious questions, which Ives answered with authority.

The strange serpent turned and writhed in her breast. Brancaster's attention to the boy so far beneath him in station raised a vein of feeling, sad and sweet together, that she couldn't identify.

And the boy himself. Looking at him tapped a wave of bittersweet regret. There was no doubting his paternity, with the sun gleaming in his black hair and bright eyes. In another version of her life, he might have been Leda's child. She might have had a husband who was kind to her and they raised a child together, tending the land and home that in time they would turn over to him.

"He's a fine boy," Leda murmured.

Betsey answered with a fond smile. "Aye, that he is. Hale and sprack, and never a bellock from him about his chores."

Leda turned to the woman, once a maid in her house, a woman who, for a year and a half, Leda had simply given orders and never bothered to know. "Did we do right? To keep you here? He should be in school."

Betsey moved to the garden and tugged at a clump of purslane. "Where's a school about, mum? The Moravians have a girl's school over at East Tytherton, and there's a Sunday school runs in Chippenham now and again."

"I cannot afford a private tutor, I'm afraid, nor one of the public schools." Leda stripped leaves from the burnet, not yet in flower, and placed them in her basket. "But there is a Free School in Chippenham, and in Gloucester the Crypt School or Sir Thomas Rich's. I've made inquiries."

Betsey glanced at her son as if already anxious to lose him. "I suppose he'll need schooling. If he's to inherit his father's estate."

"If that is what you wish, Betsey. This is your life, and your son."

Panic squeezed Leda's heart in a cold fist. It was her life as well. Her penance. She had crafted a new identity on the model of the woman she wished to be, but she could never walk away from what she'd done. Or the people who'd been hurt by it.

Betsey tore roughly at the tops of beetroot, frowning. "'Tis what it's all for, isn't it? The reason you were to claim him as yours. So he could have what his father would deny him." Her voice shook.

Leda held quiet, letting Betsey compose herself. She'd forgotten, in the clutch of her own nightmares about her marriage, that Betsey had suffered, too.

And she'd known, for the ruse to succeed, she would have to deal with Toplady someday. She'd always known.

"That plan was rather hastily revised, as we know. You came here in a panic, all of you, while I was—well. Let us say, incapacitated. We have time to think now. To do what's best for you all."

Betsey gave a cucumber vine a savage twist, freeing the tender fruit. "I want to do it. I want to die with my son in that house, living grand as a gentleman. His rotter of a father owes him that."

Leda fingered the small pin of a bean, not yet ready to pick. "He ought to have had it from the start, but I never accounted for Eustace. My husband's nephew was very eager to claim his inheritance, wasn't he? And to have me committed to the madhouse." Leda stared at the garden beds, a bright green blur.

Betsey straightened and narrowed her eyes. "Mum. You didn't do what he said. None of us believe that."

"*He* does. The judge did," Leda whispered. She caught her breath as a new thought struck her. "What if Eustace uses that to challenge our claim? That I am...mad. He always claimed..."

Her throat closed as the old nightmare rose up, darkening her vision. The house in shadow, quiet as death, only the ticking of the case clock as she padded barefoot across the carpet. The blood dripping from her hands, soaked rust-brown into her gown. Nothing alive, nothing moving, save for her and the knife she held.

"Mum. Mrs. Wroth. Caledonia." Leda snapped out of her trance to find Betsey before her, lightly shaking her arms. "Gor, you gave me a turn. Are you poorly?"

"No, just muddled for a moment." Leda gripped the other woman's forearms. "I promise you, I am not out of my mind."

"None of us believed you were, even when you went to that place." Betsey turned to examining peas. "Though how could we blame you, not us that'd seed what you went through. 'Twas a scramble setting up here at first," she added, "but now we muggle along the three of us. Watching Ives grow."

Waiting for the day of reckoning, Leda thought, then realized she'd spoken aloud when Betsey nodded.

"Aye. When that old garley-guts mucker gets his due. And the nephew, too."

Leda laughed at her friend's savage tone and blinked her eyes quickly to clear them. "I shall be proud to visit you both at the Hall when that day comes."

"Nay, mum, you'll live there in splendor too, won't you? As his mother?"

"That is your right, Betsey. I am only his mother to the world; you are his mother in truth. Unless you find some handsome man to set up your own household." She winked.

Betsey loosed a yip of merriment. "Get on, you! We'll all of us live off the lad, like three harpies, vexing him to keep us in style, as merry as the day is long."

Leda nodded, the twinge in her chest pulling again. She wanted that. Lady Plume had softened her, spoiled her, smoothed out the rough, ragged marks that years of despair had left on Leda's soul. She could spend her twilight years in company, in a warm household filled with laughter, ruled not by the whims of a fickle employer but the care of children and one day grandchildren. Not of her own body, but close enough.

She swallowed the lump growing in her throat. "It's been so long since I've been in a garden, Betsey. Do I take the outer leaves of the Silesia lettuce, or pluck it whole?"

"Here, Mother. I picked these for you. Them's gillyflowers."

Leda blinked at the cluster of wildly pink blooms with their feathery petals. Ives watched her with an anxious expression.

"Why, thank you, Master Ives. These are beautiful. You would say 'They are' gillyflowers, but the thought is lovely nevertheless." She took the bouquet from him with a heartfelt smile. "And how lovely to hear you call me mother." The word felt as strange on her lips as it had sounded on the boy's.

Jack studied them closely, his eyes moving back and forth. Did he see there was no resemblance, no sign Ives bore her blood? Would a magistrate see the same?

"You're to pick the green gooseberries for a pudding, and get them as ripe as you can find," Betsey advised, handing Ives a basket. She faltered when she glanced at Brancaster. "Your lordship may do as he pleases."

Jack took the basket. "I'll hold the basket and you fill it," he suggested to Ives. "Can you believe I've never tasted a gooseberry?"

"Don't eat 'em raw!" Ives advised, leading his new friend to the bushes draping the garden walls and forming a stand beneath the canopy of trees. "They'll taste fine in a pudding. The currants ain't ripe yet, neither."

"Are not ripe yet, either," Jack murmured, and Ives dutifully parroted the correct speech before continuing his lecture on what they might and might not eat.

Leda tried to decipher the look Brancaster flashed her and could not. An English lord, a peer of the realm, the most intriguing man she had ever met, picking gooseberries in a cottage garden. Beside the bastard son of a man dead in his prime, a boy being raised as a pauper in rural Wiltshire.

The bastard child Leda meant to pass off as a gentleman and a gentleman's heir, no matter what it cost her to make the lie real.

Eustace Toplady was looking for him. For her. She knew it in her bones the way she had known, when her parents introduced him as her husband to be, that Bertram Toplady was cruel. And she feared his nephew might be even crueler.

She and Betsey took their gatherings inside to help Mrs. Blake prepare the dinner. Leda laid the table with their best cloth and arranged the gillyflowers in a vase in the center. Betsey passed over the pewter dishes and brought out the tin-glazed earthenware and pewter cutlery for the table, giving the elaborately painted faience plate to Brancaster. "Our one fancy plate," she said proudly. "Le—Mrs. Wroth sent it us a bit ago."

"And thank goodness it wasn't broken in the mail." Leda set the table. "Lady Plume has asked me once or twice who my friends are in Wiltshire, as she knows I lived in Gloucestershire, but thankfully she is not too curious." She flicked a glance at Brancaster, who had come inside with Ives to deliver gooseberries. "One of her many kindnesses to me, I should add."

"Let me help." Brancaster went to the hearth, where Mrs. Blake was wrestling a pan of roast birds in one hand and a stewpot in the other. She gave him a grateful smile as he wrapped his hands in a rag and took the stewpot.

"Your sprawny's a good one, to be sure," Mrs. Blake said to Leda.

Leda laid out the pewter spoons. "He is not my sweetheart."

"That is interesting brick in your hearth," Brancaster remarked. "I haven't seen that red around here."

"'Tis made here in Kellaways, or close about," Mrs. Blake said. "You'll see it in many a kitchen."

Brancaster examined the bricks. "It must be a local stone, different from the limestone. This looks to be a sandstone."

"Kellaways rock, is what we call it, and more than that I can't say," Mrs. Blake replied.

"His lordship likes stones and brick making," Lede explained. "It was a feat getting him here past all the monuments. He wanted to inspect St. Giles."

"Do you, then!" Ives exclaimed. "Would you want to see my snake stones, sir?"

"Milord," Betsey corrected him as the boy scampered up the stairs to the room above. He came down directly with a small wooden box and headed to the table with it.

"Not your dirty old stones on the table we're about to eat from!" his mother scolded. "Take it elsewhere."

Ives dutifully veered to a side table, and while the women laid out the food, Ives showed his lordship his treasures.

"Found 'em near the riverbank," Ives reported. "They's all over. We calls 'em snake stones as for the lines in them. Like snakeskins, see?"

"These are fossils," Brancaster said. "We see them all over Norfolk, too. The going theory is that these are evidence of the Flood. Ancient sea creatures stranded on land when the waters receded, and so trapped in layers of earth."

Leda joined them and was given a whitish stone to inspect, heavy enough to fill her hand. She marveled at the shape printed inside, curled like a snail but with a striated shell. "A fossil?"

"Some small, strange beast wiped out by the deluge," Brancaster said. "Their like no longer exists, not that any living fisherman has found."

"How strange to think the earth was once so much different," Leda said.

"But we can learn about it. The evidence is contained

within our rocks. Some buried beneath the earth, and some beneath the sea."

Leda lifted her gaze to his and caught the full impact of his gray eyes, kindled with the light of excitement. He cupped his hands around the stone she held, with one hand tracing the print of the creature, the other cradling her knuckles. His skin was warm.

The air between them disappeared.

"They're not just stones," he said. "They're stories. About the world unseen around us."

"Fascinating," Leda breathed.

"Eat before it gets cold," Mrs. Blake called, breaking Leda's momentary trance.

Their meal was as merry as could be, all of them gathered around the table. Ives, who had never been relegated to the nursery as he would have been in a gentleman's home, joined in the lively discussion about Leda's new life in Bath.

"Many famous people come for the waters," she told the boy. "They call it the Royal Crescent now because Prince Frederick, the Duke of York, stayed there for a time."

"Did the king ever visit?" Ives wanted to know.

"Not that I know of. The king prefers Weymouth for the sea bathing, I believe. But the Duchess of Gordon is in Bath as we speak, and she is a great friend of my employer, Lady Plume."

"And this lady is good to you, aye?" Mrs. Blake asked. "Not setting a gentleman's daughter to making her possets or sorting her embroidery silks."

"I would do those things if she asked me, and many gentleman's daughters have ended in far worse circumstances," Leda replied, heaping her plate with purslane. Fresh greens from the garden were a treat she'd forgotten. If she ever had a home of her own, she would surround it with gardens. "And you are happy here, all of you?"

"Aye, it's a fine place," Mrs. Blake replied. "Kellaways isn't much for a village, but there's Bremhill on one side and Chippenham when we wish a jaunt, and some fine lady in Bath sends us money for all we need. Betsey's earning a bit working at the girl's school for the Moravians, enough to buy her bits and bobs, and our eggs and butter go well at the market. We look after ourselves, and that's more than I can say for you, mum."

"I live in the lap of luxury, I assure you. If I could, I would bring you all to Bath with me."

"I do not see my Aunt Plume as the maternal sort, reigning over a little family," Brancaster observed, his mouth lifting in a wry smile. Leda reminded herself not to look again at his mouth.

"Does she serve you birds?" Ives eyed the two pair of roast larks adorning the adults' plates. "Not even sure how you eat those."

"With one bite, bones and all." Brancaster demonstrated, and Ives grinned at the satisfying crunch.

"I say! I'll get my slingshot and catch you all the songbirds you want, Mrs. Blake. And maybe a hare or two, if I can catch 'em. This civet's a bully good one."

"You ought to thank those who do for you, Ives, but do not say 'bully,'" Betsey scolded. "You say 'fine' or 'splendid.'"

"Or, if you must express yourself in mixed company, 'cracking,'" Brancaster suggested.

Ives nodded, absorbing this instruction. His lordship's interest apparently set him to a confiding turn of mind. "I needs to learn proper speech and manners," he informed their guest, "because there's a house I am to have, and a grand gent I'll be, but only if I say my name is Toplady, and Miss Leda my mother."

"Mrs. Toplady, and perhaps we should not speak of this," Betsey said, shooting a swift, covert look at Leda.

Leda cut her sliced hare into tiny pieces and considered

them while her stomach twisted and hissed. How much dare she confide in Brancaster? How safe was he?

"So Mrs. Wroth has adopted you." Brancaster's tone was even. He took a second tatty, much to Mrs. Blake's delight, and inspected it. Then his eyes lifted to Leda's.

"You know an adopted son cannot inherit property," he said softly. "At least, not if it is entailed. I beg your pardon if the news is unwelcome."

Was he taking her side? Leda couldn't be sure. The purslane bit in her mouth.

"That is why I will say she is my mother to the world. Though this one," and Ives patted Betsey's hand with a fond look, "is the mother of my heart."

Leda put down her fork, an awful thought visiting her for the first time. It was as if the usual paths of her logical mind were trapped with thornbushes and quicksand whenever she came to this subject. She had not thought anything through, not with her usual clarity. Perhaps she *had* been a touch mad when she conceived this project.

"Do you mind it, Ives? It is a deceit we are asking of you. That *I* am asking of you."

He was eight, and though Leda had not much experience with children, she recalled her own childhood self being righteously, almost religiously honest. She'd rebelled at falsehoods, even into adulthood. It was why she had fought so hard not to lie and say she wished to marry Bertram Toplady.

How ironic. She's once been so pure, and now look at her.

Ives shared a look with his mother, then Mrs. Blake, that told Leda they'd discussed this topic, many times. "But the fancy gent was my father," he said. "It is for fathers to provide for their sons." Leda heard Betsey's argument in his words.

"And," the boy added, of his own invention, "then I can set up Mum and Mrs. Blake in the fine house, and they can be waited on, not serving, and I think that'd be a bully fine thing, don't you?"

"What they deserve, I agree." Leda picked up her own lark, determined to enjoy it. "And you've only a few more years to wait. Until you can hold your own against any argument."

Ives frowned and turned to Betsey. "Will they still believe she's my mother if she's not Mrs. Toplady too?"

Leda's stomach flopped in the most appalling fashion. She'd changed the name to escape, to be free, to have nothing of her old life following her. She would have to explain all of that to a judge and pray for sympathy.

"The magistrate will believe her, lad, with Mrs. Blake and myself as witnesses. Or the assize judge, if it comes to that." Betsey calmly spooned rhubarb onto the boy's plate with another serving of hare.

Brancaster cleared his throat. "Not to provide more unwelcome news, but an inheritance dispute might be taken to Chancery. If the current possessor of the property disputes the lad's claim."

Leda gazed at him in despair. She'd not thought of *that*, certainly.

She couldn't afford a suit in Chancery. And what would happen to her little family here if Ives did not inherit? She'd never imagined his claim, backed by her word, would not be accepted.

Would they live out their lives here, if Toplady denied them? And where would Leda go?

Ives set his chin. "I'll make it happen. For Mum. She deserves a fine house and those to do for her. She's drave like a stone carver here, doing for me."

Betsey's cheeks reddened. "Nay, Ives. I was only quanked that day, worn out from the washing. You're not to think I feel that way always."

Brancaster turned to the boy at his elbow. "I have a daughter near your age. But you have two mothers, and she has none."

Ives shook his head. "Now that's a right shame. You ought to find her one."

"He needs a housekeeper as well, for his big house." Leda dabbed her lips, savoring the taste of the roast lard.

Ives' eyes widened. "How big?"

"Have you seen the big house on St. Mary Street, behind St. Andrews Church, near Market Square?" Jack asked.

Ives scrunched his face in thought, then nodded, lighting on the image.

"Much that size."

Ives regarded their visitor with new respect. "That's big."

"Now, imagine that house not on the gentle River Avon, but on a hill, with steep cliffs dropping down to the North Sea."

Ives' expression said he was trying and failed. He had no conception of the sea. "Can you see where the Norsemen came from?"

"On a clear day? No. But if you stare long enough, you can imagine. Did you know I live in the one place in England where you can watch the sun rise over the water and set in the water on the same day?"

Ives narrowed his eyes. Brancaster laid his right hand on the table. "Norfolk sticks out in the sea, like this. And I live here." He pointed to the outside of his index finger. "So from Hunstanton, we look west to what we call The Wash, and east to the North Sea."

Ives shook his head. "I'd fancy that. Living with the sea all around you, and big cliffs, and boats with Norsemen. I've never been beyond Wick Hill."

"Perhaps you can visit someday and meet my daughter. Muriel."

Leda said the name softly to herself. Brancaster was opening up with Ives the way he had not with her, or his aunt.

He seemed easier here in the country, in the open air. In town he'd been stiff and wary as a cat. Here his shoulders relaxed, and his jaw unclenched. She'd spotted him emerging from the garden in just his waistcoat with his shirtsleeves rolled up, and the sight of his bare forearms, with their line of muscle, momentarily robbed her of breath. He was a powerfully built man, but the taming veneer of civilization returned when he slid on and buttoned his coat.

She'd caught his conversation to Ives, explaining that a gentleman never let a lady see him undressed, unless she was his wife. She'd been only marginally composed when he and Ives came inside, Ives carrying the basket of gooseberries as his prize. Even now when Leda looked at him she saw his arms in his shirt, the way the waistcoat drew tight across his shoulders and hugged his lean waist and broad chest.

She looked back at her plate.

"So you grew up there, on the cliffs." Ives sat back with the men while the women cleared the table.

"We've a second course today, like fine folk." Mrs. Blake laid out an array of smoked herring and homemade cheese, then set down a tray of sliced pink meat. "And his lordship's to try the Bath chaps, since Norfolk won't have such things."

"After smelling pork from our companion in the coach from Bath to here," Brancaster said, "I am not sure how much more of it I will want in the next days. But I will try a slice to please Mrs. Wroth."

"Pig cheeks, pickled in brine, then boiled and cooled," Leda told him. "Mrs. Blake adores them, so it's quite fortunate for you she's willing to share."

"It cannot be worse than the raw gooseberry Ives dared me

to eat," Brancaster said, accepting the slices the cook heaped on his plate.

Ives giggled. "His lordship's face! Shoulda seen it," he told Leda.

She smiled, warmed by their exchange. So many men of her station didn't have time for those beneath them, children, servants, tradesmen. Brancaster was a different creature, like a lynx of old loosed among British shorthairs.

"I didn't grow up as a baron's heir," Brancaster said to Ives, giving the boy one of his chaps. "Lady Plume had three brothers, and the eldest inherited. The second son had only a daughter, my Aunt Dinah. The baron's son, my uncle, never married, though his sisters all made high matches.

"But the estate is entailed to heirs of the male line, so my many cousins were passed over when the estate came to my grandfather's line. With my father passed away, the title fell upon me. If I die without a son, it will go to the Crown, the male line having died out. I think that is the only reason one of my cousins hasn't seen me tumble off a cliff."

He winced as he said this, as if the words pained, and Leda flashed back to Lady Sydney's revelation about his wife's death.

Fallen...or pushed?

Ives patiently waited for his lordship to try the chaps before he ate his own slice. "Your cousins ain't happy for you? I always thought it'd be jolly to have family."

Leda studied the table. Poor Ives, the lone child. She hoped there were at least other boys living nearby. She herself knew what it was to grow up feeling alone and apart, though she'd had a sister.

"Ah, but I'm a disgrace, you see. My grandfather entered the military, but my father did not. He wanted to support a family properly, so he became a shoemaker. Quite a good one, I might add. The finest folk in Norwich sought him out."

Ives made no attempt to disguise his astonishment. "A shoemaker's son a baron!"

"You see why my cousins despise me and never visit. I fear one or two of my acquaintance in the Smithdon Hundred likewise do not wish to entertain a shoemaker's son in their gracious homes."

Leda's throat pinched. *The Mad Baron.* He was born a gentleman, but his father had sullied the family name with building a business instead of amusing himself, and living in debt, with gentleman's pursuits. He held the title, but Jack would never be found worthy of it. He could never redeem himself from that pit.

Just like Leda.

Betsey and Mrs. Blake, enjoying their herring, listened attentively. "Who looks after the girl now, milord?"

"Herself, at the moment. Le—Mrs. Wroth is coming to Hunstanton to help me find a governess."

"You could marry Mrs. Wroth, and your girl would have a mother," Ives suggested.

"Not you, too." Leda pursed her lips.

"If you would woo Mrs. Wroth for me, I'd be grateful," Brancaster said to the boy. "She'd make a fine mistress of Holme Hall. Go quite a bit toward establishing my place in the neighborhood, I should think."

Mrs. Blake and Betsey exchanged knowing glances.

"But I believe Mrs. Wroth fancies her freedom," Brancaster went on. He speared a chap and regarded it thoughtfully. "Don't we all?"

"Her more than most," Ives said seriously, "as she was locked up for a time against her will and all. Bad times and bad people, Mum says."

Brancaster stopped chewing and stared at Leda.

In the silence a hen squawked outside, and a songbird swooped across the window. Wind rustled in the oak.

"I was thought mad for a time after my husband's death," Leda said lightly. "We have that in common, milord."

THEY DID NOT STAY for tea, but rather left to take advantage of the daylight. The sun lowered toward the west as they set out over Maud Heath's Causeway, dinner filling their bellies. Brancaster did not ask her questions, for which Leda was grateful. Her heart was as full as her belly. Ives hugged her before she left, and the print of his small body lingered against her heart. Then Brancaster swept her into his arms and carried her across the underwater planks in the river meadow, and a far different warmth curled and teased at her insides.

"Do you suppose a chaise will be waiting?" she asked as they entered the town.

"I hope so. We can set out for Swindon tonight, unless you would rather stay at the Angel. Or find somewhere quieter in Chippenham."

"I would rather not stay in Chippenham."

"Your friends were very welcoming." They paused on the city bridge as a fancy carriage rolled past. "I enjoyed the afternoon," he added.

Leda raised her eyebrows. She ought not provoke him to examine the topic any further. But matters would have to be dealt with eventually.

The sun and wind of the day blushed his forehead and cheeks, and his neckcloth was a wilted knot. He looked rugged from his exertions. Appealing. While the women washed and put away dishes, Brancaster had helped Ives clear the heavier deadfall from the copse and make a tidy stack of firewood. He had done the laborer's task without a murmur of complaint.

She had put the lives and livelihood of her friends in his hands, yet she didn't doubt for a moment that she could trust him. He was as solid and steady as this stone bridge.

"You might guess why I do not speak of them," she murmured. "Not even Lady Plume knows."

"I gather that Ives is Betsey's natural son by your husband." He turned toward the road. His shoulders seemed broader with the gesture. A trace of pollen from the blackthorn tree dusted his coat. "And you mean to convince a court he is your child so he might inherit your husband's estate, as you have no children of your own."

"His father's estate," she said on a sharp exhale.

Fool. She'd been a fool. What gentleman, a lord of the realm who lived by the iron rules of primogeniture—who had won his titles and estates because of them—would allow her this pretense? She had brought in the wolf who would destroy their lair, devour them all, leaving her friends—and her—with nothing.

"Which is currently held by a nephew, I take it."

She bit her lip and nodded, and he went on. "Who also, I deduce, is that man who spooked you when you saw him in Bath."

"He didn't—" She snapped off the lie. Toplady's appearance had terrified her. And Brancaster had seen.

He saw too much.

"I understand why you would disapprove." She curled her fingers into fists, following at his side as they entered the center of town.

He would turn her off, of course. Say her services were no longer required. And then what would she do? Return to Bath and Lady Plume and put herself in Toplady's way? Her whole mad plan, born of desperation, would come tumbling down, and Betsey would be the most hurt by it. And Ives. They'd land exactly in the disgrace and penury she and Mrs. Blake had wanted to protect them from.

They stepped into the hard-packed earth of Market Square, with the square tower of St. Andrews looming, topped with its Gothic spire. Leda never would have looked at the yellow-gray stones of its façade, wondering about their source, if Brancaster had not made her aware of building materials.

"I do not hold the common view on illegitimate children." Brancaster held the heavy front door of the Angel open for her.

"Meaning?"

"I know bastardy is supposed to be a moral stain the child inherits from the mother's lack of continence." He stared straight ahead as they walked through the small foyer. "But I do not see why a child should be held accountable for the sins of its parents. Nor denied a father's care simply because he did not, or could not, marry the girl."

His lips pinched as he delivered this line, and a vein in his neck suggested he clenched his teeth. His views explained why he had been kind to Ives, but not his distemper now.

"Thank you," Leda said softly.

He paused and faced her. The world around them pulled away like rolling bits on a stage. He was not much taller, but he felt so *present*. The outline of his body, the shape of his face, were burned on her inner eye.

Spending time with him today, seeing him relaxed and at his ease, had been a dangerous seduction. She had no defenses against a man who was *good*.

"My God." The cry, high and breathless, in a woman's voice, came from behind Brancaster. "Caledonia? We thought you were dead."

Before her stood another ghost, filling the doorway to the private parlor.

Another figure who had been torn from the fabric of her life, stripping Leda of her identity. Another once-loved companion lost to her the moment she came to her senses with the knife in her hand.

"Emilia." The word wisped from Leda on a breath.

Brancaster stiffened, his eyes cautious but his chivalry in place. "Good evening."

"Emilia, this is the Baron Brancaster of Holme Hall." Even stupefied, the courtesies did not desert Leda. They would hold her up while her ship sank beneath her. She searched her mind for her married name. "Brancaster, this is Mrs. Hector Crees of Chippenham. My sister."

Brancaster absorbed this new information quietly. Emilia's eyes burned into Leda.

"I thought Haines was lying when he said he saw you. That he was imagining things."

Age and time had descended harshly on her older sister. Lines framed her brow and pursed mouth. Strands of grey wove among her dark hair, the color of the black walnuts that came from America. She had Leda's nose, Leda's proud chin, and all of Leda's flinty breast.

"Ah. I thought I recognized your man. Shall we have this conversation elsewhere?" Leda motioned toward the dark, wood-framed parlor, currently empty.

Her own calm astonished her. Inside she was a shrieking, keening child. She had looked up to her sister. Admired her. Emilia knew the ways of the world that Leda did not, had early on passed through the gates of womanhood. Her one support, Emilia had been spirited away into marriage just when Leda was beginning to bud herself, and needed her.

"Six years." Her sister's voice shook. The parlor had no fire and the windows turned away from the late afternoon sun, leaving them in gloom. "Six years, with no word to our parents. To our mother. To me. You let us think you dead."

"It was better you thought that." Leda held her fisted hands to her middle, hoping to quiet the roiling sensations there.

"And you never once thought to write—not me, not our parents—to tell us we'd been lied to?"

"Would you have let me live freely? Or would you have made me go back?"

Emilia set her jaw, and Leda had her answer.

"So you are hiding. Because the law, if you were fit to stand trial, would hold you responsible for your crimes. You ran away and assumed a false name, and you are living freely at your ease, while—

"While what?" Leda broke in. Her heart wept, but her back stiffened. "What have you suffered? In your fine house with your wealthy husband and your children and your drawing room papered in hand-painted prints. Everything you wanted. Everything our parents insisted I must want, too. They would prefer me dead."

She pulled hard at her fingers in their traveling gloves to gain command of herself, so she did not dissolve into tears. "They would have preferred Bertram kill me before I could tell the world what he did."

"It would have spared us the shame," Emilia snapped. "Do you know that shadow follows me around? Even now. I can never lift my head above it. That is Mrs. Crees, they whisper. Do you know the tale?" She swung on Brancaster, her mouth taut with fury. "This is what they say: She is the one with the sister who was locked in the madhouse after she murdered her husband and newborn babe."

CHAPTER TEN

Murder.
　　　Madhouse.

The words bounced in Jack's head as he and Leda mounted the hired chaise and set out on the road to Swindon.

It would be past dusk by the time they arrived, an invitation to gentlemen of the road, were any lurking, but he could not ask Leda to stay in Chippenham. She was in agony after the confrontation with her sister. Jack had wondered what could overset the unflappable Mrs. Wroth, and now he knew.

A sister. It seemed Leda's family was alienated from her just as much as Jack's, and for similar reasons: because she had disgraced them.

She was locked up for a time, Ives had said, almost off-hand with the knowledge.

For murder?

Was he riding in a carriage with a woman who had killed a man?

Leda stared out the front window of the chaise into the falling night. He had given her the right side, with the clearer view, since the post boy, a compact man old enough to be someone's grandfather, rode the near horse. After her sister swept away with her back straight as a rod, Leda had paced the courtyard of the Angel while Jack supervised the loading of their luggage onto the post chaise. The sister lived nearby, mistress of some great house—the ostler had given her a deferential nod—but she clearly harbored no intentions to invite the travelers to her home to entertain them, nor interrogate the sibling who had risen from the grave.

"Mrs. Crees," the innkeeper had greeted her cordially. "How was your excursion today? The horses sweet goers? I hope our carriage served while yours was being repaired."

Emilia had been gruff in her answer and ascended the cabriolet waiting for her, the ribbons held by the man in dark livery who had accosted Leda earlier. The one who had addressed her as Mrs. Toplady, which, Jack now realized, was her married name.

Leda had done in her cruel husband by some means, then bundled her cook and maid, and the maid's bastard baby, away from the house. So they could not be made to testify? The nephew had taken over her home, and Leda had been locked away. In a madhouse.

She was no longer in the madhouse, but she'd been hiding from her family—and the nephew—all this time.

The sister had mentioned a murdered babe.

He was taking this woman to his home. To meet his child.

It was if she read his thoughts, or the agitation rippling from him. Leda stirred and drew a breath that fluttered the scarf tucked into the collar of her smart riding jacket. Jack tore his eyes from her bosom and trained them on the back of the post boy.

"The babe is alive," she said. "You met him. Ives."

The weight of fear left his shoulders. A wren trilled and chirped from a beech as they passed. Jack didn't see many wrens around Holme Hall, but he remembered an odd fact about their mating habits. The male wren made nests around his territory, and the female chose him for the accommodations he could provide. When she consented to be his mate, they selected a nest for breeding and lined it together.

Exactly what Jack had hoped for from Leda Wroth when she agreed to come with him.

"Why would your sister believe the child was murdered?"

"They said so at my trial, and we let everyone believe it. We hid Ives so that my husband's nephew could not find him. We feared what he might do."

At least she had not killed a child. He also wanted to know if she had murdered her husband, but he wanted the other mystery sorted first.

"Your sister thought the child was yours."

'That is what we let the world think. After Bertram...when Betsey fell pregnant, I was still childless. Despite his best efforts," she said, bitterness lancing her tone. "It was an outrage to me that he meant to turn off my maid and a babe of his blood, instead of accounting for his actions. So."

She drew a deep breath. "I pretended to all, including to him, that I was pregnant. Betsey and I increased together. We had no country estate to hide at, and I could not go to my parents or sister, so we kept to my rooms. Bertram—worsened. I think he suspected what I was about, and it set off some demon in him.

"Then the babe came early, and it was difficult. Betsey nearly died. In the middle of the uproar, my husband's nephew arrived, and they quarreled. I do not know what about—Eustace was upset he would no longer be the heir, made no secret of it. Even his own family hated my husband. I remember standing in the kitchen, making a tincture for Betsey, and then..."

He waited. The chaise dipped and jolted over a rut. One of

the horses snorted and tossed its head, jangling its harness, and the postilion scrubbed its neck. A tawny owl called from a hollow in his oak, *too-wit, too-wit.*

"I don't know what happened." Leda looked at her hands, tugging her fingers within their gloves. Her voice was a wisp of smoke. "I woke up in my shift, covered in blood. There was a pool of it in my bed. I was barefoot, and my prints traced from my bed to the front parlor, where—" She gulped and struggled. "Where my husband's body lay. Then my tracks led away, into the hall. And I was holding the carving knife that had plunged through Bertram's heart."

Jack said nothing.

"And neck," she added, as if pressed to confess all. "And stomach as well. He had several wounds. The coroner—" Again she struggled. "The coroner said this was characteristic of a crime committed in a fit of madness. And since I could remember nothing, what could they conclude but that I had killed him?"

"You would have been hanged if you were thought sane." A tight band constricted his throat.

"The madhouse was little better than a prison. Eustace was not going to pay to keep me at one of those places that are like a country home. I was a criminal, to all eyes. He said I must have murdered my babe as well, since I could produce no child."

"Where did they put you?"

"An asylum in Gloucester. Fortunately, I was not one of those locked in a cage for people to come look at, like in Bedlam. I was not an entertaining madwoman, and my crime was too horrid to be believed. I was kept hidden."

The sides of her mouth pursed, as if she tasted raw gooseberries. He knew that sensation.

"How did you escape?"

"An accomplice, a gardener I befriended. He smuggled me a

tool to loosen the bars on my window. It took a long time. Then I threw myself out the window into a hay wagon, and he drove me away. I bribed the warden to say I had died of typhus and my body burned to stop the spread of the disease. I traded my shoes for a boat to Bristol and from there walked barefoot to Bath and found an angel in the form of a school mistress named Miss Gregoire, and she gave me my life back."

"As Mrs. Wroth." Jack stared out the window. The urge to touch her was strong. He wanted to slide his palm around the nape of her proud neck, sink his fingers into her hair, rub his thumb over her satin cheek. Tell her how astonishing it was that she had survived.

Soothe a possible murderess for what she suffered because of her crime?

"Why that name?"

Her lips turned up, at least on one side, and Jack saw the smile, detached, amused, that had so captivated him in the Upper Assembly Rooms the first time he saw her.

"You have not heard of Lady Mary Wroth? That is indeed a shame. She was a true courtier of the Renaissance, poet, patroness, a marvelous dancer. I read a fabulous poem she composed, though I could only ever get my hands on part of it."

"Why her, though?"

"She endured tragedy and survived. Her firstborn son died young. She struggled most of her life with the debts her husband left. She had a passionate affair with her cousin, in fact bore him two children, though he was never faithful. She was forced to retire from court because the wife of James I, Queen Anne, was jealous of Lady Mary's sophistication and beauty. She has always impressed me as a woman who lived life on her own terms. Who left her mark."

"And escaped the shadow of her husband." Few women did. Anne-Marie hadn't. Jack tried to picture Anne-Marie climbing out of a window or walking barefoot for miles to find a life of freedom. She'd walked, but only as far as some neighbor's house, possibly right up his bedroom, and then she'd thrown herself off a cliff when the man was done wanting her. It was the only way she could escape Jack.

But Anne-Marie had not been in full possession of her faculties, Jack was sure of that. Leda was.

And if she were indeed *compos mentis,* as her sister had claimed, she could be hauled before a judge and held accountable for her crimes.

No wonder she was running away to Norfolk.

She looked him squarely in the eye. Once again it was as if she read his thoughts, or read him accurately enough to guess what his thoughts were.

"This is the woman you are bringing to Norfolk, to your home," she said. "If you wish to abandon me in Swindon, I will understand."

The coach jolted in and out of another set of ruts. Jack's dinner swirled in his belly, threatening to make its reappearance.

He was bringing this woman, a woman who claimed to have blacked out in a feverish moment and come to her senses with a knife in her hand and her husband's stabbed body in the house, to his home, to his daughter.

He studied her face, the arch of her cheekbones, the curve of her brow. Her eyes were violet shadows in the growing darkness.

The thought of leaving her, going on without her, hurt much worse.

When Anne-Marie betrayed him, then betrayed her children, Jack had vowed he would never again let another person throw him into such turmoil. He'd gathered up his acrimony and recriminations and agony and regret and stuffed his feelings into a great traveling trunk in his mind, where they were allowed to reek endlessly, a slow, quiet poison that infected his life. He'd accepted that he was a man who would not be bound to a woman, who would not have the kind of warm, interested affection his parents had shared, nor the wild doting that his sister felt for her architect. He'd accepted that he would remain untouched, likely for his whole life, and become the bitter, misanthropic recluse that, by all accounts, the previous Baron Brancaster had been.

Yet here was this woman calling herself Leda Wroth who had stepped into his life and in the span of mere days—hours, really—made him feel that perhaps there were things he could not live without. That there was a difference between existing, which he had been doing, and relishing life in its full, rich plentitude, with a pleasant companion at his side.

With the hope of other pleasures he had only dreamed about.

He'd watched her with Ives while the boy showed Leda each one of his snake stones, heard how she subtly drew out the boy's interests and a picture of his life. He'd heard her patiently answer the boy's questions about Bath, about the life Ives had been raised to expect when he took over the great house that ought to belong to him. Jack saw that she wanted to prepare him for a great future yet also wanted to keep Ives safe and shielded in his rural refuge. She was crafting a life for him built on a lie, but he could also see she didn't intend to force the boy to her will.

It was a strange plot, for certain, but no more sordid than others he'd heard about. Or had experienced in his own life.

He was absolutely certain she would not hurt Muriel. Nay, the more he was with her, the more Jack longed for Leda and his daughter to meet. For Muriel to see that a woman could be intelligent, educated, graceful, self-possessed. Clever as well as beautiful. From Leda, Muriel could learn that a gentlewoman of maturity was wise as well as kind, capable of humor and discernment. Leda could show Muriel that a woman could be motherly, calm, steady, loyal, interested in those around her. A pillar of good sense, a pillar of light. Leda was all of these things.

As well as, possibly, a murderess.

Jack didn't care. He would take the gamble of waking to a knife in his chest if he could be near Leda Wroth a while more. As long as she would let him.

"I want you."

The words came out more roughly than he intended, and in an inappropriate place, the courtyard of the inn in Swindon where they disembarked. The horses led off, the luggage taken down again from its basket, he had not even let her enter the inn before he answered her question.

"I beg your pardon?"

It was full dark now, and the torches lighting the innyard suffused her face with a haunting glow.

"To come with me. To Norfolk. I want you."

She paused, then drew in a short breath. "Let us discuss it inside. We must decide where we wish to arrange a room."

In the end they settled on staying in the coaching inn, though it would be a noisy night with the horns blowing at every arrival, the shouts of the ostlers and the neighs of horses and the clamor of travelers on the night coach. The innkeeper had two rooms available, tucked side by side beneath the eaves of the second floor, and a private parlor where they could take a light supper. The maid had lit candles, stirred the fire against the chill of the spring evening, and laid a white cloth over a small table when Leda joined him.

She'd set aside her capote and shawl and had repinned her hair, once again anchoring the strands that persisting in sliding free. The traveling gloves had been exchanged for short cotton mittens. Leda Wroth was in no way conventional, yet Jack guessed he would never see her other than neatly dressed.

Unless he ever had the great good fortune to peel her smart attire from her and take her, naked, to his bed.

His body throbbed at the thought, the hectic heat banked beneath the surface of his skin. On the walk through the countryside, in the chaise, during dinner, other sights had pulled his attention away. But in this quiet, candlelit room, there was nowhere else to focus except upon her, and the way she made his senses come alive.

Her eyes were enormous when she met his gaze. Not afraid —he doubted he would ever see Leda Wroth afraid of anything. Not a woman who had survived the detestable horrors that he heard most madhouses were, with the suffering treated like animals, the food poor, the conditions deplorable, and the workers as well as doctors forgetting that their patients were yet creations of God, even if the sense that good Lord imparted to most his human creation had left them.

Sense was a fragile state anyway, as Jack well knew.

"You said you wanted me." The words floated like a whisper, flickering like the candles in their seats.

Yes, he wanted her. Yes, again, and yes, for eternity hereafter. He simply nodded.

Her eyes widened. "You trust me with your daughter?"

Reality slithered in. Jack stood behind the wooden chair, holding its back. Should he tell her this scheme was madness itself, that he must be overcome by the sight of her? Ought he warn her that he held to restraint like a fragile thread and he might, at any moment, lose the leash that held him as a gentleman, abandon courtesy and pull her into his arms, claim her mouth with his, press that delectable body to every inch of him, plunge into her sweet depths and climb with her to the gates of heaven—

The door opened without warning, and Leda tensed like a deer. She mastered herself in a moment, but Jack detected that she had responded like a wild creature, not sure whether to crouch or flee.

What had her husband *done* to her?

Jack nodded to the entrant, the innkeeper's wife, but a new wave of emotion rolled over him, the same tenderness he felt when he watched Muriel, uncertain and fearful, confront something new. He would not lose his head and ravish Leda, not without her full knowledge and enthusiastic participation. He would protect this woman with everything in him. He wanted the privilege of protecting her, guarding her, cherishing her, to the end of his life or hers.

He reeled at the sudden surety. He'd leapt from a near future with Leda in his arms to imagining lifetimes now?

As the roaring in his head receded, he realized Leda was chatting as calmly with the innkeeper's wife as she did with everyone else.

"—a nice plump shoulder, my Will said we'd save it for someone fine, and here we are with a lord and baron in our house, and I hope you will find it as welcome a house as any you've been in, milady." Their hostess flicked an inquiring glance at Leda, who promptly clarified the matter.

"I am Mrs. Wroth, a widow of Bath, and companion to his lordship's aunt, Lady Plume. His lordship and I are truly grateful for your hospitality, and this splendid fare you have arranged for us at a moment's notice." She looked with appreciation as a pair of maids, following their mistress, laid the table with covered dishes and a pewter salt cellar. Jack knew that coaching inns typically left a hank of meat to toughen in a stew all day, and the rest of the food could be indifferent at best. But word had spread to the Crown's kitchen that a lord had made his appearance—even if he was a baron, the lowest rank of peer—and the kitchens responded accordingly.

As the chatter continued, the maids stealing glances at him as they set out pearlware plate and pewter cutlery, Leda held out her hand and coaxed the mistress of the establishment into it, with just the right balance of command and friendliness, and a wink at women's secret ways. The maids followed promptly, their admiring looks turning from Jack to include Leda as equally.

The matron shook her head. "And to be such a friend to the family, to travel with his lordship so you might personally arrange a governess for his poor daughter. Not many would be as kind, and put themselves to the inconvenience."

Jack, guilty, tried to catch Leda's eye. He was not typically forthcoming with tradesmen, but he'd needed some explanation, at the innkeep's inquisition, for why he was traveling alone with a woman not his wife or immediate relation. The truth had sufficed, he hoped.

"And with not even a maid to tend ye?" the matron went on, looking Leda over. "You must feel right put out, I should think."

Leda nodded. "Of course, if Lady Plume had been able to join us as intended, we should have had a maid and perhaps one of her footmen as well. But she was, alas, compelled to remain in Bath. She is very sorry not to meet her niece, but his lordship and I must struggle on. It would not do to leave Miss Burnham too long without the loving oversight of her father."

The matron nodded in approval. "And this Lady Plume," she probed.

"The relict of Sir Dunlap Plume of Bristol, who made his fortune with the East India Company and did not live to enjoy the comforts of his old age. Fortunately, her ladyship chose me to be the prop of her days, and her good friend the Duchess of Gordon is in town for a stay, to amuse her while I am gone."

Knights, barons, duchesses, and ladies apparently satisfied the matron that her establishment was serving the finest sort, and she signaled to the maids to conclude their business. "If you need a lady's maid or one to do for you on the road, we might find you a miss as is keen to travel. One good with young children to boot."

Leda nodded graciously. "Our thanks, mistress."

When the door shut behind her, Jack stood yet, clutching the chair, astonished by relief. He hated this, the fuss and attendance that his status stirred up whenever he set foot out of doors. He still felt the mantle of lordship was false, that the title of Brancaster and possession of Holme Hall was some absurd test, which he was failing, and someone would eventually step in to put the family's legacy in better hands. Underneath the pomp of peerage he was still Jack Burnham, shoemaker's son of Norwich, as common as milled grain.

But with Leda arranging things, providing the conversation, pleasing the curious with just the right words, everything was easier. The pressure was off him to perform as a baron ought. And now she was rearranging the table to her satisfaction, seating herself beside rather than across from him, reordering the plates so all sat within Jack's reach, and filling a plate from the assorted dishes with the quiet grace of a woman bred her whole life to preside over a table.

"You'll carve?" She cast him an inquiring look. Jack sat in his chair and took up the carving knife.

He flashed on the image Leda had planted in his brain earlier. Her, trailing gore, wandering the halls of her home in a stained shift, holding a knife, while her husband's body lay soaking blood into the parlor rug, stabbed in multiple places.

He pushed the image away and cut into the shoulder of mutton. When he laid a strip of meat on the plate she passed him, her gaze met his, and he guessed she knew exactly what was in his mind, in that uncanny way she had of reading people.

"You don't fear I would hurt Muriel? Now that you know my story."

She spoke her name as if Muriel were real to her already, not Jack's appendage, not a shadowy concept, but a person taking shape in her mind.

She offered him the plate she held. She had filled his plate first, not her own.

He couldn't remember the last time any person—any woman, outside his darling, distracted mother—had made an effort to see to his comfort.

He took the plate. "I believe Muriel would be better off with you than she is with me," he said frankly.

She filled her own plate almost as full as his. Leda Wroth was not one of those ladies who pretended not to eat in company so she might be perceived as delicate. The candle on the table flickered, casting a veil of light over her cheek.

"I was the Mad Baron even before my wife—" Jack let the sentence end there. "My uncle had petitioned Parliament for an Act of Enclosure in his benefit. I stopped the proceedings when he died and opened the common land back for grazing."

"Thereby injuring your profits, no doubt," Leda observed.

"And leaving my tenants something to live on, like the old ways, having pasture to graze their own animals, and a place to collect fuel for their homes." He forked up a stalk of asparagus, swimming in cream. "Most of the tenant farms were in shabby condition, as my uncle had left off improvements. I believe I was seen helping the thatchers now and again, and repairing one or two brick hearths with my own hands."

She watched him, wide-eyed, nibbling on a pickle. "Truly, the act of a man who has taken leave of his senses."

"Or a baron not fit for his title." He winced. "Then I wooed

Anne-Marie, who had turned down every man who approached her. She was known to be contrary. Dreamy. They said she would never make a gentleman's wife, and I was mad to think I could make her a lady."

"Contrary and dreamy are two of my favorite attributes in a young woman," Leda said. "I would have been enchanted, too."

Jack savaged his mutton, tougher than it first appeared. Anne-Marie's face, at their small wedding in a smaller church, had not been of bridal enchantment. She'd worn the stricken look of a bird caught in a snare, debating whether to injure itself to get free.

And he'd not been enchanted either. It seemed a lie to let Leda believe so, and yet—would it make him desirable in her eyes, if she thought him a normal man, with a heart that could be charmed and softened by a woman?

She would hate him when she learned the truth. Everyone did.

"We did not entertain much during our marriage," Jack said. "Anne-Marie disliked crowds of people. Disliked their judgments about her. After she...died, with Muriel being so small, I did not accept what invitations came. I knew the whispers going about and did not want to face them. But by the time I emerged, when I realized Muriel needed more people than just me in her life, the whispers had turned into established fact. And there were no more invitations."

"Did you kill your wife?" Leda asked in the most reasonable of tones, as if she were asking him to pass the salt cellar.

"No!" Jack's gaze leapt to her face.

She nodded, as if that decided the matter. "Then I shall keep my promise to accompany you and arrange proper guidance for Muriel. I do not fear gloomy households, and if I do not need fear being murdered, then you offer me a better situation than I had in my marriage."

Jack laid down his knife, haunted. "You thought your husband might kill you?"

Had Anne-Marie feared him that way? Was that why she'd chosen the path she did?

Fury reared in him, shockingly sudden. His wife had never known him at all. Had never given him a chance to woo and win her, a chance to offer her the life she wanted, a chance to please her. She had decided against him from the beginning.

While he'd done everything in his power to please her, and Leda's husband had put her in fear of her life.

"I was seventeen when I was betrothed," Leda said, spooning gravy over her meat.

"That seems the usual threshold." For gentlemen's daughters, at least, which she seemed to have been.

"Most girls." Leda nodded. "Alas for me, I was the dreamy and contrary type, too. When my sister married, the anchor was taken from my world. My mother only cared that I show well in company and hired a governess to teach me. She was a lovely woman, Miss Elam, frightened of her own shadow, and thought she would lose her post if she opposed my will, so I spent very little time cultivating the graces and more of my time tramping the pastures and reading poetry in the orchard."

"What poems?" Jack asked, fascinated. She did not appear to him to be lacking in any of the graces, but then, he was the last person equipped to judge such things.

"Milton. Donne. Herbert, Marvell, Herrick. I imagined myself another Susanna Blamire, composing verses in a meadow by a stream, pinning my poems to trees."

"Then, let me guess. You married a man who had no soul for poetry."

"My parents chose me a husband who had no soul for poetry, but a fine house near Cirencester which he had bought from a widow whose husband had died in the Americas.

Bertram was several years older than I." Unabashed, she took a second helping of pudding, offering Jack a scoop as well. He accepted.

"I, for my part, imagined I would run away to Gloucester and find work in a shop. But my parents held the key to the lock on my bedroom door, and my sister implored me to believe they knew what was right. I let her persuade me I would be settled and content in time, as she was."

"Were there any times? Of contentment," Jack asked softly.

She dipped her head, staring at her plate. "When he was gone." She drank the rest of her wine in a long swallow. "Mrs. Blake had worked for the previous family and stayed on, and she was a comfort. He hired Betsey when we married. I had friends nearby, though none I could ask for help, and the friends I could confide in lived back near home. Miss Elam—I wonder what happened to her? I had no reply from my letters."

Jack tried to imagine it: a young woman, trapped in unkind circumstances, isolated from her loved ones. Anne-Marie had gone mad with it, and she'd had a child to live for, and a husband who was not unkind.

Leda Wroth was as different from Anne-Marie as sand from flint.

He drained his own wine. "Do you believe you killed him? Your husband."

She looked up, her eyes full of shadows. "I had the knife. I suppose you think I should turn myself in, and let justice be done? But if he can hurt no one else, then I say justice *was* done." She pushed away from the table. "Please excuse me. If we are to travel tomorrow, and you trust yourself in close confines with me, it will be a long day."

Jack shot to his feet. He couldn't let her leave like this, the same haunted look with which she had parted from her sister. Not if he had the power to comfort her. "Leda."

She whirled from the door, eyes wide with surprise.

"I know I have no right." His voice rasped. He had no right to use her given name, no right to approach her as he was doing. But the hurt in her face drew him like a siren's call.

"I believe you have paid your price." If she had taken a man's life, that was a sin for which her Creator would call her to account. "And I see now why you are an unmatch-maker." She had been locked away in a madhouse, her freedom further denied her, and now that she was at liberty, she had dedicated herself to keeping others from couplings that would injure their happiness. Surely that penance counted for something.

He caved to the impulse that had rode him hard all day and curled a hand around her forearm.

She was slight but substantial. Present. Real.

Now that he'd touched her, he couldn't stop. He cupped her elbow, slid his other hand from her wrist to the shoulder of her other arm, tugging her gently toward him. She smelled of wine that had stained her lips ruby. He bent his head, bringing his face close to hers.

"But you cannot let the judgments of others rob you of happiness now. Believe me when I say it does no good to wish you could change the past. That will truly drive you to madness."

She searched his eyes with that direct, unhesitating gaze of hers. "You are no more mad than I am."

"I think I will part from my senses completely if I cannot kiss you again."

He waited for her to express dismay, or revulsion. She had spurned him earlier. But she tilted her head and lifted her chin, and when her mouth slid along his, he could have roared with triumph. Instead he squeezed his hands, gathering her to him, and claimed her mouth fully.

She tasted of berries and sugar, and her lips were smooth

and cool while inside her mouth was smooth and warm. He closed his teeth around her lower lip, tugging gently, and she met his kiss with increasing ardor. Heat licked up his thighs and bulleted his groin. She was warmth and silky softness, and her breasts against his chest made his breath stop. A murmur rose from the back of her throat, and the sound pierced and heightened his ache.

The door was near and when he pressed her against the wooden surface he could lean all of himself against her. He propped his elbows against the wood and plunged his hands into her hair, angling her chin so he could stroke his tongue into her mouth. She murmured again, the sound a small moan, and dug her fingertips into the back of his shoulders. He was as hard as the door and he swore she pressed back against him, her hips lifting ever so slightly, enough to cradle his groin with hers. Heat fogged his brain, strangling all thought of caution. She met his tongue with hers, a tentative lick, and fire roared into his belly.

Relief was a few centimeters away, the thickness of fabric, her skirts, his breeches. And she was responding to him, welcoming him. She was trying to tug him closer still, though there was no space between their bodies, hers curved tightly and sweetly against his, her thighs fitting around his manhood. Ah, God, it had been so long, and no woman he'd touched had been this soft, had tasted this sweet. He sank against her, rolling his hips, wanting to fasten her to him entirely.

She went taut and still, her body vibrating like a drawn bow.

He lifted his head. It took a moment to find his voice. "Did I hurt you?"

"No."

He blocked the light, leaving her face in shadows, only the curve of one cheek and the slope of her neck glowing like cream. He wanted badly to taste her.

"Will you come to my room?"

"No."

Somehow, though his body was wood, he leaned back, and she eased away from him. The delicate skin around her mouth was smudged pink from his evening stubble.

"No," he said stupidly. To his own ears he sounded like a beast in pain. He was going to explode from the agony of extended arousal and he would be no good for a woman again, if he ever had been.

Leda did not want him, either.

"I do desire you," she whispered.

He leaned his head against the door frame, struggling for composure. Damn her for reading him so accurately.

"But."

"But we cannot dally."

Dally. The word sounded so light-hearted. A walk through a river meadow on a warm spring day, blackbirds calling, the snake's head fritillary abloom. When he ached for her with a force that could rend stone, shoot geysers of lava from the earth.

"Why not?" He forced the words through gritted teeth.

She touched the scarf at her throat, now crushed from their embrace. "Because when a man and women are—intimate, certain expectations arise. He makes demands. He wants her to comply with his wishes." She straightened her shoulders. "I have had my freedom for six years, and I find I wish to preserve it. I do not wish to be in a position where I am bound to please a man." Her voice dropped to a whisper. "Even you."

He opened the door and she slid past him. The scent of almonds teased his nose.

He dealt with himself in his room, quietly, fiercely. It wasn't nearly enough to relieve the agony. Anne-Marie had not wanted to be bound to him, either. Was he incapable of pleasing a woman? Or had he caged his wife, without meaning to, and she found the chains so vile that she was willing to kill herself to be free?

Only when he was finally drifting off to sleep, one ear straining to hear sounds from the next room, did he repeat her words and understand their meaning. She said she'd had her freedom for six years. She'd been widowed for eight.

She'd spent two years locked in a madhouse. No wonder she valued her freedom above all else.

CHAPTER ELEVEN

Holme Hall was the wildest, loneliest, most isolated place Leda had ever seen.

It was also the most beautiful.

The landscape had changed when they left Cambridgeshire and entered the Fens, low-lying marshes that could not decide whether to be land or sea, and which reeked the rich smell of growing things. They passed the town of Ely, with the towers of its great cathedral climbing the sky, and Jack made her laugh with stories of his eccentric schoolmasters.

At Lynn Regis, the air smelled of salt, and the spires and towers of more medieval buildings combed the heavens. They traded their comfortable chaise and the turnpike road for a dog cart and a rutted track that led north through pasture and common and small flocks of trees, and the smell of salt marsh came with them.

Jack pointed out the long, grey outline of Castle Rising, where Isabella of France, the guilty widow of Edward II, had lived out her exile. They passed Snettisham, which he said was the nearest market town, then small cliffs like curled waves where chalk had been dug from the ground, and a scatter of ruins he called Ringstead Parva.

He pointed to a wooded clump to the east where sat Hunstanton Hall in its park, home of the ancient Le Strange family and currently the domain of the Reverend Armine Styleman. Then the lane turned east and the thin line on the horizon advanced into a band of blue Jack called The Wash, and Leda felt she'd arrived at the furthest reaches of the known world.

The house rose straight from the ground with no gracious setting of sculpted parterres or naturalized landscaping, simply walls of stone angled up from the earth in the blocky Jacobean style. Crenellations lined the roof, their forbidding outline offset by homey chimneys sprouting along the length, one quietly breathing smoke. The tall arched windows were set with red brick facing, accenting the blocky gray stone of the walls, lined with what looked like large pebbles.

"Flint," Jack said, watching her study the building. "It's a common building material around here, as much as brick."

Brick walls encased the front and sides of the building in concentric rectangles, holding off the wind to shelter gardens, a regular set of treetops that suggested an orchard, and most likely animal pens. As they approached the rock-clad outbuildings came into sight, organized into a neat horseshoe at the rear of the house. Holme Hall seemed enormous, framed against clumps of gray clouds that drifted and spun out overhead. The wind carried sea spray, salt marsh, and the high *brr-eek, brr-eek* of curlews.

Leda shivered and pulled her cloak tight to her shoulders. She wasn't cold, but the wind rushed through her as if she were hollow, awakening a sudden ache.

The place was austere, but it was a home. She hadn't had a home in so long.

Jack turned onto the pebbled drive fronting the house. The

boy they'd hired in Lynn Regis to return the cart, who was currently riding the near horse, stared as curiously as Leda.

"Oi, so here's the place as the Mad Baron lives!" he marveled. "Yew ain't afreard he'll do yew in, sir?" He twisted around to regard Jack. "A thack on the hid, a toss ore the cliff, and downards you go." He whistled as he curved his hand through the air, mimicking a falling body.

Jack winced. "Famous all the way in Lynn Regis, is he?"

The boy nodded solemnly. "Int many ghosties an'orl in these places. They's the Edward Queen in Rising and the Henry Queen in Blickling, an ta. The Mad Baron's bride." He gestured toward the house.

Leda bit her lip. Anywhere else, she'd have caught Jack's eye, shared a smirk of knowing amusement with him. But here, in the shadow of his home, he was not amused. And the wild air about the place made Leda feel very far from the stately, civilized rooms of Bath, where under the light of many candles and the crowds of gracious revelers, superstitions held no purchase. On these cliffs and fens, where the land stood so empty all about, a specter might take form, grow teeth.

Bird calls pierced the air, a noisy chorus, but the house sat quiet. No shadows passed before the windows inside, and outside, nothing moved save for the wind in the branches of a lone holm oak holding its crooked arms toward the sky. A brown goose with pink feet poked through the scrubby grass that lined the drive.

Leda hadn't been this nervous about meeting her husband. She'd known at the time she wouldn't get on with Bertram Toplady. But she very much wished for Muriel to like her, and the worry crashed through her stomach like the sound of waves not far away, somewhere out of sight.

Jack seemed nervous, too. He'd been stiff and scrupulously correct through their entire second day of travel, sitting upright in the chaise as if he feared he might slump and accidentally touch her. They took their supper at opposite ends of the table in a private parlor he arranged and said a formal goodnight at the door of the separate rooms he paid for.

And she had a chaperone, of sorts. Early in the morning before they left Swindon, Leda had entered the kitchens of their inn and before the bread was finished baking found a girl willing to travel with them as their maid, lending an air of respectability. With as quickly as she was ready to leave, Leda sensed that Grace Haycot was escaping something, or someone, and she had half expected the girl to peel off in Cambridge, or Lynn Regis, ready to seek her fortune in town.

Leda also suspected that young Grace carried a secret that would, in five or six months, make her ineligible for service in a genteel household. But as Grace had not broached the matter to Leda, Leda would not raise it to her. Instead, she watched as the girl hopped down from the dog cart, collecting her string bag.

"What's that and all about a ghost?" she asked the boy.

"A local superstition, I gather." Leda turned to find Jack holding out his hand to her.

Sometime in the journey, he had stopped being Brancaster in her mind and become simply Jack. Perhaps it was watching him teach Ives how to hold his fork and cut his meat like a gentleman. Or that dazzling kiss. The memory rushed through her in random moments, raising her blood, making her skin tingle like a coming storm.

She'd grasped any reason to push him away, could barely recall now what slender excuse she'd given that they shouldn't indulge in attraction. Yet it hadn't quelled her response to him, and her chest heated with a blush as he watched her. His hand was so strong, as was all of him, solid and firm to the ground. His gray eyes matched the sky. He was a man a woman could lean on, if she dared.

Leda didn't dare lean on anyone. But he clasped her hand firmly, placing his other hand on her elbow as he helped her step down from the cart, and the ache opened wider, deeper.

She could not afford to be daft. She took a deep breath and faced the house.

Atop a low wall to the side of the house lay a line of bricks of assorted colors and sizes. Two had swelled with moisture to the size of loaves. One had split apart. Another looked as if had melted.

One, a pale rectangle, Jack picked up in his hand, and it crumbled back into sand. Another just like it performed the same way.

He sighed. "Wrong again."

"What are you attempting?"

"I'm convinced the soil around here would be good for making bricks. The Romans knew the secret, which is why so many of their ruins survive, but it was lost during the Dark Ages. The Tudors found it again, with the help of Dutch and Flemish settlers. You'll see many of the great houses hereabouts have been redone in the last century. But the recipe is different depending on the soil, and I have not found the knack of it here."

"And these are the experiments you are teased about," Leda observed.

"Once, it would have been my trade. Could I manage it now, it'd be a business that could keep an estate alive, were it in difficulties." He swept his gaze over the house and grounds, still but for the keening wind.

Was his estate in difficulties? Struggling to produce, burdened with debt? Lady Plume had spoken with affection of the graciousness of Holme Hall, and as they entered through the wooden front doors, Leda could see the bones of its former splendor. The domed ceiling of the vestibule dangled an enormous chandelier above the floor, stone inlaid with marble. A wooden staircase led to the floors above, and arched doorways led to state rooms on either side.

The far wall, beyond the staircase, held a tall case clock, a polished occasional table, and a vast oil pointing of a Cavalier knight astride a rearing white charger. Beside it a small, discreet door opened and two women spilled out of a hall Leda guessed led to the service rooms and, she hoped, a water closet.

"Cor blarst me, 'tis himself," one was saying as they bustled forth. "May, stand ahind me and dint you jiffle." The elder pushed the younger at attention before the table, both of them patting aprons and caps into place before the elder bobbed a curtsey, then elbowed the younger to indicate she do the same. "Yer lordship. We hant thought you coming today."

"I had hoped to send warning, but we traveled as fast as the mail," Jack said cordially. "Mrs. Wroth, this is Mrs. Leech, my cook and housekeeper, and May, our maid of all work. I have brought Mrs. Leda Wroth of Bath, lately companion to my Aunt Plume, to arrange a governess for Muriel."

Both women dropped another curtsey. Mrs. Leech rose with a slight shake of the head, as if she were unconvinced of Leda's ability to take on this task. May, too, looked doubtful, but nonetheless offered a polite greeting. "How you goin,' milady?"

Leda struggled to follow the accents. Norfolk speakers moved their vowels back in their throats, unlike the round open sounds of Somerset. "I am very well, thank you."

Jack looked around. "Where is everyone else?"

"Henry went to Thornham to do for his mum, and the misses is out on a wander, sir," Mrs. Leech reported. "They arst if they might, and I dussent keep 'em in to craze us. Where do we put the lady, sir?"

It was a delicate probe as to her status in the household, and

Jack didn't realize it. Leda tried to catch his eye, but, bear-like, he blundered straight into the trap.

"I'll have Henry take Mrs. Wroth's things to the mistress's suite, and you may make up a room above for her maid. This is —" He looked, wide-eyed, to Leda.

"Grace Haycot. She came with us from Swindon," Leda said. Grace, craning her chin this way and that to peer into the state rooms, brought herself to attention and made her greetings.

Mrs. Leech looked her over with a sharp eye. "Well, come alonga me and spare the gawping for later, mawther," she said, shooing the two girls down the service hall. "Mind you, there's to be no mardle, no slummockun, and you don't steal a skerrit. May'll larn you how we do, and himself int too finicky, bless 'im, so…" Her instructions, which Leda could comprehend in their gist if not their specifics, faded as the door swung shut.

Jack offered a lopsided smile. "Mrs. Leech runs as tight a ship as Nelson. Tighter, I think, as she gives no quarter, and delegates nothing."

Leda followed him into an inner hall, a spare, lofty chamber. "You needn't give me a fine suite. I would be happy with something next to the nursery, near Muriel."

He blinked, startled. "You are a guest in my home."

"And your servants will conclude I am your mistress." Cool air touched her neck above the collar of her cloak. The fireplace in the corner stood empty and, from its state of cleanliness, had not seen a fire in some time. The room was scarcely used.

Jack flushed as red as the bricks she'd seen outside in his collection of experiments. "We—"

"Should have anticipated this. Traveling alone, and I am staying here without a chaperone?" To spare his embarrassment, and her own, she looked around at the display of family treasures. There were fewer of them than she might have expected, and not particularly tasteful.

She ought to have foreseen how their arrangement would appear to others, like the innkeeper's wife in Swindon, like his staff. Customarily she was awake on all suits. Seeing Eustace had rattled her wits badly, turned her into a wild creature fleeing for its life.

Being thought Jack's mistress gave her the sudden, unwise urge to become so. He looked so flustered, dragging his fingers along his jaw, coming out again in stubble. It was his gesture when he was nervous, and she knew that about him now.

She knew he snored lightly when he was overtired, that he disliked the taste of eel, that he had once been accidentally shut overnight in the west chapel of Ely Cathedral when he and a school chum snuck in to see the Saxon bones, hundreds of years old. He and his friend had spent the night awake in terror, convinced the bodies of the ancient dead would rise, or their ghosts would haunt them for disturbing their rest.

He set his jaw. "I could contact my Aunt Dinah, I suppose. She lives in Middlesex now."

Of the little Leda had gleaned of Jack's family, he was, aside from his siblings, on corresponding terms with only two members of the greater Burnham family: Lady Plume, who took an interest in everyone and everything, or at least knowing about them, and his aunt Dinah, who as a woman had been left out of the line of inheritance and excluded from most of the family struggles as well.

"Would she come to stay?"

"I could ask. If you are concerned about your reputation."

"I am not concerned on my account." She stepped into the next room, a large formal parlor. She wished she had the right to take his hand, soothe the worry from his face. "I am more concerned how it might reflect upon you and Muriel if my time here causes gossip. Perhaps I ought to stay elsewhere."

He showed her the rest of the rooms on the ground floor, the dining parlor and beyond it the kitchens, a smaller parlor that served as a family sitting room and library. Above, on the first floor, he pointed to the nursery and Muriel's bedchamber, then his own down the hall. Doors opened to a powder room, now unused as Jack wore no wig, and a bathing chamber alongside. The mistress's suite lay at the end of the hall, with windows on all three walls that stared out to sea.

She'd never seen so much water in her life. It looked like it could swallow the world.

Jack spoke from behind her, his voice soft with unguarded longing. "I want you to stay here."

She turned to regard him, standing in the doorway, ever the gentleman. Or at least, the gentleman now. He hadn't been chivalrous when he kissed her in Swindon. He'd been overwhelming, demanding, an inferno of roaring heat. She could close the door behind him and step into his arms, offering herself again. Her breasts tingled at the thought, aching, and a heat roused low in her belly, a restless hunger.

She couldn't give into passion. She couldn't trust herself when she did.

Jack's face changed, tightened. His eyes darkened as he stared at her. Leda's skin prickled. He knew what she was thinking, sensed her desire. He was ready to unleash his. She need only show the smallest invitation and that inferno would roar again to life, all that strength and heat and maleness of him against her, surrounding her. Consuming her.

His face changed. "There's Muriel."

Leda followed his gaze out the window and saw a girl trudging across the lawn. She let herself through a gate in the first wall, stepping into the orchard. Her straw hat bobbed between the trees, and a dark blue skirt flapped about her legs. She looked small and determined.

"I'll meet her downstairs," Jack said. "Will you join us?"

"In a moment." Leda untied the ribbon on her hat and set it on a table, her gaze still fixed on the window as Jack departed down hall toward the stairs.

The sea heaved in gray humps, rippled by the wind, and short grasses along the cliff bent and nodded. A steep path led down to the beach, a wide strip of sand dotted with clumps of rock crowned with green seaweed. Between the field of rocks and the high cliffs, banded with cream and red, lay a broad path of sand untouched by the tide. On it were two sets of footprints, small and distinct.

Muriel must have been walking with her nurse, but where had the maid gone? The girl made her way alone through the inner garden to a door beneath Leda's window, which must lead to the kitchens or a room attached to them. There seemed a dearth of servants for a house this size, only the cook, one chambermaid, and this Henry. If Jack's fame as the Mad Baron had spread to Lynn Regis, or beyond, she didn't doubt his difficulty retaining servants.

Something about the vast sky and the haunting call of the sea made the strange feel possible. Made it seem that a darker, wilder world, one full of ancient things not yet tamed, lay but a step away, across a layer of sand and mist. While inside this house, moaning in answer to the wild wind, lay a still, empty shell encasing a grieving widower and a motherless child.

Little wonder she wanted to put her arms around Jack and hold him close. He didn't seem the Mad Baron to her. He seemed lonely.

CHAPTER TWELVE

Leda's heart gave a small kick against her ribs as Jack clicked to the horses and the market cart rolled away from Holme Hall. It took her a moment to place the sensation: excitement. The sky stretched broad and blue gray above them, dotted with birds swooping along the shoreline and feeding in the marshes, their calls echoing in a continuing musical chorus. The scent of salt braced her senses with its bouquet of sand and cordgrass and seaweed, the wind scraping her skin. She hadn't felt this wild and alive since she sailed toward Bristol and saw if she kept going she'd reach the wide sea, leaving behind everything she'd known. Norfolk unrolled before her in the same way, like an enamel box opening to reveal treasures nestled within.

The man beside her in the driving seat had something to do with her excitement. Being near Jack brought her to attention, as if she were an instrument being tuned by a skilled hand.

"My mother took me to market in Snettisham with her all the time," Muriel announced. The girl sat between Jack and Leda, her back straight and determined, hands clasped around the small cloth pocket she carried, which she had not attached beneath her dress. The fabric, scraps of silk brocade in an elegant weave, were held together by knotted thread and showed the wear and dirt of steady use. Leda had never seen the girl without it.

"What is your favorite part of the market?" Leda asked lightly.

Muriel set her tiny chin. She was a small child, built like a reed, with her slender limbs and tufts of hair red as the bands of stone that lined the cliffs. There was no doubt she was Jack's child, with that hair, and something about her chin suggested his features as well, but her fair skin and green eyes came from her mother, or so she had informed Leda. In the two days since they had been introduced, Muriel's mother fell constantly from her lips. Leda knew it was a challenge and reminder, the girl's one defense against this stranger whom her father had brought, without her knowledge or permission, into their home.

"A peddler would sometimes come, and my mother liked to look at his buttons and pretty ribbons and pins."

"What do you want from market, Mere?" Jack asked, glancing down at his daughter.

His look sliced Leda's chest. There was something protective and hopeless blended in it, inviting her confidence, and doubtful he would be gifted with knowing the secrets of her heart.

Muriel did not return his look, but rather studied her pocket with great attention. The cart dipped into a rut into the road, and the girl stiffened and pulled away as the motion tipped her toward Leda. The slight stung. Leda was accustomed to people trusting her within moments, sometimes on sight. Muriel would not be easily won.

"Would you also like a ribbon, Muriel?" Leda asked. Not that she meant to woo Jack's daughter with treats.

The girl's attire was frightfully plain, a simple cotton frock of dark blue with only one ruffle on the short sleeves. The white tucker at her neckline and the apron at her waist were clean white linen, but her muslin cap had no ribbon to lace it, and her straw bonnet had nothing to adorn it but a strip of scarlet silk, matching her red woolen cloak. Her shoes were clean, but the leather showed scuffed and worn above a set of wooden pattens. Leda had been furnished her own set of pattens before they left —she guessed they might have belonged to the former lady of the manor—and they served a warning that the market might be a muddy as well as crowded affair.

Muriel drew a small doll out of her pocket, an oddly shaped figure woven of dried corn husks. "Nanette would like a ribbon," the girl said.

Jack stiffened and stared straight ahead. Mrs. Leech, seated in the back of the cart, abruptly stopped her stream of steady commentary and instruction directed at Grace, who nodded and took everything in.

Something about the mention of Nanette, the doll, had brought them all to swift attention. Did Muriel ask for so little?

"Then we shall look for a ribbon at market," Leda said. "Is that a corn dolly? She is pretty."

"My mother always won the corn dolly in the fall. The workers made it for her. She was the queen of the harvest." Despite the proud note in her words, Muriel stuffed the dolly back into her fabric pocket as if she meant to bury it.

"My mother was the most beautiful lady," Muriel added. "Everyone loved her."

"I am very sure they did," Leda murmured.

Jack's jaw had gone as hard as the cliffs that fell down to the beach outside his house, a hardness that could weather centuries of wind and wear.

"I'll never want a different doll." Muriel looked Leda full in the face, her expression as tight as her father's. "Never."

Leda trained her gaze on the rough track ahead of them.

The wind cut through her cloak, made for the sheltered, stone-walled streets of Bath, not this wild, empty country where grass stretched out endlessly to one side of her and the other rolled to marshland dropping bare and open to the sea and sky.

"Not a different," Leda agreed. "But perhaps another, in time?"

Muriel set her chin and stared straight ahead. "No."

"She will warm to you." Jack came to Leda's side after he stopped the cart south of Heacham to inspect a brick kiln there. A chalk pit dug out a hill across the road. Leda watched Muriel wander to the edge of a pond, where shovelers and teals floated in pairs on the water. The girl looked so small, framed against the green-gray marsh.

"She is on her guard. I can understand that."

As a girl herself, Leda had been open and trusting, at least when it came to her sister. She had learned early to be wary of her mother's motives, but had for the most part found the world a hospitable place, right up until she met the man her parents meant her to marry.

Muriel had been betrayed young by her mother's death. She would not see the world as a warm and welcoming place at all.

Jack stood beside her, and Leda's stomach did that strange dance it reserved only for him. "She's usually so biddable," he said. "I've never seen her this—mulish."

Leda looked at him in surprise. "Milord Brancaster, your daughter is nothing but mulish." She had needed less than ten minutes in Muriel's company, on the occasion of their first meeting, to see that the girl was mostly hair, pale skin, and backbone. If she was biddable, it was only for her father.

Because perhaps she thought that was what he wished. Or what she thought was necessary to her survival.

Jack looked as if she had struck him, his gray eyes capturing the range of colors in the sky. He was made of this place, and belonged here. In the countryside, he didn't walk like some leashed predator, his power strapped in and contained. Here, in these wild open spaces, he was at home.

"How is she for you?" Leda asked softly. As Jack watched his daughter, she saw again in his eyes the bewilderment of an otherwise capable man who didn't know the first thing to do with the small creature placed in his care. Her heart ached for Muriel, losing her mother, and for him, who had lost near as much.

He turned away. "Today, in the cart, was the most I've heard her speak in months." He paused, his back toward her. "She speaks to *you*."

"Perhaps she is still grieving," Leda said. "How long ago did her mother die?"

"Six years." He looked again toward the pond, as if it pained him to see his daughter distance herself, but he couldn't look away.

Six years was not a recent loss. Time enough for the first wounds of grief to scab over, as she knew. Some men moved on once their year of mourning was complete, or even before then. Jack's walls were as high and firm as his daughter's.

What had happened to this family, that the surviving members locked themselves away?

And what had led milady Brancaster to jump? To leave what the world would see as her comfortable home, her beautiful daughter, her handsome and no doubt quite doting husband?

Madness. Or desperation, like Lady Sydney had said.

Jack moved away, and she felt his departure like a physical diminishing. "Have you ever been in a brick kiln?" he called over his shoulder.

Leda wavered. She understood that where she chose to stand would indicate her alliance in this household. Did she move toward Muriel, standing in for governess, holding guard as the girl trailed her fingers through blooming knapweed and purple moor-grass? Or did she wait near the cart, like the servants?

She ought to keep her distance from Jack. Regard him, if not as an employer, then her employer's nephew. Family acquaintance, no more. Despite that kiss.

But that kiss had happened. Kisses. So had their dance, and their walk on Maud Heath's Causeway, and their many dinners, and shared miles and hours in the carriage, sometimes talking, sometimes drifting in a silence that felt shared and serene, demanding nothing. All of those moments bound her to him with small sure threads, tight as the knots on Muriel's pocket.

He paused at the rim of the kiln, a pit dug into the earth, and turned to her, his eyes glowing like sun rising behind a veil of fog. He rippled with aliveness, with that alert but quiet intensity she had noticed in him from the first.

"Coming? You've seen nothing like this in your West Country, I promise."

She made her choice, a declaration to the others of where her loyalties lay. An admission of sorts, for she was helpless to resist him. He lured her like the flicker of a warm hearth on an icy day, the call of a candle in the window across a heath dark and cold with storms.

He beckoned, and she followed, as if she had no sense of self-preservation whatsoever. As if he hadn't led another woman to her doom, and Leda might be next.

"JUMPED," one farm wife said confidently, bundling asparagus for Leda. "Though if you arst others, they'll say *pushed*, tha will." She sent a glare toward another goodwife, sidling over with her apron full of cauliflower sprouts and turnip tops.

"Oi say pushed, and thas the right of it an'orl." The second woman peeped open her apron for Leda's inspection like a smuggler sporting stolen wares.

"Thassa lud a squit," a third woman announced, plunking a basket of pears on the first woman's table and leaning in. "It warnt neither. He thacked her on the lug, dint he, and tipped her ore the edge. An she never made a deen, the poor mawther, tha she dint, jes sank her down to a watery grave."

"Hold yew hard," said the first in irritation. "She warnt in the water. They found her bones all frooz the next day on the shingle."

"Who found her?" Leda asked, agog at this wealth of information. The farm wives of Snettisham didn't hold a bit with the coy crosstalk of Bath parlors or assembly rooms. The moment she had shown up in the broad dusty triangle of the market, where the sellers vied to place their carts or blankets beneath the spreading branches of a great oak, the good women of Snettisham had been talking over one another to answer Leda's questions about the mad baron Brancaster and his late, little-lamented wife.

A silence fell at this last, however. The second woman shook her head, her white cap peeking out beneath a straw bonnet. "The little mawther founder, thas her daughter, and she hant been the same after."

"And his lordship went all titchy, too," the first goodwife added. "Tha say he went mad."

"If he went mad after finding his wife dead," Leda said, "that would seem to suggest he did not kill her."

Her group of informers met this with silence, each grappling in their own way with Leda's logic.

Finally, the third spoke in a hushed tone. "Do y'spose someone else mighta kilt her and blamed it on himself?"

"She jumped, dint she," the first farm wife said firmly, rearranging the cabbage heads on her folding table. She had staked a prime place beneath the tree, sheltered by its branches but well within sights of the crossing roads, and Leda guessed she had trucked into town well before dawn, pulling her handcart with her table and wares, a Norfolk version of Maud Heath.

"I wonder why," Leda murmured. "Milord Brancaster seems the sort of husband that a woman could go on with."

The others leaned in.

"He's a masterpiece, tha he is," the second wife confirmed. "When he moved here, every mawther in the hundred set her cap for him. An he won't see none but Anne-Marie Waddelow, the only one who dint make sheep's eyes." She sighed. "Thas the way of it, hintut? We wants the ones as don't want us."

Leda's heart turned over, and she darted a guilty look about the market. It was a quiet day, vendors sparsely scattered around the open areas and along a line of beech trees that shielded some great house from prying eyes. She spotted the top of Jack's black felt hat, the hat of a common laborer, as he spoke with great animation to another man Leda guessed to be a cooper, by the casks and barrels scattered about him.

Grace idled by a woman setting out an array of colorful items, perhaps feathers and ribbons, while keeping an eye on Muriel, who was stalking a chicken. Mrs. Leech was engaged in a hearty discussion with another farm wife, shaking a bundle of watercress in her fist. Leda guessed she was negotiating the best price she could, all too aware that her budget would not stretch as far in these days.

The members of the household being out of earshot, Leda was free to gossip. She felt no compunction about mining these good wives for information.

"She was very lovely, I'll wager," Leda prodded, keeping her voice confidentially low, and that was all it took.

"As the day is long," said the first wife, whose name was Ellen. She described a dark-haired beauty with mother-of-pearl skin and eyes the color of seablite that grew along the coast. A woman who floated like a fairy and seemed untethered to earth. Every man wanted her, yet none won her from her parents until Brancaster came along with his hall and his title and his square jaw and broad shoulders, a lion among donkeys.

There'd been some whispers, some secrets that were shushed up when the young lord came calling. Leda gathered there might have been some protests on the part of young Anne-Marie, overruled by her older and wiser parents. Well she knew how such a conversation would go. So young Anne-Marie, who might have wanted more from her life than to be given in marriage to a hall and husband in Hunstanton, Norfolk, was bound will she nil she, and bore him a child in short order.

"And thas when she..." The second farm wife, Jane, twirled a finger outside her ear in a gesture Leda knew all too well. She winced.

"What were her symptoms?" She wondered at her own fascination with this woman—the woman Jack had loved, wooed and won, who became his wife, the mother of his child, the mistress of his home. She wanted to know everything about her.

How he had touched her. How he had longed for her. If Anne-Marie felt the same way when Jack kissed her—as if the top of her head were floating away, her body caught on a magnificent tide.

"Wandered the cliffs, blarin' streams of sea water from her eyes," reported the third farm wife, Mary. "They'd allus been quiet folk, but no one saw inside that house save the servants. Such a kelter she'ud get herself into. Tried agin and over to have her folks take her back, or anyone. But they allus said no and sent her back to him, dint they."

"She tried to leave him?"

"She was badly afore the babe," Jane offered. "And then the next un..." She clamped her lips together.

Leda pounced. "There was another child?"

"Naught that we're in the know of," Mary rushed in. "But she was a primmicky sort from the first. Allus puttin' on her parts."

"Botty," Ellen added. "Liked the attention, dint she. 'Specially from the bors."

"Yet she never had folks callin, did she, not even the grand families heres about," Jane argued. "When she useter to be at all the great dews afore she was married."

Mary tapped the side of her nose. "Himself dint care to share her, I shink."

"Ah, you do run on." Jane shook her head. "She wasn't a furriner, mind, but it was us she dint want no truck with."

"She was from here?" Leda asked in surprise.

"Aye, from Hope House, she was. That great block acrorst the way."

Ellen nodded in a direction leading down the street, toward a house with the local red brick and a black tiled roof. Leda counted five bays around the central porch, framed with its classical pillars. The Waddelows were of no mean stature, it would seem. And what gentleman's family wouldn't want their daughter to reach high above their station, however she felt about the marriage.

Jack had moved on from the cooper and was deep in conversation with another man, shorter and bulkier than he was. He spoke with animation, his hands sweeping through the air as he made shapes to accompany his words. Curls the color of the dark brick of the buildings about them poked from beneath his hat, and she wanted to curve her hand over the nape of his neck. Lean close and inhale the scent of him, wood and smoke, salt and cedar.

The strangest heat bloomed in her belly. She wanted to twine her tongue with his in another soul-consuming kiss, feel his hard body pressing her against a door, as if he could mold her softness to his hard frame and each could balance the other.

How could a woman, knowing the heat of his embrace, the safety of his arms, ever bear to part from him? What could possibly have driven his wife away?

Leda cleared her throat. "Why do they call him the Mad Baron?"

Her conspirators considered this question, looking to one another for assistance.

"He's the one as drove her to it," said a new voice at Leda's ear.

Leda turned and saw a girl, barely to her shoulder, clad in a prim printed calico. Dark hair lay pinned beneath a straw bonnet, and a white tucker like a child would wear filled the neckline of her gown, but a black ribbon tied around her throat lent her a more mature aspect. Leda guessed she was thirteen, perhaps fourteen—a girl on the cusp of womanhood, and seemingly, from the unease in her stance, unsure how she felt about it.

"The mad-making baron, then," Leda said.

The girl nodded, her eyes narrowing. Their color was startling, the green of seaweed that speckled the shore. Leda had seen that color. Recently.

"You think he drove her to despair?" Leda questioned. The girl's serious demeanor roused her curiosity.

"Such a barney he had to get her," Jane said thoughtfully, shaking her head. "Then to find she's not keen to the shackle."

"Thas all mardle, hintut," Ellen said. "Nowt but gossip and talk. How you goin, Miss Nora?"

The girl raised her chin. She had a fine-boned beauty to her, like expensive porcelain. "None too sadly. It's a tidy place I have, when the missus isn't titchy."

"Nora works for the Waddelows," Mary said, hushed as if it were a secret. "In the house we shewed yew." She nodded toward Hope House.

"Where Anne-Marie grew up?" Leda asked, surprised. "Did you know her?"

The girl stiffened. "I was a babe when she married," she said. "A foundling. And the Missus said I wasn't goin with her when she married, so I'm a maid of all work now, aren't I."

"Good of Missus Waddelow, warnt it," Mary remarked, with the air of someone rehearsing a fact she didn't quite believe.

Jack lifted his head and looked over the market, searching for something. His eyes paused on Leda, and his lips half-lifted, as if he smiled despite himself. He did have a delicious mouth, that man.

Then he noticed Nora, and the smile froze.

Leda's skin prickled, and she looked around. Muriel had given up on the chicken and she, too, stared, not at Leda, but at Nora, as if the girl were a wild creature chained to a stake. Nora stared back at Muriel for a long moment, her lips tightening into a line.

A cool wind swirled through the marketplace, winter on the back of it, as if spring were yet far away. Leda was glad she had worn her flannel petticoat.

"You have some lovely ribbons on your bonnet," Leda said, struck by one of those intuitions she didn't question. "I've been searching out ribbons for Muriel. Can you help me look?"

Nora softened and started toward a table across the way,

where a woman sat behind a small folding table drifted over with trimmings, feathers and buttons and bows. "That girl needs a treat, she does."

"You know her?"

"We've never spoken."

The two girls converged before the ribbon as if they'd made an assignation. They stared at one another, both with the same mother-of-pearl skin, the same light green eyes, Nora's dark hair beside Muriel's red, the color of fired clay.

"Hello, Muriel," Nora said. "Your lady friend said you wish for a ribbon."

Muriel clamped her lips together. "She's not a lady, an she's not my friend."

"That is true," Leda said, though her stomach pinched like she'd been poked with a pin. Muriel would resist even the smallest overtures, it would seem. "Our acquaintance at this point is very slight."

"And she will *not* marry my da and carry him off with her, howsomever," Muriel said.

"That's a caution did she do," Nora answered. "You'll want a green for your eyes, then? Or a red to go with that sash on your frock."

While the girls discussed colors and textures, Leda turned to the peddler who had come alongside. Pans hung from the sack slung across his back, and he had the weary, wizened look of a man worn down by the elements. A sparkle entered his eyes when he heard Leda's request, and in short order he had located her item within one of his many packs.

"No *vonga*. No money." He held up a hand as she reached for the pocket inside her skirt. "That *chavi* needs to smile. She is so sad."

Leda blinked, recognizing the Romani words. There'd been a caravan that came near Cheltenham every so often during her childhood, and every time she'd defy her parents' warnings and run off to spy on their camp.

There were so many currents in this place that she couldn't begin to untangle, a history piling up over her head. She felt as if she were a bather inching into the Wash, sure at any moment the sea floor would fall away.

"You know the family?"

He nodded. "Walked the Peddar's Way many times, have I. A straight old noble Roman road." The peddler sobered as he watched the two girls, with their same slender arms, same pert nose, though Muriel had Jack's forehead and the stubborn slope of his jaw. "The *daj*, the mother." He shook his head.

"Some say her husband drove her to it." Leda tugged three hairpins out of her coiffure and handed them to the peddler. His eyes lit, and he slipped the pins into a pocket, patting the fabric as if it held treasure. Her acquaintance with Jack was costing her many a hairpin, Leda observed.

"You can mend a pot," her new friend said in accented English. "But will it hold the same, after?"

Jack arrived at her side, and the peddler melted away. So did Nora. He appeared not to notice, focused instead on his daughter.

"You have made purchases I must pay for, I see."

"I hope you will allow me," Leda said. "It was my idea."

"I insist upon the honor. That color will flatter you, Mere."

"Did you choose one for Nanette?" Leda asked.

Jack stilled, and so did Muriel. His daughter's gaze searched his face, hers fretful, wary. He looked above the top of her head and withdrew a few coins from inside his coat.

Nora reappeared at Leda's side, holding back from Muriel now that her father had arrived. Her gown was fine for a servant's, but she kept her head bent and her hands, lacking gloves, were chapped. Leda thought of the extra cotton gloves in her bag, back at the hall. She ought to have brought them.

"At least he cares for his daughter," Leda observed, keeping her voice low.

"Who's to say he didn't care for her, too."

Leda knew of whom the girl spoke. The woman was still on everyone's mind. If nothing else, Muriel would not let them forget her.

"Maybe he never done her in a'tall," Nora whispered. "Maybe he's locked her away in the attics." Her eyes shone despite the cloudy day, her gaze sharp as the edge on a knife. "Haven't you heard the voices? The Hall is full of ghosts."

CHAPTER THIRTEEN

Leda heard the voices, drifting down the hall from the nursery.

Muriel's suite, with the schoolroom and her bedroom, lay toward the east arm of the house, and the mistress's suite to the west, with a view of the Wash. The house had a north-facing entry, which Leda had thought odd, for here the Hall faced nothing but water on two sides and flat grass on the other, with the sharp line of carrstone cliffs on its flank rearing eventually down to a gentle sandy beach. Now, having seen how the south side caught the light and let the house brace the brunt of the wind, she understood why the stableyards and many gardens lay in that direction.

A main stair that circled up from the state rooms below let out on a landing across from the master suite, Jack's domain. Leda stepped quickly past it. Though she knew Jack was out, peering into his rooms, his sanctum, would be like touching his body.

She longed to do so, and knew she must not.

Muriel was having quite a conversation with Grace, who

despite being hired as Leda's companion had taken quickly to the role of nursemaid for the child. May had surrendered her childcare duties without a protest, muttering something about preferring to beat carpets and haul fuel than wrangle with a stubborn little mawther.

Muriel was certainly stubborn. In the days since Leda's arrival, the girl had refused to bend an inch to her father's plans for her. She had a complaint about every local family Leda had called upon as she attempted to learn the neighborhood—complaints, Leda guessed, rehearsed from remarks she had overheard from some unknown source, not her father. She found fault with every local woman Leda proposed pursuing an acquaintance with.

On the whole, it seemed this pocket of Norfolk had a noticeable dearth of unmarried daughters and spinster sisters the likes of which could be found anywhere else in Britain. There was no workhouse or boarding school to plumb for orphans, no agency to request referrals. There was only the Hall among its cliffs, a few stately homes here and there buried in their parks, and scattered villages perching on the crests of small hills or wading into the marshland that stretched into the North Sea. It was land that had been cultivated for centuries, populated many times over by waves of settlers coming by sea, yet Leda had never lived in a place that felt so wild and empty and open to the sky.

"—with three big chandeliers simply *dripping* with candles, and musicians in a balcony perched high above, and they danced the minuet."

Leda paused at the sound of Muriel's voice, hearing a story she had told one night at dinner. She had suggested to Jack that they allow Muriel to dine with them, in part so she could see the girl's manners in order to properly warn a governess of the work ahead. In part because Jack's relationship with his daughter so clearly needed mending.

And in part because, when she was left alone with him, Leda lived in that memory of their kiss in the dining parlor of the coaching house in Swindon. She lived in that memory at many other times, also.

"The minuet's a stately dance. Lots of intricate steps. Here, I'll show you."

A bustle followed, then the sound of footsteps striking the wooden floor. Leda imagined Grace humoring the girl, letting her make up the steps of a dance neither of them knew, and had likely never observed. Muriel had presented a rigidly unimpressed façade as Leda described how she'd met Muriel's father, yet the girl had clearly been listening.

Giggles followed a larger thump, as if something had been knocked to the floor.

"Well, one of us has to be the lady! Is it you or me?"

Leda smiled to herself and knocked gently on the nursery door. Perhaps she was getting through to Muriel after all. "Is there an assembly within? I would very much like to—"

A screech cut off her words, and the door slammed against her, pushing Leda back into the hall. The noises inside the room resembled the flutter and flight of frightened hens when a fox entered the henhouse. A rustle of fabric, the beat of hurried footsteps, then a slam. Leda pushed the door open.

"What in heaven's name?"

Muriel stood in the center of the room, panting, her eyes spitting defiance above pink cheeks.

She was alone.

"What do *you* want?" she said in challenge.

"Where did Grace run off to?"

Leda looked around. Schoolbooks sprawled open on the table, the history book Leda had suggested for Muriel and a primer for one beginning to read. The shelf held its neat line of toys and books and a teapot with a jagged, broken spout. The immense wardrobe loomed with doors snugly shut, like a matron crossing its arms. The rocking chair in the corner, below the window, swung gently back and forth, as if rocked by a breeze, or a ghostly hand.

The door to the inner bedroom stood open, but the room was empty.

Muriel breathed in short pants, like a frightened animal. She glared at Leda, unblinking.

Footsteps rang from the hall, near the servant's stair, and moment later Grace appeared in the doorway, a pile of fabric in her arms. "Mrs. Leech found your cloak, Miss Burnham, but says she don't know where your bonnet coulda got to. I be thinking—oh, good day, Mrs. Wroth. Are you ready for our airing, then?"

The hair on the back of Leda's neck rose. "How did you come from the hall? I thought I heard you in here."

Grace regarded her warily. "I were downstairs, mum, fetching the things."

Muriel's nostrils flared. "I was *alone*, miss."

"Mrs. Wroth," Grace corrected her sternly, coming into the room. "Will you change your apron to see your da, or go along like a flamtag in your dirt?"

Muriel raised her chin. "He's playing in the mud, innit he? It'll be my dirt, then."

Grace fussed with outfitting Muriel, reporting that Mrs. Leech anticipated a fine drizzle. Leda closed the books on the table and capped the ink, which had been left open when the dancing began. A blob from the quill had been left on the page which held the beginnings of Muriel's report on her book.

Next to the primer lay a slate in its wooden frame and a piece of chalk beside. The slate bore the beginning of letters: a shaky A, a large looping B, a C with the curve of an unpracticed hand.

"This cannot be your slate, Muriel? You already know your letters. Were you teaching Grace?" Leda wondered sometimes if Muriel would respond better if she addressed her as Miss Burham, but Jack had made her feel as if the child were Leda's own family. Someone it was upon her to look out and care for.

"I were in the kitchen all morning, mum," Grace said nervously. "I hope it's all right, but I asked Miss Burham to look after herself a moment. The peddler came round, and Mrs. Leech wanted a minute to look his things over."

Muriel crossed her arms, creasing her fresh tucker. "I told you. I'm the only one here."

Leda spotted the corn doll on the edge of the table, bound in one of the ribbons Jack had bought his daughter at market. Muriel had worn none of them save the one that Grace had fastened to her good hat. Leda wondered if this was because the girl suspected Leda had a hand in their acquisition, or if she was adamant about refusing overtures from her father.

"Are you bringing Nanette?" Leda asked.

Muriel recoiled as if Leda had slapped her. Her eyes flared, a combative light springing into them, and her entire body tensed. Then she followed the direction of Leda's gaze and sprang forward to grab her doll.

"I'll bring her."

There was some unholy connection between Muriel and that doll. Something about Nanette that made even Grace flinch and dart Leda a look of apprehension, as if steeling herself, not for a fine drizzle, but a full-on storm.

Leda fastened the tapes of her cloak, shaking her head as they descended the stairs. She was not mad. She could trust the evidence of her ears and eyes.

Or at least, she hoped so. What, then, was Muriel hiding?

Nora had offered one explanation. *The Hall is full of ghosts.*

. . .

LEDA EXPERIENCED the strangest sensation as she stepped off the small front porch of Holme Hall, tugging on the leather gloves she would use for driving. She had not had occasion in years to wear driving gloves; driving a horse was something her father had taught her when she was young, and she had barreled around in the pony cart until her parents banned her from gollumping about the neighborhood proving she was naught but a hoyden, as her grandmother would say, though she put it in less kindly terms. Leda had enjoyed her grandmother's strict house even less than she appreciated her mother's many rules.

What they thought when she went to the madhouse for killing her husband, Leda couldn't say. They'd stopped speaking to her.

And with a husband stricter than her grandmother, then being locked up and running away after, Leda hadn't been on a horse, nor had her hand on the ribbons of any sort of conveyance, since those long-lost days of hoydenhood. Her heart expanded in her chest with a sense of fullness, like the tide rolling in.

She heard the water all the time now, and the cry of the shore birds, especially the migrations that came through in swarms that could block the sun. And a small, high call out on the water that she couldn't place, but might be mermaids. She'd seen small sleek heads breaking the surface just this morning as she watched the water from her window.

Mermaids. She chuckled to herself at her fancies.

"Alright, me kiddie?" she asked her companion.

Muriel narrowed her eyes, not drawn in by Leda's light tone. Now the dialect of her youth was coming back, too. She felt younger here than she had in years. The land was made for flinging one's arms out and twirling. One could *breathe* here as one couldn't in Bath, where the muck of the street waste and the coal smoke from so many chimneys hung heavy in the air.

And Eustace would never find her. Not here.

Henry stood at the head of the horse, harnessed into the market cart and waiting patiently. "The bor's botty a'smornum, and he'll allus pull left if you let um." He held the ribbons as if reluctant to share. "S'name's Pontus."

"God of the sea. We'll get along, won't we?" Leda scrubbed his muzzle with her knuckles. The big gelding blew and butted his forehead beneath her hand. Leda scratched between his ears, delighted. She'd forgotten she loved horses.

Henry helped her settle on the board that served as a seat and handed up the reins. "Dew yew keep a' troshin, miss."

She heard this phrase often among the servants, and Leda gathered it was a mixture of "fare thee well" and "mind how you go." *Keep threshing*—an injunction to carry on, no matter what. Because one day, one might step out of a grand old hall that felt like a home—the first home one had had in ages—on the way to meet a strapping man who sent up flutters beneath one's stays at the sight of him. There might be a pale sun peeking out behind clouds, and the wilding scent of salt and sea, the edge of the world falling open.

And there might be a quiet, troubled girl beside one whose heart Leda longed to know. Almost as much as she wished to know that of her father.

"So it seems I must teach you the minuet." Leda concentrated first on getting a feel for the harness and horse, and keeping her seat, but when she'd assembled some level of confidence in her own abilities, she thought to speak to the girl sitting beside her.

"I won't need it." Muriel looked away, pointedly indicating her lack of interest in conversation.

"You don't expect you will dance at assemblies, or have suitors who will want to dance with you?"

Wasn't that every girl's dream? Although Leda's girlhood

dreams had not tended toward men or marriage. She'd wanted to read all the books she could lay hands on. Travel to the remotest corners of Britain, and then beyond. To go to school—how she had longed for school—and make friends who would be hers for life, like happened in the books.

"I won't." Muriel said this firmly.

"Don't wish to marry?" Leda probed. "Or don't wish to dance?"

The girl's head swiveled toward her. A field vole shot across the path, and the horse's ears flickered back. Worried he would shy, Leda took a moment to comprehend Muriel's answer.

"I won't have any of those things," she snapped. "Who will offer for a mad woman's daughter?"

Pontus snorted and tossed his head, and Leda realized she had pulled back on the ribbons. At once she loosened her hands.

"Your mother was not—" Leda chose not to finish this thought. The woman had abandoned her child. What frantic thoughts had preyed on her mind to force her to such a choice?

Although, if one listened to certain farm wives of Snettisham market, Anne-Marie Burham hadn't jumped from the cliffs. She'd been pushed.

"And my da, too," Muriel went on ruthlessly. "I'm the mad baron's daughter, aren't I?"

"Your father is not mad," Leda said in a sharp tone. This she was certain of. Jack Burham was as sane, as *solid* a man as it was possible to find.

She concentrated on keeping her hands light on the ribbons, but something of her distress must have communicated itself down to the leather to Pontus. He flicked his ears, then picked up the pace into a trot.

Muriel held on to the seat on both sides. "Of course you think that. You want him to marry you."

The girl stared straight ahead, her tiny jaw clamped tight. She was such a picture of her father in that moment that Leda felt stabbed in her heart.

"I'm here to find you a governess."

"You want my father." Muriel dashed a knuckle across one cheek. "He had to go far away to find a woman who wouldn't care that he's mad, to a place where you all gather and talk about getting husbands. And I suppose you'll want other children, too."

"I won't marry again," Leda blurted. "I'll have no child of my own."

Muriel blinked, her eyelashes heavy with tears. "Don't you all want that?"

Leda's heart twisted and thrashed in her chest, like a landed fish. Her lungs compressed, bereft of air.

"Many do," Leda said. "But I won't have them. Just like you."

Muriel scrubbed at her eyes. "Why not?"

How could Leda explain to a child that she didn't trust herself? That she might go blank again, who knew when, and wake with a knife in her hand and a body in her house. She'd never feared it with Lady Plume, but then Lady Plume did not unsettle Leda the way Jack Burham did. Make her long for things she couldn't have, so much that she might indeed go mad with the wanting.

Jack made her long to have a home of her own with a husband who smiled at her over dinner, who touched her hand as they walked through town. To have a child to hold to her breast. A woman like her, with madness buried within her—she couldn't risk having those things. The demon might come out and destroy them.

Because I am just like your mother, Leda almost said, but

knew better to let the words emerge. She must keep Muriel safe. The moment she feared that madness was threatening, she'd flee Holme Hall the way she left Bath. She'd leave Lord Brancaster without looking back.

"I suppose some women are shaped for such things, a home and babies and fixing tea," Leda said finally. "And some are made for other purposes."

It wasn't madness, yet, the things that were stirring inside of her, like rumblings from the depths of the earth or waves from the deeps of the sea. This felt like freedom. A surfacing of parts of herself she'd thought lost to her, buried under the years of fear and want. It wasn't darkness rising in her but something fierce and bright, a joy she'd thought no longer possible for her.

When she topped the ridge and found Jack, exactly where he had said she might find him, that bright thing rose like a golden shower, shaking loose more pieces that had bricked over all the girlish dreams and desires and pleasures of her youth. She had the strangest sense that she had arrived precisely where she was supposed to be, and had always known she would find him waiting for her.

LEDA WAS HERE. The day brightened, the sun that had been teasing all morning finally emerging from the clouds in full glory. The woman brought light with her, and the sense that a drab, winter-dead world was only dormant, about to burst into full bloom.

Jack stood quietly a moment, letting the new knowledge settle, absorbing its rays. She wore a round gown of sprigged muslin, the color of a new-blown rose, and a spencer of cherry red, lined with white fur, that hugged her bosom and lovely arms. Cherry blossoms from a tree that some ancestor had lodged in the hall gardens adorned her straw hat.

She pegged the ribbons over the seat as if she'd been driving for years, hopped down with a lively little spring, and came around the horse, sparing a pat on the muzzle for Pontus, to help Muriel descend from the cart. As they turned toward him, the woman holding his daughter's hand, Jack felt as if the huge horse had kicked him in the chest.

This woman. She was smart and well-dressed for any occasion. She carried herself with confidence and composure. She was past her first blush of innocence, that was clear by her complete lack of shyness or guile. She was a woman who knew her mind and would speak it as the occasion called for. She was fully formed, so secure in herself, so *complete*.

He'd never known a woman to possess such ease, such surety. Certainly not his wife. Anne-Marie had never seemed fully present, her mind always elsewhere, her heart driven by longings he couldn't fulfill, restless fears he could never assuage for her.

Leda Wroth looked fear in the eye and stared it down.

He watched them approach, enjoying the sight of Muriel holding Leda's hand, which she had not yet let go of. Leda paused and plucked a yellow flower, waving it beneath Muriel's chin.

"Do you like butter? The buttercup can tell us."

Muriel giggled. *Giggled.* Jack drank in the sound.

"That's cowslip," Muriel said.

Leda gazed at the bloom in mock despair. "Well, now what shall I do with it? Wait a moment." She tucked the stem into the new ribbon tied to Muriel's hat. "There, all smart and proper. What does your father think?"

"I've never seen anything more lovely." Jack spoke the honest truth, betrayed by the hitch in his voice.

As if she'd just spotted him, Muriel stiffened. She pulled her hand from Leda's and turned away. "I'll wait here."

"Don't you wish to see what your father is about?"

Muriel muttered something Jack couldn't hear. Leda's lips tightened, but she did not chasten the girl as Muriel moved toward a path of wildflowers. She only called, "Watch for stinging nettle."

"That's dead nettle." Jack forced out the words. "It oughtn't sting."

Muriel moved along the ridge, her small frame nearly swallowed by the waving meadow grasses, red curls a banner down her back. The sun retreated behind the clouds again.

Jack looked to Leda. "She laughed with you." Something had shifted between them; something had lightened Muriel's gloom and drawn her to Leda, if only for a moment. But she wasn't about to yield the same softening toward her father.

"A first." Leda moved closer to him. He smelled blossom, then her beneath, the almond scent of her skin. "I doubt she'll allow it to happen again."

Jack turned and walked back to his frames and pots. "She laughed all the time as a baby. Constantly. Everything I did made her giggle."

"Losing her mother would hurt. Would still hurt."

"It was well before that when she stopped. She learned young to tiptoe around Anne-Marie. To take on her sadness. We all did."

Leda waited a moment. He appreciated that. She didn't press him. She didn't utter platitudes. She didn't try to chivvy him out his grief or momentary despair. She simply let the confession float between them, let him understand for the first time how much of his own happiness he had held in reserve, tamped down, put aside, because Anne-Marie was always so distant and sad.

She touched his arm, and her steady warmth flushed

through him as if he were a sponge drawing water. "Show me what you've done."

She took an interest in everything: in the kiln he had, after the pattern of the one at Heacham, cut into the side of the ridge, with a space alongside for the ovens that would heat the bricks. "I'll make these first bricks extra hard as they'll provide the walls and insulation. I've spoken to a man in Snettisham about getting a cast iron door for the furnace. For the time being I'll cover the roof with wooden planks, as that gives me options for ventilation. Later I might build a brick roof, like the lime kiln at Thornham. The gravel in the barrow there is for lining the floor."

"And you simply put the bricks in here to bake them? How long does it take?"

"A day at least to get the kiln hot enough, sometimes two. A day or two of keeping things hot. You arrange the bricks in columns to create chimneys that will move the air and distribute the heat. Then another day or so to cool, and your bricks should be ready."

"And then what?"

"I sell them," Jack said. "And feed my household on the income until this agricultural depression is over, if it ever is."

She peered into the square hole in the ground, where the boys he'd hired to help him were gleefully hardening the dirt floor of his kiln by tramping about, cuffing each other or mock wrestling as they passed.

"How will you fire the bricks to line your kiln? I imagine they need to be especially hard."

He grinned, something joyous loosening and rolling in his chest. She was interested. In him. In his plans, his creation. "I'll fire those bricks in Heacham, or see if the old kiln by Thornham is still working. But I want my own kiln so I can experiment."

"Experiment how?"

He led her to his workstation, where he had labored all

morning. Muriel dallied along the ridge, glancing now and again at the men building the shed, seasoned laborers with their jackets shed and sleeves rolled up as they hammered and sawed. They'd softened their language when Leda arrived, but hadn't moved to dress, and Jack wasn't going to demand it. Leda nodded pleasantly at the men and didn't seem anywhere near fainting at the sight of male forearms bared to the air.

She hadn't fainted when Jack kissed her, pressing her body against the door of the dining parlor in Swindon. She'd pressed back, fitting her hips to his, melting that delectable bosom against him, drowning him with her delicious mouth. A tight heat shot to his groin, pure want, as she bent to peer at the piles he'd made. The breeze molded her skirt to her legs and a sweet rump he wanted to curve his palm around.

Time to get a rein on his animal instincts. His daughter was present, for God's sake.

"What's all this?"

"I need to find the right mixture for my bricks. I'm testing whether this is brick earth."

She leaned over and sniffed the mass of reddish earth. He loved her curiosity. He wanted to pull her into his arms and wrap his body around hers. Absorb her into him and hold her there. Keep her always.

"You'd think there would be experts about who would want to share their knowledge, but they've been hard to come by. The only one I've found who will talk to me is the bricklayer who helped Rolfe rebuild Heacham Hall a few years ago, but he can only advise me on technique, not the recipe. The masons here are more interested in cutting and using the local carrstone than in making bricks of their own. I've been in touch with some from my old apprenticeship program in Norwich, though, and they've helped somewhat."

Leda put her hands on her hips, like a housekeeper surveying the items she would assemble into a feast.

"That's brick earth?"

"I hope." He scooped a handful of the clay soil. "Brick earth needs no mixing, can simply be tipped into molds and fired. I've heard they have it around here, but so far, all the areas I've tested have yielded what you saw the day we arrived. Failed experiments."

He rolled the earth around in his hands, learning the texture. "You start with clay of the right consistency. Soft enough to be molded. A bit of give when you poke and prod it. You can feel when it's right."

Without hesitation Leda stripped off her leather gloves and sank her clean, dainty fingers into the red earth. "Indeed you can," she murmured.

Jack swallowed. "The right mixture will have a trace of sand in it to give the right shape and texture. There needs to be a bit of lime as well to help the sand melt and fuse when fired. The earth around here is mostly clay, you can see, but with the chalk layer, it often contains its own lime and silica. I may need do nothing more than fill my molds and have all the bricks I could want." As if anything in his life turned out as he wished.

Leda's eyes gleamed, the color capturing the endless blue gray of the sky and reflecting it back as violet. "I want to make a brick."

"You'll get soil on your hands."

"I want to *make* something." She unfastened the button that wrapped one end of her spencer over her bodice. The cherry red brocade with its fur trim fell away. "I want to shape something with my own hands that will be useful. I want to build something that *lasts*."

Again he took that sharp blow to his chest. "That is exactly what I want."

She pushed back the ruffles at the edge of her short sleeves. "Show me."

"It sticks enough that you can simply make a ball with your hands." He shaped and pulled a large handful of clay from his pile, about knee height.

"Not that pile," he called as she went to a far mound. "That has to be sifted yet to shake out the pebbles."

She bent and took from his pile, inhaling the scent of rich earth. "I love this smell."

He loved that she was doing this, diving without a qualm into his world, his interests. He moved to the table he'd built of a few planks. "Then you press the earth into molds."

He showed her, tamping the reddish clay into the wooden frame. He'd built these, too.

"It's like bread dough," she said, her voice lilting with delight. "You want it to have enough pull that you can coax and stretch it. If it's stiff, you've teased it too much."

He grinned at her, catching her enthusiasm, alight with it. This woman fired him like nothing else. "I suppose the same is true here. Too much lime, and the brick melts in the kiln. If the lime is not powdered enough, it will swell when moist and break the brick apart. It's the rich red color that tells you the mix is right. Too much iron, and the bricks will be black or dark blue. They turn up yellowish, and you know they will shatter at the first blow."

He showed her how to tamp the earth into the corners of the mold, then scrape the top flat. "If there is anything alkaline in your soil, like soda or potash, the bricks will twist and warp when you bake them. Any vegetation that works its way in will catch fire in the kiln. Pebbles will make your brick weak and porous. It will soak up moisture and crumble, or swell and break after the first frost."

"There's so much to account for." Leda followed his

example and scraped extra clay from her brick, leaving the top smooth and flat. "How does one ever find the right recipe?"

"Trial and error," Jack said. "A great deal of it. Do you wish a pattern in your brick?"

She raised her eyebrows. "Might I?"

"There are many ways to dress a brick. You've seen them in town. Most of the time the mason breaks bricks in half to make that smooth facing. When the bricks alternate color, as you'll see on some of the grander houses, that's Flemish bond. You can carve lines into the facing side, or create all sorts of wonderful designs. The chimneys at Hampton Court Palace are an example. Once the substance of your brick is right."

"I've never seen Hampton Court Palace," Leda said. "I want a plain red brick. Simple and serviceable."

He smiled, glancing at her from the corner of his eye. Nothing about Leda Wroth was simple or serviceable. She watched as he tapped the red clay out of the molds onto a plank that topped a wheeled hand cart parked alongside his table. Perfectly symmetrical they were, side by side. Evenly matched.

"I'll fill this plank with bricks, then wheel them into the drying shed, which the men are building." He nodded in their direction. "In some climes they let their bricks dry in the open air, but I wouldn't dare that here. When the clay dries, we'll stack them in the kiln."

"And have sound, strong bricks for building," she murmured.

"God willing."

He handed her a rag, and she wiped her hands clean, digging under the nails to remove clay.

"You adore this," she observed. "This is a passion for you."

He opened his mouth to object—the word *passion* didn't fit him. He was not, never had been, passionate about anything.

He closed his lips on the denial, considering. He needed

this to work, and he was more desperate than he allowed her to see. Masonry was his one skill, the trade he'd trained for. A tether to the life he'd had, and the future he'd been building before the black-edged letter reached his mother and a title he'd never thought of came along with it.

There was a world a baron was supposed to dwell in, he knew, a gentleman's world of horses and hunts and card parties and debates in the House of Lords. But Jack only wanted this: the Norfolk countryside, a task that occupied his mind, something he could build with his bare hands. A safe home for his daughter, food on his table, an estate that yielded enough to keep everyone upon it alive.

A woman like this beside him, working with him. Standing here so lovely with the breeze blowing her gown against her curves, teasing dark locks from beneath her hat, her hand to her brow as she watched Muriel. She didn't shiver in the cold or shrink from the sun. She played in the dirt with him, then rebuttoned her spencer, inspected her fingernails, and pulled on her gloves, reassembling her ladylike attire as if she'd never shed it. Not a veneer at all, but a sign of the grace that ran deep within her, and the easy way she adapted to any place, any circumstances.

"Will you clean yourself up, then?" she teased. "We oughtn't show up filthy if we're to call upon the Stylemans. They are quite the family in this area, I understand."

Jack wiped his fingers and cleaned his nails while Leda went to the cart and pulled out several packets wrapped in oiled paper.

"Mrs. Leech packed lunch for your crew. Pickled pig parts, eggs and asparagus, oysters with vinegar, and bread with preserves. She packed a Norfolk cheese in yours, and shortcake in everyone else's."

"Why did I not merit a shortcake?"

She passed him a packet. "Muriel wanted yours as we drove over, so I gave it her."

"You're a motherly sort," Jack said, guessing that Leda had had a hand in the lunches. Mrs. Leech did not typically send Jack on his way with more than day old bread and perhaps a chutney.

She turned from him, and her entire demeanor changed, stiff bombazine where she'd been easy silk.

"I am not motherly in the least," she said shortly. "Only I am acquainted with a man's temper when he is hungry, and we can't meet the Stylemans like that. I am counting on Mrs. Styleman to have relations, or friends of friends, who will leap at a chance to be governess to a mild-mannered child in a great house with a cook like Mrs. Leech." She waved Muriel in, then laid the lunches in a neat row along the plank where they'd set their bricks to dry.

She'd make the brick, but would she stay to bake it? Turn it into something lasting that could shelter one against wind and water?

He held Pontus while she helped Muriel into the cart. Then she ascended to the seat, taking the driver's place.

"I would have shared my shortcake with you also," he said.

She took the ribbons and looped them around her hands, not looking at him. Pontus shifted his head and stomped one foot.

"I do like your Norfolk shortcake, with the currants added, but I like your vinegar cake better."

"I meant to say nurturing. You are the nurturing type." Jack swung up beside her and tackled his lunch. The cheese sank under his teeth, soft and sweet as the skin on Leda's neck and throat. "You'd make a grand governess."

"You are forgetting our bargain, Lord Brancaster."

That she would leave. That she would fix his problem, set

him on his path, as she had so many others, then depart, never to see the fruits of her labors.

Muriel perched in the belly of the cart, braiding a daisy chain for her doll.

"What will it take to keep you?" Jack asked bluntly.

Leda glanced over her shoulder at the girl, who was pretending not to listen to them.

"For me to have a different past," she said, and looked away.

CHAPTER FOURTEEN

"I should be a family of note in the area," Jack remarked as they neared Hunstanton Park, encased in its woodlands and centuries of acknowledged power. "The Burnhams, I mean. Styleman is a reverend and the son of a gentleman, and his mother was the daughter of a baronet, but we are barons, even if the title is young."

"Have they been in the area long?"

Leda steered Pontus through the line of stately oaks and beeches, the ground a purple-gold carpet of comfrey and celandine. She'd lost the easy companion who had shown her the ways of brick making and gave her a glimpse into his ambitions, his heart. Beside her sat the baron in truth, upright, polished, distant. Negotiating his place in the world, picking out who was above him, and who below.

"The first L'Estrange sailed over with William the Conqueror," Jack said. "The family gained lands here, and here they have been ever since. The sixth baronet left no issue, so the estate passed to his sister, who married a Styleman.

"But L'Estrange was an upstart to the Burnhams, established here in Saxon times," Jack added. "There's a tale that

L'Estrange claimed lands as far out into the Wash as a knight could ride at low tide, then shoot an arrow. One day a Burnham challenged that he could shoot an arrow further. He did, and won the land where Holme Hall now stands."

"The families have been friends?"

"My uncle kept few friends," Jack said, the words clipped with disapproval. "And his sisters even fewer."

"You have written to your Aunt Dinah? What does she think of my stay in your household?"

"She is happily lodged with a friend in Middlesex, and not inclined to think ill of your presence." He set his lips, that mouth that lent a hint of softness to his face, and which Leda spent too much time noticing. "In fact, in her last, she said she agreed with our Aunt Plume and I require a mother, not a nurse, for Muriel."

"I have a mother." The cry rose from behind them. "Had. I don't need nor wish another."

Leda took her eyes off the road long enough to assure herself that Muriel was in a fury. Jack turned to placate her. "Mere—"

"I won't." She curled her hands into fists. The bloom Leda had added to her hat shook with the force of rage. "I don't want it. Her or anyone. You can't just buy a new mum at market."

"Mere, I know. I never meant—"

"You did. You *did*. You wanted her gone from the start, because you didn't like her. And now you have things just the way you want them, don't you?"

"Muriel Marie. I never wished for you to be motherless."

She traded him a challenging glare. "And I didn't either. But here we are."

Leda swallowed a laugh that might very well become a sob. She herself said that all the time: "And here we are." Muriel was borrowing Leda's sayings without being conscious of it. Her heart pulled apart for Jack, for the look on his face as his daughter defied him. Muriel would not approve no matter what he chose.

But she also couldn't ignore the warning that the girl's words tapped into her shoulder blades. *You wanted her gone.*

"My word," Leda said, slicing through the tension, "what a great lot of bricks went into the building of this house. Only look at this gate and wall."

Jack turned and, with an effort, brought himself to the conversation. Ever the gentleman, even when he had a dagger in his heart. Leda wanted to place her hand on his cheek, rub those tired lines from his brow. But she hadn't the right, and Muriel was watching.

A wife would have the right, even if Muriel were watching.

She pushed the thought away and flicked Pontus through the archway. The pillars on either side followed an Italianate design at odds with the medieval symmetry of the great house and the crenellations marching along the roof. The tracery of the family coat of arms, with its swirls and vines, stood out as much for its delicacy as for its lighter color.

"Now that gatehouse looks like Bath stone to me," Leda said lightly, "while the walls are much older." A straight dirt lane arrowed through a lawn studded with ornamental trees, some in delirious blossom. A wall not much higher than a man filed around the garden, the crenellations mimicking those of the house. To the east stood the stable block, a long low wall of small square windows with a thatched roof.

"That archway is the work of Thomas Thorpe, master mason, in the style of Inigo Jones," Jack said. "The wall of the house is coursed carrstone, at least a century old. Pieces of the Hall, they say, date to the time of the third Edward."

"Late medieval, then," Leda guessed, trying to remember her history lessons and the reign of the English kings. Her mother had engaged a governess for the girls for precisely this reason: so they could engage in conversation with a man, and have a chance to enchant him.

Jack twisted on the seat, and his shoulder brushed hers. Leda did her best not to thrill to the contact, and most certainly not to let a blush show on her face, like some debutante riding out with a favored suitor.

"The middle portion of the hall, that's the gatehouse. At least three centuries old, judging from the style. Native carrstone, that's why it's red. The wings, Jacobean era. Built early in the last century, I'd say. That checkerboard pattern, gray and white, that comes from clunch, a kind of limestone, and knapped flint. Very common building materials around here."

Leda watched him grow animated, forgetting the checks and challenges of earlier. She wished she could cup her hands around his fire and shield him from the world while he burned. He cast such a light.

She let Pontus fall to a walk, giving Jack time to look around. Neighs and whickers came from the stable block, the estate horses sensing an intruder; human voices sounded in response. "You must have grand plans for Holme Hall, with all this building knowledge."

The light dimmed. "It would take money to enlarge. Hamon le Strange had enough to buy a baronetcy for himself and his sons. Cost around four hundred pounds, so they say."

"And how did the Burnhams achieve their elevation?"

He peered down a lane of trees, straight as a plane, to the blank wall beyond of undressed brick.

"By acquiring wealth through shipping interests in King's Lynn, first, then aspiring to the rank of gentleman upon it, and standing members of Parliament. Queen Anne made a favorite of Judith, my great-grandfather's wife, but only noblewomen could be attendants in the Queen's bedchamber. So she looked about for an available title and made Judith's husband Brancaster. My worthy progenitor hopped from the House of Commons to the House of Lords, the family set up a house in London, and the two women were thick as thieves until the Queen's death."

"Clever Judith," Leda murmured.

"If only her grandson had been so. The second Brancaster lived well on the favors his mother had earned the family, managed to prove he was not a Jacobite, and so kept his wealth and position. But my uncle, having been born to it, had no mathematical sense. He apparently believed that his income was an inexhaustible stream that would not cease no matter how much he drew from it. His sisters depended on his support, even after they married, and their families continue to assume that the income from my farms exists only to fund their pleasures and wants.

"For that I blame my grandmother, whose father had been a maltster, and whose first husband the vicar had been a Nonconformist, and whose chief accomplishment was adhering to the standards of beauty of her time. But to see her, you'd have thought she'd been born wrapped in purple, and the title invented solely so she could marry the man who held it."

"I venture to guess that your pleasures and wants go unregarded," Leda said.

He faced her, and the sun picked out silver highlights in his eyes. His neckcloth had become disarranged, and Leda kept a firm grip on the ribbons so her hand would not stray and be tempted to tidy him.

"Yes." A single word, but she heard so much behind it: dormant longings reawakened, dreams once extinguished stirring to life. Just like hers.

He had wants, and he could name them. She sensed, she *knew*, that some of those wants were attached to her. Just as the tendrils growing inside her reached for him.

"Look." Muriel pressed between them, an arm held out. "Swans. On the moat."

Two enormous white birds floated down the canal as if they were clouds come to life, their feathery hulks leaving barely a ripple in their wake. A mated pair.

"I intend to name my doll Judith," Muriel announced.

"No longer Nanette?"

At that name, both her companions stilled, as if they'd fallen under the gaze of a witch. Pontus clopped across the bridge spanning the moat, each step of his shoes a blow on the flint cobbles. A square shadow pulled over them, trailing cold over Leda's shoulders, as they went through the gatehouse. Then they were in the courtyard beyond, where a pale sun lifted above the rim of stone chimneys and trees, and a servant came forward to take the horse.

Jack swung Muriel out of the cart, and as soon as her feet hit the ground, the girl shied as if she could not stand his touch. Jack's face was like a whip had fallen across his skin, and Leda spoke before she could debate the wisdom of pushing in. She was a child, true, and a hurt child. But she could not go lashing about at the world and expect it to remain a safe place for her. She must learn that lesson swift and early.

"Miss Burham, we are here to discuss if Mrs. Styleman knows of any prospects for a governess for you, therefore I expect you shall be on your best behavior," Leda said in her crispest tone. "I expect civility in your answers when you are addressed. If you have a quarrel with your father, you will save it for discussion at home, in private. Here, you will be a good guest, and a good guest makes themselves pleasant and cordial to their hosts, on whose hospitality they are intruding."

Muriel's eyes widened, her surprise evident at being chastened. "But he—"

"Is your father, and deserves to be addressed respectfully.

As ladies, we must learn how to express our strong feelings in ways conducive to achieving our aims, while also showing consideration for those around us."

Muriel snapped her mouth shut and hugged her doll to her chest. Leda saw the girl's struggle, torn between mutiny, purely on principle, and awe at being handed a secret to the mystifying world of womanhood.

But she would not give Leda the pleasure of having the last world. Her little chin tightened in that manner so like her father's.

"He put you in her room," she said. "But he hasn't told you *anything*, has he?"

JACK *HADN'T* TOLD her much of anything, about himself, about his family, about his wife. The reminder stabbed at Leda's confidence as she settled in for a coze with her hostess.

"That little Muriel is a cunning baggage," Mrs. Styleman announced the moment that Jack, on the pretext of taking Muriel to see the swans, left them alone in the small parlor.

Hunstanton Hall, from what Leda had seen, was a great sweep of polished woodwork and painted plaster, built on medieval lines lacking the classical symmetry Leda was accustomed to seeing in Bath. Its mistress was just as imposing. She was a matron of at least five decades, wearing a heavily embroidered brocade open robe that was years out of fashion, and piles of scarves, shawls, and a lace cap to ward off the cold of the room, where there was no fire. The tea was fast cooling, the footman having trundled from the faraway kitchens to deliver it, and Leda drank from the remaining warmth.

"I believe Muriel to be no slyer than any other girl of nine," Leda said, remembering the small bits of cunning she herself had been capable of that age when it came to nicking Mrs.

Chubb's brandy snaps from the kitchen or inventing reasons she hadn't come in from out of doors when her mother called.

"Dear Brancaster. He doesn't know the first thing how to take her in hand, of course. And her mother! What could one expect of a child, with such an example before her?"

Despite herself, Leda sat forward. She was no stranger to gossip. People seemed inclined to confide in her; she was not sure why. Perhaps her sincere desire to help, to fix problems, provide clarity on vexing matters that entangled the heart and clouded the thinking.

But this interest was not motivated by a charitable instinct toward Jack. She wanted desperately to know what had drawn him to Anne-Marie. And what had ruined him completely when he lost her.

"But then, I oughtn't carry tales, ought I?" Mrs. Styleman raised her teacup to her lips. The Delft blue reflected on her chin, giving her a faintly wolfish look.

Leda sat back, trying not to let her vexation show.

Mary Styleman was the kind of woman Leda might herself have become if marriage had made her more solid, and not mad. Lacking children to amuse her, Mrs. Styleman had surrounded herself with fine things. The parlor was done up in floridly rococo design, heavy with cream and gold, vines and twirls and sunbursts filling every pane of the walls and ceiling, so that the eye had nowhere to rest. A pair of enormous urns reared from the mantelpiece. Above it reposed a dark oil painting of a man and woman standing in a park, he watching her with a satisfied expression, she, in a smart scarlet riding habit and jaunty hat, patting the neck of an expensive bay mare.

"Henry commissioned that for our marriage," Mary remarked, studying the painting as well. "A man can come across so *jaunty*, can he not? When he is young and fresh and strong of limb, and he sets asides portions from two of his favorite estates just for you, and looks at you as if you are the most clever, the most lovely thing in all the world."

Leda sipped her tea and found herself unable to swallow. Jack had regarded her with exactly that expression as they stood by the pits and his kiln and clay, and he showed her how to make bricks.

"I imagine that is how Lord Brancaster won Miss Waddelow," Leda said, setting all shame out the window.

"The stranger thing is that he chose her," said Mrs. Styleman, "given her past and all."

Leda swayed forward, unable to stop herself. She knew that to invite confidences, she must set down some crumbs of her own. "I met the most curious girl in Snettisham, living with the Waddelows in Hope House. Nora, I believe she is called."

"Ellinore." Her hostess nodded. "That'll be Anne-Marie's child, the one as she had with the gypsy."

Leda swallowed her tea, struggling valiantly not to choke on it. "Anne-Marie was married before Ja—before Brancaster?"

"Oh, there was no blessing upon that union, mind you me. Missus Waddelow, great as she'd wish to rise, put it about that they adopted an orphan, saved the mite from being sent to the house of industry over in Gressenhall. But we all know who comes along Peddars Way, don't we? And how many moons turn about between the getting of a babe and the birthing of it."

"But Ja—Brancaster did not take the girl into their home?"

Mrs. Styleman tilted her head, looking at Leda from beneath lowered brows. "What lord wants a canary in his nest? Especially if he's some rust to scrub off the family name, after the last one dragged it about. Everyone told him to pick a girl who was true, so he could be sure that his heir was a Burnham. But she had a pair of fine eyes, hadn't she, and that wisp-o'-the-will way about her. It was rather romantic, I suppose, like one of those tragedies in the books. He thought he could refine her with his love, and she..." She shrugged, creasing the expensive lace tucked about her bosom.

"Left him," Leda said, thinking it wise to remain delicate.

Mrs. Styleman lifted her brows. "Threw herself at every man within reach of Holme Hall, is what I heard. And then ended herself when no one else would carry her off, and she had to lie in the bed she'd made."

LEDA REMAINED quiet as Jack drove them home. He wondered what Mrs. Styleman had said to her. She watched, her lovely head tilted, as a harrier skimmed its way along the placid River Hun, which spouted deep in Hunstanton Park and meandered its way north to the town of Holme-next-the-Sea. She looked and nodded when he pointed out the old wooden lighthouse, cutting the air with unmistakable authority, a landmark for customs officials and smugglers alike.

"I spoke with the lodge keeper at Hunstanton Park," Jack said. "He's a heap of stone from the old deer keeper's house that he'll give me for my kiln. It'll save me a great deal of time, and I'll be able to fire my first set of bricks as soon as the mortar dries."

"How lovely," Leda said.

"Clever Judith," Muriel, in the back, crooned to her doll. "Sweet, clever Judith. I'll give you a swan to lead on a silver chain and more ribbons than you have hair."

Jack paused Pontus next to the ruined chapel that stood at the edge of the sea. The footprint of a nave and chancel stood outlined in stone among the green lawn, grazed short by sheep, his sheep. Sweet violet and chickweed bloomed along a section of a brick wall that erupted proud and alone from the ground, a cluster of clunch and white chalk, its bricks undressed flint and carrstone and whatever the medieval builders had turned up on the beach. An arched doorway led to nothing but empty air, as if the world beyond lay hidden to human eyes.

Leda roused as he held up his arms to help her down. Her weight in his hands was so solid, so real, the firm plump of her hips, the nip of her waist, her ribs a smooth line within her stays. His head swirled as she gained her feet, and he had to flex his fingers to loosen her, let her go. Her eyes were on the ruin, not him.

"That's a witch's doorway," she said. "A fairy portal. You'll step through that and disappear."

"This is ground consecrated to Edmund the Martyr," Jack said, a touch indignant. He turned to Muriel, noodling her doll along the stepstone of rocks left exposed in the ancient wall. "He landed here to be crowned King of East Anglia in 855, a proper Anglo-Saxon king, was Edmund. Fought with King Alfred of Wessex against the great heathen armies of the Norsemen. Of course, they captured and executed him when he wouldn't renounce his faith. His remains are in Bury St. Edmunds, both his body and the head the infidels parted from him, which his followers found through the help of a talking wolf."

Muriel looked up. "A talking wolf?"

Jack nodded. "Fluent in Latin, no less, who called *hic, hic* when Edmund's subjects came looking for him, if the life of St. Dunstan is to be believed."

"Wolves in Norfolk." Muriel appeared skeptical. "With the hiccups."

"*Hic* means this, or here," Leda said absently. "As in *hic jacet*, here lies. *Hic jacet rosa mundi,* the rose of the world. *Hic jacet Arturus, rex quondamn, rexque futurus,* Arthur, king once and king to be. *Hic jacet* so-and-so, beloved of someone else."

"*Hic jacet* my mother, beloved of me," Muriel said.

Jack flailed. He wanted to ask Leda how she knew Latin, or

at least bits of it. He wanted to know everything. He wanted those violet eyes turned toward him again, with that look of delight she'd worn when she worked beside him shaping clay into his brick molds, sharing his work, his life. That look of admiration that made him feel ten feet tall and strong as a bear.

"Of course you know the tale of Arthur, but Norfolk too has a sleeping king who will rise again," Jack said. "King Gurgunt, son of Belinus, who ruled Britain long before the Romans came. Gurgunt founded Norwich and built the castle to keep an eye on the pesky Danes, whom he invaded and subdued after they refused to render him tribute. Geoffrey of Monmouth said he was buried in Caerleon, because Geoffrey of Monmouth knew nothing of the world outside Wales. But Gurgunt came here and took his seat in his robes and crown on his great throne in a mound beneath Norwich Castle. He fell asleep there surrounded by his jewels and gold and all his treasure, and he will wake again when Britain has need of him and come to her defense."

Muriel regarded him with great calculation. "And how do you know this?"

"I grew up in Norwich, pet. Do you want to hear of the Wild Boy of Bridewell Alley?"

"No, I don't wish to hear of boys, wild or otherwise." Muriel shook her head.

Leda stood as still as the lighthouse, face turned toward the west, where a frill of green shrubbery edged the blue sky, a faint darker blue line the only sign of the heaving, restless sea. The breeze threaded her dark curls. A redshank shot past her, flashing its white rump and bright legs, trailing a high, flute-like call as it dove over the edge and disappeared.

"It's as if the earth simply falls away," Leda said.

"These are the cliffs where my mother fell," said Muriel.

There was little to say after that, and they drove in silence the short way to the hall, Pontus picking his way through the sheep lanes lined with comfrey and cow parsley. The sky darkened, as if someone had let down a shade. Mrs. Styleman was responsible, of course. She would have filled Leda's head with all the tales, of how he was the mad baron, how he was cruel to Anne-Marie.

And Leda, sensible as she was, wouldn't know what to believe, for what did she know of Jack, really? What had he allowed her to see, other than a man who had failed as a husband and father, as a landowner and a mason, failed in every part of being a gentleman or a lord of the realm?

He was nothing but a man who had woken to the needs of his body, to longings that he dared not name or frame a thought around, to the feverish wish to press his lips against hers and wrap her softness around him and lose himself in her body, sinking into her as if he could be carried away by the sea, enveloped, transformed, made new by her touch.

Holme Hall stood with its mouth tight shut and its eyes lidded, the windows a dull silver against the clouding afternoon, safe behind its curtain walls. Jack wondered if the brick and stone of his home would stand as long as had that one piece of wall from St. Edmund's Chapel, five centuries old. How odd that the doorway had proved the strongest part, the curved passage through which worshippers came to draw strength from the saint before returning to their worlds without.

A woman stood at the cliff's edge, in a posture just as Leda had assumed. Black tresses seethed between her straw hat, and the wind sucked her skirts against her legs, slender and strong. Behind him, Muriel hissed in her breath and lurched forward.

"Mother!" she screamed. Before Jack could stop her, or pause to make her hear reason, Muriel had cast herself from the cart like a leaping deer and was running toward the still figure. *"Mama!"*

Jack rubbed his eyes. The woman turned. For a moment the face was Anne-Marie's, the same pale, dark-lashed eyes, the same restless twitch of her hands. Then the face changed.

"That is Nora, the girl from the market," Leda said. "She lives in Snettisham, with the Waddelows."

"Yes," Jack said.

Leda turned to him, finally, and it was as if her face were overlaid on the face of another woman who had so often turned to him with questions, with unspoken longings, with a need in her gaze that he couldn't identify and could never fulfill.

"And you knew that she is Anne-Marie's daughter, her first daughter?"

Jack watched another form moving up the beach, several feet below. A metallic gleam winked from the pack on his back, from the threads of gray in his ink-black hair.

"I always wondered," he said.

CHAPTER FIFTEEN

"It is good of you to take her in."

Jack stood when Leda entered the dining parlor. The sight of her hit him with a physical impact, as if his vital organs were organizing around a new center.

She glided toward him.

"We could do no less. The peddler walked with her from Snettisham, which is quite a ways, and everything she owns in the world is in that box she brought. I will send word to the Waddelows that she is here, and that we have asked her to stay with us."

With us, she said. As if they were a unit. An *us*.

He gripped the back of her chair to keep from reaching for her as she neared. She had long ago eschewed sitting at the far end of the table for their dinners and instead sat to his right, like an honored guest. She took her seat, and he smelled violets. A small knot of the flowers peeked from a glossy coil of hair and from the neckline of her dress, a simple round gown of innocent white but with a long tunic draped over her shoulders, trimmed with green vines and subtle flowers.

She had dressed for him, for their simple dinner together,

and dabbed toilet water behind her ears. He saw directly down her bosom—the reason the custom had been invented, no doubt, for a gentleman to hand a lady into her chair. His groin tightened.

She was learning his secrets, all of them. Peeling away and exposing to air the truths he had tried for years not to look at.

"The peddler said her father is dead, poor soul." Leda fidgeted with a fork beside her plate, edging it into alignment. "He knew him and his people. They camp over by Bircham for part of the year."

Jack stared at the cloth covering the table, pressed white and crisp with the industry of Mrs. Leech. Nora's red-rimmed eyes stared back at him, her cheeks two stabs of bright color in her pale, anguished face. How had she been standing right at the spot where they had discovered Anne-Marie's body? How had she *known*?

"Nora had been living with the Waddelows all this time hoping he would eventually come to claim her. But now, with no hope...she came to you."

"She came to you." Jack's voice grated his throat. "She trusts *you*."

Nora had not, in all this time, come to Jack, though she knew the truth and he had pretended not to. What was it about Leda Wroth that drew bruised, seeking souls like iron shavings to a lodestone?

"What will you do?" she asked.

"Keep her here, of course. And find a governess for thr—two girls."

He would not make Anne-Marie's daughter a housemaid, not as the Waddelows had. For certain, natural children were not always accepted, but they need not be hidden away. Edmund Rolfe, rolling round and well-fed among the brand-new bricks of Heacham Hall, had got a son on a Swiss girl he met during his Grand Tour and brought the boy to England to marry a gentleman's daughter. The bastard was a lieutenant-general in the Army, last Jack heard, and had two children himself, and when Rolfe died the world would say he had left his estate to a fond acquaintance when really it passed to his grandson, because a family that had begun as tradesmen in King's Lynn did not put an entail on their properties as if name were to be prized above the cunning to take an opportunity that presented itself.

Ellinore would be Jack's ward. He should have insisted on it in the first place, rather than letting Anne-Marie keep her veil of secrets. He had seen Nora's chapped hands, her forearms beneath the short sleeves of her gown little more than tendons and skin. That harm lay at his door, another sin piled atop the others.

He should tell Leda the truth, in its entirety, now. The words poised on his tongue. But he did not like what the truth said of him, and once it emerged, he would not see that look of warmth and admiration from her again. He would like her to adore him a little while longer. One more night.

Leda canted her head, studying him. "It will make the task of finding a governess harder, with a cuckoo in the nest."

Even peers needed to pretend to a certain respectability, though the world watched closely enough to see their dirty laundry as it came out the back door into the yard for airing.

"No one would say a word if you married me," Jack remarked. "That would be the greater wonder. A fine, clever woman with the world at her feet, choosing to marry a mad widower baron who lives with his bricks at the edge of the world."

Her eyes glimmered round and sad. "Jack." She said his name; it dropped like a ripe plum from her lips. "I've said I won't marry again. You or anyone. I—cannot."

"Yes." The bitterness spilled from him. "So you've said."

"Doesn't it help, knowing it's not you?"

"It would be better if it *were* me. Then I would have a reason."

Henry entered the parlor wearing the livery in which he had served the previous baron, antique breeches and a tailed coat. It had never occurred to Jack to tell Henry he might put the suit aside if he wished, for who would see him here? Jack never entertained—Anne-Marie had disliked crowds of people—and he would not have Leda for his helpmeet, a beautiful, clever wife who shone in company, who drew people to her like moths to flame.

She smiled at May, the housemaid, as she trundled in after Henry with the tureen of soup, placing it as carefully on the table as if she were serving the queen.

"Is it a great fuss for you downstairs, May, if we take in Miss Nora?"

May's eyes widened. "Thas alright, tha is. Her's a right mite, so thin and tiny, but she's useter work, so she won't get primmicky, and she'll fit in the upstairs with Miss Muriel for now." She shook head. "Hant a scrap with her but her bag. It went sadly with her in the town, I shink."

Jack winced, feeling this report on Ellinore's state a further accusation of his neglect. He'd assumed the child was better off with her grandparents, even if they didn't acknowledge her outright. Anne-Marie hadn't really cared for the company of children; she liked to sew and do fine work, take long walks in her own company, and she could seclude herself in her dressing room for hours, trying on different adornments.

Anne-Marie, come to think, had possessed that same self-containment he saw in Leda, but where Anne-Marie had been cool and remote, Leda was warm and approachable. It was like her to notice that taking in an orphan would create more work for the servants, and like her to broach the subject directly.

Anne-Marie, like most of her class, had assumed servants existed to do the job for which they had been hired, seeing to her comfort. Leda saw the human creature within. Jack hadn't missed how his aunt's butler in Bath had chivvied his ladyship's companion, and that the man would dare showed he considered himself one of the household, not a stick of furniture that moved about.

Nevertheless, as soon as the dishes had been laid, Jack sent the servants away. Leda stirred her soup; Jack regarded his wine.

"I knew Anne-Marie had a past when I courted her."

Her eyes were a deep gray in the candlelight, like a tidal pool at dusk. "And you approached her despite that?"

"Because of it, I think. I knew I must have a wife, and I was attached to no one. I didn't see a risk that I would become attached to anyone. I was ridiculed when I arrived. A baron's coronet on the head of a shoemaker's son? The very foundations of the earth should tremble and fall."

Leda applied herself to her soup, sipping delicately as she listened. The woman didn't hide her appetite. Jack wondered if meals at the asylum had been inadequate, and that was why Leda openly savored her food.

"You didn't think you would find love?" she asked softly.

He met her gaze. "Did you ever imagine you would?"

She took up her fork and pried at the shell of a lobster. "We are discussing your courtship. I've been told she was very lovely."

"She was. Many had tried for her hand. I was told to harbor no hope. But I had that coronet, you see. The best on offer around here are baronets and vicars."

She lifted her brows. "That swayed her?"

"It swayed her parents, certainly."

"Ah."

The flame of the candle in its stick before him flickered as Leda passed him a dish of buttered asparagus. "But were you happy?"

"Not in the least. Nothing I did could please her. I was as kind to her as I knew how to be." He caught the flicker of Leda's eyelids, the narrowing of suspicion, there and gone. "But I, even with the title, was not enough. She was rarely content. I thought a child might cheer her, but when Muriel was born…"

"A difficult birth? I saw one with Ives, remember. You will not turn me off my food."

He smiled with one half of his mouth. No, indeed, from the way she tackled the dish of cauliflower, she was not squeamish about talk of childbirth.

"It was the melancholy that gripped her." Jack drew in a deep breath. Even now, these shadows held teeth and claws when they sprang out again at him. "It was dark. Deep. I knew no way to draw her out of it. She had no interest in the babe, she would not nurse—she could scarcely leave her bed. I feared she would starve to death under my roof."

Leda chewed, then chased her bite with a swallow of wine. "I have heard it goes ill for some women. Motherhood is not every woman's sole mission in life. And not always the rarefied joy that the church fathers would have us believe."

"She did not wish me to touch her thereafter." Jack swallowed hard. Shame tasted tart, like the horseradish Mrs. Leech had used to flavor the leg of mutton with oysters. "And I respected her wishes. I feared what another childbirth would drive her to. But then, of course…"

His lips closed over the words. This shame, he could not share. Despair choked him, the oyster turning cold and gummy in his throat.

"So it is good that you decline to marry me," he said, his voice hoarse with the burn of the sauce. "I made my wife's life a misery. I should no doubt do the same for you, and make you loathe my touch."

"Jack Burnham. My lord Brancaster." Leda set down her fork, tapping it against her porcelain plate, and the clatter rang like a shot through the quiet room. "I do not loathe your touch. I crave it."

He raised his goblet, saw his hand shaking, set it upon the table again. "I see no evidence of that. You hide it well."

She watched him, a level look, that calm consideration he had seen in her as she watched the ball in the Upper Assembly rooms when he had first come upon her. A woman of remarkable poise and elegance, who looked upon the field before her as if she were assessing each of the actors. Deliberating where the danger to herself might arise, and how to defend herself if it did.

She glanced toward the door, which stood open to admit the servants. She rose and walked across the room with the deliberation she always showed, the edges of her long tunic fluttering against her gown like wings she kept tucked to her sides. She shut the wooden portal, and he saw that her hand trembled slightly, as his had done.

Then she returned, circling the table, rounding her chair to his. He half rose, finally conscious that a lady was standing. His heartbeat rang in his ears. She drew a deep breath and held his eyes, as if she were asking something. Whatever she wanted, his answer was *yes*.

She pushed him into his chair and settled her beautiful rump into his lap, and Jack's vision blanked for a stunned moment. She slid her fingers through the curls clinging to the nape of his neck, and his mind started to gallop—he would have to ask Mrs. Leech for a trim. The contact unleashed something feral in him, a fierce, hot rush of triumph, of possession, of need.

She whispered the words against the side of his mouth. "Touch me, Jack."

Her mouth was warm and sweet from the lobster sauce, her tongue as silky soft as the violets in her hair. He fell upon her like a man arriving at a pool of cool, fresh water after months, after years of drought. He stroked her jaw to tilt her chin so he might plunge his tongue into her mouth, and she shivered. She met his invasion with a soft probe of her tongue, tasting him, and he was lost, drowning. She smelled of almonds and her hair was spun silk and her body was as soft and firm as a ripe summer plum. He wanted to take every part of her into his mouth and consume her. Possess her utterly.

He splayed a hand across her collarbone, exposed by the gown. A pulse drummed at the base of her neck, that smooth, proud column. She didn't flinch as he trailed his roughened fingertips over the damask of her skin.

"I can touch you here."

"Yes." She breathed hard, kissing him back, kissing him with a hunger that matched his. *She wanted him.*

He slid his hand to her bosom and cupped one breast, feeling where her softness met the firm slope of her stays. He traced the skin along the edge. "I can touch you here."

"Yes." She shifted position, throwing one leg over his to straddle him, turning her body toward him, pushing her breast into his hand. She *wanted* him. "Oh, yes."

He dove into her softness, putting his mouth everywhere he could reach. She shuddered when he kissed along her jawline, nipped the shell of her ear. The soft hollow below, that was where she dabbed the almonds. He nuzzled his face into her neck. Her short, fast breaths pushed her breast against his hand and he cupped it mate with his other, glorying in her surrender. He found a tiny mole on the side of her neck, as if the artist had marked his glorious canvas. She gasped as he kissed along the ridge of her collarbones, moved lower.

"I can kiss you here."

She tipped her chin back. A coil of hair fell from its pin, brushing his shoulder, the back of his hand at her breast. "Please do."

"I can kiss you here?" He brushed his mouth over the tops of her breasts, swells of softness. She had dabbed almond water here, too, and the scent nearly drove him to frenzy.

Her eyes flew open. "There?"

Had no man ever kissed her properly? Had her husband had this splendid body before him, all these luscious curves, and never feasted, as was his right? Jack growled at the waste.

"These are *made* to be kissed." He kneaded his fingers, and her shoulders melted, pushing her breasts toward him. He swallowed another growl of satisfaction.

"If you don't like it, tell me, and I'll stop." He would stop, though it would kill him if he failed her. Right now she was completely with him, soft clay in his hands, yielding to his touch. She looked dazed and heated, tossed on the same wave devouring him, and he wanted to push her further, to the brink of passion.

The drawstring neckline untied easily, and he simply shoved down her stays. Two beautiful breasts spilled forth, her beige skin slightly marked by the stays, her nipples like the brown pebbles he found on the beach. He wrapped one arm around her back to lift her and gorged on the banquet before him.

"*Jack.*" She tossed her head, another lock of hair sliding free, as he curled his tongue around a nipple and pulled it into his mouth. Her pulse raced like a deer over a field. "Oh."

"You don't want me to stop," he growled, the words muffled by his tongue against her skin.

"Oh, *please* don't."

She was so responsive. Her short catches of breath, her fingers digging into his shoulders, the way she arched her back over his arm as he licked and nipped. He caught her wildness, fed on it. She thrashed in his arms as he shaped a soft breast and sucked, hard. She whimpered and bucked against his leg, her thighs clenching. His groin hardened, the ache its own pleasure, spurred by his awareness of her desire.

"Will you come for me, Leda?" he murmured, pursing his lips around a nipple, wine-sweet. "Will you give me that?"

She tossed her head to the side, clinging to his shoulders as he moved to the other breast, the nipple taut and begging. She whimpered as he suckled. "I don't—I can't—"

"You like this." His growl was guttural. He felt like a wolf homing in on its prey. Here, *here*, this woman in his arms, she was all that mattered in the world.

"I do," she mewled. "I *do*."

He lifted his thigh, pressing against her. "Then ride me. Take your pleasure. Use me, beautiful Leda."

"But I don't—we're—"

"*Take it.*" Take *me*, he wanted to beg. If he could bring her to peak, make her climax, if she could have pleasure because of him, it would mean everything. He tossed aside her muslin skirts and gripped her knee, covered in a silk stocking. "I'm going to touch you here."

"Oh," she gasped, nudging her hips toward him as he swirled his tongue around her nipple.

"And here." He slid his hand up her thigh, past the edge of her stocking, over her garter, to the sweet, firm flesh, hot and smooth as cream. He stroked his way to her inner thigh, pressing against the smooth fabric of his pantaloons, so thin a barrier between them.

Her entire body shuddered. "*Oh.*"

He paused and caught her eyes, pools of violet shadow, hazy with desire. For him. "Shall I stop?"

"No," she whispered.

"I want to make you come," he rasped. "Just like this."

She closed her eyes as he bent again to her breasts. She shivered as he traced a path over the damp flesh, pinkened from his mouth. He'd found now what she liked and pulled her into his mouth, sucking and licking. She squirmed, allowing his hand to move up her thigh. Her skin was so warm and in a moment he found the soft curls, damp with need. His cock swelled in his pantaloons, reaching for her, for this heaven.

He didn't know a woman's body. She would perceive that and pull away. But as he slid his fingers over the unfamiliar flesh, moist and slick and hot, she inched her hips until she settled a tight bud of heat against his finger. The catch of breath in her throat, her moan almost near despair, told him he had found the key.

"Take what you want. Use me, Leda. Find your pleasure." *With me. Because of me. In my arms, and no one else's.*

She bit her lips and dug her fingers into the muscle of his shoulder. Then she began to rock against his hand.

Her ecstasy was beautiful to behold. She shivered as she strove, bucking against him, writhing her back and rolling her hips. Moisture pearled on his finger. His groin throbbed with an ache of pain and he wondered if he would come too, just from the feel of her, the taste of her flesh, his hand buried at the core of her, the scent of her arousal, rich and sweet, and her wild, keening moans. He rubbed his finger against her secret pearl and she dug in her nails.

"Like that," she whispered. "Just that."

He wanted to watch her forever, relish her wild seeking, but all of a sudden she went stiff, head thrown back, her entire body quivering, and he felt it in his hand, the tremor of her release.

She gave a soft, quiet moan and he watched her face as the sweetness of her climax suffused her. His body throbbed in tune with hers, his breath harsh and rasping to match her soft pants. She dropped her chin to press her forehead to his as she calmed, and he simply held her, clamping down on his own need, enjoying the wonder, the primal triumph he felt.

"What," she whispered, her breath on his cheek, "*happened* to me?"

He grinned. He wanted to shake his fists and roar, but that would mean letting go of her, his soft, beautiful, pleasured woman. "You never came with your husband?"

"Not even close."

"But you can bring yourself—surely?" She'd known how to fit herself against him. She'd known the rhythm she liked.

"Not like that," she said, the words barely a whisper, but they raised a shiver on his skin. "That was—*you*."

He wasn't less than a man, then. He could please a woman. Even if he had offered nothing more than his body to use, she was *with* him. He felt the tendrils sinking into him like weights on a fisherman's net clawing into the sand. She belonged to him now.

A hesitant, ponderous knock sounded at the door, Henry's knock, then May's anxious voice behind it. "Milord, are you badly? We've the fricassee of chickens here, and the trifle coming directly."

Leda uttered a curse and slid off his lap, skirts trailing. He missed her heat at once. With swift hands she yanked up her stays and the bodice of her gown as she slid into her seat. With two vicious yanks she stabbed her loose locks of hair back into their pins.

"You may enter," Jack called when she had hid the evidence of their tryst, all but the radiant flush of her skin. "We needed a moment. Mrs. Wroth had a—confidence to share."

The door opened and the servants came in, glancing between the two of them, and Jack knew his grin surely told them more than they needed to know. Leda began a conversation, sharing a whimsical tale Mrs. Styleman had told her about the rug in the parlor of Hunstanton Hall and her mother-in-law's attachment to it. Jack listened and made the appropriate remarks, aware of the throb in his body, the flush of her skin, the memory of her trembling beneath his mouth and hands. He wanted to be alone with her again, as soon as possible.

All at once it didn't matter that he had another mouth to feed in his household, when he so desperately needed to repair his income. It didn't matter that all Norfolk and his fellows in the House of Lords thought of him as the Mad Baron. It didn't matter, right now, if whispers still ran that he'd pushed his wife off the cliff. Leda Wroth had found pleasure with him, and all that mattered now was that she not leave him.

She couldn't abandon him. Not now, not after he'd tasted her. He'd never be able to let her go.

CHAPTER SIXTEEN

Leda paused outside the half-open door of the nursery, hearing the murmur of girlish voices within. Part of her hesitated to intrude on the happy circle, not certain she'd be welcomed. She'd come to ensure that Ellinore felt at home, that she'd been seen to and put at her ease. She also wanted to show Muriel that she cared about the girl for own sake, and not because Leda was desperately fascinated with her father.

Yet she hardly felt she should be among innocent children after what she had just done downstairs with Jack. The indecency of her actions might be writ on her face, and they would perceive the signs her lust and not be innocent any longer.

Lust. Pleasure. Ecstasy, really. She felt flushed with it, her body languid and humming. She'd been a complete wanton, pushing herself at him, but she'd been seized with the powerful wish to erase, if she could, the self-loathing on his face. She couldn't bear that he was not supremely confident in knowing, down to his fingertips, how wonderful he was, how fine his character, how noble his heart, how sound his intellect, how splendid—so very splendid—his body.

A kiss had seemed a logical way to show him all this. One

kiss of reassurance. And instead, she had been transformed with a new knowledge of her body's desires. He'd unleashed a side of her she'd never acknowledged, primal, full of passion.

And, heaven help her, now that she knew what pleasure was with him, she wanted it again. And again. And again.

"—doesn't know?" Ellinore's voice, hushed and curious. "Hant no one told her?"

"She'd leave my father flat." This from Muriel. "She wouldn't want him anymore. It's why no one here does."

Another noise followed, a creak as the wooden rocker shifted, then a sound between a sniffle and a hiss.

"Thought that's what you wanted," Ellinore said. "For her to be on her way."

Silence stretched out, and then another voice, one she didn't recognize. Not Grace. Not May. A low, guttural utterance, more like a moan.

"I do *not* like her," Muriel flared. "I said I want her gone, and I do."

"But she bought ribbons for Nanette, dint she?" Ellinore said. "Here, chick, come about and I'll fix tha proper."

Leda told herself to leave, go to her room, as she'd told Jack she was doing when she left him in the small parlor downstairs after dinner. No good would come of eavesdropping as the girls discussed her. They had a right to their own opinion of her, whether they knew of her shamelessness with their father or not.

She'd paused in her step, dallying in the hall outside the nursery, because the exchange of confidences between sisters made her nostalgic for a tender time in her own life when she and her sister had stayed up nights whispering to one another about anything and everything, while the moon floated past their window like a double Gloucestershire cheese that monthly was eaten and then filled up again.

She'd been so pleased, absurdly so, when it had seemed Muriel wanted to name her little corn dolly Judith, after Leda had remarked on the woman's cleverness. She ought to have known better.

Muriel made an outraged huff. Through the slit in the door Leda saw her dart forward, lift her hand, jab at something. She came back holding a ribbon. "That one's for Judith," Muriel cried. "You can't have them all, you little greedy guts."

She busied herself tying the ribbon about the little doll. "Clever Judith," she crooned. "Pretty Judith."

"Whiff, now you've made her mad," Nora said. "Is the little cat going to bite us?"

Muriel tossed her head. "Dint you see all the marks I have from her? You'll have your share soon enough, I shink."

Who was with them at this hour? Leda wondered. Grace and May, after work from dawn to dusk, ought to be well in their beds. She'd sent the tea things back with May an hour ago for precisely that reason, so someone wasn't waiting up for her while she sat in the parlor, spinning out all the time she could with Jack.

"Whiff, don't let that Grace hear you speak Norfolk." Ellinore moved behind Muriel, both girls visible now through the slit of light falling through the door. Leda was ashamed to realize she'd inched closer. "Though how we're to understand a word in her Wiltshire dialect, I'm bound I don't know. Worse than Nanny."

A response to this came from deeper within the room, a point which had fixed both girls' attention. It was a low drone of a voice, but Leda couldn't make out the words. Whatever their content, they made Muriel laugh. Ellinore shook her head with a rueful smile.

"But your da hant said a thing neither? I don't see how the all of you—"

The door creaked beneath Leda's hand. She only wanted a peek. The girls were looking at someone—who was with them?

The girls whirled toward the door, Ellinore's face surprised and wary, Muriel's full of horror. A muffled sound came within, much like the mewl of a kitten, then a thump. Leda pushed the door further.

"Is ought amiss?"

Muriel's mouth worked but produced no speech.

"You've just caught us heading to bed, missus," Ellinore said. "That's what we're about, innit, Muriel?"

Muriel rolled her eyes about the room like a frightened rabbit. Leda followed her gaze. The door to the inner room, the bedroom, stood open and dark. Leda had never been inside there but saw the outline of a cot placed near the wall, no doubt an addition for Ellinore. They would have to see about getting her a proper room; she was old enough for it. The wardrobe in the nursery was shut up, the bookshelves all orderly. Three plates and cups sat on at the little table, their tea things not yet put away.

Leda walked across the room, spotting a splash of color. The wooden floor creaked as she bent and lifted a length of ribbon.

"The mate to the one you're holding, I believe?" She turned to Muriel. "For your doll, Nanette?"

"Her name is Judith." Muriel took the ribbon with great caution, as if Leda might nip off her arm if she drew close.

Leda flushed. She would never do right, not where Muriel was concerned, and she detected Ellinore's look of gentle pity. Waves crashed on the beach outside, the tide embracing the rocky shingle. A sliver of chill wind crept around the window panes.

"Oh," Leda said. "I thought I heard you refer to a Nanette."

Muriel's mouth dropped open and her eyes flared wide, but again, words failed her.

"Oi, you know how tha do, tha wee ones," Ellinore said. She moved a finger at her temple, as if drawing an invisible string. "With the friends you don't see."

"Made-up friends." Leda nodded. "I had many when I was Muriel's age. I also tried to make a pet of a cow, a hedgehog, our local badger, and a hare that lived beneath my mother's dog rose."

Muriel wrinkled her nose. "A badger? They bite."

"And thus I do not recommend attempting to befriend them. I am sure you wouldn't be so unwise."

Her skin prickled with the oddest sense that she was being watched, but the door to the hall stood empty. Jack had not yet come to bed. She wondered if he sat in the parlor still, brooding before a dying fire. He'd spoken so sanely to her, of Norwich and the neighborhood and Lady Plume and bricks, as if at dinner his hand had not delved into her private place, and if he had not devoured her breasts like sweet cakes. Her body still savored the ease following her release, yet her chest flushed with heat, with new longing.

The girls said nothing to encourage further conversation. They simply watched, waiting for her to leave. She wasn't wanted here.

Cold slipped around the panes in her own room, carrying the nip of the sea. Moonlight floated on the waters. A small head broke the surface, a small pointed face. Another joined it. The mermaids at their play.

They belonged here, in the cold sea, with the sea thrift blooming above the cliffs and the great broad vault of the sky. Leda didn't belong here, though. She wondered if she belonged anywhere.

MURIEL DIDN'T WANT HER, but Norfolk embraced Leda.

Mrs. Leech consulted Leda to plan menus, showing great satisfaction at Leda's acknowledgment of the cook's undisputedly superior knowledge of local cuisine, especially the seafoods. Leda nodded along to every proposal, made an occasional suggestion so Mrs. Leech would know Leda was making an effort, and was rewarded with delicious, warm meals, beautifully presented, and Mrs. Leech's confidences whenever the housemaids needed guidance or correction, stores were low, or she thought Henry had been too long at his task of checking over the late baron's supply in the wine cellar.

Leda sensed that Mrs. Leech pitied her about something—or sympathized? The staff often watched her as if they were waiting for something, the proverbial other shoe. Did they expect her to learn something about Jack, or the family, and run screaming from the hall?

Did they know her history, and were waiting for *her* to run mad? But their manner was all respectful warmth, and an unexpected deference, as if she were the lady of the house already in their eyes.

Jack said he had never eaten so well and confirmed that the staff were turning themselves out to impress Leda. Even the boy in the stables made an extra effort to brush out the old draught horse's mane when Leda was taking the cart.

"I can't think why any of them should regard me with favor," she told Jack one night over a dish of Stewkey blues, a special cockle fished only from the dunes near Stiffkey, and acquired by Mrs. Leech on a special trip to the town of Burnham Market. They had a unique blue cast to the shell and, dressed with vinegar and a dash of lemon, Leda found them delicious.

Jack pried open a shell with his fork. "You don't see it? You make me respectable. It's clear you're a sensible, steady sort of woman who isn't prone to fancies or freaks of the imagination.

Everyone hopes you will marry me and reform me, chasing my madness away. Or, if reform fails, live with me as I am, turning the mad baron only slightly eccentric."

She suffered freaks of imagination in spades, Leda wanted to reply. And she was the last person on earth to offer a cure for madness. She was more likely to infect him with hers, did the demon inside her awake.

She distracted herself with the stack of invitations that had been pouring in, which she had brought into dinner to discuss with him.

"You do seem to be invited everywhere lately, when I thought you were the pariah of the neighborhood. I suppose everyone wants to take my measure."

"How many of them have warned you off me?" Jack asked, squeezing lemon onto his next shell. "And how many have recommended you marry me at once?"

"I hear all of that advice, from nearly everyone," Leda reflected. "The ladies warn me about you, then point out all your marriageable qualities. It significantly hinders my quest to locate a governess, you know, when the conversation turns always to our wedding."

"Perhaps you should take that their counsel and accept my suit." Jack speared a round of pale flesh and popped it into his mouth.

She felt the blush, the heat of it, climbing her collarbones and neck. Jack wanted her, too, and the elegant panels of the parlor, painted in a deep blue gray that matched the cockle shells, bore witness. He showed his care in the way he sought her out when he returned home from his bricks, washing off the dust and clay. He showed her affection in the clasp of his hand on her arm or waist when he helped her in and out of the market cart as they made calls. In the looks of admiration he cast her over the dinner table, over the tops of the wavering candles, and in the pleasant conversations they had in the parlor in the evenings, often with the girls keeping company.

Ellinore was improving her reading, and Muriel her sewing, and their quiet chatter was the dearest thing Leda ever heard. She often thought Ellinore might wish to linger with the adults, learning their ways, but she went up to the nursery when Muriel wished it, leaving them alone, when Jack inevitably stole a kiss or two. Each kiss turned her to pudding in his arms. He made her lose her senses entirely.

Leda sensed that, if she showed the slightest invitation, he would gather her close and pleasure her again as he had in the dining parlor that night, or more, whisk her off to bed. He wanted only a sign from her.

She sensed also that, did she but demand, he would, without hesitation, throw himself at her feet and offer her everything he had, all of him.

How did he dare, knowing what she was?

"We've seen all the great families hereabout, I think," Leda said. "Mrs. Styleman's sisters are all married well and provided for. Mrs. George Hogg of Thornham Hall would never leave a female relation of hers to earn her own keep." She made a face at this; Mrs. Hogg had learned, through the gossip mill that fed neighborhoods like theirs, that Leda worked as a companion for Jack's great-aunt, and made her disapproval clear.

"Mrs. Catherine Daly of Ingoldsthorpe Hall said she would inquire after anyone suitable, but she was more interested in instructing me how I might win over Muriel as a mother. Mr. Rolfe of Heacham Hall only wanted to tell me you will make no headway as a brick maker and might as well give it up before they laugh you out of Smithdon Hundred. And Caley Hall, which I thought held by a family, is now housing for customs officers who are chasing the smugglers along the coast."

She moved on to a dish of buttered samphire, her cockles

depleted. "There are more families I could try, the Henleys of Sandringham, or the Fosters of Old Hall. I thought Mr. Nicholas Styleman of Snettisham Hall would be more useful, as the Stylemans seem to be a large and well-connected family. But they merely asked me about the ghost."

She had thought Jack would laugh at this. Instead he went pale as chalk and dropped his fork. "Ghost?"

Unseen fingers walked across her shoulders. She ought to have brought her shawl with her; this house could be drafty, sitting on its hill with its face to the wind.

"Because they suppose you murdered Lady Brancaster, and so her ghost must walk the halls. Their descriptions are much like what I've heard about Queen Isabelle, whom I've heard haunts Castle Rising. A woman in a white dress wisping through rooms, echoes of maniacal laughter, that sort of thing. I daresay they didn't put much imagination into the conjecture."

Jack's color changed to something slightly green. If she didn't know him better, she would say he looked guilty about something.

"I did not kill my wife."

Leda picked apart her roast partridge. "So you assured me, and so I did not abandon you in Swindon. But it is odd." She put down her knife. "I do hear voices abovestairs. And sometimes footsteps, when I would swear the maids and children were downstairs."

Jack reached for his glass of wine and took a long swallow. Red stained his lips.

"There is something I did not tell you about Anne-Marie."

Leda curled her hands into her lap. He did not push his wife off the cliff. He did not drive her to madness. He had not been cruel. She was certain of these things, she told herself. Certain.

He pushed his plate away, crumpling the linen cloth

covering the table. "I have told you, after Muriel was born, she would not let me touch her."

Leda nodded. She herself, after she had conceived her plan to pass off Betsey's child as her own, had insisted Bertram not touch her. She'd welcomed the reprieve from the pawing and prodding that left her sore and raw the day after, and sometimes bleeding.

She'd never known those parts of her were capable of the pleasure she'd found with Jack. It explained a great deal about human behavior she had observed over the years.

She forced herself to sit quietly as he straightened his shoulders and drew a breath.

"She did, however, let other men touch her."

A gasp escaped Leda against her will. "She was unfaithful?" The woman must truly have taken leave of her senses, to prefer any other man to Jack.

He jerked his head. "I didn't know who. I suspected everyone. Hogg. Rolfe. Styleman, for all he's a reverend."

"Ellinore's father?" Leda guessed.

This had clearly never entered his mind. Jack stared at her. Shadows danced along the ribs of the plaster ceiling that curved overhead, rippling down the corners of the room like a whisper.

"The gypsy? He left her. Pregnant and alone. Why would she go back to him?"

Leda shivered at the anguish in his voice. "If she loved him," she tried, but she didn't understand. What woman, given Jack Burnham in her home, in her bed, would want anything, anyone else? Leda would sell her soul to belong here with him. To have him like this for dinners and evenings, for travels whenever the whim called. For the right to lie in his arms at night, wrapped in the embrace of husband and wife.

She put her hands over her face. She *was* going mad, to want such things, when she knew she could not have—did not *deserve* them. Not after what she had done. Not knowing what she was capable of.

"I am hearing voices, Jack," she whispered.

He jerked again, as if taking an invisible blow. "Ellinore will be finding her feet. And that girl, that maid we brought from Wiltshire."

He didn't understand. He couldn't. He was as sane as a brick, as steady as Pontus the work horse. However Anne-Marie had hurt him, she'd scarred his heart, but not his mind. He'd not suffered what Leda had suffered.

He wasn't a murderer.

But Leda was.

THE HOUSE WAS DARK, but far away, she heard the high, shrill cry of a babe. A cold rug pressed against her feet. Cold swirled around her bare legs beneath her shift.

"You're a sight to frighten the devil."

Toplady stood at the end of a long, narrow hallway, a hulking outline in the dark. Not Bertram, her husband. Bertram lay stabbed on the floor of his library, his eyes dull and open with shock. Eustace stood in the hall, his dark hair greasy with sweat, his teeth a gleam in the shadows.

She was dreaming. A nightmare. She must wake.

She looked down at herself and saw what she knew she would see. The ones fading to rust were from the maid, where they had cut her to free the babe struggling to emerge. The midwife knew what to do, but yet, so much blood.

There were fresher ones, though, bright red, sticking to her bodice. Her hands were sticky, too. She examined them, the red smudges on the blade and handle of the knife. Why was the *carving* knife in her hand?

Wake up, Leda!

"I didn't kill him." She stood as she was before the magistrate's table, bloody shift, bare feet, the knife. The room crowded with spectators gawking, whispering her guilt.

"Not in her right mind." The judge was so large, so fierce as he glared at her. Troublesome woman. "Lock her in the asylum and see if they might cure her madness."

Eustace at her side as she was loaded, hands in manacles, into the prisoner's cart, the way revolutionaries had been carried to the guillotine in France. Such a good nephew. Such a caring man, placing her valise with her one gown and shoes and hairbrush and the Bible that had belonged to her grandmother. Who had packed the bag? Betsey was gone. Mrs. Blake was gone.

The babe was gone.

"Where is it?" Eustace leaned close, hissing in her ear like the geese in the yard. "The child."

She'd killed it. They told her so. They couldn't find the body, but they said she had borne her babe and slain it, and then she had killed her husband, before or after. Childbed madness. It happened to some women, pitiable creatures. She couldn't be let around good people, of course. Not sane, godfearing folk.

"The babe is dead." She was lying. *Wake up*, she urged herself as Eustace leaned in, his onion breath stirring her hair, lank and unwashed down her back.

"It had better be," he said. "And when I am ready, I will come for you. I will take you for my own and redeem you, you miserable creature. Once they've broken some of that pride." He grinned again, showing the rot in his teeth, the plump satisfaction of a man who lived only for the surfeit of his bodily desires. "And then you will have a *real* master."

He rubbed the bulge in his breeches, his black eyes sharp and satisfied as they gazed on her. There was the knife again in her chained hands. She raised it, pointed it toward his throat. She struck.

Someone screamed, and wept. *Wake up*!

It was the mermaids calling. Their sharp, weeping cries drew her to the rim of sleep, surfacing.

She lay in the mistress's suite in Holme Hall, looking out at the Wash. There were no chains, no blood, no knife. No Eustace. She wanted to cry with relief.

Moonlight outlined the waves, gently heaving. A sharp edge dug into her side, and Leda shifted on the mattress, then sat up. The mermaids had murdered her sleep, like Macbeth. Sleep, the balm of hurt minds. Or the source of nightmares. Leda rose, reaching for her dressing robe and slippers. Her cap had fallen off her head, as usual, and she let it lie on the pillow, like a weary thought.

Anne-Marie had slept in this room, tossed on this bed, kicked these covers with her restless longings. She had perhaps paced these floors and looked out on other moonlit nights, thinking of her lover.

Perhaps Jack had come to her in this bed, seeking her warmth. And his wife had turned him away.

How could she have left her children? Leda wished she could understand the woman's mind. She must have been truly desperate.

The memory clawed its way out, a monster from the dark, and Leda wasn't seeing the scene out her window, the sandy beach studded with worn, smooth stones and seaweed. Her fingers froze around the hilt of a kitchen knife, the great blade used for carving joints, for rending bone and sinew from flesh. Her bare feet pressed the cold floor of the house, Toplady's house, which had never felt like hers, not even the rooms allotted to her. Her hands were damp and crusted. And her heart beat so quickly, quivering in her chest, as if she'd drunk poison. Far away, in a distant part of the house, a baby shrieked, jolted into cold air from the womb that had safely held him all this time.

No. *No.* She would not go back to that nightmare. She would not let that woman into this house, Jack's house. Not with the girls here. Leda blinked, trying to clear her thoughts.

Her arm ached. She must have stabbed him. She must have stabbed him many times, from the gashes in his waistcoat, from the blood splashed on the carpet around him, part of a table, the cushion of an overturned chair. How easily the great knife must have sunk through the fabric to the soft, pale flesh beneath. How cool his skin had always felt, even when he shuddered above her in her bed. Cold sweat fell from his brow as he worked her, striving to sow his seed. She had always washed herself after, and no matter how cold the water in her basin, it had felt warmer on her skin than her husband's flesh. He was a creature entirely lacking in human warmth.

But that didn't mean she should have killed him. She was mad, as they said. So mad she could not submit to her imprisonment, which she deserved, but had spilled herself out of the window like Rapunzel following her hair, had fled like a wraith across the fields and meadows to the ship that could carry her away.

To here. To a place surrounded, embraced by the sea, knit up with legends, laden with ghosts.

A song came from afar, a singing, but not the mermaids. The blurred, wordless moaning she'd heard from the girls' room when she watched them, and swore she had heard since. It was tuneless, haunting.

There was no light beneath Jack's door, but farther down, at the end of the hall, silver light spilled from the nursery door, partly open. The singing came from there. A shadow moved across the slit of light, a weaving pattern. As she neared Leda heard the creak of the floor, the quiet pad of feet. She pushed the door open as silently as she could.

The ghost was dancing. She whirled and twirled a ribbon over her head like a maid at the May fair. She leapt from side to side, a clumsy hop. Dark waves of hair spilled down her back, and her tiny feet were bare.

Not a woman, nor the ghost of a woman. The ghost of a girl. A tiny girl, bone thin, with eyes that captured the darkness. She turned and saw Leda and froze mid-step, a silent pillar, moonlight from the window falling about her, shining through her white gown. The ribbon fluttered to rest, dangling from her small fingers, which looked translucent.

It had happened, just as Leda feared: her mind had truly cracked. She had gone mad again, this time seeing apparitions. At least she didn't have a knife in her hand.

Leda backed away, shaking, her entire body cold with shock. She couldn't stay here with Jack, not now that what she feared had come to pass. She had to run again. She didn't know where. She had nowhere to go that was safe. Nowhere that would take her.

Jack. Leaving him would be agony.

She stumbled to another door, but not her door. It opened.

His room, too, lay silvered with strange light, as if the furniture, the hearth, the rug before it all lay on the border between this world and another. A door to his dressing room on one side; the door to her powder room on the other. The great bed loomed like a ship at anchor, curtains fluttering in a breeze from the window, which stood open a slit. Cold crept around it, clenched her body. So cold. She needed warmth, and safety, and someone to hold her even if she were mad. She needed Jack.

"Leda?" His sleepy voice slid from the silvery dark as the mattress dipped beneath her weight. Soft, like feathers. His mattress had been turned and plumped, not like that in the mistress's room, flat and hard and empty for years.

"I'm dreaming. Hallucinating. I saw a ghost." Her ghosts *and* his. There were too many ghosts to account for. The shadows inside the bed curtains were warm and quiet and smelled faintly of a rich spice. Of him. She moved closer.

"You're real." He touched her arm, slid his hand from elbow to wrist, then back up to her shoulder, ruffling the sleeve of her dressing gown and the bedgown beneath.

"There's something in the nursery."

"Shh. You're safe. Everyone here is safe." He kissed her, and she sank into his bed, into his body. He was so warm. He threw heat, like the stove in his kiln, searing her skin.

"The girls," she tried again when he moved to kiss her neck, her collarbones.

"Are safe. I promise. It's all right."

She shivered at the delicious slide of his mouth, more heat. It seeped into her, erasing the chill. There were no ghosts here. There was only Jack, solid, firm, *safe*.

Kissing her. She squirmed as he pressed her onto her back, tugged the fabric away, and kissed her breasts. Her nipples hardened, reveling in his mouth, better than memory. Heat reached into her core, curled tight, longing. He slid a hand down her ribs, down her belly, between her legs, cupping her there, where the heat coiled and seethed, as if he knew.

She clamped her thighs together, remembering the pleasure. She was not sure she could bear it again. She wanted it more than anything.

"Tell me you'll stay with me. That you want this, too. *Faire l'amour.*"

To make love. She whimpered as he sucked on her breasts, tugging a nipple between his teeth. That place where his hand was ached for him. Without meaning to she rubbed against him.

"Let me please you, Leda." He took her mouth again, his tongue plunging inside, and she melted, thought receding like an outgoing tide. He muttered the plea against the crook of her neck and shoulder. "Let me see what it can be like."

He wanted her. This beautiful, darling man craved *her,* with her madness, with her spotted past, with all her ghosts. He desired her, and in his arms she felt beautiful, and powerful as the moon with its pull on the water.

"Show me," she whispered, and parted her legs.

He didn't dive straight in, as she expected, as she thought men did. Instead he kept kissing her. He kissed all over her breasts and below, pushing fabric out of the way. Then he pushed the fabric of her skirts up, baring her legs, and she squirmed.

"What are you doing?"

He kissed down one thigh, down her knee, and she trembled. That wantonness was washing over her again, its own madness. She felt damp between her legs at the very thought that he might fill her.

"I want to try something. I read about it. They say—it is very pleasing for a woman." He pushed at her hips, and she jumped at his hands on her flesh, warm, his fingers slightly callused. "Scoot up on the bed."

"I don't—what are you—"

"Ssh. It's just a kiss. And if you don't like it, tell me to stop."

"But how can you kiss when you are down—there...*oh.*"

He pushed her thighs apart, gently, and now she knew what he meant. Leda covered her eyes with her hands as he probed with his lips and tongue the parts of her he had discovered with his fingers. She moaned at the indecency.

"Stop?"

She kept her eyes firmly covered. "You—may proceed."

If he wanted this, she would try it, for his sake, but she felt so exposed, so naked. So *seen*.

He proceeded. She quivered, and he raised his head. "How does that feel?"

She had no words. "It is...pleasant." There was discomfort, but a welcome discomfort, if there were such a thing. A restless wanting. She squirmed again, her hands squeezing the bedclothes as she sought something, she didn't know what. He licked inside her secret place with his tongue and it became *quite* pleasant, and she lay still, thrilled at the new sensations. After a while it became necessary, urgently so, that he not stop, that he keep doing *that,* right *there,* and he obliged, reading her soft moans, the lift and seek of her hips. Then all at once her thighs tensed and the soft bud exploded beneath his tongue, and the shock of it rippled outward all through her body, like a star exploding in the sky.

"So it *is* pleasing."

Leda opened her eyes, gasping, and saw his smug grin, his eyes alight with silver, as if he'd caught the moonlight.

"Yes," she whispered.

"Good."

She tugged on his arm. "I want to please you. Do you want... more *l'amour*?" She didn't know another word for it beside the delicate French. Making *love*.

"Beautiful Leda. I want all of you. Every part." He kissed her neck again, and the scrape of stubble on her tender skin delighted her. "But—if there could be a child?"

"There won't." She stared at the canopy of the bed, a scarlet shadow. She'd been married for two years, and her husband had tried regularly to breed her, with no success. She was one of those women with a barren womb, and she accepted it. She would never go through what Betsey had.

As if he sensed her brief withdrawal, he stroked a hand

along her sides, her belly. "Are you certain you're ready? I don't want to hurt you."

"Jack, you are the one person—the *only* person in my life—who has never hurt me." There was no fear she would be like Anne-Marie, going mad from children she did not want to keep. There was no fear Jack would hurt her. He was *Jack*. She tugged him toward her.

He reared over her again and slid a pillow beneath her head, beneath her bottom, and she had a moment to wonder if she would regret this, if he would hurt as Bertram had. She wanted to give this to him, to please him, and a restless ache grew, even on the heels of the starry shower that still pulsed through her body. There was something *more*, and she wanted it with him. When he probed her entrance with his manhood, she took a breath and slipped her arms around him.

"You want this?" he whispered.

She squeezed her eyes shut and nodded. "I want *you*."

He pushed gently, then slipped inside in one long, slow glide, like rolling an evening glove up her arm, the delicious slide of silk, and a warm fullness that reached to her core. Her eyes popped open.

"*Leda*." His groan of pleasure thrilled her.

This was so different from anything she'd known. He found his rhythm and she surged in his arms, the pleasure deeper, keener, more urgent than she could bear. He thrust and she bucked against him, biting his chin, frantic with the intensity. And then she burst again like a seed bud in summer, breaking into pieces, flying apart, soaring. He groaned her name as he arched his back and joined her at the summit, their bodies pulsing, melded so deeply together she could not tell where she ended and he began.

At long last, he rolled to his side and cradled her. Moonlight shone through the bed curtains as he drew the covers over them.

"That," he said with great satisfaction.

She nodded, feeling she could barely move. Her body was a cloud, airy, boneless.

"You found it with me," he said. "*La petite morte.*"

"Mmm." She wondered why the French had the words for this act and its parts, while English only offered the crudest euphemisms. Because the French understood it was an art, it was poetry, when it felt like this.

He lifted his head, searching her face. "I pleased you."

She trailed her fingertips along his jaw. How Anne-Marie had failed to find delight with him, when he was *this*, she would never understand.

Perhaps because he hadn't been meant for Anne-Marie. Perhaps he was meant for Leda.

She stilled the path of her fingers and stared into his eyes. "Everything about you delights me, Jack."

He grinned. "So. Not a useless nodcock after all."

He rolled onto his back, rubbing a hand over her shoulder, and she let him revel in his triumph while she discreetly dabbed between her legs with her shift. She would wash the stain out herself, later, so the maids didn't know what she'd done.

What had she done? Jack drew her into the crook of his arm, holding her there, and she understood he wanted her to stay with him as he drifted off to sleep. How strange, to share a bed with someone again. She hadn't been this close to another person since her sister left home to be married.

A bundle of feelings she couldn't name curled and tightened inside, like a wrack of seaweed tumbled up on shore. Jack breathed in peaceful slumber, and she breathed with him, battling the despair that crept around the edges of her bone-deep bliss, sending out shoots of doubt.

How could she leave him, after this?

Yet how could she stay, if she were destined to hurt him?

CHAPTER SEVENTEEN

Leda's boots sank into the soggy brown sand of the beach. Each step tugged at her sole, leaving the shape of her foot imprinted on the shore, dotted with small impressions from the hobnails. Jack's father had been a shoemaker; he could tell her if she were ruining her favorite boots—her only boots. But she couldn't decline a walk along the beach, especially since the girls had invited her.

They fanned out ahead of her, Ellinore bending to peer along the rocky shingle, Muriel following the waves as they sucked themselves back into the sea with the receding tide, leaving small streams and rivers among the humped rocks crowned with seaweed. To her left the cliffs reared far above her head, a layered caked with green at the rim, the rugged stripe of white chalk, the brick red carrstone buttressed below.

So high those cliffs. So far a tumble, especially for a small woman. Leda wondered that Muriel could come here. That she did not see her mother's ghost wandering the rocks crumbling the base of the cliffs, or sitting atop a shorn boulder, weeping.

"Have you seen the ghost in the nursery?" Leda asked this

in the most conversational tone she could affect as she neared Ellinore.

The girl straightened quickly, clenching her fist around what she'd found, and stabbed a look in Muriel's direction. Leda turned just in time to catch the frantic shake of Muriel's head.

Ellinore looked out to sea, the ribbon ends of her bonnet flapping beneath her chin. The air carried the morning chill, and the wind snuck around Leda's ankles beneath her petticoat, smacked her skirts against her knees.

"I donow what you mean, mum."

"You are the one who told me there are ghosts here."

The girl's neck went stiff, chin up, shoulders braced, and Leda remembered she was grieving. She'd lost her mother years ago when she left to marry—she'd known Anne-Marie was her mother, thanks to the way gossip worked in small towns, no matter what her grandparents had tried to keep from her.

And now she knew that her father was dead as well. There was no one to come for her. No parent waiting in the wings to reveal they were a king or lost princess, who would come to sweep Ellinore away from the drab of her life. She had this now: Jack, Holme Hall, Muriel for a companion, and a future she could not see on the horizon.

"I was only meaning to scare you, mum."

"I saw her. Last night. She was dancing," Leda said.

Ellinore turned, her back a sharp blade. "A girl, you say."

She hadn't said that. Leda turned to Muriel, struck by a new thought that hadn't made it through her nightmare of the previous evening, and the way Jack had completely claimed her attention after.

Grace had already been in the nursery when Leda woke in Jack's bed—she'd woken to the sound of the girls' voices—and the water in his wash basin, the fresh towel on the rack, said that May had been in the master's room, too. There was no way

Leda could hide what she had done. She could only sneak through the mistress's dressing room to her own chamber, where the bed had been neatly made and water waited in the basin, still holding a trace of warmth.

The servants knew, then. Did the girls?

"Have you seen a girl up there?" Leda asked Muriel. Perhaps she wasn't an apparition. Perhaps the girls had snuck someone up to the nursery the same way Leda had slunk into Jack's room. Who was she—a local girl? A servant's child? Did Jack know?

"Do you see apparitions often, Miss Leda?"

Muriel's insolent jab was deliberate, another post hole for the fence the girl would not let her cross.

"I do not fear ghosts, Miss Burnham. Only the living. Does your father know you've had someone up there?"

Muriel faced away from her, too. Everyone was turning away from her.

"He knows."

Twin fangs of anger and hurt sank into Leda. Perhaps jealousy, too. They were all conspiring to keep something from her —she, the woman who invited confidences, the woman others begged to solve their most delicate problems, the woman who had a reputation through Bath and beyond for fixing things. Not breaking things, as Jack had first accused her. Mending. Putting people on their proper path. She had always been the one people turned to, and now these girls were shutting her out.

The birds skittered before Leda as she walked, their feet small sticks in the sand. Others wheeled overhead, calling to their own, their wings dark lace against the gray sky. A golden gleam caught her eye and she bent to see what had bubbled up beside a small rock. A leather pocket, small enough to fit in her hands, with strings curling fancifully from its corners.

"A mermaid's purse!" Ellinore peered into her palm. "Oi,

that's a great find. Very lucky, mum, do the mermaid leave her magic in it."

Leda turned over the small packet with her finger. A slit showed the innards, empty.

"Alas, this one lacks magic, it would seem." She showed Muriel, who had come to hover, too. "Shall I throw it back?"

"My mother always kept them," Muriel said. "She put them on her dressing table. Said they were gifts from the sea, and one oughtn't take gifts lightly."

Leda couldn't toss the thing onto the ground after that remark, not even if she thought it a dark omen. A woman who would keep a piece of sea wrack but had spurned the gift of her husband, if she'd never reveled with him in the kind of pleasure Leda had known last night. Even now she felt pleasantly aware of the warm place between her legs, though she went about all the normal activities of her day. Ordinary life suddenly turned on its side to show a wondrous new realm available to her, underneath the rest.

"I've heard the mermaids singing," Leda said instead. "Saw one swimming last night, in fact."

Muriel met this confidence with narrowed eyes. Ellinore raised her brows. "Singing?"

"They've small round heads and pointed noses. Very long eyelashes. And they give that high, keening cry, almost like a gull, but sweeter."

Ellinore's eyes crinkled at the corners. "Thas the seals, mum."

"Seals!"

"There's a colony of them as lives here. The winter babies will be growing now. Grey seals," Muriel said with great scorn for Leda's ignorance. "Do you go around the point that way," and she pointed north, toward the sea, "there's a place where they come ashore. Scores at a time, some days."

Leda curled her hands around the mermaid purse and slipped it into her pocket. There was no enchantment here. No mermaids. Seals, a lovely creature, but flesh and bone and whiskery seal skin all the same.

And there was no ghost either, not of a girl. Only the ghost of Anne-Marie, still looming between her and Jack, to continue looming if Leda stayed. So would linger Muriel's contempt, and Ellinore's polite distance.

A figure down the beach caught her eye. A man, standing where the rocky cliffs slowly fell to their knees and sank into a sandy stretch of beach, a place where a tumble would not break a woman's neck. It was not Jack, nor anyone else she recognized. Yet she knew him.

Every muscle in Leda's body went rigid with fear. It was Toplady. A ghost in truth. The ghost of the man she'd murdered. He stood there without cuts in his coat, without blood staining his chest, but the arrogant set of that jaw, the smirk of contempt—that she knew, even from this distance.

She was going mad in truth, to see visions of him here.

Her boot kicked up a stone as she started forward—why she would run toward this apparition, she didn't know—but she looked down and froze, seeing another omen. A smooth gray stone, roughly oval in shape, with a hole straight through it the size of her finger. She plucked it from the sand, a cool weight in her palm, and stared.

"What is it?" Ellinore gaped, too.

"It's a hag stone." Muriel's cry was sharp as a seal's, fearful, she thought. Cold darted down Leda's spine. "And why should *you* find it? I've been looking for one all my life."

"What does it mean?" Leda asked.

"It can cure poison and keep away witches," Muriel said. "And if you look through it, you can see a witch, or a fairy."

Leda held up the stone and looked through the small window at Muriel. "You're not a fairy."

Muriel's knit brow eased, and her lips curled into a smile before she caught herself. "Boo."

"And you're not a witch." Leda swung toward Ellinore.

The girl stepped back, wide-eyed, shaking her head. "What d'you see, then?"

"Nothing. Sand."

On a mad impulse, Leda looked down the beach to where the ghost from her nightmare had appeared.

No man was there. A sea swallow darted above where he had stood, its cap a streak of black, its serrated wings cutting the sky.

No ghosts, and no magic. No world of enchantment lay through this lens. The wind swooped under her cap, stealing her breath.

Grace met them as they climbed to high land and circled back along the cliffs. "Did you know there are seals here?" Leda asked her.

"Aye, mum. I hear them singing at dusk. A sight we've never had in Wiltshire, I do say. Will the young ladies help me find raspberries?" She held out a pair of small baskets.

Muriel took hers cautiously, Ellinore with a cordial, "Of course." The three of them turned and walked along the sheltering wall of the back garden to the thicket of bushes near the orchard.

Leda wasn't included, though she loved raspberries. Perhaps Grace thought Leda would spend her afternoon out again, making calls, and that was why she was not invited.

Leda dallied back to the house, which stood hunched in its red stone against the cool spring air. Away on the fringe of the sky, to the east, was a lightening, but Holme Hall would lay a while longer under clouds. Jack was around here somewhere, digging in random places about his land, testing the earth, testing if his experimental bricks could hold against strain and weather.

How lovely it would be to walk the beach with him, her hand in his, his firm body her shield against the wind, his deep voice speaking to her of the thoughts in his mind and heart.

Somehow she had no interest in visiting today and asking the families about for likely governess candidates.

Her heart tugged in her chest, like a sheep caught on a bramble bush. She wanted to stay with Jack.

Her footsteps echoed on the wooden stairs as she climbed to the first floor. She must be sensible. She could not stay and be governess herself, not after she'd been in his arms. She'd never resist him, even if she took a salary from his hands, and she could not set that example for the girls, could not conduct herself in such a fashion beneath his roof. She could not stay and be his mistress.

She could set herself up nearby, find some way to support herself, and then she could be his mistress. She wouldn't care about talk. She would care only about being with him.

She would care, deeply, when the talk led to cuts for Ellinore and Muriel. When they were looked aslant in circles where they had the right, as the daughter and ward of a baron, to hold their heads high.

Leda set her cap on the dressing table, then the mermaid's purse, and sat on the side of the bed with a sigh.

There was nothing left of Anne-Marie in the dressing table or in the room, unless she had chosen the deep green brocade for the curtains and the patterned rug for the floor. The small Sheraton dressing table with its satinwood inlay was bare of the personal trinkets Muriel had said her mother kept. Jack, or the servants, had swept the room clean of memory.

There was no art that gave her insight into the woman,

either. No bridal portrait with a delicate glow, no wedding portrait of the couple, no lavish oil of a young mother doting on her infant. No samplers on the wall with trite marital verses or sentimental adages to bear her through the day. There was nothing of Anne-Marie here at all.

A hard edge dug into her hip and, with a huff of exasperation, Leda turned on it. The flaw in this mattress had chafed her on more than one night; she would have it out once and for all. She considered reaching for her sewing scissors to cut a slit in the fabric, but saw that a slit already existed. She thrust her hand inside, among the goose feathers, and jabbed her fingertip against a hard surface. A book, the wooden cover bound with leather.

She pulled it free. The front cover bore no words, only a floral design tooled into the brown calf. The flyleaf bore the declaration, in faded brown ink: *Anne-Marie Waddelow. Her diary.*

Astonished, Leda turned to the first page. It was dated the fourteenth of June, 1786.

Dear diary: Today my life begins. Today I met Bohamos.

Leda could not have stopped reading to save her life, even if she were intruding on the private thoughts of a dead woman. Anne-Marie was sixteen. She had never been more than a few miles outside Snettisham, save for the one time her father took her to Norwich to buy her fabric for her first evening gown. She knew of her parents' hopes for her, beautiful as she was, their only and cherished child. She was restless and unhappy in her tiny town, when such places as London existed in the world.

And then a caravan came through the Peddars Way, on their seasonal circuit. There was a man among them, a real man, over a score of years, nothing like the green boys who blushed and stammered when they tried to speak to her. He wore a red scarf at his throat and had a scar by his brow from tumbling against the edge of his family's caravan one day when he was a boy. He taught her how to fish in the River Ingol and how to catch plover with a weighted string. He taught her the names of the constellations as they lay on their backs in the meadows on a bed of saxifrage.

He kissed me. And more. And I became stardust.

Yes. Leda thought of Jack. *Yes, that is exactly how it feels.*

She would have read the whole way through, pulling on the strings of Anne-Marie's life for answers, but the singing came again from the nursery, low, mournful, lacking words.

He vows he loves me, and he knows I love him. But he is promised to a girl of his own kind. It will cost him his place in the family if he refuses. And he says I must marry my own kind also, a barbarian, an Englishman.

I never will. There will never be any man for me but Bohamos. Nothing about our love is wrong. And no child of our love can be wrong, either, no matter what the neighbors say. I will love him unto death.

A giggle broke the low hum of singing, and it broke Leda's spell. She set the book on the dressing table and followed the siren's call.

The girl sat on the window seat playing with Muriel's doll. She was no ghost. She wore a small tucker and apron and had pushed off her shoes. A smear of jam marked the crest of her sweetly curved cheek. She might have been four or five, tiny, her face and frame turning from baby to girl.

She swooped the corn dolly through the air, crooning to it. Her voice had a closed-off sound to it, coming from her nose and far back in her throat. It was a sound Leda had heard from others in the madhouse, those who had stopped speaking, or had never spoken real words.

"Nanette?"

The child didn't look at her, only continued her tuneless

hum. Leda walked across the floor, the heels of her boots drumming the planks. The girl's chin snapped up and her eyes flew wide.

This time, Leda wasn't imagining things. The girl was as real as day, as solid as the bench beneath the window.

Her eyes darted to the wardrobe, as if gauging how quickly she could reach it. Leda thought of the other times she had come by surprise into the nursery and saw that wardrobe buttoned shut. Certainly it was large enough to hold a child.

"They have been hiding you from me," Leda said softly. "Why?"

The girl's eyes were the light green of seablite, the same shade as Ellinore's, as Muriel's. Anne-Marie's eyes. She watched Leda's face, her mouth.

"Who are you?"

The girl wetted her lips and swallowed. She took care in pronouncing the word, pointing to herself for emphasis. "Nan."

"Hello, Nan." She wasn't certain what to say. "I am Mrs. Wroth."

The girl's gaze flitted from Leda's mouth to her eyes. "Raw."

A girl with Ellinore's eyes, Ellinore's dark hair. Muriel had Jack's auburn hair and his chin. This girl was Ellinore in miniature, minus a few years.

"Cor blarst me," came May's voice from the door. "You've gone and found the little 'un."

"Yes," Leda said softly. "What I don't understand is why I've not met her long before."

She turned to find May behind her, clutching a dinner tray. Boots clattered up the stairs, the girls surfacing first, Grace behind them. All three stopped in a troop behind May, facing Leda.

Muriel's face went completely white when she looked into the room.

"So," Leda said. "I've not been seeing ghosts, nor hearing them either, though you all let me believe it. I take it Nanette is not some local child come to play? She lives here?"

The dishes rattled on the tray as May placed it on the table. Four plates, for Grace would take her midday meal with the children. Three settings for the children's supper, when Grace would take her dinner downstairs with the other servants.

"Her has lived here since a babe, Mrs. Wroth," May said. "His lordship took her in as a mite, as she had no one else."

This wasn't the place to demand the girl's parentage. The clues lay spelled out before her, like letters in the sand. Leda shot a wounded look at Grace, the girl who had entered this house the same time she did. "You knew?"

Grace nodded warily. She moved a protective hand over her belly, an instinctive gesture. "Aye, mum."

"You've all been keeping this from me," Leda whispered. "Why?"

"That's as for his lordship to say, mum," May answered, as nervous as the others. "'Twas him axed us not to blar t'yew."

They all feared what Leda would do. Why? Did they know of her episode? Had Jack thought something about Nanette would overset Leda's delicate mind, send her spiraling again into madness and murder?

Her hands shook. She *felt* overset. She felt suffocated.

Jack had known there was a child in the house. He'd said nothing. He'd let Leda think she was seeing things, that her mind was rattling loose in this wild, remote place, that she was becoming unhinged from reality. He'd made love to her—*love*—but he hadn't trusted her enough to explain.

She had to run. She was trapped here, as she had been in Toplady's house with his cruelty and his lust, as she had been trapped in the madhouse by the accusations against her. She must escape.

She fled first to her room. Cap, gloves. She must not look like a madwoman, flinging her shoes out the window in a call for help. She would have Jack send her valise to Bath. He would do that much, be that decent. It was the least he owed her for his lies.

The book, Anne-Marie's diary, lay on the dressing table. With shaking hands, Leda placed the doll she had made for Muriel beside it. She would take only what was hers. Memories. Ash in her mouth.

Henry walked Pontus along the drive, the cart hitched and ready. "Mum. Arnt you ameant for to go with his lordship a'smornum?"

"Not today, Henry. Thank you." She hauled herself into the cart without assistance, kicking her heavy skirt from beneath her boot. A month ago she hadn't known which end was what on a horse harness, and now she was a dab hand at the ribbons. Norfolk had given her one thing.

It had given her Jack. And then it had taken him away. Her chest felt like she was strapped in an iron cage. Held to a bed by the leather bands they used at the madhouse for the fighters. Leda had suffered that once, and never again. She would not be at any man's mercy, not ever again.

"Mind how yew go, mum," Henry said, a furrow in his brow as he regarded her, as if he could sense her mood.

The dream-like state was descending again, that fog. It muffled sound and made her vision narrow, moving everything far away. She was Caledonia Hill again, her parents explaining to her that Bertram Toplady was a gentleman and a prime catch, the best a hopeless girl like herself could hope for, and the reward she owed her parents for their years of thankless care.

She was Caledonia Toplady beneath a thick veil at church, hiding her shame when she heard the whispers of what her husband had been up to in the neighborhood, felt the scorn drifting from the people who would otherwise have been her friends, her support.

She was Caledonia Toplady, maniac, *non compos mentis*, hearing the clang on the iron lock of the door to her chamber, seeing the iron rings in the floor where she would be chained if she screamed and thrashed against this handling.

No. She was Leda Wroth. She had walked away from that place shaking hay from her hair. She had changed her name and buried her history, buried Caledonia Toplady atop Caledonia Hill in a tomb with no markings. That starved girl, cut from her herd and forced to the chopping block, she no longer existed. Nor did the woman who had walked her own house in caution, fearing her husband's contemptuous wrath, plotting to thwart his viciousness and his greed.

Nor was she the woman watching thin plates of food shoved through a hinge in the door, shivering in her shift after the cold baths to clear her mind, stripped of her hairpins, jewelry, and garters so she could not cut or strangle herself. That woman had died.

She was Leda Wroth, and she was in full possession of her faculties.

She was a woman betrayed, but not by her own mind. By a man, which was far more mundane, one might even say inevitable.

She would go to Mrs. Styleman. The wind teased Leda's cap and the folds of her cloak. She was not dressed for calls, but Mary Styleman would help, would be pleased at the status it granted her to be the first to know of Leda's flight, that the mad baron was driving her from the hundred, just as everyone believed he would.

Mrs. Styleman could direct Leda to a coaching inn. She would go to London and then to Bath. She would throw herself back on the mercy of Lady Plume, and wonder how long she might keep her position when her ladyship learned Leda had not aided Brancaster as promised. She could find other work. She knew families in Bath, those who lived there, those who came to visit. There was always a place for a woman who was not too proud to work.

Of course, her sister knew she was alive, and by now would have notified her parents. And Eustace might still be in Bath. He might not have connected Leda Wroth, had he heard talk of her, with the woman he had known as his aunt by marriage, at whom he had leered when he came for hunting and meals and an advance on his allowance.

But if he saw her, he would know. She had not changed all that much in eight years. And neither had he.

Leda looked around, realizing she ought to have reached Hunstanton Park by now, crossed the river long ago. The ruins of a church stood in a field to her left, in better shape than St. Edmund's chapel, able to boast all four walls, if no roof and nothing inside. It stood like an etching against the landscape, like a long-forgotten thought. If she turned her hag stone upon it —the omen lay in her pocket—the ruin might vanish into the other realm from which it had come.

Leda shook her head to clear the fancies. This was not fairy-made; this was chalk and flint, a human-made building long outlasting its use. This was Ringstead Parva, a medieval village wiped out by the Black Death. Jack had told her the story. Now the village church stood naught but an empty frame, a monument to lost safety and the illusion of refuge. It stood exposed, the entire roof lifted off, its inner life whisked away, leaving a husk.

Much like Leda would be when she left here, leaving Jack behind. How had she become so attached to the man, and so quickly? Why did she understand, just as a besotted Anne-Marie had written in her diary, that the bliss they had shared was to be found with him, and him only, and once she left him, she would be bereft for the rest of her life?

Hunstanton Park was north. Leda turned down the next lane she found, heading east, determined to turn north as soon as she might. Pontus flicked his ears and trotted nervously, picking up on her distress through the narrow leather strips. She must rein in her emotions. She must keep control of her mind.

She could not show up in Mary Styleman's parlor ranting like a madwoman. It would reflect badly on Jack, and his reputation was strained enough, baron though he might be. He was struggling already to keep his estate afloat, and he had children —*three* children—to support. He had to keep his standing in the eyes of his neighbors, and his credit with the tradesmen about.

Pontus flicked his ears backwards, and a prickle along her spine made Leda glance behind her. A man on a horse appeared in the lane—the drift, they called it in Norfolk. He was far back, but riding at an uneasy canter. Jack had found her already?

She must reach Hunstanton Hall. She would keep her wits about her in the company of the Stylemans. She would remember he had not trusted her to learn of Nanette—for good reason, perhaps, knowing what she had done to her husband, though she had never hurt Ives.

Jack did not trust her, and she did not trust herself. The only solution was a break. Which meant he could not come after her, lure her back. She urged Pontus to a trot, and the large horse reluctantly obliged.

She passed a farm, a yard, a gravel pit. This wasn't right. Where was the lane to head north? Then the land on either side of the lane rose suddenly into grass-covered downs, with white walls forming a large sunken amphitheater before her, and she realized where she was. Jack had brought her here once, on his tour of brick making in Norfolk. This was the Ringstead chalk pit, one of the great scooped-out pits that pocked Norfolk, and there was nowhere else to go. She would have to turn and face him. Or hide.

She glanced behind her. It wasn't Jack. It was the apparition from the beach. Black hair a blot of grease atop his pale, doughy face. Dark coat flapping around his barrel of a chest. He was large, strong. He had found her. This time, she had no knife.

There was a kiln set into the face of the pit, with an iron grille of a door to keep out animals, brigands and vagabonds, and to prevent smugglers using it to hide untaxed goods. She did not care to lock herself in such a place.

But tunnels opened in the white walls like gaps between teeth, tunnels formed to follow seams of flint deep into the hill upon which sat Ringstead Magna. They were worms of darkness creeping into the hillside, and who knows how deep they ran. She could hide there until he went away. A ghost could not touch her, only haunt. She would whisk herself into the darkness, and he would disappear.

She could be lost in the hill forever, like the sleeping king beneath Norwich Castle.

She cast a look of despair behind her. The rider neared. His face, his grim smile, was pure malevolence. She halted Pontus and threw herself to the ground, then tossed the reins into a broom bush to hold the horse. He wouldn't like it, but she needed a way to find shelter once the ghost left her.

If he had found her here, he could follow her anywhere, to the edges of the island, to the far reaches of the sea. She would never be free of this ghost. Leda sobbed as she stumbled toward the kiln, frantic with the need to hide.

"Caledonia!" The voice was strange, not quite Bertram's bellow.

The door to the kiln was locked.

If he killed her, left her body here, her bones would never be found. No one would ever know what had become of Leda Wroth.

"Leda." He crooned the word, the name she had always preferred to call herself, and claimed for herself when she decided she was no longer mad.

"Stop. Be reasonable, I beg you."

Leda whirled and gaped at the man who dismounted the horse. She didn't recognize the animal; he must have hired it somewhere. He pulled down the waistcoat riding up over his large belly, then looked around for a place to tie the horse. Seeing none, he simply dropped the reins and turned toward her.

The word escaped her in a gasp of shock. "Eustace."

CHAPTER EIGHTEEN

He had changed. He'd been nearly thirty when she married his uncle, yet a selfish boy weary of living on his uncle's sufferance, wheedling for a raise in his allowance, for a piece of the property to sustain him. Leda had heard the rows rising from her husband's library when Eustace's debts and scandals grew costly.

There were whispers about him, too, worse than Bertram, who was ever dabbing his wick in places it wasn't wanted. There'd been a woman in Eustace's village, a woman known for bartering her body to keep her children fed, found strangled early one morning behind the pub. There'd been a girl, a younger sister of a woman Eustace was courting for marriage, who'd been bundled away swiftly to a faraway school.

There was a little scullery maid, freshly hired, who had come to Leda with a bruised wrist the morning after Eustace ended a visit and said, not meeting Leda's eyes, her mum was ill and she was needed at home, directly, to see to the babies. Leda, still naïve then, had let her go, but had felt the urge after to look up the girl and help her household, except no one could say exactly where she lived, where she had come from, or where she had gone.

Eustace, a colder, older Leda now knew, was a worse monster than Bertram had been: the cast and mold of his uncle, but without the thin veneer of respectability, that slim leash of caring what his neighbors thought, of pretending he could demand their respect. Eustace did not care for anything but his own desires.

He breathed heavily as he regarded her. He had gained two stone in weight in the years since she'd seen him, had gone from stocky to portly. His cheeks flushed as his eyes moved over her, lingering on her bosom. He licked his lips.

"Hello, Auntie. You've been a difficult woman to find."

The opening of the nearest tunnel was some distance from her, an open maw gaping in the shaved white sides of the cliff. Grasses and weeds grew up the sides of the bank, just as shrubs and small trees had begun filling the basin, nature creeping over the scars left by man. There was one lane into the pit, and Eustace stood in the center of it, trapping her as if she were a vixen at bay.

Leda hugged her arms across her chest. "You were never supposed to find me. They were to say that I died."

He held a riding crop and tapped it lightly against one bulging thigh. His boots were crusted with sand, the tails of his coat damp with mud. It *had* been him on the beach that morning. She hadn't been seeing apparitions, not Nanette, and not him. She was sane as the morning.

"And yet here you are. In the living flesh," he said. She shivered at the way he examined her, his eyes dark and beady, cold yet covetous. Tap, tap went the whip.

"You little fool," he added. "Living buried in Bath all this time? I was going to rescue you from the madhouse, you know. Only needed a bit of time past to make it seem respectable. My mourning over. You recovering your wits. I would have made you a very pleasant offer."

He lumbered closer, and Leda sidled away. He smelled like must and old sweat and spoiled mutton.

She must not anger him. He was big, and he was angry, a giant badger to her field mouse. "How very generous of you. I hope you are well-settled now. Married? Any children?" The thought of any woman having to submit to Eustace revolted her, but she had felt the same of Bertram and survived.

He huffed, the sound not of amusement. "Imagine my surprise, after all this time, when I went to a wedding in Cheltenham and heard all about the friend who had advised the bride to take her groom. A handsome woman named Leda, with a crown of dark hair and violet eyes. An interesting description, I thought. How many women have I known with violet eyes? And I wondered, has my dear aunt arisen from her pauper's grave?"

Leda gulped down the lump in her throat. "You came to Bath looking for me."

He loomed. "Where is the boy, Leda?"

Her throat closed. There would be no swallowing anything. "Ives—the boy died. I killed him, remember?"

"Then why would your cook and that feral bitch of a housemaid run away? She wouldn't let me touch her, though my uncle enjoyed her now and again."

Bertram had "enjoyed" many women. Leda doubted they had enjoyed him.

"They ran because I was mad, and a killer." If she reminded him of her crimes, he would back away. He would leave.

He would not demand anything. And he would not send her back to the asylum. The mouth of the tunnel was nearly at her back. She would never enter a place like that madhouse again. She would bury herself in this hill first.

Eustace snorted. The sound might have been a laugh; his second chin shook. There was no way to dart around him, and if she tried, she would not get to the horse in time. He had a longer reach, with his whip. She could only retreat.

"You'd best come with me," he said softly.

Cold brushed the back of her neck, the continuous wind, bearing the chalky damp of the hill. "I don't see why."

"They won't take you back. Not that old beldame in Bath. Not after I told her about you."

"What did you say?"

"No more than the truth." He sneered. "But why go back to her when you've made yourself a nice nest here. A baron to keep you, mad as he might be. I suppose you think it a good trade."

He could hurt Jack because of her. Fear lodged high in her chest, cutting off breath. "He's a friend of the family. I've only come for a visit."

"He won't want you now. Not after *he* knows. And I'll make sure he does." He whispered the whip against his breeches, leather upon buckskin.

"What do you want, Eustace?"

"The boy, first. And then I have other demands."

"The baby died. You said I killed him. You swore before the magistrate that I stabbed him when he emerged from the womb, and that accounted for the blood."

"Then I wonder why the man at the White Hart says you send so many packages to Tytherton Kellaways. And I found your sister in Chippenham—so surprised was she, to learn her dear Caledonia was not dead after all! There were many to say they'd seen a violet-eyed woman and a lordly kind of man walking Maud Heath's Causeway that day."

"No one would know the shade of my eyes from that

distance," Leda said weakly. Her sister had spoken to Eustace? Then she had also told their parents Leda was not dead.

And if she lied about her own death, she might be lying about Ives. He could hunt him down so easily, Eustace and his dogged greed. He stepped closer.

"You didn't kill a babe any more than you killed my uncle."

His nasty smile poured a cold shower of horror down her spine. "I didn't? Then who did?"

"Oh, I'm sure any number of people had it in for that rat-faced bastard. It's a blessing to the world someone blotted him. And enough time has passed, I'll forgive his mad wife. I'll take in his poor, sad relict and give her a home." He leered. "I am certain I can teach her to please me."

The triumph in his gaze alerted her. It was the only explanation that made sense, really. "You killed him," Leda whispered.

His eyes narrowed to dark slits, like the eyes of a snake. "You'd best keep that between us. For you're the one to benefit, after all. You'll be the mistress of Norcott Hall again, but with a young and fitter husband, one who forgives your madness. You'll have all that you wish if you prove a good, smart, quiet, loyal little wife."

Fear dug talons into her throat. He was so close. "I won't marry you, Eustace."

"You were *supposed* to marry me." He lashed his leg with the whip. "You were supposed to be sleeping your nice little laudanum nap while I took care of things for us. But no, always a meddler, weren't you? Had to come downstairs and surprise me. I had to put the knife in your hand. You're lucky you didn't fall on it and kill yourself while you stumbled around in your fog. A hard one to put down, you are, Caledonia Hill."

She hadn't killed Bertram. She hadn't murdered anyone.

Leda's heart beat so fast the rush of blood made her dizzy. "Why would you tell me this?"

"Because a wife can't testify against her husband in court. No one will believe you anyway. I'm the generous one, taking in a poor, mad woman whose family won't have her back. Giving her a home. And she'll show her gratitude." He leered, his hot breath wafting toward her. "I'll breed my own children on you, proper heirs, and you won't dare shame me, will you? You know what it's like to be a woman alone, at the mercy of her own wits. Best cast yourself on my mercy instead."

He put a hand to his groin, adjusting himself inside his breeches, aroused by whatever images his words conjured in his dark mind. Shame and fury scorched Leda's cheeks. It was the same threat he'd made when he saw her carted away to the madhouse, her wrists bound in chains. He would never make such a gesture before a lady.

He would never admit his crimes, either, not where they could come back to him. He didn't mean to marry her. He didn't mean to let her live. He wanted to confirm where Ives was, and then he meant to kill her.

"You don't have the mercy of a stone," Leda said. She turned and plunged into the tunnel.

"Get back out here," Eustace roared. "I'm not going to chase you." She heard the slap of his crop against his thigh as he vented his frustration. He would use it on her if he could.

Eustace was afraid of the dark; she knew that. Leda wasn't. She had made friends with the dark as a girl, all the nights she sat curled at her window weaving dreams from the stars. She had made cold truce with the dark in the madhouse, where they took away the candles for fear of fire.

"What do you suppose you're doing, you foolish bitch? You have to come out sometime."

But she didn't. She could wait him out. She could stay in

here until she fainted of thirst, and then she would crawl out on her knees, triumphant.

"Caledonia Toplady!" he bellowed.

The tunnel she was in went straight for a while, casting a dim carpet of light before her. Gray sparks glinted from the walls now and again, like secret eyes. The floor wasn't smooth, clods of chalk breaking apart beneath her boots, dust sliding along her soles. She put a hand to the wall so she could find her way out. Just like walking a hedge maze. The earth smelled fresh and damp and powdery, like Jack's brick mixture.

Jack. If she died here—if she died in the tunnel like a rat, or Eustace found and killed her, which would be worse—how would Jack know what had happened? He would know only that she had left him. Like Anne-Marie.

Her heart jammed in her chest. Of course, she *had* left him, but she meant to send a long letter explaining why. Because he had not trusted her with the truth about Nanette, and she knew she deserved that. She had not trusted herself.

But she wasn't a killer. She could scarce wrap her mind around this new reality. She'd never lost her senses and attacked a man with a knife. She'd been drugged, and Eustace had murdered Bertram.

Of course. Why hadn't she seen that all along? She wasn't strong enough to drive a carving knife through a grown man's ribcage. The worst she could have done is nicked his skin even if she penetrated the thick cloth of his coat. It took another man, younger, stronger, full of murderous rage. The man who stood to gain everything if Bertram died.

As long as Bertram's so-called heir died with him.

A string of curses exploded behind her, Eustace's voice a bit muffled. "That ties it. I'm coming in after you. And you're not going to like what happens to you if you don't meet me halfway."

That was a laugh. She wouldn't like what he would do to her in any circumstances. She had thought Bertram's use of her something to endure. Eustace would hurt her and delight in her pain. He was that way.

She bit off a cry as she collided with something, a hard jab of wood against her shoulder. She felt along the surface with her hand, the light too dim to make out much. A plank of wood propped up the ceiling. Perhaps the roof of the tunnel was weaker here. She squirmed around the brace and kept going.

Behind her another curse ricocheted, an echoing quality to it. Eustace was in the tunnel.

Leda pushed herself on, keeping her breath shallow and remembering to pick up her feet so a stumble or pant didn't tell Eustace where she was. She'd said goodbye to her parents ten years ago, when they married her to Bertram despite her tears. She'd said goodbye to her sister when the locked door closed on her in the madhouse and she knew her family would try to bury the shame. There were only a few others she'd miss.

There would be no one to tell Mrs. Blake and Betsey and Ives, unless Jack eventually learned of her fate, buried in this hill, perhaps if a stoat or a polecat found and ferreted out her bones. The women would protect Ives to adulthood and set him on the best path they could, she had to die believing that, but she would never live to see fruition of her plan.

And Jack. She would never be able to tell Jack she loved him.

She would never see him repair his relationship with Muriel, or see Ellinore and Nanette flourish in his protective care. She would never know if he succeeded with his dratted bricks. Lady Plume would find a replacement companion, of course. The social round of Bath would go on. So would life at Holme Hall and in the Smithdon Hundred, and they might speak of Leda Wroth once in a while as that West Country foreigner who visited for a time.

Would Jack fall in love with someone else? Marry and be happy with her? Would he ever find a governess who would suit Muriel and teach her aright?

The tunnel forked, and Leda paused. To one side, her left, lay a faint sliver of light: daylight. She could head that way, escape. Take Eustace's horse and Pontus and ride—where? Anywhere. Back to the farm she had passed on the way. Could she escape outside without his hearing him? He blundered behind her, swearing, trying she guessed to worm his bulk through the small tunnels. If he saw her leave, he could follow and catch her. She was safe in here.

Right it was. She kept her hand along the wall, wincing when her palm grazed a sharp outcropping. She was shredding her gloves. She wished she could tell Jack: she wasn't a murderer. She wasn't mad, perhaps never had been. If she could escape, if she could tell a magistrate what had happened, Eustace would be tried and hanged for a murderer, and the house—what would happen to the estate? Could she persuade the justice to give it to Ives?

She would try. She would live, and she would try. She had to find a way to outwit Eustace.

"Leda? Leda! Where are you?"

Her knees went weak at the sound of Jack's voice. Jack was in the chalk pit. An intense joy flooded her chest and, for a moment, overswept her good sense. "Jack!" she screamed. "I'm in the tunnels!"

"Caledonia!" Eustace roared from behind her.

Leda whirled and scurried deeper, away from him. She tripped over another wooden plank holding up the ceiling, recovered herself, moved on. She could not go back that way. There was air in here, dank, ripe with earthen smell, and these tunnels would not have pockets of poison, not like a mine. But her breath grew short nonetheless, panic using her air. She must escape Eustace and get to Jack.

"Who is that? Who's there?" Jack called.

Leda shrieked as a sudden shower of pebbles rained on her. "Don't come in here!" she screamed to Jack.

"Time to come out, come out of the hill, Caledonia!" Eustace shouted behind her. "Run to your lover's arms. See what he thinks when he sees the thing you truly are."

"At least I'm not a killer!"

"Then you didn't murder the boy. *I knew it*. Where is he, Leda?"

She pressed a fist to her mouth to keep herself from screaming, wasting more air. He could not hurt Ives. She would not let him. The tunnel kept curving—she could tell by the tilt of the surface—and she had no sense of direction. She couldn't go back; Eustace was coming. And she couldn't get out.

He could get out first, get his horse, escape. And find Ives.

"You have to stop him, Jack!" Leda called.

"I will. Come out of there, darling. Those tunnels are—there's good reason they stopped digging. Leda, please. Come to me now."

The wall fell away and she groped in darkness. She was lost in blank space, teetering. She put her arms out, afraid to fall, more afraid to stay where she was. Another groaning sound, then the creak and crack of wood. Eustace was blundering his way toward her, pushing down the wooden supports as he went, as unstoppable as a maddened bull.

You must get out of here. But how?

She wanted to sob, to scream, fall to her knees and beat the earth. She couldn't lose her mind, not here, though everything was so dark it robbed her breath, dulled her hearing. It seemed a great echo rose about her, the earth itself growling.

Think, Leda. You escaped a madhouse. Think.

She couldn't throw a shoe out a window. Jack wouldn't see it. She held very still, breathing. *Think.*

The king under the mountain would awake one day when he was needed. She was needed. She needed to arise. How would the king know?

She held still and felt it: the cool touch of air on her cheek. Left cheek.

She turned, spread her hands out either way, and found the edge of the tunnel, the branch with the breeze. She plunged into it.

"What the devil?" Eustace cursed. "The bloody ceiling is coming down! Leda, what did you *do*?"

She felt the shake and the shudder, then an odd hollow thump. There was hardly a noise as the earth swallowed. But she smelled it, heard the ground behind her collapsing, felt the dust drifting from the tunnel behind her, airy and light.

"Leda!" Jack bellowed. "The hill is caving in. *You need to get out now.*"

She ran. Rocks collided with her feet, the edges of flint stabbed her palms, once she hit her head on a low outcropping and saw stars dance across her vision. She paused and shook her head until the ringing cleared. But it wasn't a ringing, just a slow rumble. Gathering behind her. On her heels.

"*Leda.*"

The tunnel turned sharply, and she crashed into the side. A swift, sharp slice on her cheek, a sudden sting. Her toe throbbed. She groped with her hands and saw the turn, the oval of light. She threw herself at it. And then, as the oval started to shrink, a dark curtain falling before it, she threw her arms over her face and dove through.

"My God. My darling. Leda."

Jack had her. Jack scooped her up and before she could find

her feet she was pressed against his chest. So sturdy, so firm. So warm. He smelled like currants. He clamped one arm like a band around her and the other pushed through her hair, then across her face. His knuckles slid through the damp on her cheek, came away bloody.

"Oh," Leda gasped. "I'm bleeding."

"You're alive. Come away now."

Before she could squeak he swept a hand beneath her legs and lifted her in his arms. Leda clung to his shoulder and watched as the hill caved in. Not a landslide, like when a chunk of sea cliff fell into the water. Just a maidenly sigh as a sinkhole formed in the green dome above, and one tunnel, then another beside it, fell in like a closing mouth.

Leda clung to Jack's shoulders. "Eustace is in there."

"Who?"

"My nephew."

"How did your nephew get in *there*?"

"Because he was following me. Jack, he murdered Bertram, and he was going to murder Ives, and possibly me. We have to save him."

"*What?*"

She struggled against his grip. "I can't let him die in there. He's Bertram's flesh and blood."

"You stay here. Not another step." Jack threw the words at her as he set her on her feet, his jaw clenching as he turned toward the walls of chalk. "Don't you dare go back inside."

"Don't you go in, either. What if more collapses?"

"Hallo in there!" Jack framed his mouth with his hands. The shout echoed around the pit, ringing with shrubs and greening trees, the dome of the gray sky pressing down like the lid of a teapot. "Can you hear me? Any chance you survived in there, mate?"

They waited. Jack held Leda's gaze. She scrubbed her face.

Her gloves were tatters, her hands filthy, and she smeared dirt in the cut on her cheek. Brilliant. She must look a madwoman indeed.

"Leda..." Jack took a stick and tested the fall of dirt and white chalk that filled the mouth of the tunnel. "If he survived the cave in, I don't know that we can dig him out before he suffocates."

She curled her hands into fists, her palms smarting and raw. A great tremor seized her, like a terrier shaking a rat to break its neck. Cold followed in its wake, as if she were caught in an undertow. "We must try."

Jack bolted forward and caught her just as she fainted.

CHAPTER NINETEEN

Jack took charge. It was such a lovely thing, someone else taking charge for once. Leda sat in the cart next to him as he drove Pontus, leading Eustace's horse behind. He would ask around, find where it was hired, and return it, he told her. He would hire boys to dig out the tunnels and recover Eustace, if he was alive.

She nodded. He wouldn't be.

"I will have to send his body back to Cirencester," she said. "Or take it myself. The Toplady crypt is in a cemetery there."

"A proper burial is more than you owe him. He killed your husband because he meant to seize the estate from the child he thought you were carrying?"

She formed words through chattering teeth. This had happened to her before, after she realized Bertram was dead and Mrs. Blake and Betsey had fled who knew where with a just-born babe. She waited in the cold wooden cell that was used to hold those coming before the magistrate, and it was if she stood on the beach against a rising tide, cold dousing her, freezing her veins, and trembling that would not stop.

Jack snaked an arm about her, and she leaned into him. He was so firm, so present. So calm.

"He wanted the house and estate. He would have been the heir, without a child. He said he had intended to marry me as well. He simply wanted what Bertram had."

"And he put the knife in your hand to pin the murder on you."

"He said he had planned to take me out of the madhouse, eventually. I suppose he could have, as family. He wanted it to look as if I had been punished and was sufficiently penitent, having paid for my crimes. He wanted me to tell him where I had hidden Ives."

"Did he know?"

"He was close." Leda shuddered. "He came to Bath looking for me, as I thought, after he'd heard rumors I was alive. He found Lady Plume, and he found out about the packets I was sending to Kellaways, though I never discussed it with her."

Jack snorted. "She knows everything that goes on beneath her roof, and many others besides, but I find it hard to believe she would betray you."

"He said he asked at the coaching inn. Then he found my sister in Chippenham, so I suppose she mentioned where I was going. I think I had said I was traveling with you to Norfolk. I imagine it took him some time to find exactly where, and that is why we've not seen him before now."

Unless he had found Ives first. Cold shook her.

"You are safe now." Jack squeezed the arm about her, pulling her close. "He cannot hurt you."

She sighed and leaned against him as the cart jolted over the ruts. There were the ruins of Ringstead Parva again, but now they were merely sad instead of frightening, the relics of a bygone age and lives that had long passed into obscurity. It felt so *good* to trust another person. A warm bead formed, deep in the center of her chest, and the glow began to chase away the cold. She was with Jack, and she wanted never to leave him.

He brought her to Holme Hall as if it were her home, and the great shrug of red stone indeed felt welcoming. A thread of sadness tugged at the sight of the cliffs and the sea beyond. She thought for a moment she saw a shadow, almost the shape of a woman, but then a great flock of terns wheeled and lifted, and the shadow fled.

"Jack." Leda clasped his shoulders as he lifted her down from the cart. He pulled her against his body, and a thrill darted through her from the place where their bodies touched, her insides soaring just like those birds.

"I was running away from you. I was so angry that you hadn't told me about Nanette."

His eyelid tensed, his beautiful lips flattening into a line. He held her cradled against him as if he could not bear to set her down. "I want to explain."

"I do as well. It felt—I told you I thought I was imagining things, and you let me believe it. You let me think I could be going mad again, and if I were—if I hurt someone..."

He pressed her close. "I am sorry. I didn't think of how you might feel. I only knew, with your clever mind, you would figure out everything, and I would be exposed. And I feared you would despise me. The man whose own wife didn't want him."

She found her feet but still leaned against him. This firm, splendid body, the shape of this man whom she utterly loved. Having had him close to her, how could she ever let him go?

She touched her fingertips to his jaw, the silk of his short beard, the warm skin beneath, and the hard, determined slant of bone. There was steel in his core, but such softness in his heart.

"Let us be clear about one thing. What I feel for you is *not* contempt."

He curved his palm around the back of her hand. Her insides quivered at the intensity of his expression. "No?"

"No," she said firmly.

His head lowered, and she would have kissed him, quite willingly, there in the drive before Holme Hall, with the shore birds wheeling above them and the grasses waving in the ruffle of wind and the insects chirping as madly as if there were a coming storm. Then Henry barreled out the front door, taking Pontus' head.

"Are you right, mum? Thas a great puckaterry in the kitchen or you agorn, but I says thas a great load a squit, tha is, and you warnt ment to lollop off on us."

Leda reined in a shaky laugh. Her feet did not yet feel solid on the ground. Her balance had been thrown off in the dark of the tunnel, and she had not yet found her bearings.

"I am here now, Henry. You may tell them in the kitchen I have returned."

She didn't need to, because May was in her room with hot water for the basin and fresh cloths for her face and hands. She hovered, pretending to straighten and clean the already tidied room, while Grace herded Leda into the dressing room and made her stand on an old rug while she stripped off her filthy gown. Once bundled into a fresh shift and dressing gown, Grace shooed her into the bed, where May slid out the bed warmer with its coals and plumped the counterpane.

All three girls sat huddled on the windowsill, eyes wide as they watched Leda, while Mrs. Leech peeked around the door with a tray of treacle tart and tea.

Leda nestled against the pillows with a happy sigh and a hairbrush. "You might as well come in. All of you."

"What happened, mum? You looked queer-like asmornum, an left in a pelter, an now you come home all a muckwash, like you was dredged from the sea." Mrs. Leech doled out tarts.

"From a hill, actually." Leda made a face as she tugged a tangle out of her hair. "I suppose you'll want the whole of it, though I'm not certain your father would approve."

"I give my permission." Jack entered the room and took the upholstered chair, moving it close by the bed, then sitting and crossing one foot over his knees as if he meant to stay.

Before she had properly begun the girls settled themselves across the bed, perched like birds over the brocade counterpane. Ellinore leaned against the far post, sewing a ribbon. Nanette crept like a little cat to the pillow beside Leda and sat there, intently watching Leda's face. Muriel sat against the other bed post and watched Leda steadily, eyes narrowed, her new doll cradled firmly in her arms. Mrs. Leech served them all treacle tart, her ears wide open, while Grace and May dawdled in the door of the dressing room, pretending to fold frocks.

They were all here, her new little family, and that bright, small window in her chest opened further. How could she ever leave them?

Leda said as much as she thought she could. How she married young to a man who had not been kind to her, who had a malicious nephew who wanted his land. How the day that his heir was born, the man was found murdered in his own library, and the magistrate thought Leda did it. How she was sent for a time to a madhouse, and then she left, and took work with Jack's great aunt in Bath, and ended up here, in search of a governess. But her nephew followed her, and when she left earlier he had trailed her to the chalk pit, and one of the tunnels had caved in around him.

"An heir?" Grace said when Leda was finished. She moved a hand over her lower belly, where a slight bulge was forming beneath her apron. "Your babe? And you left him behind you, mum?"

Leda bit her lip and nodded. "I had to. I hid him away so

Eustace wouldn't learn about him. I feared what he might do, and as it happens, my fears were founded."

"But he'll be safe now, won't he. Will you go back to your house? Now that you're not mad?" Grace asked.

"I will have to set things in order after Eustace's death," Leda answered. "The property will go to Ives, I hope, for him to take over when he is of age."

"So ye'll be leaving us."

"I hate to go, particularly when I have not finished my task. I have not found a governess." Leda smiled at Nanette. "His lordship should have told me right away there were *two* of you. I would have adjusted my search accordingly."

"Twee." The girl pointed to Ellinore. They were unmistakably sisters, down to the shape of their faces, the set of their ears.

"Yes, three of you now. This will require some thought."

The girl, though cautious, showed no fear of a stranger. She held up her dolly for Leda's inspection, the little corn dolly that Muriel had treasured. "Judit," she said in a serious tone.

Leda smiled. "Do you know, I thought the dolly was named Nanette. I suppose that was why it took me so long to figure things out. But I wonder. Why did they hide you from me, my pet?"

Jack shifted in his chair, rubbing tart from his fingertips. "You will think my reasons foolish, I suppose. But I'm hoping no one knows Nanette is here. That no one in the neighborhood knows she was even born." He glanced at Muriel, then at Leda. "I don't know who her father is, you see. I feared if he knew about her, he would take her away, or insist she be put somewhere because—well. They might say she is simple, or worse, because of what her mother did. And I simply couldn't guess who the man was. Rolfe, or Styleman, or even Hogg—Anne-Marie didn't visit, but she wasn't a recluse. And she was very beautiful."

Leda tamped down the pang of jealousy. Anne-Marie had been gifted with three children, three beautiful, graceful daughters, and she hadn't clung to life for any of them. While Leda, who adored children, had been given none.

"Simple?" she questioned. "She's understood me when I spoke to her."

"Sometimes she do, and sometimes she pretend you never spoke a'tall. Here, mite." Ellinore bit off the end of her thread and handed the scarlet ribbon to Nanette. "For Judith."

With evident glee, Nanette crawled across the bed and accepted the gift. At once she began twining it around the corn dolly's neck.

Muriel tapped the younger girl on the shoulder and stared intently into her face. "You're to be kind to her, hear? No thacking her about or rough play."

Nanette nodded, eyes wide, and began trying the ribbon more gently.

Leda, taken with a hunch, crooked a finger at the girl. "That is a pretty ribbon in your hair. May I see it?" She lured the girl close with a piece of tart and, as she took it, ran a hand over her dark curls. Then, quite deliberately, she snapped her fingers behind the girl's left ear. Nanette didn't turn a hair.

Leda smoothed the girl's other braid and snapped behind her right ear. Nanette turned her head a shade, flicking curious eyes up at Leda, then back to her tart.

"She's not simple," Leda said. "She doesn't hear well."

"What do you mean?" Jack sat forward, his voice catching.

"I saw some women like this in the madhouse," Leda said. "Sometimes it is damage, or illness. Sometimes they are simply born that way. What happened?"

"When she was very small..." Jack cleared his throat and blinked his eyes. He looked at Mrs. Leech like a drowning man who had just seen a boat appear on the horizon.

The cook shook her head and wiped her eyes. "You orter tell her, sir. They all should know."

Jack swallowed. "One day, when I was away, and Muriel was staying with Anne-Marie's parents, Anne-Marie gave the servants the day off. Then she took Nanette and went somewhere. I don't know where; we've never learned. But she came back the next morning and said nothing to Mrs. Leech, only went and locked herself in a room.

"Nanette came down with a fever the next day, and a terrible, racking cough. It might have been scarlet fever, or whooping cough—we don't know. Mrs. Leech nursed her through it, and she survived, but the illness damaged her hearing and possibly her vocal cords, we think." He swallowed again. His eyes looked desperate, sad.

"Anne-Marie had nothing to do with the baby, not when she was ill, and not after. She locked herself in her room and sank into despair. I couldn't reach her. She wouldn't see Muriel. Her parents could do nothing—no one could. A week or so later…" He cleared his throat. "She jumped."

"Fell," Muriel said, sitting up, her eyes flaring, fingers clenched around her doll.

"Fell," Jack amended. He met Leda's gaze. "I've always assumed she tried to run away with her lover, and he turned her down. That is why I thought it was someone near here."

"But perhaps not someone you know," Leda murmured. "Nora, my dear, will you hand me that book on the dressing table? Next to the mermaid's purse."

"My mother's diary," Muriel said in hushed, reverent tones.

"I found it in the mattress. It's been under my nose all this time. When was Nanette born?"

"June 1794. She'll be six this year."

She was small for a six year old, but illness or neglect could slow an infant's growth; she'd seen that in the madhouse, too, of the women who came with babes in or outside their belly. Leda skimmed through the dates in the journal with its scant but vivid entries. Her heart clenched as read through the fall of the year before Nanette's birth, Anne-Marie's wild joy palpable. She was a woman desperately, thoroughly in love. Then the spring, and news of the baby, and the infinite, equally wild despair.

Leda looked up at Jack, her eyes brimming with tears. "May I tell you what I've found? I think Mrs. Leech is right. You all should know."

Jack sat at the edge of the chair like a man ready to start a race. White lines bracketed his eyes. "Tell us."

"Anne-Marie was in love with a man named Bohamos. Desperately, wildly, completely in love. She fell for him when she was a young girl and watched him for years from afar. When his family came through one fall, she approached him. He loved her back."

Jack glanced at the older girl. "Ellinore."

Nora sat on the bed, back straight, knees curved gracefully beside her. She blinked quickly. "Bohamos. He was not from around here?"

"He is one of the Roma, part of the family that travels through this tract of Norfolk in the fall and winter. They have done so for decades, maybe centuries."

"Of course my grandparents would not let her be with a gypsy," Ellinore said.

"That is not what they call themselves," Leda reminded her. "He was betrothed to a Roma woman and meant to marry her. He could not break that oath. When Anne-Marie learned he had married, a year or two later, she—" Leda paused. "She fell into a deep melancholy. Very deep. I think you saved her life when you offered to marry her, Jack."

"I wish I could believe that were the case," Jack said quietly. "But I don't think the melancholy ever left her."

"It wasn't you." Leda leaned forward, wishing she had the right to touch him. But the servants were still watching, pretending to tidy as they listened to the story, and the girls were riveted, Nanette closely watching Leda's face.

"And me?" Muriel asked. She looked sad, lost, and determined to know. Her expression, her very face, was the image of Jack's.

"I think there is no doubt who your father is, Muriel," Leda said gently. "Who else could have given you red hair?"

Muriel gave her father a look full of caution and longing intertwined. A wistful hope nipped at Leda's heart. With this reassurance, perhaps Muriel would feel softer toward Jack. And perhaps he would be able to reach her with his love. The girl needed it so badly.

"But Nanette," Ellinore said quietly, tugging on one of her littlest sister's curls.

"When the travelers came through one fall, Anne-Marie went to Bohamos. She pleaded to join them. Be a second wife. His mistress. Anything to be with him. He still loved her, she believed, but he would not take her with him. It was against his custom. And he had children with his wife. I guess Anne-Marie went to him that day she left, trying to use his child as persuasion, but he broke with her instead. She had to give up the hope that she could ever be with him."

"And if she could not have him, then she felt her life was over." Jack's voice trailed away. "She was that unhappy with me?"

"I don't think she was well, Jack. There are some women...I saw them in the madhouse, too. After they have a baby, something happens to them. It is as if their reason is stolen away. They might try to hurt themselves or—" Leda caught her breath, recalling the worst story she'd heard. "Or the baby. It is truly a type of madness. Not their choice."

"And it happened to Anne-Marie?" Jack asked.

"Worse with every birth, her diary would suggest. After Nanette...I suspect she was simply overcome. She writes about the pain she was in." She closed the journal, silencing its anguished cries.

Jack sat back, dropping his head into his hands.

"She *fell*." Muriel's voice wobbled, and she clung to her doll tightly.

Leda glanced at Jack, who didn't look up. He was wrestling with whatever this knowledge meant to him. Leda focused on the girl.

"Of course she fell, darling. She would never have left the three of you. Or your father. It was a terrible accident that robbed you of your mother. I am so sorry, my dear."

Muriel clutched her toy to her, blinking rapidly. Then she said, "But you made this doll for me, didn't you?"

"Yes, I bought the carved wood for her head from the peddler in Snettisham, and then I made the body. I used old rags of yours for her frock. I hope that is all right. I can make her a different dress if you wish."

Muriel hugged the doll. "I like her just as she is." She pursed her lips. "Are you going to leave us?"

Jack didn't lift his head, but he tensed. Leda said carefully, "I will need to take my nephew's body back to be buried in the family crypt, I think. There is not much left of the Toplady family, but they will wish that for him. And I have to ensure that Ives—that is my son—" The lie came uneasy to her lips— "I must see that he inherits the estate that is meant for him." The estate that she had lied and cheated to ensure he would have. She had stayed in the madhouse for two years, pretending to pay for the crime of killing her child, until she had been certain Ives was hidden and safe.

"My heart alive, the time," Mrs. Leech said mildly. "The girls will be wanting their denner, and then the master and missus, I shink." She shooed the maids, then the girls, into a little flock before her.

"May I—?" Ellinore hesitated, fingertips hovering over the diary with the twined roses stamped on the cover.

"I think his lordship should read it first, don't you? And then share it with you when he believes the time is right."

"Very well."

"You could stay." Muriel looked astonished at herself for blurting her words, her eyes wide, her cheeks flaming with two spots of color on her pale skin. "You don't need to leave. You could stay here."

"Thank you, Muriel. It means a great deal to hear you say that. But I think I shall have to discuss that with your father."

Nanette regarded her soberly. Then, puckering her lips, she clambered onto the bed, planted a kiss on Leda's cheek, then clambered back down, satisfied with herself, and let the others bustle her out the door. Leda placed a hand over her cheek, waiting until they were all gone to let the tears well.

Jack lifted his head, then the rest of him, and came to the side of the bed, reaching out a hand to her. Leda gave him hers willingly.

"Don't you dare put your chalky boots on my covers," she murmured.

He smiled, and that smile, sad as it was at the corners, tugged at her heart. In a moment he shed his coat and boots. She lifted the counterpane and he slid into the bed beside her, his arms curving around her, and she melted against him like warm butter. In an instant desire lit her like a fuse. He needed only to touch her. To be near.

He kissed her temple, smoothing back her hair. "You could stay. I need someone to advise me what to do with these girls."

She turned her face into his neck, inhaling his scent. She didn't understand how she could feel so completely content, warm and safe, and yet impatient with desire at the same time.

"Ellinore could go to a school in Bath I know. Miss Gregoire's. It would be just the place for her. And Muriel, when she is ready." She thought a moment. "Nanette, too. She is reading our lips, and Muriel has begun to teach her letters. I am certain Miss Gregoire's would be able to work with her. She could have every opportunity deserving of a baron's daughter." She lifted her head to meet his eyes. "You *are* going to keep them, I hope?"

"I think you know the answer to that." He growled and kissed down the side of her face, toward her ear. "But I can't raise three girls on my own. I'll need a great deal of help. A very clever, sensible, capable sort of woman to be my wife. Someone who knows how to solve most any problem." He nibbled on her ear, and Leda caught her breath on a shiver of delight. "It will help if she is very beautiful, and I want to keep her in my bed all day."

"I thought I had to leave," she murmured as his lips moved down her jaw. The shivers darted everywhere. "I was afraid none of you were safe with me." She paused. "Did I kill Eustace?"

He nipped her chin. "No. He is his own king under the mountain now."

A tear fell. "Then I am free." No more fearing. No more hiding. No more lies. She could live in the light and not always be peering into shadows, waiting for judgment.

"Free to marry?" he muttered against her skin.

"Who?" She gasped as his hand came to cover her breast. Her nipple curled into a delighted bud, begging.

"I said when I met you I could give you a title. I believe I proposed to you upon our first meeting."

He kissed her then, deeply, with complete possession, and she opened her mouth to the seek of his tongue, to the heat and the fire and the sweetness.

"Brash. Some might say mad." All of her opened to him. She was warm syrup in his arms.

"Marry me, Leda. You beautiful, clever, maddening woman. Say you'll never leave me."

She gasped as he moved his mouth to her bosom, lavishing her breasts with the attention they were begging for. "Stay and be the mad baron's bride?"

"You set people on their path, do you not? You save lives. Save mine."

He moved to kiss her lower, pushing the counterpane and the dressing gown and all the many layers separating them aside, and she bloomed for him like a flower. Like a woman who had been a prisoner for years in her own lies and follies, who had shed one identity after another, who could now be fully herself.

"Yes," she breathed, threading her fingers through his thick, unruly hair. This man. This love that bound them. She could not see their future together, not clearly, but she felt the strength of this bond, the ebb and flow that would hold them together, as dependable as the tide.

"Yes," she said. "I believe I will."

CHAPTER TWENTY

"So the owner of Norcott Park is deceased. This is his death certificate?" The magistrate, brow furrowed, perched his bridge spectacles on his nose and regarded the sheet of parchment his clerk had furnished him, which Leda had furnished the clerk.

"Yes, your worship."

Leda sat in the ladder-back chair that had been set aside as a witness stand, though this was not a courtroom, only a very curious sort of inquest. A private parlor had been requested, and granted, in the King's Head in Cirencester, and its situation in the Market Place, sandwiched between other inns and public buildings within a main route of a bustling city, suffused the room with the harmonious lull of a continuous stream of traffic. Signs of a busy world of commerce and life taking place outside while Leda sat suspended, waiting to see if she might return to her life, or if she would be condemned, again, to the madhouse.

The magistrate presiding over events was not the one who committed her; his predecessor had become Earl of Bathurst around the same time Leda escaped the madhouse he had put her in, and while she swam south to Bristol, the new earl had jauntered off to London to take his seat in the House of Lords and the family's elegant London home. Mr. Michael Hicks Beach, son of one baronet and heir to another, had replaced him and held his position through a hotly debated election, so she'd heard.

Leda knew already, from having lived here, that Mr. Hicks Beach had bought the expensive Williamstrip Park a few years before her marriage; had himself married a wealthy heiress who brought him a tidy sum and the adopted surname Beach; and had sired two sons and two daughters to be brought up in the English manner. He was a man who had done all in the usual style and was climbing his way steadily to a position of influence without the dramatics of family deaths, bouts of madness, and questionable heirs popping up unannounced. It was clear he was taking Leda's case with extreme suspicion.

Eight years earlier, Mrs. Hicks Beach had not called upon the new Mrs. Bertram Toplady, not even a card felicitating their marriage. Leda suspected Bertram had done something untoward, like proposition a married lady, and she had cut him from her acquaintance because of it.

"And the death is due to accidental causes. The coroner at Snettisham confirms this." The magistrate scanned another piece of parchment, remnant of another inquest, short and brief, conducted under the watchful eyes of all the families of standing the Smithdon Hundred, who were curious about the excitement this foreigner, Leda Wroth, had brought into their quiet lives.

Mr. Hicks Beach peered at Leda over his spectacles. She straightened her back.

She had worn the primmest of her old gowns, a simple robe in the nightgown fashion in a soft dove gray. She would be eager to get rid of the thing as soon as her new gowns arrived. May could wear it marketing and preen like a hawfinch in it.

The maid currently sat in the back of the room with Jack, who had insisted on attending the hearing, and the girls, who had insisted on coming as well. May was enjoying her turn as traveling nurse and governess, while Grace despite her growing belly had taken the position of lady's maid, as the rank of a baron's wife required one. Henry had come as groom, leaving Mrs. Leech to set up her feet and direct the hall boy and little scullery maid to such tasks as needed attending at Holme Hall while the family was away.

Leda's sister sat in the back of the room as well. Leda had not yet ascertained what Emilia thought of all this, but when she learned of the proceedings that would reinstate Leda's standing in the neighborhood or condemn her again to the asylum, she insisted on coming from Chippenham.

Her parents, in Cheltenham, had not sent a note.

"And the deceased has no surviving issue. His nearest family would be..."

"My son, your worship. Ives Toplady."

Emilia flinched.

"Ah, yes, Master Ives." The magistrate turned his gaze to where Ives sat between Bestey and Mrs. Blake. Ives, too, straightened his back, and Leda bit her lip in fear. He looked so small and brave, his hair flattened with Jack's pomade, new clothes for his appearance in court. He had Bertram's hair, Bertram's heavy jaw, and what threatened to become, in a few years, Bertram's nose. She would swear, in the month since she'd seen him, he'd grown taller, his face filling out.

"Yet there is no record of the boy's birth or baptism in the parish registry. This is the boy you were believed to have..." The magistrate shifted his gaze over the women and children assembled. "Erm."

"My husband's servants hid the boy after his birth, your worship, a task with which I assisted. I had reason to believe that Eustace meant the boy harm. He admitted as much to me."

As there was no possibility of questioning Eustace, the magistrate could only take her word for what it was worth. "And Mr. Toplady—Eustace—admitted to causing the death of Mr. Toplady—Bertram. Your husband."

"Eustace told me he had killed Bertram, yes. He had drugged me with laudanum so I could not interfere, but when I woke too early, he feared I would accuse him and so put the knife in my hand to make it appear that I had—well."

No need to go into the lurid details before children. She had suggested they all stay at the house, but her good advice had for once gone unheeded. She had been alone in this box of accusation the last time. Her family had insisted she not be alone again.

"Mr. Cripps." The magistrate turned to the coroner. He had been in attendance at Leda's last hearing; she remembered how he'd never met her eyes, as if madness were catching and he might take it home to his wife. "You examined the, er, body at the time of, um, Mr. Toplady's demise. Is it possible that what Mrs.—what her ladyship claims is true?"

The coroner blinked at the reminder of Leda's status. She had entered her name in the records as Leda Burnham, Lady Brancaster, formerly Caledonia Toplady, née Caledonia Hill. They were not dealing with a poor, mad widow this time. They were dealing with the wife of a peer of the realm, and the peer himself sat on a hard wooden bench in the back of the room, appearing relaxed in his superfine cloth coat and pantaloons, but alert to every word of the proceedings.

"Erm. It is very likely that Mr. Eustace Toplady is responsible for the, ah, state of the body. The wounds were, ah, at a depth and placement that suggests a man delivered them, and not a mere female."

How different her fate might have been if someone had raised that point eight years ago, Leda thought.

The magistrate nodded and moved on. "And you yourself, Lady Brancaster, are not deceased, though your family was informed of your passing six years ago, by the proprietor of the madhouse—er, the asylum in Gloucester, we thought?"

"I believe the information about my death was given out to cover the fact that I escaped," Leda said.

That was changing the facts a little; she had paid the proprietor of the private institution, trading the bits and bobs of jewelry and other possessions he had locked in the strongbox on her behalf for the promise not to pursue her if she disappeared. Very likely, if questioned, he would not admit to having made that dubious arrangement.

Six years. The connection sent a strange trill down her back. Six years ago, Anne-Marie Waddelow Burnham had died, and six years ago, Caledonia Toplady had died, too. But Caledonia got to rise again as Leda Wroth. Anne-Marie Burnham was reduced to a ghost, haunting the edges of her former life.

The life which Leda had taken over as Jack's wife, as the mother of his daughter and the keeper of his wards, as the mistress of Holme Hall. The lady of precedence in Smithdon Hundred, though she had a ways to go to rival Mrs. Styleman as a hostess, given the vast richness of Hunstanton Hall.

"So you have not, in fact, committed any murders," Hicks Beach concluded.

"No, sir."

"And you are not mad?"

"I am in full possession of my faculties, your worship. *Compos mentis*."

Except for certain moments in Jack's bed, in Jack's arms, but that was between her and Jack. Heat singed Leda's ears at the most recent memory.

"And you wish it confirmed that Master Ives Toplady come into possession of the estate of Norcott Park, including the house and home farm, as well as all the duties and obligations of the estate, at his majority. Until which time, you and Lord Brancaster will hold the property in trust."

"Yes, your worship."

Hicks Beach glanced at Jack. "Know the Earl of Bathurst, do you? Since you're both in Lords."

Jack shifted. "I have not occupied my seat as much as I'd like. I'll be there when the First Parliament of the United Kingdom forms, however."

There would be much to prepare to move the household for the opening of Parliament and the Season. Finding an affordable house to let in a respectable part of London. Arranging for the girls to have a proper governess, since Leda would be busy as a hostess, consolidating connections for the Burnham family. And, she hoped, continuing her side interest of ensuring that independent women were able to remain so, and did not fall prey to fortune hunters and thieves of hearts.

All this awaited her as long as Mr. Hicks Beach did not see fit to lock her away. But she was a lady now, a baron's wife, not a poor mad relict of an unliked man. What a difference a title made.

What a difference love made, Leda thought, watching Jack. No wonder she'd had to strive so very hard, with some of her young mentees, to steer them away from unsuitable men. Desire flattened common sense the way a herd of frightened sheep could trample a fence and stile.

"I have every confidence you will be a good benefactor for Master Toplady, milord, and will be looking out for the boy's best interests." Mr. Hicks Beach swept aside his papers and handed them to the clerk. "I believe we're done here, are we not? I, for one, am for a pint, if mine host will bring it."

"Stop." Emilia rose with a rustle of white satin skirts. "She is lying to you."

Leda swung her head, sitting up at the edge of her seat. "I am not mad."

"And you have no child. Ives is not Leda's son, your worship. His mother is that woman beside him."

"Emilia," Leda began warningly.

"What's this?" Whatever the source of his outrage—being delayed in his pint, or learning his witness had committed perjury—the emotion was writ clear on the magistrate's face.

"She wouldn't know," Leda said swiftly. "She never visited. She never saw me—"

"You know I did. And I know you were not breeding. A mother knows." Emilia glared in turn at the magistrate, seated at his table, the coroner, who shuffled in his seat, and the wide-eyed clerk. "I cannot permit the lie to stand."

"You have no reason to doubt me." Leda fought to keep her voice calm.

"I do, if you claim him as your son. Our father might decide he deserves to inherit some of his property, rather than leaving it to my children, his blood. You would make my children claim a relationship where they have none. You might put a cuckoo in your husband's nest, but not in mine, Caledonia."

Leda stared. Where was the companion of her childhood, her guide and advisor, her first great love? She didn't know this cold woman.

"Ives is Bertram's son," Leda said swiftly. "Only look at him."

Betsey, almost too terrified to speak, blushed as red as a rhubarb stem as every eye tuned to her. She swallowed hard. "He were fathered by Bertram Toplady, that he were. As God and Patience Blake are my witness."

Ives looked as if he'd eaten a raw gooseberry, his lips set, his eyes bright.

The magistrate frowned. "The boy cannot inherit if he is a bastard."

Jack broke in with a mild tone. "To whom would Norcott Park go without an heir, Hicks, and without an entail or last testament?"

Hicks cleared his throat. His gaze moved, with considerable surprise, to Leda. "To his wife, by law, as the nearest surviving family. To be under your control, as her new husband, Brancaster."

"Then let it be known that my wife, being declared *compos mentis* and restored to full rights under the law, inherits all of Norcott Park, its duties and obligations."

"To be administered by you, I take it." Hicks peered over his glasses, brow furrowed.

"To be dispensed with however my wife wishes," Jack said silkily.

"To be granted in full to Ives Toplady, at his majority," Leda rushed to say. She slanted a narrowed gaze at Jack, challenging him.

He nodded, a smile tugging the side of his mouth. He'd grown a short beard on their travels, and while she would make him cut it the moment they returned home, for the moment it made him look rakish, a pirate in a gentleman's suit. Her heart beat faster.

"I will insist on it," her husband replied, and Leda nearly melted in relief.

"His name is not Toplady," Emilia said.

"Then the lad can take whatever name he likes, or petition to take the name of his sire," said Hicks with a touch of irritation. "Do you object to any of these arrangements, Mrs. Crees?"

"Of course not." She subsided into her chair, not looking at

Leda. "I have no objection to the boy being provided for. I only wanted the truth out in the open."

Leda's hands trembled as she linked them in her lap. It was out in force, the lies she'd told, the people she'd tricked. The hoax she'd meant to perpetuate on Bertram and the English laws of primogeniture.

Hicks Beach checked the watch hanging from his coat by a chain. "Am I permitted at last to close the proceedings, or does anyone else have any surprises?"

Leda bit her lip, holding her breath, until Hicks rose. "Brancaster, are you at your leisure?"

"I'll join you in a moment," Jack said. "I must congratulate my lady on her inheritance."

"Fine thing, to marry rich." Hicks nodded. "Recommend it to anyone. Cripps, you can stay for a round if you like." And he exited the parlor.

Leda staggered to her feet, feeling the room spin. She was thrown off balance. The chains of the past had been loosed suddenly, when she'd been dragging them so long.

Betsey reached her first, sniffling, and threw her arms around Leda. "We'll do what you wish, mum. We'll live where you say."

"You'll live at Norcott, of course." They were already installed there, Betsey and Mrs. Blake and Ives. Mrs. Blake didn't quite know what to do with herself, being the mistress of her own domain, and tended to harry the cook-housekeeper whom she was training up. Betsey sometimes forgot she was the lady of the house and Leda had caught her pulling a cloth from her apron to polish a plate, rather than calling to the young chambermaid, who had become a different person once she learned Eustace was dead, as if she, too, were a prisoner freed to the light.

Ives had his own bedroom, with a shelf for his snake stones

and all his other treasures, and he invited Leda in at least once a day to view them. She meant for the house to belong to Ives, and she would see it done if she had to fight her own husband to do it.

Mrs. Blake shook Leda's hand, and Ives shook her hand, then flung his arms around her waist. Leda squeezed him gratefully. He was a strong, bright boy, and he would grow up to be a strong, sweet man, God willing, and a pillar of his neighborhood.

Ives's right to Leda's person was soon challenged by the Burnham wards and daughter, who wanted it made clear that their claim to Leda was as close as his, if not closer, and crowded in to congratulate her.

"He's to inherit that fine house? That young stripling?" Ellinore sounded disbelieving, and she looked at Ives with all the scorn a budding young woman could show a high-spirited boy.

"But you'll live with us, still, won't you?" Muriel squished her doll against Leda's waist, unable to let her toy out of her arms even for that.

"I plan to, if your father permits it," Leda said, tamping down a wild laugh.

"Mum," Nanette said, squeezing her knee.

Atop the heads of the girls, Jack, with that lazy, satisfied smile of his, leaned in to kiss her cheek. Leda let out her breath. She wouldn't have to fight him for what was right, nor for anything he wanted. This man had given her the world, handed her life back, and he would serve up the moon and stars if she asked.

"Do you object if I stay and drink with your justice? Or shall I drive you all home?"

"Stay and make friends. He is an important landowner here, and he will likely stand for MP again in the next election. We will want friends for Ives. I can drive the chaise."

They'd hired a carriage for their journey, along with horses, and Leda felt a great sense of freedom as she learned to navigate the vehicle. Before she'd been restricted to where she could walk with her two feet; now all of Britain lay open to her, if she wished to roam.

Though she didn't wish to be anywhere but here, in Jack's arms. She leaned her cheek into his kiss and smiled at him. Then she turned to see her sister's faintly sour expression. Leda wondered if it was the open gesture of affection that displeased her, or something else.

"You wish me back in the madhouse, I suppose," Leda said, trying to keep her voice light.

Her sister's lips turned down. "Of course not. The shame of it, for one. I am very glad you are exonerated, and I shall feed the news to all the Chippenham gossips at once. And those back at home at Cheltenham, too."

"Speaking of those." Leda patted Muriel's shoulder as the girl gave her another squeeze. "Did you tell Eustace I was traveling to Norfolk?"

Emilia's eyes widened at Leda's tone. "I thought he had a right to know. He was as shocked as I to learn you were alive, and he said he wanted to help you. Was I wrong?"

"*He* was," Leda said. "He had some mad notion to marry me. I was fortunate to escape."

"Yes, to him." Emilia's gaze wandered to Jack, who, having been commandeered by Ives, was thereafter besieged by all three of the girls, who refused to grant the interloper precedence. Betsey and Mrs. Blake replaced the parlor chairs as if they could not, even now, set aside long habit.

"Your husband does not seem mad in the least," Emilia observed. "Do you know, our mother was still dining out on her woes of having a poor, lunatic daughter and the affliction to her nerves, up until the moment I shattered her again with the news of seeing you alive and well. I think the only way you could have redeemed yourself by coming back to life was to marry a peer. A young, handsome one. Very easy on the eyes, though I for one would never have taken the risk, given his history." Her gaze lingered. "Is he wealthy?"

"Obscenely," Leda murmured. It seemed she was not yet done with lies, but she could not resist the urge to needle this new, self-important Mrs. Crees, when Leda was the one who had fetched her compresses and fresh clothes when she was laid up with her monthly courses, who had shared her devilled kidneys because her sister loved them, who had pretended to see nothing every time a boy tried to steal a kiss from Emilia behind the village church. She was glad that Muriel would grow up with sisters.

"Yes, well. You're in the honeymoon still. Give him a half a year, and you'll see his true stripes." Emilia touched the curls beneath her cap to ensure they held their place.

"Norcott will go to Ives," Leda warned her sister. "I hope you can accept that."

"I told you, I have no problem with the boy. Only when you are burdening the family with lies, trying to pass off a bastard as your own."

Leda nodded. Her plan had been a wild hope, born of desperation, and the wish to bar Bertram from her bed. "I simply wanted Ives to have what should be his."

"Which is the same I want for my children." Emilia smoothed her gloves. Leda felt a pang that they should part this way. This had once been the dearest person to her. Her sister had once known all her secrets, and now, they knew almost nothing of one another's lives.

"My Patrick is only a year or two older than Ives, you know," Emilia said. "I have no compunction with him being friends with a natural son, if the boy is being raised right."

Leda blinked. "Does that mean you will come to dinner on Saturday?" It was Leda's birthday. She had invited her family to what she had hoped would be her resurrection, but she was not sure they wanted to see her.

"Of course we will be there, Hector and I with the children, and Mama and Papa plan on coming with us," Emilia said. "Mama and I are dying to see what Eustace did to the inside of that house."

IT WAS strange to be mistress of Norcott Park again, Leda thought as she walked through it Saturday morning, ensuring it would meet her mother's exacting standards when she arrived. Mrs. Hill had always been prone to place more value on the appearance of a thing than its substance. Leda had ordered a complete and thorough house cleaning when she arrived, hiring help from the nearby village, and some of Eustace's less lovely acquisitions were still being tidied away.

Lady Brancaster, newly arrived in town, and newly exonerated of both murder and madness, had enjoyed a steady stream of callers. Ives and his mothers would have a very different experience living here than that Caledonia Toplady had known.

Here was the library where she'd found Bertram's body. The rug was different, and one chair had been reupholstered, but Eustace had kept things almost the same. He hadn't wanted to remake Norcott in his own fashion; he'd coveted his uncle's fine things.

After his father had died under a cloud, Eustace's mother had remarried to a man who didn't much like Eustace, and certainly could not keep him in the manner of a fine young gentleman about town. Another young man might have tried to ingratiate himself with his rich uncle, but Eustace hadn't felt it necessary to make that effort; he'd demanded what he felt he deserved, and then killed to acquire it when he wasn't getting his way.

Leda shuddered and left the room. She would let Jack borrow what books he liked, then let Betsey decide what she wanted to do with the chamber.

Here was the parlor where she'd spent so many days mauling her embroidery, wishing someone would call to relieve the monotony. Wishing she could go out in their small village and feel welcomed, rather than having to travel to Cirencester, where she was not known, for her business.

How different this small, oak-paneled room was from the room they had made the family parlor in Holme Hall, which was a glowing seashell rose and gently cluttered with the girls' many projects: Nanette's slate with her letters, Muriel's book of French exercises, Ellinore's attempt at netting.

Leda walked past the bedchamber that had been hers when she lived here. She'd given it to Betsey. She and Jack had taken the master suite. Leda had suggested a smaller guest room would be enough for them when they were in residence, but Mrs. Blake had insisted. She wanted one of the smaller rooms for herself.

Jack appeared outside the door of their dressing room, his shoes sinking into the soft runner along the hallway. He had not yet finished with his toilette and wore only his waistcoat, with no neckcloth, and her gaze riveted on the strong line of his neck and throat. One of her favorite places to kiss.

His voice was warm, husky as he surveyed her dressing gown. "Everything just as you want it?"

The servants were downstairs busy in the kitchen and laying the table with the china Leda had brought with her ten years ago. She had married on the instant of her eighteenth birthday—so naïve, so resentful, knowing even then there was something wrong about the barter of innocence to feed greed. May had taken the girls for a turn in the overgrown gardens to settle them before guests arrived, and Betsey and Mrs. Blake were dressing Ives, then redressing him again so he would meet the approval of the Hills.

Leda was quite sure little would meet with their approval, and nothing about her. Leda's mother had sent her off to marriage with no better advice than to keep her own set of accounts so her housekeeper did not cheat her, never air her dirty linen in public, and accommodate her husband without complaint in everything he should require.

How much more she knew, this time around. And how different it was to delight to accommodate a husband, and feel he looked after her as well. She stepped toward Jack.

How different to have an anchor in her life now. A compass point, rather than living by her wits alone.

"I am walking with my ghosts," Leda admitted. "It's not as if I can feel them here—I know they're gone, both of them. But something—lingers." Memories. Regrets.

"Come into our dressing room. I put something away that I found when we first arrived. I've been thinking of moving them to the attics, but I wanted to see what you think."

"Are you luring me into an interlude, milord? My parents are bound to arrive early, and I am not yet dressed."

"Then you can't mind if I muss you first." He beckoned her into the room.

The dressing room was as large as a bedchamber, built to accommodate the powdering apparatus and furniture-sized skirts of a previous era, the extra space occupied now with their luggage.

"What did you do with Grace?"

"There was a last-minute spill on a prized tablecloth, or

some such, and Grace knows just the thing to get it out. But I've no doubt she will be reminding everyone belowstairs she is a lady's maid now, above such household tasks, and she shares these nuggets of knowledge out of the goodness of her heart." He ran a hand through the fall of her hair, unbound and left to dry after the morning's washing. "You've made a great many dreams come true, my love."

She stepped into his arms and raised her face for his kiss. "You flatter me."

"Not at all. Ellinore came to us because of you. She trusted you from the first moment. So did Muriel, though she had her little claws out, I know, and might still bite you now and again. Nanette has never known mothering. You seem a veritable goddess to her."

"Pooh." She tilted her head to allow his kisses along her neck.

"A goddess to me as well," he whispered, and she shivered at his warm breath on her skin. "Of course, I was half in love with you from my aunt's letters, well before we met."

"What do you mean?" She hummed with pleasure as he skimmed his lips over her shoulder, pushing aside the neckline of her loose gown. His beard was soft, his lips softer.

"Aunt Plume would not stop going on about her clever companion, her wondrous Leda. I suspected she was trying to entice me. Insisted I come in person to talk with you about finding a governess. And when I saw you in the Assembly Rooms, in that gown trimmed with scarlet, so calm and queenly, with a queue of people lining up for your attention and advice—I knew why my aunt made me visit."

"You didn't like me one bit." Leda shivered as she recalled their first dance, and the spell he had wrapped around her. The way she had longed for him instantly. Had she known then what he would come to mean to her, that he would be the element of life that she'd never known she sought? Had she been looking for him all that time—lover, companion, her solid rock, her sure refuge, the piece that made her heart complete.

"I kissed you under my aunt's roof when I had known you less than a day. Do you suppose I am in the habit of falling upon women in libraries?"

"Not anymore," Leda said. "Only me."

"Yes." He kissed above her breasts, and the fire, always banked for him, began to burn. "Only you," he said. "Now—who do you suppose procured these?"

He pulled the cloth from a set of four prints leaning atop one of the dressing tables. Leda put a hand to her mouth, suppressing a giggle. All of them depicted nude couples in the midst of sexual congress, in varied and interesting positions.

"Oh, these are Bertram's. He was very proud of his collection. He spent a great deal of time—admiring them."

"I believe Eustace admired them well. They were on full display in here, no doubt for his own delectation." Jack slid his arms around her from behind, and his mouth was beneath her ear again, trailing hot kisses. "Which one of them is your favorite?"

"I've never tried them. I saw these prints once, when I entered Bertram's dressing room to tell him something, and he bellowed at me to go away. A wife wasn't to be—entertained in this fashion." He was still at the edges of the room somehow, his glowering presence, his animal scent, meaty and rank.

"What an utter fool." Jack pulled a low stool toward them. "Put your foot on here."

"What, now?"

"I'll make short work of it, I promise." He bunched the back of her skirts up to her waist and slid a hand over her bottom, bare beneath the shift. "If you're willing, I think number four."

Leda twisted at the waist to kiss him. "I suppose I won't know if I like it until I try," she said demurely.

His eyes lit, a gleam of silver. "That's the spirit."

He was hard already, and a few tugs opened the fall of his pantaloons. He moved his hands to her breasts and Leda sighed as the arousal washed over her. She was wet and wanton and ready for him.

"Beautiful Leda," he whispered, his voice hoarse in her ear. She felt his hardness pressing against her backside, the thick length of him. "I would have taken you in my aunt's library if you had permitted it."

"Far too forward." She leaned forward on her knee, shamelessly baring her bottom to him. Her head fell back as he tested her entrance, put his hands on her hips to adjust. "Far too—" She caught her breath as he entered her. "Bold."

He moved inside her, and the fullness was different, the pressure in new places. She sucked in another breath, light-headed.

"I would have taken you against the door of the pub in Swindon." His voice, a low growl, spiked her craving for him. "Just like this."

"I was facing you that time." She threw back her head and reveled in the new sensations. Jack with her, filling her, the pleasure rising in new ways, that spiral that lifted and carried her. He pushed every fear, every regret out of her head, leaving only him.

"In the carriage on the way to Chippenham. With you on my lap. How I dreamed of moving your skirts aside and having you ride me. Very shocking for the Clutterbucks, I daresay."

He thrust deeply, and she cried out as he nudged a place of pure sensation inside of her. He clamped one hand on her hip and the other to her breast, and the pleasure spouted like a geyser, drenching everything. Every wisp of her past whisked itself behind a curtain, blotted out.

"The mad baron, indeed. If I'd only known." She rocked with him, pressing herself into his hand, back against his body, arching her body to take him deeper. Need scattered her senses, but she didn't fear the surrender. She could set aside her relentless self-control, her constant guard. She could let herself come apart, and Jack would catch her. The tight burn all through her body gathered and grew.

"Having you in my house. If you only knew. Every dinner, I imagined spreading you across the table and dining on you. I imagined coming to your chair and lifting your skirts."

"Oh. Only think what Mrs. Leech would say." She keened softly with pleasure as he pinched her nipple. She writhed against him, then, wanting to be closer still, slipped her hand between their legs. He groaned as she cradled his bollocks. There was something wild about connecting this way, feral. He was not simply a pleasure but a need, a necessity.

"I thought I couldn't please a woman," he whispered. "I thought I had failed my wife. And then...you..." He surged inside her, and Leda cried out. "I didn't know pleasure like this existed."

"I didn't either, my love." She hung her head, panting, straining toward that peak. She wanted this never to end, to live in this rapture always. Be joined with him, swimming this sea with him, always.

"Touch yourself, my Leda. Take your pleasure from me. With me."

She was wanton and without shame. And she wanted to seal him to her. Here in this house where she'd been Bertram's rug, she wanted to be Jack's woman. She wanted every other memory blotted out.

Unsure at first, she touched that quivering nub, and gasped

as the pleasure deepened, soared. He filled her like the tide, riding them both to that delirious height, and she let herself be lifted and flung past the edges of the known world. She cried out as the rising tide slammed her, towering through her, and felt his trembling as he joined her on the edge of madness. They hung in a world suspended, composed of only the two of them, and stardust.

He dropped his head to her shoulder and held her close as they rocked together on the waves of bliss, their breath slowing as the waves receded, until they were finally quiet and still, joined in completion. The pulse rolled through them both, fastening them together.

"Leda," he whispered. "You are the dream I never knew was possible."

She blinked back tears and twisted to kiss him. Then she disengaged herself to embrace him firmly, her bare breasts against his chest, her naked legs twined with his. "You are for me as well, dear."

She kissed him long and hard, cradled in his arms, in the satisfaction of desire, in the fulfillment of a promise. He had given her a new name, and he had given her new life. In his arms, she was remade.

"And now you are going to make me face my parents knowing I just did *this* with you," she added.

"We can try the others whenever you wish." He rubbed his face in her hair.

"We will have it all, my love. Everything. In good time."

"In the most sensible, rational, conventional manner. No more madness for either of us."

"Not a whit," she agreed, and kissed him again.

She felt it, that bright spot in her chest, only it wasn't a floating bead any longer. It was a bloom, and the stem of it ran all through her, down into the ground, like a root. She had to search far back in her memory for the last time she had felt this blithe sense of being tethered to something, firmly attached, and deserving of it. She knew it then for what it was.

Leda Wroth—now Lady Brancaster—finally knew where she belonged.

All of her ghosts were gone.

EPILOGUE
HUNSTANTON, NORFOLK, 1801

"Unbreakable." Jack smiled with satisfaction as he rapped his knuckles against the brick he held up for display. "Stands up to rain, frost, thunder, heat. We tested them all last summer and winter, and not a warp, not a fracture, not a bit of swelling. Sound as can be."

"Strong as a brick," Lady Plume said dryly. "How fascinating." She looked around the churchyard. "Where is that baby?"

Jack managed a smile, acknowledging that he had not impressed his great aunt. "Leda took him for a feed before the ceremony. It won't take long. He's a fast eater."

His aunt sniffed and rearranged the cape covering her shoulders. She sat, uncaring of the disrespect, on the headstone erected to an excise man slain in a skirmish with a smuggler more than a decade ago. The September air still held the summer's warmth, and clouds trailed like powder through the sky.

Jack scanned the churchyard for the sight of Leda. Just the thought of his wife brought him joy. So did the thought that his aunt had traveled all the way from Bath, though she hated travel, to be at St. Mary's for the babe's baptism. She had only remarked a dozen times on the oddness of the circumstance, that Jack should wait a whole two months for his child to be baptized, with Leda already churched, and furthermore to make a family party of it. His aunt had also remarked more than a dozen times that it was not the done thing for a baron's wife to nurse her own infant like a nanny goat.

"Here she is now." Leda came from the church porch, where she'd stepped for a bit of privacy, and his heart swelled at the sight of her. She wore a red satin robe over her shift, the bodice cut low to accommodate the demands of the baby, and a small lace veil drifted from the back of her head, crowned with flowers. She looked the very image of Madonna and child, cradling a puff of white lace and muslin in her arms. One of these days his heart would burst from the knowledge that this woman was his wife and he could have her always.

If he did not drive her away. He scanned her face, the old fear breathing on the back of his neck. She came to Lady Plume and held out her bundle so that her ladyship, who did not dandle babies, could complete her inspection. The baby lay with lips slightly puckered after his meal, one small fist pressed to his cheek. The dark hair tufting his head at birth had not fallen out but rather filled in, Leda's hair, but his blue eyes were lightening, and Jack suspected they would be gray.

Leda's eyes reflected the blue of the sky about her head, and while her smile was sleepy, due to interruptions at night, her aspect was calm contentment. She had not fallen into melancholy before the babe's birth or after. From what he understood, she had been as efficient and pragmatic about that experience as she was everything else. She had decided it was more practical to feed Jay herself, rather than arranging a wet nurse, and she carried him about wrapped to her like a peasant woman in the fields, when he was not in the hands of a doting servants or his admiring sisters.

Leda had joyed in every moment of her pregnancy, or most of them, quite astonished it had happened to her at all. He didn't see any signs of desperation or despair. On the whole she seemed quite pleased with the addition to their family, and satisfied that Jack now had an heir, which validated his position considerably. He was, less and less in the neighborhood, the upstart shoemaker's son who seized a set of peer's robes for himself. He was the lord of the carrstone hall perched upon the sea, with the clever wife and the handful of daughters. He was the progenitor of an heir to his empire.

"Did you see they used your bricks to repair the wall?" Leda gestured to the low barrier separating the church yard from the lane beyond and the pond, where the swans floated like notes of music on the water. Leda, thinking ahead as always, had brought day-old bread so the girls could feed the birds, and their daughters clustered near the wall in their white gowns and fresh tuckers like a bunch of meadow saxifrage in bloom.

His daughters. And now he had a son. And a wife who ran his house and their social circle, who took an interest in his brickworks, who presided over his table and was a source of endless pleasure in his bed. Sometimes Jack feared to look too hard at them, as if the transformation were a fairy spell and might dissolve if he breathed a harsh word.

"You named him John, of course." Lady Plume laid her hands atop one another on her walking stick, which she still pretended was an ornamental accessory rather than a necessity.

"Yes. We call him Little J for now, or just Jay," Leda answered, smiling at her son.

"And you'll have more, I imagine."

"We shall see what heaven sends us. I did not expect this one, frankly."

"Queen Charlotte gave birth to fifteen, and I don't see why you should aspire to anything less." Lady Plume, who would have nothing to do with the plain new fashions, fanned out her ornamented skirts. "Jack, is that your mother at last? She does like to make a spectacle of herself."

With surprise, Jack watched the carriage approaching. A line of coaches, actually. They had sent invitations, but he'd not heard a response.

"Jack! Yoo hoo! We made it, finally, though I didn't think we'd survive those ghastly ruts from Fakenham. Do you not believe in turnpikes in this outpost of the world?"

His sister waved at him from the window of the lead coach, which slowed to a stop on the gravel drive. Henry stepped forward to take the ribbons, but then looked in alarm at the several coaches behind, a parade of grandness the likes of which Hunstanton had not seen since the baron's marriage.

"They *all* came," Jack said in wonder as coaches began to dispense their contents. He glanced at his wife. "Did you know about this?"

Leda stared also, hitching the baby close to her chest. "Susan said she wanted to surprise you. Who are these others?"

His chest tightened as Jack realized that, while only his mother and sister had attended their quiet wedding last summer, the entire Burnham family had come in state for the christening of the heir. His sister, visibly pregnant, was helped down by her husband, who handled her as if she were a delicate fall bloom. Behind Susan came their mother, then his father's sister, now widowed, with her two sons, whom she always said should have gotten the barony. From the coach behind a troop of children poured out, his three nephews making a beeline for the water, their baby sister toddling behind with her nurse.

"Another one?" Lady Plume lifted her brows, regarding Susan's swelling middle.

"Yes, well, when Leda wrote that Jack was producing number four, I thought I must stay ahead of him." Susan came to Leda first and hugged her, then tugged back a fold of lace to stare at the baby. "Oh, dear, that's going to be the Burnham jaw. I fear it's the family curse."

"I adore that jaw." Leda glanced at Jack, her eyes merry.

"It's very telling, isn't it? You always know when you've provoked him. Hello, Jack." Susan moved to kiss him on both cheeks. "Well done. You've done *very* well for yourself."

"Everyone came?" Jack stared in disbelief as he watched the others assemble.

His Aunt Dinah had brought her friend, linking her arm with a lady her age with the same proprietary gentleness Susan's husband showed her. He saw the families of his other three aunts, the daughters whose families had been skipped over after his great-uncle died, due to the crime of being female. He had not received cards from any of them when he took up residence in Holme Hall or married Anne-Marie. He had over the past year received cards from all of them, congratulating him on his marriage to Leda, but he'd thought that only a hint of thaw, not a capitulation. Yet here they were.

Jack turned to his great-aunt, who regarded the growing mass of plumed hats, embroidered skirts, and noisy people with a look of satisfaction, but a betraying sheen in her eye. "You did this," he guessed.

"Did what? I wrote some letters. I might have suggested it is time the Burnhams show some solidarity, especially if they'd like to have some influence over the new government. It is certainly not your fault Seymour chose to never marry and cloud the family name with debt and disgrace."

"I'm the black sheep," Jack said. "The mad baron."

"The brick baron, now," Lady Plume said briskly, "and don't think every one of them won't be looking for a share of the profits, now that you are making a name for yourself. Give me the child so they must come to me to admire it."

Leda gave her old friend the infant, but remained nearby for swift extraction should the need arise. Jack stood with her, taking the moment to compose himself before he met the family who had once shunned him.

"You are gracious," Leda murmured to him. "You are the lord here, and this is your manor. You dispense favors to secure their loyalty. You are benevolent and wise."

He didn't feel wise, but he appreciated that she guessed his thoughts, as usual. He glanced down at her, letting his gaze linger on the soft curve of her neck where tiny curls fluttered. How he adored that firm curve of her jaw, those lips so often turned in a smile. Those changeable eyes that took in everything, and reflected adoration back at him.

As if he were worthy of all this. As if he deserved any shred of it.

"All this because I finally learned to make bricks?"

"The best bricks," Leda confirmed. "I may have mentioned, in my letters, how very much in demand your bricks are. And not just Norwich and King's Lynn. The Cathedral at Ely is using your bricks. Cambridge University is using your bricks. You have builders in London calling you up to build houses for dukes and seats for bishops."

"Then Aunt Plume is no doubt right, and they're hoping rise by my seeming success. Surprising how growing profits can cover up the stink of trade."

All he cared was that he could keep a roof over the heads of the people he loved and, now, support a growing family. But it did lend satisfaction to know he'd succeeded in the work he'd apprenticed to all those years ago, in another life. As soon as Jay could travel, Jack would take them to Norwich to show them where the family bricks were being used to build grand things. Monuments that would last as long as the ruins of St. Edmund's chapel, or the bridge over the Avon where he had once thought of kissing Leda Wroth on a spring day not so long ago.

"We must take the children to Norwich when your next niece or nephew is born," Leda murmured, watching the crowds mill around Lady Plume, returning greetings with smiles and nods. "You can show us where you grew up. Where the brick baron had his beginnings."

He smiled, no longer astonished that she practically read his thoughts. It was very efficient, especially when she could read a lascivious thought from across the parlor and excused herself early to bed. On those nights Grace would gather the girls, who sat with them evenings when they weren't out or entertaining, and take them up to the nursery where her own little babe lay in cradle, unaware how his clever mother had procured much finer lodgings for him than an inn in Swindon, and much lighter work for herself.

The Burnham girls, finished with their bread and establishing hierarchies with the newcomers, drifted by with their new flocks of cousins.

"Is Nanette baptized?" Leda asked out of the blue.

Jack felt the old punch of alarm that had once attended him so often. Though much diminished, Anne-Marie was still haunting him, it seemed.

"I am very sorry to say I do not believe her birth is recorded. Anne-Marie did not want to pretend she was mine so simply decided to hide her upstairs."

"And what about Ellinore?"

"I am not sure of that either."

Leda called the girls over and had a quick discussion with them. She bent to put her face close to Nanette's.

"Do you want to be baptized with Baby J? The vicar will put a dot of oil on your head, here," Leda touched her. "It will tell everyone that you are God's child, and he is watching over you. Then the priest will write your name in a book, along with those of your parents."

"Me," Nanette said somberly, nodding in agreement. She still declined to speak much, but Leda was studying ways to work with those of little hearing, and they were making progress.

"And you, Nora? Were you baptized, you suppose?"

Ellinore shrugged. "I might take a splash if he's giving it out. If you are sure you want my parents known." Her eyes sparkled at the thought of being the center of attention. Jack knew Leda could not bear to part with the girl quite yet, but she'd said the other day it was growing time to send Ellinore to school. Leda knew just the place, back in Bath, and Jack was content to trust her judgment.

"I am sure I could bear the weight of one more scandal," Jack said. "It will be a ripple on the Wash compared to the tidal waves before."

"But who will you put for Nanette's parents?" Muriel asks anxiously.

Leda glanced at Jack. "The same, dear. Baptism is a sacrament. It is best, I think, to be truthful in the eyes of God."

"Then you won't put you? But you are our *belle-mère* now."

"Belle," Nanette said fondly, stroking the silk of Leda's skirt.

Leda had hit on using the French term when the girls wondered what to call her, and Jack thought it a fine solution. Leda crouched to be level with Muriel, whose doll had also gotten a new dress for the occasion, the lace stitched by Muriel herself. Leda had made sure Jack noticed and admired.

"I have the great privilege of looking out for you, Muriel," Leda said. "But I am not, and will never replace, the mother who gave birth to you. We will respect her name, and her life, by putting the proper names on the register. Alright, me kiddie?"

"But you will put Papa's and your names on the paper for Jay Jay," Muriel said, glancing anxiously at her father.

"Yes, because I have the honor of being his mother by blood, which is almost as good as being your *belle-mère*."

"Producing the son and heir? Given the crowd of folk here, thas quite an accomplishment, that is," Ellinore said with amusement. "Greater jollificearshuns here than the harvest fair in Snettisham."

"No speaking Norfolk in the church, dear. Proper English."

Muriel fastened her doll to her chest and regarded Leda solemnly. "I don't mind, you know," she said, her tone anxious still.

"Mind what, dear?" Leda murmured, half an eye on Aunt Plume, who was doling out views of Baby Jay as if he were peeks at the Crown jewels.

"That you are my *belle-mère*. I am very glad Papa persuaded you to marry him."

Leda looked at her and smiled, that beautiful, all-encompassing smile that made Jack feel, every time, as if the sun had slipped out from a cloud. "I am glad to hear that, sweetling."

Muriel slipped her hand into Jack's, and a lump closed his throat. She hadn't done that since before her mother died.

He felt the last brick in the wall between him and his daughter give way.

"Glad you approve, Mere," he said gruffly.

"She's all right," Muriel conceded. "Much better than a grumpy governess."

Jack merely nodded. Leda was the sun and moon and all the lesser stars, the entire firmament of his life. He almost feared it, how much he loved and needed her. He had never thought he would find what Susan had with her architect, that kind of open love, riddled with laughter. Nor yet the quiet communion between his aunt Dinah and her companion, a secret they kept from the world.

Yet this. This churchyard full of colorful people, chatting and milling and waiting impatiently for the vicar to finish his preparations. This had all come to him because of the woman at his side.

Muriel drifted away to play with the others, and Jack stood for a moment alone in the crowd with Leda. He slid his fingers through hers.

She glanced at him, reading the emotion in his face, and squeezed his hand lightly.

"For me as well, you know," she murmured.

"Impossible." He could not have brought her nearly as much as she did him.

She shook her head lightly. "Ask your aunt. I had my room in her garret, and I had her company, and it was more than what I'd had in the madhouse, and more freedom than I'd had before. I never guessed...never *dreamed*..." Her words trailed off.

"Missus," said a new voice. "I hear you're to be congratulated."

Jack looked around and saw the peddler he'd seen Leda speaking to in Snettisham. For a moment his heart seized, then relaxed. It wasn't his rival, the man Anne-Marie had loved instead of him. Silver threaded the man's hair, and a red scarf knotted at his neck kept the dust of the road from his face.

"Her ladyship now," Jack said, though not in reprimand.

The man nodded. "It is good, the *chavo*. The child. Extending the family. It is good."

"They are well," Leda said to the man as he leaned on the wall, watching the crowd of people. "The girls. Did—did Bohamos know of them?"

The man blinked and looked at her, taken aback. "That is his Roma name."

"Anne-Marie called him that, in her diary," Leda said. "What is—was—his, er, English name?"

"John."

Jack suppressed a groan. Of course.

"Did he know of them?" Leda asked again. "Did he ever wonder?"

"He wondered." The peddler glanced at Jack. "But he could not give them the red string. That is how a father acknowledges a child, in our clan. It was not permitted."

"His wife? Does he—have other children?"

"They are well also."

Leda nodded. "May they so remain."

The man focused on Jack, his dark eyes wary. "I brought something."

Jack stiffened. "This is not the time, but if you come to the house, my lady—"

"She gave this to him." He withdrew a small pouch of lace tied with a ribbon.

Jack's hands were too numb to lift them. Leda took the pouch and delicately unwrapped it, then showed him the contents.

A thick lock of hair, growing brittle with passing time but still the hue of ripe wheat, lay curled like vegetable peelings in her palm, catching the light of the overhead sun.

"She gave him her hair?" Jack swallowed.

She'd never given Jack a lock of her hair. She'd never given him any keepsakes, come to think of it. And he'd not thought to cut locks from the remains of her when she was brought up, broken, from the beach. He'd kept scraps of her clothing, some bits of jewelry for Muriel, whatever Anne-Marie's mother had not taken when she came for her things.

Leda touched the golden strands with a fingertip. "I'll braid these into a brooch for the girls," she said. "One for each of them. Thank you."

She tied the pouch and slipped it into her pocket. "You are welcome to join us in the church, if you wish. Or come to the hall after. Mrs. Leech has been cooking for days."

He nodded in acknowledgement. "I'm for Holme-next-the-Sea, but I'll knock on your door on returning, should you need any pins or baubles."

He moved away as the vicar opened the church door, and people started streaming in. Lady Plume handed the baby back to Leda, who rearranged the swaddling and touched the tiny cheek. He had slept through everything.

"She truly loved him, didn't she?" Jack said as he and Leda stood another moment alone, watching his family assemble—hers too, now—and the crowd poured through the church doors. Something long knotted about his heart eased, the final tangle cut clean through.

Leda, guessing his thoughts again, met his eyes. She nodded. "The kind of love the poets write of, I think. Juliet for her Romeo, and all that."

"I would never have won her," Jack realized. "I never even came close. Nothing I could have done would have made her content to settle for me."

Leda squeezed his hand and brought it briefly to her cheek. Her skin was smooth as whipped cream and the smell of her steadied him. She added almond extract to her toilet water. He knew her secrets, now.

"I pity Anne-Marie. That poor dear. Her melancholy, her despair overcame her. She couldn't fight it. But Jack..." She hesitated. "I would wish nothing otherwise. Because she left you for *me*."

He studied her face. Her eyes had gone violet, deep and pure and clear, the shade of the night sky just turning to dawn.

"I didn't drive her to her death." He felt a great load shift to finally say it.

She leaned her cheek into his palm, shaking her head. "You did not."

"And you're not going to leave me."

"Never."

He believed her. He would not drive her away. He would have Leda in his life, could depend on that as he could depend on the sun rising over the North Sea and setting on the Wash, the only place in England one could see the sun rise and set on the water. This woman loved him with her whole heart. He felt the depth, the steadfastness of it, of her. She had made a promise and she would keep it unto death. And she would not hasten her death, either, because she wanted to spend every moment she could with him. Like this.

He leaned down and lightly kissed her forehead, then that of their child's. This gift she had brought him, the crowning triumph of his world made right.

"Then all the ghosts are laid to rest at last," he said, and she smiled.

ABOUT THE AUTHOR

Misty Urban fell in love with stories at an early age and has spent her life among books as a teacher, scholar, editor, writer, and bookseller. Her favorite stories take you new places, teach you new things, and end with a win. She especially likes romances about unconventional heroines who defy the odds and the unexpected heroes who woo them, so that's mostly what she writes. When she puts down the book she likes to take long walks, drag her family to new places, or hang out around water, dreaming up new stories.

Visit her at mistyurban.com
Join author's newsletter

ALSO BY MISTY URBAN

Ladies Least Likely

Viscount Overboard

The Forger and the Duke

The Painter Takes an Earl

The Mad Baron's Bride

Contemporary Novels

My Day As Regan Forrester

My Thing with Timothy Kay

Milton Keynes UK
Ingram Content Group UK Ltd.
UKHW031836290724
446271UK00004B/259